The Devil's Angels MC
Book 4 – Vex

Lola Wright

Contents

Contents i
Acknowledgements vi
Preface vii
Chapter 1 1
Chapter 2 9
Chapter 3 23
Chapter 4 37
Chapter 5 47
Chapter 6 63
Chapter 7 71
Chapter 8 83
Chapter 9 93
Chapter 10 103
Chapter 11 127
Chapter 12 145
Chapter 13 169
Chapter 14 185
Chapter 15 197
Chapter 16 211
Chapter 17 227

Chapter 18	239
Chapter 19	245
Chapter 20	269
Chapter 21	289
Chapter 22	309
Chapter 23	327
Chapter 24	353
Chapter 25	381
Chapter 26	405
Chapter 27	417
Chapter 28	443
Chapter 29	475
Epilogue	481
About the Author	491
Also by Lola Wright	493

First published by Lola Wright 2020

Copyright ©2020 by Lola Wright

All rights reserved. No part of this publication may be reproduced, stored or transmitted in any form or by any means: electronic, mechanical, photocopying, recording, scanning, or otherwise without written permission from the publisher. It is illegal to copy this book, post it to a website, or distribute it by any other means without permission.

This novel is entirely a work of fiction. The names, characters and incidents portrayed in it are the work of the author's imagination. Any resemblance to actual persons, living or dead, events or localities is entirely coincidental.

Lola Wright asserts the moral right to be identified as the author of this work

Lola Wright has no responsibility for the persistence or accuracy of URLs for external or third-party Internet Websites referred to in this publication and does not guarantee that any content on such Websites is, or will remain, accurate or appropriate.

Designations used by companies to distinguish their products are often claimed as trademarks. All brand names and product names used in this book and on its cover are trade names, service marks, trademarks and registered trademarks of their respective owners. The publishers and the book are not associated with any product or vendor mentioned in this book. None of the companies referenced within the book have endorsed the book.

Adult Content Warning: This book is intended for readers 18 years of age and older. It contains adult language, violence, explicit sex and may contain triggers for some people.

First edition

Editing by Pam Clinton

This book was professional typeset on Reedsy

Find out more at reedsy.com

Acknowledgements

Cover Photographer: Sorsillo @ Dreamstime.com

Cover Design: Cal5086 @ Fiverr.com

Editor: Pam Clinton @ pccProofreading.com

Preface

Vex

I've lived my life free and easy. No attachments, no entanglements. I easily move on after an evening with a woman. For a night, they get all I have to give. After that, it's time to go. They're warned ahead of time, so tears and ploys have no effect on me. I love my MC family, The Devil's Angels, and my bikes. Not much else. Certainly, none of the various women I've known.

Then I meet someone who changes all my rules, thoughts, and beliefs. But as luck would have it, she's the unattainable one. She seems immune to my charm, and that tweaks my ego. After being warned away from her, I try to push her to the back of my mind. She doesn't stay there for long, though. Now I'm determined to have my night with her, consequences be damned.

Taja

Trying to raise my sister, working any job I can while fighting to keep a roof over our heads, I don't live the life of a normal woman my age. I don't have time for dating, sex, or men. Especially a member of an MC. My father's an MC President, and I want nothing to do with that lifestyle. Not even for the gorgeous biker whose nearly golden eyes follow my every move. Common sense tells me he's in it for a night, and that's not my style. Best to keep my head on straight and ignore what my body's craving.

Actions have consequences, and fate has a way of messing up the best-laid plans.

Chapter 1

Taja

I brace against Tessie's weight as she leans heavily into me. I absorb her slight frame by wrapping my arm around her shoulders and leaning my head against hers as we watch the coffin being lowered into the grave. Our eyes are dry as they've shed all they had over the last few months. Watching someone you love die slowly and painfully takes everything you have to just hold your head up most days. Both Tessie and I have held our heads high through everything, but today's taking its toll.

After the coffin has settled into its final resting place, we step forward and each drop a white rose on top of it and stare down at what's left of our mother. A beautiful white coffin with her emaciated remains locked inside. Our rock, our best friend, and she's lost to us forever. I mentally say a quick prayer that she's now without pain and will always be looking over us.

"It's done, honey. Let's go home," I whisper to Tessie and feel her shudder before nodding her head in agreement.

We turn away from the grave and walk hand in hand past the small group of people who came out to be here for us during this time. Neighbors, nurses, and fellow cancer patients who came to know and love our mother showed today even though the temperature's cold and the wind is strong. We hold onto each other, as we always have, and walk slowly to my car.

Looking up, I spot the man I saw earlier today at the church. He's at a distance, but I can still tell he's wearing a biker's cut. I can't read the club patch, but I know what club he's from. I'm uneasy as to why he's here or if he'll approach, so I pick up my pace to get Tessie inside my car. After we both get settled in, I start the car and blast the heater. I shiver, and it's not all from the lack of heat.

"We'll be okay, Taj," whispers Tessie while eyeing me with her dark brown eyes.

"Yeah, we will be," I whisper back.

"Love you, sis."

"Love you more, Tessie."

"You shouldn't be working tonight, Taja. You need a few days off. We both need a few days to catch our breath," Tessie quietly tells me as I'm putting on the uniform that Suki dropped off yesterday on her way to the airport.

"I know, Tess, but we can use the money, and it'll keep my mind busy. At least for a few hours," I respond.

"It's only been two days since the funeral. Are you sure you want to deal with strippers, drunks, and perverts already?"

"I never want to deal with them, but Suki really needs these shifts covered, and I promised her. She's done so much for us, and I know she'd understand if I didn't want to work them, but the tips I'll make will help with the medical bills. I'm sorry for leaving you home alone, though. Are you sure you'll be okay, or do you want to stay with Mrs. Peterson until I get home? She said it's fine with her, and she loves spoiling you."

"No, I'd rather just chill out here. It's nice of her to offer, but I don't really want to be around people right now, you know? I'm just worried because it's a strip club owned by an MC."

"I'm bartending, not stripping. And Suki swears that they're good guys and don't allow anything to happen to the women there. I'll be fine, and I'll be home right after my shift. Call me if you need anything."

"Okay, Taj, but be careful. Are you stopping at Suki's to feed her fish on your way to work, or do you want me to run over there?" Tessie asks.

"I'll stop on my way. I've got to get going. See you later, honey."

I hate to admit it, but I think Tessie was right. I should've stayed home tonight instead of covering these three shifts for Suki. My headspace isn't where it should be to deal with whining strippers and groping drunken patrons. But I promised my best friend weeks ago, and nobody knew that my mom would worsen so quickly. The money I'm making is better than I'll make all week doing homework assignments for lazy college students. Those two reasons are keeping me from bolting for the door and saying to hell with being a responsible adult.

Suki and I used to bartend together at a club in downtown Denver before she quit and took the job here at Dreams. I'm still bartending downtown part-time, but I can see now why she made the move to Dreams. The tips are much better, and the security is top-notch. Freddy, the manager, greeted me and showed me around as soon as I arrived. He expressed how grateful he is that I'm filling in for Suki since they're running shorthanded right now on staff. And he was kind. Extra kind, in fact, so I know that Suki must have told him about my mom.

"You doing okay, darlin'?"

I look up and meet Freddy's eyes. I nod my head and give him a small, fake smile. I'm not okay, but I'm working hard on not letting that show. Guess I'm not being successful at that endeavor.

"If you need anything, you let me know. If you need to leave, I'll deal with that too. Much respect for honoring your promise to Suki, but you've had a hell of a week. Family comes first," Freddy quietly tells me.

"Thank you, Freddy. I actually don't have much of a choice but to be here making money. Medical bills have piled up, and I have a sister to keep fed and clothed. I appreciate you letting me cover these shifts. The tips will help out a lot," I answer him just as quietly.

"Dad not in the picture?"

"God, no. He split the first time Mom got sick. It's best that way, considering the type of man he is. Just hope he stays gone."

Freddy stares hard at me for a moment before placing his hand on my arm. I can see anger moving in his eyes, but I know it's not directed at me. Any decent man would be angry at another man who bails on a sick wife and two small kids.

"Like I said, Taja, you need anything, you let me know. You want a full-time job here, it's yours. Tips are better, and we pay great wages. Suki sung your praises, and I can see she was right. You're welcome to work here anytime, girl."

With that being said, he gives my arm a slight squeeze and walks off. I battle and win against the tears his kindness brought to the surface. Taking a deep breath, I release it slowly and get back to work.

Lola Wright

Chapter 2

Vex

Pulling into the parking lot at Dreams, The Devil's Angels MC's strip joint, I back my bike into its parking spot and dismount. I should've driven my truck tonight because of how cold it is, but I couldn't resist getting some bike time. With winter on its way out, I've taken advantage of any day that I can ride instead of drive. But I'm chilled to the bone right now and in need of a few shots of Crown Royal to warm my ass up.

After entering, I speak with Rod, the security guy I'm relieving for the night, and catch up on what's going on at the club. When that conversation runs its course, I move directly to the bar. Parking my ass on a stool, I look for Suki. Instead of her, I spot a new face behind the bar.

And what a face it is. As I take in her features, everything in me perks up. I expected the usual boring shift of watching the same tits and asses shaking for all they're worth, but this could be a fun change of pace. There's absolutely nothing about this woman that isn't perfection in human form.

Different shades of golden blond hair pulled up in a high ponytail with long bangs sweeping to the side of a delicate face. Arched brows in a darker shade frame wide eyes that I can't tell the color of from this distance. Full lips in a rosy pink color that I want to see in action. High cheekbones that accent her bone structure and how well put together her features are. She's taller than average, maybe 5'9" or 5'10", with legs that go on forever. Full, but not overly large, breasts that fit her body style to a T. She has my attention, and I want hers.

After sliding a drink in front of a customer, the new bartender walks to my end of the bar. Stopping in front of me, she speaks in a husky tone that I want to hear screaming my name.

"What can I get you?"

"Crown, straight, please."

I watch as she silently walks away, and I'm intrigued. She's gorgeous, but there's something off about her whole being. Her face and body language scream that she doesn't want to be here, but she's trying to hide that shit. Now I'm even more curious as to what her story is and why she's here instead of Suki.

Setting the drink on a cocktail napkin in front of me, she turns to walk off, but I speak up in time to stop her.

"Name's Vex. Working security here tonight. And you are?"

"Taja. Filling in for Suki for a couple of days. Enjoy your drink, Vex," she answers before she completes her turn and saunters back to the middle of the bar.

I have to admit that I'm a little surprised that I didn't get the usual double take from this Taja chick. Young, old, and everywhere in between, women take notice of me. I'm not sure how to take this from her, so now I'm intrigued more than before.

I finish my drink and make my rounds of the club while keeping one eye on Taja. I want to know if she's cool to everyone or just me. I see Freddy chat with her a few times, and she seems fine with him. It suddenly dawns on me that I'm a little irritated I didn't get more of a reaction out of her. Guess my fragile male ego just took a hit it's not used to getting.

"Vex, baby, you're here. I was beginning to wonder if you'd taken the night off," coos Kristy as she approaches and presses herself against my front.

"Usual shift for me, Kristy. Nothing new about what time I get here," I answer as I take a step back.

I made the mistake of tapping her ass one night months ago, and she's been determined to claim me ever since. I may be a man whore, and I own that shit, but this one is way too clingy and not someone I would ever consider having a relationship with. Once was more than enough, but she's failed to see that I have no interest in her now.

I've never lied to a woman to get her into bed, and I've always been up-front that it's going to be a one-night deal only. That doesn't stop them from getting their feelings hurt or demanding more from me. You'd think I would've learned sooner to not sleep with the women that work where I do. But I've finally learned that lesson and no longer consider any of the women here as potential bedmates. Nope, I get my strange in other places or hit up a club slut when I need to get my dick wet now.

"I get off in an hour. Let's hit up one of the private rooms, and I'll help you get off too," Kristy offers with a coy smile.

"Sorry, not interested. Told you before that we're not going to happen. Let it go, Kristy," I say back to her before I walk away.

"What's your problem, Vex? You're always blowing me off, and yet I know you loved it when we hooked up!"

I turn back to face her just as she stomps her foot in anger. She crosses her arms over her enhanced breasts and pushes them nearly to her chin while her mouth pouts at me. I take a long look at her and wonder now what the hell I was thinking when I slept with her before. She's pretty, but everything is artificial. She's shallow, self-centered, whines about everything, and isn't very nice to the rest of the staff here. I realize that I don't like her very much and that I'm sick of her bullshit.

"We had one fuck, Kristy. That was it. It was adequate enough to get off, but that's all it was. You and me? There's no such thing, and there never will be. It was a one-time deal, and you knew that going into it. I'm sorry if you believed anything different was going to happen, but I'm tired of you acting like you own me. All you have to do now is your job. We're both employees here, and that's the extent of our relationship. Back the fuck off."

With that being said, I walk away, listening to her hissing obscenities to my back. What-the-fuck-ever.

After a few hours and a few more rounds of the club, I take a seat back at the bar and wait for Taja to look my direction. When she does, I motion for a drink by pointing at the beer tap directly in front of my seat. When she finishes up with the order she's filling, she walks to the tap and fills a glass. She slides it in front of me, and we make eye contact. She has gorgeous dark blue eyes that seem to be hiding a lot of turmoil.

"How long is Suki going to be gone for?" I ask mostly to keep her standing near my space.

"Three shifts. I'll be here the next two days for her too."

I'm loving her husky voice. It has a slight rasp to it, and I want to continue hearing it, so I keep asking questions.

"Do you bartend elsewhere when you're not here? You seem to know what you're doing."

"Yeah, I work part-time at Zero. Suki and I worked there together before she came here."

"So that's where you know her from?"

"No, we went to school together and then had a few college courses together as well. We've known each other since tenth grade. Best friends ever since," Taja says softly. She's speaking so quietly that I can barely hear her over the music thumping in the background.

"Suki's good people. She's well-liked here. She does a great job. Has Freddy approached you about working here full-time? We're short on staff if you're interested. I'm sure he'd consider you for more hours."

"Yeah, we spoke earlier about a permanent job here for me. I'll give it some thought and get back with him on it. I need to talk it over with my sister before I make a decision. It would leave her home alone at night a lot more than she is now. But I'm definitely thinking about it," Taja replies.

"How old is she?" I ask.

"Fifteen going on forty," Taja answers with a small smile.

"Are you going to get me a fucking drink or just stand around flirting with the pretty biker?" barks a man a few stools down from where I'm sitting.

Taja moves to stand in front of the dicksplat and waits silently for his order. When he gives it, she turns immediately to make his girlie-ass drink while I glare daggers at him. He smirks, and I know right now he's going to be a problem tonight.

"You want a drink in here, mister, you ask nice, or you get the fuck out. Nobody treats our staff like shit. Got it?" I spit back at him while walking to stand next to his stool.

"Yeah, biker, I got it," he says without conviction.

Yep, he's going to be a problem. Taja sets his drink in front of him and moves away to work on a large order from one of the waitresses. I move back to my stool and wait for what I know is coming.

It's only a few minutes before the man finishes his drink and slams the glass onto the bar. Taja's in front of him with another drink before he can even open his big mouth.

"I see I have you trained now, little girl. How come your ass isn't up on that stage? You'd make more money being the pretty little thing you are than behind the bar slinging drinks. How much will it cost me to get a lap dance from you?" the man slurs.

"I sell drinks, not myself," Taja responds evenly.

"Everyone and everything's for sale. Name your price. I'd like to see you without so many clothes on," he says.

"Not me. Not going to happen."

Before Taja can move away, the jerk grabs her wrist and drags her toward him over the bar. I'm on my feet, hand wrapped around his wrist and squeezing hard before he sees me coming. Taja jerks out of his grasp and steps back while my other hand grabs the back of his shirt, and I hoist him off the stool. Bending his arm behind his back, I head for the exit.

"What the fuck, man? Let go of me!" he bellows.

"Rule number one here is no touching the ladies. You're out. Don't come back," I inform him as we reach the door.

"What fucking ladies? They're all whores and get what they deserve for working here!"

Ash opens the door and smiles wide as I shove the man through it and follow him outside. Ash lets the door close behind us as he gets in close to watch this particular shitstorm. He genuinely loves to watch a good brawl, but he'll be disappointed tonight. This guy isn't the type to fight. Not a man, anyway.

I give the man a shove away from me and drop my hands to my hips and wait for his mouth to say more stupid shit. I don't have to wait long.

"You biker boys take good care of your whores, don't you? You must make good money off of them. Keep the pretty ones for yourselves and pimp out the rest. Is that how it works? Is she your own personal cocksucker?"

"Get gone, douchbag. Don't come back," I calmly tell him. I know his type well. They have to save face, so they run their mouths so they can tell themselves they're badass.

"Fuck you, bik…"

As soon as I hear his voice again, I start toward him. Doesn't take him long to decide to leave the premises and to do that shit in a hurry. I stand there until his car pulls out of the lot, and then I turn around to head back inside.

"They never learn, do they?" laughs Ash.

"Nope. Stupid and drunk is a bad combination. But it keeps you and I employed," I answer.

Taja is busy with orders when I take my seat again, so I sit quietly and watch her work. After completing several drink orders, she makes her way down the bar and stops in front of me.

"Thank you, Vex, for stepping up and getting that man out of here," she tells me while looking me directly in the eyes. I note she's calm and not visibly upset over being grabbed.

"You're welcome. That's what I'm here for, Taja."

"We have security at Zero, but they're not a lot of help, so us women usually have to deal with the jerks on our own."

"Not here, doll. We look out for our own. How's your wrist?"

"It's fine. Thanks again, Vex," she says before tapping the bar in front of me and walking off to get back to work.

After helping Pooh patch the roof at New Horizons, a domestic violence shelter for women, I get cleaned up at the clubhouse and ride my bike to Dreams for my shift. Walking through the door, I catch myself looking for Taja. Annoyed at myself for doing that, I deliberately walk the opposite direction from the bar and get right into doing my rounds.

After a few hours and numerous sly looks to the bar area, I make my way over there and take a stool. Taja immediately places a shot of Crown Royal in front of me, gives me a slight smile, and moves away.

Once again, it tweaks me a little that I'm not getting the usual female response from her that most give me. I'm used to getting a lot of attention from the female half of our population. Sometimes from the males too, but I pretend not to notice that shit.

Not trying to be conceited, but I know I'm a good-looking guy. I know this because everyone tells me this shit constantly. It makes getting laid very easy, too easy, but it gets old sometimes too. Looking like I do, women seem to think it's okay to grab my ass, or worse, my junk, anytime they feel like it. Add in being a biker, and it seems to make them think there is a permanent green light for my cock.

Maybe my interest in Taja is simply her lack of interest in me. I think about this for a moment and realize that may very well be why I've been thinking about her a lot since meeting her last night. My ego is bruised, and that's all this is about. My eyes shift to her again, and I drink her in. Nope, this isn't all about my ego. She's caught my eye, but I do know it's a temporary thing. That's all it ever is, and that's all I'll allow this to be. She's an itch that I need to scratch, and then I can move on as I always do. One night's all I ever allow with anyone outside of the club sluts. While thinking this, I realize I'm already forgetting my lesson about not dipping my pen in company ink. Hmm. Maybe since she's temporarily working here, I won't actually be breaking my own rule. My male brain is already finding ways around the obstacles.

Lola Wright

Chapter 3

Taja

I'm running on fumes tonight. I'm exhausted, grief-stricken, and worried about leaving Tessie home alone again. I'm trying to balance the need for money against the need to be a good sister. Tessie doesn't really know how dire our finances are because I keep her in the dark so she doesn't worry about something she can't change. As the older sister, it's my responsibility, not hers. She knows money is tight and offers constantly to get a job, but I won't let her. She deserves to be a teenager, to enjoy high school, and not to have to grow up too fast like I had to do. I don't resent that I had to, not in the least, considering why that was the way things were.

When I was eight and Tessie was one, Mom was diagnosed with breast cancer. We were too young to understand what that meant exactly, but I wasn't too young to see Mom struggling when our worthless father split. He left her sick with two small daughters to raise. He also left her broke. He took every penny they had with no regard to how she'd feed his kids.

Dad leaving made things very difficult for Mom financially, but other than that, it was good riddance. He was a shit father and husband anyway. He worked when he felt like it, ran on mom constantly, and generally saw us girls as a waste of sperm. He wanted a son and got two girls instead. He made sure I was aware from a young age that I was worthless to him. I've always been grateful he left before he could poison Tessie with his opinions too.

Part of the reason I didn't follow Suki to working at Dreams right away is because it's owned by The Devil's Angels MC. She understood my reasons, but she's told me a thousand times that they're nothing like my dad's club, the Spirit Skulls. But

I've only known one type of biker and have never wanted to spend time around any of them.

Dad's the president of his club, and the club's filled with men just like him. They are lowlife scum that think they're complete badasses when in reality, they're just criminals who are too lazy to work real jobs. Luckily, when Dad left Mom, he moved his club to Santa Fe.

"You with us tonight, doll?" I hear spoken in a deep, smooth voice.

My body jerks and I turn to see Vex sitting on a stool directly in front of me. My mind had wandered so far that I didn't see him take a seat.

"Yeah, sorry, Vex. Want a drink?"

"Beer, please. You alright? You seem distracted," he says with a small smile that tilts up one side of his mouth.

"I'm fine, really. Just tired, I guess."

"You need a drink and a break from behind the bar. You get two breaks a shift, and you haven't taken any of them yet. Pick your poison, and I'll get Ash to cover the bar," Vex orders, and he walks off before I can decline.

I sigh, grab a Coke, and walk out the front door when Ash takes over the bar. I walk along the front of the building until I get to a low block wall and take a seat. Looking around, I notice the parking lot's only about half-full tonight. It's a weeknight, so that's not surprising. I have the feeling I'm not alone, but I don't see anyone else at the moment.

I enjoy a few moments of quiet when I hear a bike roar to life and see a headlight shining from the back of the lot. I warily watch as it creeps my direction. I stand and start inching back toward the front door of the club when the bike comes to a stop next to me. Turning to face the rider head-on, I take a step back so I'm out of reach. I know who this is, and I'm not happy to have him approaching me. He's the same biker that was at the cemetery and the same one I spot occasionally around town watching Tessie and me. His road name is Popeye, and he's one of my dad's club members.

"Call your dad, Taja. He wants to talk to you, and he wants to do that now. Not tomorrow, not an hour from now," Popeye barks at me while holding out a burner phone for me to use.

"What dad? You mean the one who walked out when Mom got sick the first time? That one? Fuck him! I have nothing to say to him that he'd want to hear. Tell him to stay out of my life like he chose to do years ago," I spit back.

"Not up for debate, Taj. Do as you're told and be a good little biker brat. Your dad's not happy that you've chosen to associate with the Devil's. He wants to speak with you. Call him, or he'll show up here, and things will get ugly," he responds.

"Like I said, fuck him."

With that said, I turn and walk quickly to the door of the club. Just before I reach the door, it's opened and out steps Vex. His eyes do a once over of me and then shoot over my head in the direction of Popeye. They narrow to slits, and I duck around his broad body and bolt through the door.

I don't get much of a reprieve before Vex is sitting back at the bar and staring a hole in the side of my head. I avoid eye contact and keep my hands busy making drinks and chatting up customers. I know he's going to ask about Popeye, and I know he'll do that the first chance he gets. MCs don't like other MCs on their turf without permission. He didn't see us speaking together, but I'm sure he read my face well enough to know I was trying to put space between myself and Popeye.

After a few minutes of avoiding Vex, I amble his direction with a beer and place it in front of him. Might as well get this over with.

"That guy giving you trouble?" Vex immediately asks.

"No. He made an approach, and I walked off," I hedge my answer.

"Your face didn't read that it was that simple, Taja. You looked pissed. Very pissed."

"I didn't like having my break interrupted by a guy looking for an easy lay," I somewhat lie.

"He was wearing a cut. You notice what club he's from?" Vex persists.

"No. I didn't waste the time looking for anything but the door to the club."

"You see him around again, let me know. Yeah?"

"Yeah, Vex, I will," I outright lie and then move down the bar to escape more questions.

I secretly watch Vex watching me for the rest of my shift. A person can be dead on their feet, wallowing in grief, and not feeling themselves in the least and still notice Vex. He's impossible not to notice. The man is beautiful from head to toe. Tall, at least 6'3", lean muscle with his broad shoulders being wider than his hips. Perfect, blinding white smile. Eyes so light brown they're almost gold in color and long, thick black lashes. Black as night hair that hangs halfway down his back. It's not straight. It's not curly. It's got a touch of wild in it in all the best ways possible. Vex often carelessly brushes it straight back over his broad, tanned forehead, and that action has drawn my eye to his hands more than once. Long, strong fingers, blunt nails, and they're simply beautiful. They're man's hands that can probably turn a wrench like nobody's business, but they should be strumming a guitar or gliding along a soft thigh. I'm sure they've glided along a lot of thighs, and all the attention he receives from the females here indicates I'm not the only one who finds him hotter than Hades. He's so out of my league, though.

Having spent most of my years taking care of a sick mom and a little sister, I've never had the opportunity to be a kid or a teenager. I've never dated or had a boyfriend. I've never deliberately made the choice to save my V-card for someone special. I've just never had a guy in my life that I cared enough about to give it up to. So, yes, here I am a virgin at the ripe old age of twenty-two. And I don't care in the least because my mom and sister needed me, and I loved being there for them.

Looking at Vex now, I realize I've led a very narrow life. I studied hard at school, got good grades, worked whatever job I could to make extra money for the family, and took care of them the best I could. And while my world has been small, it's been filled with love. I wouldn't change a thing except Mom being sick for so long and then leaving us. Sick or not, she was the best mom ever. She was mine and Tessie's world, and she's leaving a huge hole in our lives. But she taught us to be strong, independent women, and that's what we'll be. We have each other, and we'll survive losing her because she wanted that for us.

At closing time, I finish wiping down the bar, toss the dishrag into the bin and grab my purse. On my way to the door, I glance around for Vex but don't see him. It's just as well. I don't need the complication of having a man whore in my life, even for one night. I'm smart enough to recognize the fact that I'm letting grief cloud my judgment. I want and need comfort, but that shouldn't include a man like Vex. I need to get my tired mind and body home to my sister, take her pulse on how she's coping and spend time with her. A moment of comfort in someone's arms will not fill the hole in my heart. Having a moment to not be strong, to let go and just feel my emotions would be cathartic but wouldn't fix anything long-term. And Vex? Yeah, he's hot and all that, but I doubt he does comfort. Straightening my spine, I walk out the door then stop to take a look around the almost deserted parking lot.

"He's not out here, Taja," says a deep voice behind me.

I squeak out an embarrassingly girlie sound as I jump sideways and whirl toward the voice. Heart racing, I shoot a death glare at Vex. He grins while explaining further.

"I came out a few minutes earlier to make sure the coast was clear. You know, from the guy you said you didn't know. No sign of him. I'll walk you to your car, though, just to be safe."

"You took a year off my life, Vex," I grumble as I start toward my car with Vex at my side.

"Sorry about that. You're pretty jumpy for someone who simply walked away from a guy approaching you. Sure you don't know who he is and what he wanted?"

"Just your average creep, I'm guessing," I say while unlocking my car door and avoiding eye contact.

"Okay, Taja. We'll go with that theory for now. See you tomorrow."

"Thanks, Vex. See you tomorrow."

I keep my eyes moving on the drive home. I'm watching my mirrors, hoping against hope, to not see Popeye following me. I don't think I can deal with anymore tonight. I need to check on Tessie, and I need peace. I make the drive without incident and collapse on the couch when I make it through the house door.

"Long night?" questions Tessie from her side of the couch.

"Yeah, it was. How you doing, honey?" I ask as I look at her beautiful, but exhausted, face.

"Are we going to be okay, Taj?" Tessie asks so quietly I have to strain to hear her words.

I pull myself up to sitting upright and turn to face Tessie. I note the concern on her face. She's worried and that guts me.

"Yeah, Tess, we're going to be okay. It's not going to be easy, but we'll get to where we need to be. Mom raised us right, and we'll honor her memory by being the women she wanted us to be. We'll make mistakes, and we'll regret them, but we'll figure things out together," I answer her just as quietly, but I do it firmly. No room for doubt because we have no choice but to figure things out.

Tessie looks deep into my eyes, and I know she's looking for conviction in what I'm saying. I steadily meet her gaze. After a moment, she slumps back and sighs, dropping her eyes from mine. I lean in her direction and wrap my arm around her shoulders. We sit, heads resting against each other's, for several long moments before Tessie speaks again.

"With Mom gone, and me under the age of 18, do you have custody of me now, or can Dad come get me?"

I can hear the quiver and the fear in her voice, and my stomach bottoms out.

"Mom spoke with an attorney about that, and it's complicated. At your age, he said most judges would take your wishes into account, and that would have a lot of sway. The attorney is filing the paperwork tomorrow for me to be your guardian. Hopefully, Dad won't care and everything goes through without a hitch. If he does, we'll fight him. You're not going to live with that man or that club. I won't allow it, Tessie, no matter what we have to do."

"Dad doesn't care about me in the least. He doesn't care about either of us. But he will care about any money he could get from the government for me. He'll want the Social Security check he'd get if he has custody of me. He'll fight this, and we can't afford to pay an attorney for a custody dispute. How do we win if we can't hire a good attorney?" Tessie asks with a worried thread to her voice.

"Mom already paid the attorney to file the papers. If Dad fights it, we'll do whatever we have to do to win. We'll come up with the money one way or another. We'll sell the house if we need to. College classes can wait for another semester. I can pick up more hours at Zero. The manager, Freddy, offered me a job at Dreams. The pay's better, and the tips are great there. We have options, Tess. We'll be okay," I tell her while hoping like hell that I'm not lying to my baby sister.

Tessie still looks uncertain but nods her head in agreement. Now I just have to make my words come true.

Lola Wright

Chapter 4

Vex

"Meow."

Looking down, I see Duffy strutting his chubby self across the clubhouse floor in my direction. Duffy's a gray and white, humongous-ass cat owned by my President's wife, Ava.

"Hey, Fat Cat. Where's your dad?" I ask as I bend to give his head a rub.

"I'm not that fat bastard's dad, you jackhole," grumbles Gunner, the MC President, as he ambles into the room.

"Who's your daddy?" screeches Mac, Ava's very naughty Macaw, from his perch on Gunner's shoulder. "Hey, pretty boy!" he adds soon after.

"You on babysitting duty, Prez?" I ask with a smirk, totally ignoring Mac because I know that annoys him. He can't stand not being the center of attention.

"Yeah, for now, anyway. You need something?"

I indicate a table and chairs, and we both take a seat. Duffy immediately starts pawing at my leg, wanting to be picked up. The damn cat's obsessed with me, and nobody knows why. If I don't pick him up, and soon, he'll unleash his tiny switchblades on me without batting an eye. I lean down, lift him up and place him on the table in front of me. He immediately lays down and rests his head on my forearm. Then the purring commences, and he does that shit loud.

"Was working last night and had a biker with a cut on approach a temporary employee in the parking lot. I wasn't close enough to identify the patch. The employee said she didn't wait around to see what he wanted. Took off for the door as soon as she saw him coming her direction."

"You sound like you're not sure you believe her," Gunner states while raising an eyebrow.

"I don't know her, so I'm not sure whether to believe her or not. Biker took off as soon as he saw me step out the door. She looked pissed, but that could've been from anything, I guess."

"Freddy usually does background checks on anyone he hires. Anything in that indicate an affiliation with another club?" Gunner questions.

"He didn't do one on her since she's only filling in for Suki for three days. She does a great job, and I know he's offered her full-time employment. If she takes the job, I'm sure he'll have Rex do one then. It's probably no big thing, but I wanted to make you aware that another club had someone outside Dreams," I explain.

"Yeah, probably not. Keep an eye open to see if he comes back and get a closer look if possible. I haven't had any requests from other clubs to be there, so he was not where he should've been. Let Freddy and the other security guys know too."

"Will do, Boss," I affirm as Gunner stands, raps his knuckles on the table, and walks off with Mac still riding on his shoulder.

I look down at the fat, sleeping cat and know that I'm ready to imitate him. I stand, lift him and head for my room for some shut-eye.

Walking into Dreams, my eyes instantly search for Taja behind the bar. It annoys me, again, that I need to see her, but it happens just the same. When she sees me looking her direction, I notice the slight hesitation in her movements, and a smirk finds its way to my face. She's not as indifferent to me as she lets on to being.

"She's fucking hot," says Rod as he steps up beside me.

"Yeah, Freddy don't hire ugly ones," I agree.

"Too young for me, though. Guess I'll have to step aside and let you have a shot," he laughingly says to me.

"Your wife would disembowel you for even thinking of another piece," I laugh back at him.

"Yeah and with a huge smile on her face while doing it," Rod agrees with a slight grimace.

I spend a few minutes chatting with Rod and letting him know to keep an eye out for other bikers around the club. I also tell him about the biker and Taja incident. After that, I do a round through the club, then make my way to a barstool and take a seat. Within a moment, Taja's standing in front of me.

"Hey, Vex. What can I get you?"

"Beer, please."

After setting the beer in front of me, I ask, "Been quiet so far tonight?"

"Not really. It's been kind of loud with a bachelor party here. There's a lot in their group, so it's been busy so far. Makes the night go by faster, though."

I carefully look her over and note that she looks exhausted again. I know her shift only started two hours ago, so I doubt that's why she looks so drained. Too curious about her to mind my own business, I start with the questions.

"Are you working both clubs right now?"

"No, I don't work at Zero again for a few days yet," she answers.

"You're gorgeous, Taja, so don't take this wrong, but you look exhausted. Everything okay?"

"Thank you. I am exhausted. It's been a long couple of weeks, and I haven't gotten much sleep. Nothing's okay at the moment, but it will be. Thanks for asking, Vex," Taja says softly before walking away.

It's been a few hours since speaking with Taja. The club is hopping tonight, and I've been busy keeping the patrons in line. I've kept one eye on my job and one on Taja. She's not stopped moving, and I know she's not taken any breaks yet. Freddy has even helped behind the bar, and I was glad to see she had him there. When things slow a little, I make my way over to the end of the bar and signal for her.

"Take a break, Taja. Take fifteen or twenty minutes and get off your feet. If you go outside, stay in sight of Rod at the door. He'll be standing outside if you're out there, so no worries. Okay?" I tell her when she stops in front of me.

"Freddy left, so there isn't anyone to cover the bar," she tells me.

"Ash and I'll cover it. Go take your break."

I'm gifted with a grateful smile as she grabs a Coke and disappears out the front door with Rod stepping out behind her. I wave Ash over, and the two of us get busy with drink orders.

A few minutes into Taja's break, Pigeon, Toes, and Horse Nuts take a seat at the bar. Pigeon is a club brother, a fully patched member of The Devil's Angels MC, as I am. Toes and Horse Nuts are both prospects but getting close to the club voting them in or out. My guess is that Horse Nuts will definitely have the vote go in his favor. Not sure about Toes yet, though.

"Hey, Pretty Biker Boy! Drinks over here, please!" shouts Pigeon with a shit-eating grin on his face.

"What're you ladies drinking tonight?" I ask as I make my way down the bar to them.

"Beer and Jack. Line 'em up," Pigeon states.

I glance at the prospects and both nod in agreement. I set a bottle of Jack Daniels, three shot glasses, and three beers in front of them. It doesn't take them long to dive in.

After swigging down a good portion of his beer, Pigeon speaks up again.

"Who's the hot piece standing outside with Rod?"

I like Pigeon. He's a great brother, and he's always the first to volunteer to help out whenever one of us needs something. But his comment sets my teeth on edge. I bite back my first thought and take a breath before answering.

"Name's Taja. She's temporary. Just filling in for Suki tonight."

"I've seen her before, but I'm not sure where," comments Horse Nuts. "Not easy to forget a face like that."

"Or that bangin' body," adds Toes.

I feel my temperature rise a bit and again have to bite back the first thought that comes to mind.

"She works at Club Zero. Maybe you've seen her there," I murmur.

"Yes! That's it! I saw her working there with Suki a while back. Not exactly the best place for a young woman to work, though. The security's really lax," Horse Nuts says while pouring a shot of Jack.

I frown because Taja mentioned something about the security there also. I make a mental note to speak with Suki about it.

"Are these guys sexually harassing you, Vex?" Taja asks with a small smile.

I jerk around and see her standing next to me as the guys all hoot with laughter.

"Nothing I can't handle. Ignore all three. They're unimportant," I answer back, grinning wide when the laughter switches to mock outrage.

"Copy that," she replies while tying her apron back on and walking off.

"Whoa! Stop! Come back here," shouts Pigeon. "Don't leave us with his special kind of ugly! Woman! Have a heart!"

Taja continues to the other end of the bar and starts filling orders without responding.

"Fuck me. She's even easier on the eyes up close," moans Toes.

"Why don't you all take your sorry asses to a booth and enjoy the talent?" I ask.

"Seen it all before. Many times. It's more fun to fuck with you and check out the new employee's assets," grins Pigeon.

Again, I bite my tongue. Pigeon, Toes, and Horse Nuts aren't going to harass her or step out of line, and I know that. But I'm fighting this urge to be protective of her from even them. Fuck me. This isn't the normal me, and I'm not liking it one bit. I move out from behind the bar and make myself do a round of the club, putting distance between me and Taja.

Chapter 5

Taja

I enjoy the view of Vex walking away before realizing what I'm doing. I push the image of him from my mind and get back to mixing drinks. It's busy, and my hands don't stop moving, but it's not long before I find myself standing in front of Vex's club members again. I was a biker kid for enough years to know what the patches on their cuts mean. One patched member, Pigeon, and two prospects.

"Refills?" I ask as I'm already reaching for more beer bottles.

"Yes, please, hit us again," answers Pigeon before introducing the three of them.

"I'm Pigeon. Toes and Horse Nuts," he states as he aims his thumb in their direction respectively.

"Taja. Nice to meet you. Need anything else, let me know," I answer as I turn to walk off, but I get stopped when Horse Nuts speaks up.

"I've seen you at Club Zero with Suki. You still work there, right?"

"Yeah, part-time."

"That's a tough joint to work for a woman. Has their security gotten any better?" he asks.

"Not really, but I'm careful. I've learned a lot from working there. Freddy's mentioned a job here, and I'm thinking it over, though," I answer him.

"Security's tight here. Freddy's a great guy to work for. All the employees here like him. I'd put some serious thought into making the change, Taja," advises Pigeon.

I look at him carefully and see nothing but sincerity. But my long-held dislike and distrust of bikers is hard to overcome. I nod my head and get back to work.

I feel a warm hand land on my right hip at the same time I hear Vex's voice in my ear.

"Behind you. Grabbing a beer."

I still my body and enjoy the tingle that runs through my hip from his touch. I've never felt that before, and it's beyond nice. My heart rate picks up speed as his chest brushes across my back, and his breath hits my neck. Involuntarily, I lean back slightly to feel more of his heat. He's solid and warm. Yeah, I'm liking him being this close. Unfortunately, it doesn't last long. As his long, tan fingers grab the neck of a beer bottle, he moves back and away from me. With a gentle squeeze on my hipbone, he moves toward his club brothers.

I'm amazed at my reaction to Vex. I may be inexperienced in the sexual world, but I've had guys touch me like that before and had zero reaction. Nothing. Nada. Zip. Vex lays one hand on me, and I feel it everywhere. And now I can't un-feel it. The man is sex on a stick, way the hell out of my league, and I'm standing here wanting to feel more of his touch. I've lost my damn mind, and I know it. I shake it off and turn back to the drink orders.

"Break time, Taja. Grab a drink, and let's go chill for a while," Vex orders as Ash steps behind the bar beside me.

I don't hesitate to grab a Coke and follow Vex down the hall to the office in the back. He unlocks the door, flips on the light, and drops down on the couch that sits against one wall. I shut the door behind me and take a seat on the other end of the couch. I drop my head against the back of it and sigh. It feels great to be off my feet and to have the thumping music considerably quieted by the closed door.

"Last night for you, Taja. Any thought on taking Freddy up on his offer?" Vex asks while twisting the cap off his beer bottle.

He tips his head back and takes a long draw off the bottle. My eyes immediately take in the view of his throat, and even that's attractive on this man. Gah!

"Yeah, I've been thinking about it. I spoke with Tessie too. We both want to speak with Suki first, though."

"Why's it such a hard decision? Your tips have been off the charts. Suki wouldn't have recommended you if she didn't think you'd like it here. What's holding you back?"

"Honestly? Dreams is owned by an MC. That makes me a little nervous about a full-time job here. I refuse to become any club's property or anything outside of being an employee, period. Suki has said nothing but great things about working here. We're close, we're best friends, but we've had different experiences in life," I answer.

I watch Vex's eyebrows rise as I'm speaking, and I worry for a second that I may have been too honest. But that's who I am, and I'm not going to mince words now. I hate liars, and I've never been good at being deceptive. I say what I think, and I stand behind my words. I wait patiently for his response to all I just laid out for him.

Vex sits up and drops his forearms onto his knees, all while looking me in the eyes. I can tell he's carefully thinking about what I said and forming a response. I don't have to wait long for it.

"The Devil's Angels MC owns numerous businesses. We have a lot of employees that aren't members of the club. We don't consider any of those employees as club property. Nobody's asked to do anything but their job. Being an employee, you'd be invited to some club functions like cookouts or parties, but you'd never be ordered to come. Being an employee of the Devil's doesn't mean you'd be taken advantage of or mistreated in any way. Quite the opposite. You'd have someone to call if your car broke down. Or you wanted to take a self-defense class. You'd get a huge discount at any of our businesses. We offer benefits, like insurance, and our accountant is always willing to help set up retirement plans or college funds," he explains.

I listen closely, and I have to admit, it all sounds good. Much better than where I'm working now. I need to give this some serious thought.

"Thanks for explaining that, Vex. Tessie always says that I worry about the little details too much, and maybe she's right. It'd be awesome to have insurance again. And my car breaks down regularly, so it'd be great to get a discount when it does," I say with a small smile. "Though Tessie loves tinkering on it." Not having to worry about just a few of those things would ease my burdens quite a bit.

"Bottom line, we treat our employees great, and we keep them safe while working here. If someone makes you feel uncomfortable, you let one of us know, and they're gone. No questions asked. That's usually my favorite part of the job," he replies with a grin.

"I'll talk with Tessie tonight and let Freddy know if I'm going to take the job," I assure him.

Vex's grin goes into a full-blown smile, and it's amazing to see. I feel a thump in my chest region and realize the man is deadly when smiling. Hell, he'd be deadly sound asleep.

"Let's drink to the possibility of a new job for you," Vex states while holding his bottle toward me.

I clink my Coke can against it and take a sip while watching him do the same.

Vex walks me to my car at the end of my shift. Being a smidge over 5'9", I don't usually feel tiny when standing next to anyone, so it's a nice change to have to look up to see his face. I find that I feel safe when he's near, and I like it. I unlock my car door when we get to it, then turn to thank him, but he speaks before I can.

"Give me your phone number, and I'll call it so you have mine. When you make a decision, let me know. Sounds like you could use this job. Freddy and I'll get you set up and started as soon as you're ready if you want. If not, it was great meeting you. And you can still use my number if you want to hang out sometime. No pressure, yeah?"

I rattle off my phone number while staring stupidly at him. I'm so engrossed in the strong lines of his face that I'm startled when my phone rings in my hand. God, I'm such an idiot. Vex flashes his blinding smile at me, runs the back of his hand along my jawbone, and saunters back to the club entrance. He waits at the door until I'm in my car, engine started, and am pulling out of the parking lot.

I'm pulling myself out of bed the next morning when I hear Tessie scream from downstairs. I run out the bedroom door and take the stairs two and three at a time. I come sliding to a stop when I hit the living room and see Tessie standing and alive. Her back is facing me, and she's staring into the kitchen.

Assuming she saw a spider, it still takes a moment for my heart to leave my throat. She whirls her head in my direction, and the expression on her face tells me it's worse than a spider. Approaching her, I look over her shoulder to see four men seated around our table, drinking coffee.

"Grab a cup and take a seat, girls. We've things to discuss," drawls Rooster, President of the Spirit Skulls MC. Our sperm donor.

"What the fuck are you doing in our house?" I bark as I step in front of Tessie.

"Told you. Here to discuss business. Now sit as you've been told, Taja, and keep your mouth contained. Not happy I had to come here when you were told to call me," Rooster orders.

"You've no right to break into our home and order us to do anything. You gave up that right many, many years ago, Rooster," I reply.

"You need to leave, or I'm calling 911," adds Tessie.

Tats and Bear both stand and look pointedly at their chairs. I ignore the hint and turn to Tessie.

"Get dressed and get out of here, honey," I tell her quietly.

The blow to my cheekbone sends me reeling into Tessie, but she keeps me on my feet. I feel the pain explode across my face, but it does little to change my mind about needing Tessie out of here and now.

"Go! Run!" I shout at her as I feel hands grabbing me from behind. I try to block the doorway to give Tessie a chance, but I don't buy her enough time to get out of the house. I'm pulled up against Tats, and my arms are pinned to my side as I struggle to get loose. Bear bolts after Tessie and returns with her fighting him the entire way.

"If your mom had half this spunk, I might not have left," laughs Rooster.

Tessie growls as Bear slams her down into his vacated chair. I'm also not so gently seated.

"Now that the fun stuff's out of the way, let's talk money," Rooster says while looking at me. There's not one bit of guilt showing on his face for one of his men striking his daughter. He's cold as ice, and I again wonder what Mom ever saw in this poor excuse for a man.

"What do you want, Rooster? What will it take for you to stay out of our lives?" I ask tiredly. I just want them out of our house at this point.

"Tessie stays here with you. But you'll sign over any and all government checks for her care to me. That'll be done immediately after you receive each one of them. I know this house is in your name now, Taja, but you'll be paying me $1,000 a month in rent for it on the first of every month. You miss a payment, Tessie will be picked up and become club property. Young blond girls are valuable to our club, so don't think I won't do just that. In fact, two young blond girls are worth even more, so you could easily find yourself turning tricks right beside her. You'll also turn over any life insurance money you two will be getting. Basically, you'll be paying me back each month for the money I'll be out by not adding you two to the club's stable. Any questions?"

I stare in disbelief at my so-called father. I know in my heart that none of what he's saying is a bluff, and that terrifies me. I'd sell my soul to keep Tessie safe, and he knows it. No qualms about using it for his gain, either. While these thoughts are racing through my head, Rooster grins at me, knowing full well he's got me cornered.

"Done. I'll send the…" I start to say but get interrupted by Tessie.

"Taja, no! How will we…"

"We'll be fine, Tess. If money's all it takes to keep these bottom-feeders out of our lives, it's worth the pennies," I assure her before turning my eyes back to Rooster.

"It'll take a few months to get the paperwork straight. Give me a mailing address, and when the money arrives, I'll forward it to you."

"I don't care how long it takes, Taj. Your payments start on the first day of the month. Don't be late, girl, or we'll be back, and it'll be ugly," he tells me as they all stand and prepare to leave. Popeye drops a business-type card on the table in front of me, and I see an address written on it.

"Tried warning you, Taj. Learn to listen," Popeye says with a smirk before following the rest of them out the back door.

Immediately, Tessie jumps out of her chair and grabs a bag of frozen corn. She places it against my face, and we simply stare at each other for a moment. What the hell just happened?

Before we can sift through our thoughts, there's loud knocking on the front door. Tessie walks out of the kitchen and a moment later re-enters with Suki on her heels.

"What the fuck happened, Taj?" Suki exclaims as she rushes to my side and gently pulls the bag of corn away from my face.

"Our loving father paid us a visit," Tessie spits in anger.

"Holy shit! Are you serious? He hit you? Was that him and his club that I saw leaving?" Suki questions while looking my face over.

"No, one of his men did the honors, and yes, that was them leaving," I reply.

"I'm getting us coffee, and then we need to talk about Rooster and his demands," Tessie says.

Suki takes a seat at the table and stares wide-eyed at me. She reaches over and covers my hand on the table with hers. I can see the anger and sympathy in her eyes. I'm actually surprised she hasn't started screaming and busting stuff yet. The woman knows how to throw a hissy fit and isn't shy about doing it.

Tessie sets a cup of coffee in front of each of us and takes a seat with her hands cupping her own cup. She looks tired, and I don't mean sleepy. It's been a hell of a week for both of us, and the strain is showing on her face.

"You're going to call the cops, right? Report their asses?" asks Suki.

"Wouldn't do me any good. It'd only make things worse," I answer.

"How much worse can it get than them coming into your home and striking you?"

"Much, much worse, Suki. There's no level they won't sink to get their way. I cut a deal with them, and no, it wasn't something I wanted to do. But it's the best I can hope for when dealing with Rooster."

I explain the details and watch Suki's face get angrier while Tessie's gets more strained. I don't see a way out of this mess except to give Rooster what he wants. I need to call Mom's attorney and tell him not to bother filing the guardianship papers. They're just pieces of paper, and Rooster's going to do what he wants no matter what a court might say.

"I can't fucking believe this," Suki murmurs.

"I don't see how we can afford to pay him the money he wants," Tessie states.

"I won't sign up for any more classes right now. I can wait on those until we get things straightened out," I tell her.

"Taja, you only have a semester left, and you'll get your degree. You've worked too hard to stop when you're this close," Tessie adds.

"You've always wanted to be a nurse. You can't stop now, Taja. You've earned the right to finish your classes and get a good job doing what you want," Suki comments.

"Waiting a semester isn't going to change that for me. I'll finish and get a job in the nursing field eventually. In the meantime, Freddy offered me a full-time job at Dreams. The pay, benefits, and tips are way better. We'll be able to keep Rooster at bay if I'm working there."

"I'm so sorry all of this is happening to you two. You've been through so much already, and now this. I should have been here for you when your mom passed," Suki tells us quietly.

"Your sister's wedding had been planned for months, Suki. You couldn't just not show for it. You were the maid of honor, and she was depending on you. We get that. My covering for you at Dreams might be the one thing that saves us now."

Lola Wright

"Glad you took the job, Taja. If you have any questions or problems, let me or Vex know right away. Want to tell me how you got that shiner?" Freddy asks carefully.

"Thank you, Freddy. I appreciate you offering it to me. The black eye? Uh, it's no big deal. Walked into a door is all. When can I start?"

"You start tomorrow night. Same shift you were working before. You and Suki will be covering the bar together. We usually have two bartenders on duty, so it'll be nice to be back to that now that we have you onboard. If that door decides to get in your way again, let me know. I'll have a chat with it," Freddy states with a stern look.

I know he's not buying what I laid out there, but there's no way I can explain Rooster. It's easier not even trying to.

"Thanks again, Freddy. I gave my notice to Zero, but they told me not to bother coming in again, so I'm available full-time now."

"We'll keep you busy. Let's go get your uniforms, and you can go enjoy your day off."

Chapter 6

Vex

Taja: Start full time tomorrow night

Vex: That's good. You'll like it at Dreams

Taja: See you then

Vex: See ya

That makes my day a little brighter than it should. Why Taja? I've no idea why she's different to me than every other female, but she seems to be, at least for now. With my past history of hit-it and quit-it, though, that could change if I get her naked once. Time will tell, but for now, I'm going to enjoy the chase. Yes, I told myself I wouldn't hook up with anyone else that I work with, but one more can't hurt. Can it?

Walking through the clubhouse, I see Axel and Pooh hanging out at the bar, so I take a stool next to Pooh. Both are club brothers, Axel the VP, and two of my best friends.

"Beer, please," I tell Toes, who's working the bar today.

"What's up, Brother Vex?" Axel asks as my beer is set in front of me.

"Not much. Same shit, different day," I reply before taking a healthy swallow of my beer.

"We were just talking about the women from New Horizons that have been taking self-defense classes at the gym. Anytime you're bored, come teach a class. It's been busy as fuck there lately," Pooh informs me.

"I can do that. Happy to help out. How's their classes going anyway?" I respond.

"Really well. They take them seriously and really want to learn. Axel and I are hoping to get to see one of them lay their abusive ex out. That'd make great entertainment."

"Fuck yeah, it would. Love to lay a few of them out myself," I reply.

"Meow."

Axel and Pooh start laughing while I bend and pick up Duffy, setting him on the bar before me. Damn cat finds me every time I surface from my room.

"What is it with you and that chubby bastard?" Axel asks.

"No idea. Can't seem to get rid of him. He's chased more sluts from my room than I can count, though. Has saved me from listening to the moaning and tears I get when I'm telling them to leave. Guess he does come in handy sometimes," I answer with a grin.

"Saw Peaches was sporting some new scars a few weeks ago. Heard her complaining long and loud about them too. Her and a few of the other women were talking about placing a bounty on Duffy's head. Tried warning them that if they take the cat out, Ava will eliminate them from this earth. Slowly and painfully," Axel laughs.

"Bounty?" Mac questions when he flutters up to the bar top.

"Yeah, a bounty. It's like a reward. Someone pays you to do something they don't want to do themselves," Axel explains.

"Like cashews?" Mac asks while cocking his head.

"It would be like you saying you'd give me 10,000 cashews to eliminate Axel," Pooh tells Mac. "Your bounty on Axel's head would be the cashews."

"I be saving cashews," crows Mac.

"Fuck you, Mac," Axel spouts.

"Neva neva neva!" Mac responds loudly while shaking his head back and forth rapidly.

Mac strolls away, leaving Pooh and me laughing at Axel. They fight constantly, and it's always fun to see who's going to win.

"You guys want to go for a short ride?" Axel asks.

"Can't. I have to hit the shower and head to Dreams. Working tonight. Just surfaced long enough to grab something to eat beforehand," I answer.

"I got time. Let's go," Pooh says.

I get a couple of back slaps and watch them leave the clubhouse. Ambling into the kitchen, I rummage around the fridge until I find all the makings of a sandwich and get down to the task of feeding myself. When done, I get ready for work and leave the clubhouse. I'm going in earlier than I need to, and I know why I am. I refuse to admit it, even to myself, but there it is. Taja.

It's obvious Suki and Taja have worked together before because they move seamlessly through their duties. They're chatting up the customers, and everything's smooth so far. In this line of work, though, it can change rapidly. It usually only takes one loudmouth to ruin the night. I keep a close eye on all the women but especially Taja. Making my rounds, I catch myself glancing back to the bar area often.

"I've never interfered with you and the women you've fucked, Vex, but unless you're dead serious about that one in particular, keep your distance. Please. She's a good girl and has a lot on her plate already," Freddy states as he stops next to me.

I look down at his face and see that it's serious as hell. Following his eyes, I note he's looking directly at Taja. Well, hell, he's picked up on my interest in her.

"Not sure why you're bringing this up, Freddy. I haven't touched her. And you've never cared before who I did touch," I answer carefully.

"She's young, Vex. Younger than the other women here and definitely less experienced. Who you do is your business. Not trying to interfere, but you could hurt her, and I don't want to see that happen. The other women all know what they're getting into with you, but she doesn't. She's had enough of life's hard lessons already. Just let her be unless you've decided to change your ways and settle down. She's that type of girl. Not your usual. I know I sound like I'm lecturing you, and I don't mean to. I just worry about her, is all," Freddy explains.

I think over everything he said, and I see his point. I'm not ready to settle down. I like my life as it is, but Taja isn't the type to be okay with a one-night thing. I sigh, knowing he's right.

"I hear ya. I'll keep it strictly business with her."

Freddy looks at me closely, then nods, slaps me on the shoulder, and walks off.

I feel a pit in my stomach, but I'm ignoring that shit and going to do as I told Freddy I'd do. Taja's off-limits, period. Now I just have to convince my cock of that.

Lola Wright

Chapter 7

Taja

I've been working at Dreams for a few months now, and it's gone very well. Working with Suki again has been fun, and I know I'm safer at Dreams than I ever was at Zero. Best decision ever. I've been able to make my payments to Rooster, and while I hate sending money to him, it's better than having him back in our lives. Tessie and I are slowly getting our lives back to our new normal and learning to live without our mom. It's been hard, a lot of tears and anger at the world, but we're making it work.

The only problem I have at work is this insane attraction to Vex. He's always polite, nice, and funny, but my mind and body crave more from him. I know it's not smart, but I can't help myself. I spend way too much time watching him and enjoying the view. But there's so much more to him than just his looks, I've found. I don't think many have taken the time to look past the gorgeous exterior. I have, and I like who he is as a person and not just his appearance. He's kind, protective, and so easy to be around. We chat often and have become great friends. I've definitely noticed the heat in his eyes when he looks at me, but he's never made a move, and I'm confused by that. I'm assuming I'm just not his type. I don't know what his type is, though, because I haven't seen him hit on any woman since I've been here. I see them hit on him, and he always politely brushes them off or jokes his way out of their demands. What I do know is that I need to get a grip on myself and get over my infatuation with such an unattainable man. I think I need to start dating. Maybe having someone in my life like that would alleviate my obsession with Vex.

My problem with the idea of dating is that the whole idea is unappealing to me if it's not Vex. I meet dozens, if not more, men each night at work, and none measure up to him. I don't mean appearance-wise either. He's such a nice guy, and so many that come to Dreams are not. They're married, engaged, or have a girlfriend, but they're here coming on to me, Suki, waitstaff, and strippers alike. They hand out their phone numbers like a pervert does candy. They're disrespectful to women, something I've never seen Vex be, even when he's had reason to. The other members of The Devil's Angels that I've met are a lot like Vex. I can easily see why they're all in the same club. And yet, they don't quite measure up to him either as far as I am concerned.

Vex and I take most of our breaks together, even with Suki giving us the stink eye. We chat, but things always stay light. I don't want to discuss Mom and how that defined who Tessie and I are. I don't want to share all the ways that gutted us. I like our time together just being a man and a woman without heavy baggage. Vex occasionally asks more personal questions, but I've become adept at changing the subject. I can tell he notices, and I'm hoping he doesn't think it's because he's not important enough to share with. He fast became very important to me, and I value our friendship, but I don't want pity for all the crap life's thrown my direction. Vex never fails to make me smile or laugh, and I selfishly want that to continue. I haven't had much reason to either, and I'm enjoying it now.

One thing I really enjoy is Vex's texts. Every single day, I receive a good morning and good night text. We've taken to texting often, and it makes my day to know he's thinking of me at the beginning and end of his day. I often receive texts with pictures attached of something funny he's seen that he wanted to share. A bumper sticker, someone out in public wearing some outrageous outfit, or a club member caught doing something ridiculous. I even got a video of a club member getting his ass waxed, and I'm still laughing over that one. His cries of agony never fail to amuse me, and I know that's just wrong, but it's too funny to care.

Vex is slowly becoming as much a friend to me as Suki. While I adore Freddy and a lot of the other employees at Dreams, it's Vex I seek out the most. That should worry me, but it doesn't. I know that he'd never give me bad advice, and I'm comfortable being alone with him. I trust him more at this point than I do myself. I'm the one having a difficult time keeping us as friends because I think I'd like more than that, but I don't want to mess up our friendship for one night.

The Devil's Angels MC

As usual for me, I'm rushing out the door so I'm not late for work. Doesn't seem to matter how early I start getting ready for work, I'm always rushing at the end. I fly out the door, jump into my car and hear a clicking sound when I turn the key. What I don't hear is my car starting up. Damn it all to hell! I get out and jog to the backdoor. Opening it, I shout, "Tessie! My car won't start!"

Tessie's head appears over the back of the couch. I swear I see a small smile on her face. Damn kid loves tinkering on cars and is pretty damn good at it for someone who's self-taught. But the glee in her eyes is not making me happy at the moment.

"Call Suki for a ride, and I'll see what's up with your car," Tessie says as she brushes past me on her way outside.

I hit dial on Suki's contact and wait for her to answer.

"Hey, girlfriend. What's up?" she answers.

"Car won't start. Can you pick me up?"

"Sorry, babes. I came in an hour early today to cover for Angie. Hang tight. I'll get one of the guys to come get you."

"Okay, thanks, Suki. I'll wait. Can you tell Freddy I'm so sorry about this?"

"Will do. He's cool about these things. See you when you get here," Suki responds before blowing a kiss in my ear and disconnecting.

"Your starter's shot. I'll call around and see if I can find one so I can get it fixed," Tessie says as she wipes her hands on her jean shorts.

"Is that going to be expensive?" I ask nervously.

"Not too bad since we won't need to pay someone labor. I can fix it. I just need to buy the parts. Don't you get a discount on auto parts from the club's garage?"

"Yeah, Vex mentioned that once. That might save us a lot."

As I'm looking up the phone number to the Devil's garage, I hear a Harley coming down our street. As I'm saying a quick prayer that it's not Rooster, I recognize Vex as he makes the turn into our driveway and stops behind my car. He removes his helmet, steps off the bike, and walks toward Tessie and me.

"Please tell me he has a brother that's my age," I hear Tessie whisper to me.

I look down at my sister in shock. I've never heard her make a comment about any male like that. I can't help but choke out a laugh at her expression and comment.

"Suki called. Said you needed a ride. What's up with your car?" Vex asks.

"He's walking, talking porn. Damn," Tessie continues to whisper and stare openmouthed at Vex.

"Tessie! Oh my God, girl. Behave!" I whisper back.

"Starter's shot," Tessie answers Vex as he comes to a stop in front of us.

"You sure? Want me to take a look?" he questions.

"Yes. No need. I'm Tessie. You got a younger brother?"

My mouth falls open in shock at the same time Vex grins at Tessie. It's a killer look on him, and I feel it everywhere when it gets aimed at me next.

"Nice to meet you, Tessie. I'm Vex. Yes, I have a younger brother, but he doesn't live here. Sorry," he replies to her.

"Figures. Okay, so I need to pick up a starter, so I can get the car fixed for Taja. Does your club's garage carry the parts I'll need?"

"I'll have Chubs come and tow the car to the shop. If they don't have the parts there, Petey will get them ordered right away. Then I'll get you to work, Taja," Vex says.

"Thanks, Vex. Appreciate the ride," I answer. "But we just need the parts. Tessie's pretty handy with fixing things, and I trust her with our car. If you could give her the number, she can call and order what's needed."

I watch Tessie grin and stand a little straighter as Vex's eyes swing back to her.

"Number is up. Use my phone," Vex states as he hands Tessie his phone.

Tessie makes the call and walks over to the car to order what she needs. Meanwhile, Vex turns to face me, and I notice the grin's back in place.

"If she likes working on cars that much, you've got to let her go to the garage. They have a garage bay that's used by the club members to tinker with their rides. She can use that. She'd have access to every tool imaginable, and the guys would be there to help if she needed it. You won't be charged for labor because she'd be doing the work. All good guys work there. She'd be safe as hell. Trigger, Petey, and Chubs would be around, and nobody will mess with her with them nearby. I promise that on my life, Taja. Ask Suki."

"Yes! Please, Taja, please! It'd be fricking awesome to work in a real garage!" Tessie begs as she rushes up to us, apparently overhearing Vex. I'm torn. I don't like the idea of her being around MC members, but that's not being fair. I've been treated with nothing but respect from the Devil's members that I've met. I don't want to judge them based on Rooster's club, but it's hard ignoring what I know of some MCs.

"Let me call Suki and see what she thinks, and then I'll decide, okay?"

"Fair enough," Vex answers.

I step away and make another call to Suki. After the phone call, I turn to Tessie and nod my head. I still have reservations about this, but Suki was pretty convincing. Tessie's whoop, mile-wide smile, and fist bump with Vex eases my mind a little.

It's not long before a wrecker pulls into my driveway and another Devil's member steps out of the truck. Much to my amazement, he lifts a jiggly, red and black spotted pig out of the truck and sets it on the ground. The pig's wearing lime green muck boots and a t-shirt that reads: Bacon Booty. Tessie and I both laugh as it clomps its way to stand in front of us.

"That's Gee. I'm Chubs. Nice to meet you lovely ladies," the curly-haired guy says with a dimpled smile. "Hey, Brother Vex."

"Hey, Chubs. Thanks for coming. Taja works as a bartender at Dreams, and Tessie would like to go to the garage and work on their car herself. Can you make that happen?" Vex asks him while pointing to each of us.

"Absolutely! You work on cars, Tessie?" Chubs asks, eyebrows raised.

"I'm teaching myself how. I like fixing things," Tessie responds proudly.

"Good for you, girl. Great skill to have. Hey, Taja. Sorry I haven't met you sooner, but I don't go to Dreams unless the MC needs me to," Chubs says apologetically.

I like him already. I can't explain it, but he just radiates kindness. And how do you not like a guy who rides around with a pig?

"No problem, Chubs. Nice to meet you too. Are you sure it's okay if Tessie works at the shop?"

"Sure is. Petey and Trigger are going to love having someone around to teach things to. She'll be safe, Taja. I'll bring her home when she's done. No worries."

"Thank you. Call me when you get home, Tess," I say while aiming my eyes at her.

Vex walks away with Chubs to help get the car loaded onto the wrecker. I turn to Tessie and see her petting Gee. He's making contented little snorts and grunts, and Tessie couldn't smile any bigger. I love seeing that on her face. It's been a long time since we had anything to smile about.

After the car's loaded, I watch Tessie, Chubs, and Gee drive away. I can't delay this any longer. I take a deep breath while placing my hand on Vex's shoulder. I swing my leg over his bike and settle down behind him. Wrapping my arms around his waist, I connect my fingers and hold on. When I realize I'm getting lightheaded, I release my breath. My whole body's tingling, and I don't know how to get it to stop. I know being pressed up against Vex is the cause, so I try to relax and just enjoy the ride. Not surprisingly, I enjoy every second of it.

Chapter 8

Vex

I'm a dumbass. I could've run back to the clubhouse and switched my bike for my truck when Suki called, but I wanted to have Taja this close. Now, I'm regretting my impulsiveness. This is fucking torture. We're pressed tight together, and I'm loving it way too much. I'm hard in a way that I know isn't going to go away without help. So, while I'm currently enjoying the feeling of her, I know it's going to turn painful soon. Fuck me. Making matters worse for me is that Taja feels like a natural on my bike and with her arms wrapped around my body. This isn't good for my peace of mind. I'm a man whore. I need to remind myself of that and not to start thinking of just one woman. Especially Taja because Freddy will hang me by my dangling parts if I do anything he deems as inappropriate.

I ignore my inner voice that's telling me to skip work and just keep riding. I pull to a stop near the entrance door and wait with gritted teeth for Taja to dismount. She does so while giving my shoulder a squeeze, thanks me, and walks inside. I relax my jaw, take a deep breath before releasing the clutch and riding my bike to my parking spot. I'm not much of a smoker, but I pull a pack from my vest and light one up. I need a few minutes to relax before spending the rest of the night knowing I have to do this all over again to get her home. Again, fuck me.

A few hours (and one quick bathroom jackoff session) later, I see Taja looking at her phone. A huge smile appears on her face while she's rapidly texting back to whoever is on the other end. I find myself frowning while thinking that a guy might've caused that smile. I wander over to the bar and take a seat. Suki sets a beer down in front of me and leans against her side of the bar.

"Don't make me stab you, Vex. I like you, but I'll stab you if you don't keep your hands, and cock, away from Taja," Suki says conversationally.

"Already had this chat with Freddy," I answer.

"I knew I loved that man for a reason," Suki grins.

I grin back at her as I lift my beer bottle to my mouth. I'm not offended by Suki's comment. She's the best kind of person Taja could have as a friend. I admire Suki for being who she is and not being afraid to live her life as she wants. She takes no shit, no prisoners when something riles her, and she's loyal to the max. Good person, through and through.

"That was Tessie," Taja informs us when she stops beside Suki. "I haven't seen her this excited about something in months. Maybe even a year or so. She's totally loving the garage and the guys there."

"Knew she would. They're good guys," I reply.

"I don't know them really well, but what I do know, I like a lot. Freddy said she couldn't be safer than at the garage with them," Suki adds.

"Apparently, the guys have been super with her and invited her back tomorrow to finish up the repairs. And Chubs insisted on taking her for dinner with him and his girlfriend before taking Tessie home. She texted to let me know she won't be home for a little bit yet because they're eating now. Thank you,

Vex, for suggesting this for her. God knows that girl deserves to have a good day and some laughs," Taja says with feeling.

I'm curious what's been going on in their lives that going to a garage would be a good day. Before I can ask, a fight breaks out near the stage. Duty calls.

I walk into the storeroom to find a quiet place for a few minutes when I see Taja loading up a crate of different liquor bottles. I plant my ass on top of a keg and watch her move around gathering what she needs. I get a quick smile tossed over her shoulder before she goes back to searching the boxes and shelves. I admire her ass when she reaches for something on the top shelf. While the strippers obviously wear very little, the bartenders and waitstaff wear uniforms. They have a few variations they can wear, but they're all in black. Black button-downs, t-shirts, or tank tops, their choice. Black jeans, shorts, or skirts. Black Chucks on their feet. Freddy wanted them comfortable, so no heels unless you're stripping. Taja has chosen to wear the t-shirt and jeans. The jeans mold to her ass, and it's delectable. I get caught when she turns around, and her hand lands on her hip. I raise my eyes to hers and give her my best smile while shrugging one shoulder. She laughs, and my best intentions go right out the damn window. Fuck the consequences of what I'm about to do. I like and respect both Freddy and Suki, but I make my own decisions concerning my life. I tried doing as they asked, but it's not going to work. I'm too drawn to Taja to ignore it any longer.

I stand and step up close to her. I watch as her head goes back, so we can keep eye contact. Her long bangs are swept to the side, and I gently tuck them behind her right ear. I run the back of my hand along her cheekbone and feel myself start to harden when she leans into my hand.

"You're so fucking beautiful, Taja," I groan out.

"So are you, Vex," she whispers back.

I grip the side of her neck with both hands while trying to convince myself to stop where this is going. I know I should, but I don't want to, especially when I feel her hands land lightly on my hips. I pull her up against my front and drop my mouth on hers. I don't deepen the kiss yet; I just enjoy the feel of her mouth against mine. Her lips are full and so soft. Using the tip of my tongue, I trace them lightly. I feel the tremor that runs through her body, and I know not even the threat of Suki can stop me now. I angle my head slightly and take full possession of her mouth. She tastes sweet, and I need more. I take full advantage of her compliance and run my tongue along the inside of her warm, wet mouth. I crush our lips together and finally feel her tongue mating with mine. Her hands creep around my back, and her fingers dig in. I pull my mouth from hers, change the angle and dive back in. Without breaking our kiss, I walk her backward until her back rests against the wall. Things are getting hot and heavy, but I can't seem to put a stop to them. I release her neck, grasp her ass, and pull her lower half tight to mine. I'm hard as a rock, and I know she can feel it. I feel the bite of her nails in my back, and that drives me deeper into her mouth.

"Vex? You in here?" I hear from the door. Fuck!

I pull back but keep Taja blocked from sight with my body.

"Yeah, Rod. What'cha need?" I bark.

"Need you out here," he answers.

"Be right there," I say and listen as he shuts the door.

Taja instantly releases me and pulls her arms to her sides. I take one step back, letting go of her, and giving her a little space.

"This isn't over, Taja. We'll talk later when we're done for the night, okay?"

"Yeah, okay. I've got to get back before Suki comes looking for me. Um, okay then, chat later, Vex," Taja answers quietly before bolting past me, grabbing the crate of booze, and walking to the door.

I make it to the door in time to open it for her and watch her walk out. Damn. She wouldn't even look me in the eyes.

That worries me a little because I've gotten to know Taja fairly well over the last few months, and she's never afraid to make eye contact with anyone. She doesn't divulge much of her personal life, but she does open up about a lot of other things. She clearly adores her little sister, and they're super close. She talks about taking college courses and how much she likes them. She has a great sense of humor and takes most everything in stride. She's not a party girl, and she has no idea how gorgeous she is. She's confident, doesn't have low self-esteem but is in no way conceited. She truly believes the guys hitting on her would hit on anyone, and it has nothing to do with her own appeal. I'm surrounded by women who use their beauty to earn a living, many with over-the-top opinions of themselves, so Taja's lack of that is refreshing. One thing I certainly like is she's careful about chatting up the customers. She's friendly and helpful but never crosses the line into being flirtatious. It's like she has an invisible shield up that keeps men at bay, and yet I don't feel it in place with me unless I ask too personal of a question. When that happens, Taja will change the subject, and it's not long before we're laughing about something Suki or Tessie did. For now, I'll let her have that space she still feels she needs.

We text constantly, sometimes even while at work. She'll shoot me a text about a customer that's starting to get out of hand. She texts so she doesn't alert the customer and cause a bigger scene. I like that she's smart in those ways. I also like that she's cautious about her safety. Head up, eyes alert. She doesn't walk to her car or take breaks outside while busy on her phone. She pays attention to her surroundings, and while I like that, I also have to wonder why. Most women her age have their noses in their phones, completely unaware of what's going on around them, and she doesn't. I'm hoping it's good lessons her mother taught her and not bad lessons she learned the hard way.

I'm finding it more difficult to keep a friends-only relationship with her. Over the last few months, I've barely noticed other women, and when I do, I compare them to Taja. They always end up lacking. When I first noticed I was doing this, it was disconcerting, to say the least. Now, it's the norm. I'll listen to one of the strippers telling me about some dramatic thing going on in their life, and I know instantly how Taja would handle it. Or know that she'd never allow the drama to get that far to begin with. For being in her early 20s, she's got her head on straight and her priorities set. I admire her, and that's new for me. While I love my own mom, I don't admire her or her choices at all. But Taja can't seem to take a misstep in my mind. I've placed her on a pedestal, even though I know I shouldn't, but that's where she rates amongst the women in my life. Problem with that is this pull to her and the distraction she's become to my peace of mind. Something needs to give and soon.

Lola Wright

Chapter 9

Taja

I need to get myself under control and smooth out my expression, or Suki will know something happened. She's a bloodhound when it comes to sniffing out stuff. I need to think about what happened with Vex before it gets forced out of me through Suki's impressive interrogation skills.

I take a deep breath, hold it for a few seconds, and release it slowly. I consciously relax my face muscles and approach the bar with the crate of booze.

"I'll help you get this stuff put up, and then I'm hitting the road. It's been a long-ass day," Suki says while reaching for bottles in the crate. She's distracted, and that's great news for me.

"Okay, sounds good," I answer her brightly.

Working quickly, we get the job done. Suki removes her apron, grabs her purse from under the bar, gives me a quick hug, and leaves for the night. I'm on my own, but it's slowed down some, and it's manageable.

"Give me a Coke and rum. Heavy on the rum," I hear.

Turning my head, I see it's Kristy. She's rude, bossy, sarcastic, and catty to everyone but the men. Freddy's probably the only person here that actually likes her. I mix her drink, slide it across the bar to her, and note the pissy expression on her face. I know cutting sarcasm will be making an appearance. I'm not wrong.

"How'd someone like you get a job here? Too young, too tall, and too damn mousy. Freddy must be into the helpless look now," Kristy says, making her sentiments known. "You blowing him?"

I lean my forearms on the bar in front of her and respond calmly.

"No. Not my style to blow someone for a job. I've never been that desperate. I'll never be that desperate. My mom raised me to use my brain, not my body, to earn my keep. Hard work, not on my knees, is how I keep my job. So, Kristy, who are you blowing to still be employed here?"

"You couldn't earn your keep with that body. Maybe it's a good thing you've decided to use that brain of yours to be a bartender instead of a dancer," she replies cattily.

"Before your boob enhancement, butt lift, and thigh reduction surgeries, I'm guessing yours looked like a twelve-year-old girl's," I say sweetly.

"Fuck you!" she screams while slamming her fists on the bar.

"I'll leave that to all your 'friends' named John, thank you very much," I say with a smirk as I walk away. I hear a screech behind me, and my smirk changes into a smile.

I like most of the women who work here, including the strippers. There are only a few I don't. Most are just trying to earn a living, and I get that. I really like that Dreams is different from other strip clubs in that they don't allow sex. There are private rooms for lap dances, but they're monitored closely. The customers aren't allowed to use their hands even during those dances. If the women choose to hook up with a customer, it's after hours and off property. The MC doesn't encourage or benefit from those encounters. I know a few of the women collect phone numbers and meet up with clients after the club closes. Kristy's one of them who has chosen to make extra money by prostituting herself. The club also does random drug tests on all employees. A strung-out stripper doesn't make them money and only causes trouble. Test positive for more than pot and say goodbye to your job here.

"Let's go, Taja," Vex orders as I step out from behind the bar after finishing my closing duties.

We walk silently out the door and across the lot to Vex's bike. Out of habit, my eyes scan the nearly vacant lot looking for any sign of Rooster or his club. Seeing none, I relax and breathe easy. I didn't realize that my actions were obvious until Vex speaks.

"Someone in particular you looking for or looking to avoid, Taja?"

"No. No one at all. Just being cautious, you know. Walking out of a club at night, you can't ever be too vigilant," I answer without looking at him.

When we reach the bike, Vex sits sideways on the seat. He grasps my hips and pulls me between his thighs. I drop my hands to his biceps and enjoy the firm definition of them.

"People keep telling me to keep my distance from you. I get why. I know they mean well, but that's not working for me anymore. I'm not a relationship kind of guy, and you need to know that up-front. But we're going to happen, Taja. For a night, maybe a few nights. I need a hell of a lot less distance between us. I need your clothes off and my mouth touching all of you. I want to be inside you more than I've ever wanted anything. Where's your head at with all that?" Vex informs me in his deep, smooth voice.

I like that he's direct and isn't playing games. After working around him for the last few months, I've found there's a lot to like about Vex. Not just his looks, but all of him. I'm attracted to Vex. Anyone born with a vagina would be. A lot born without one would be too. But am I ready for certain heartbreak? We're worlds apart on the experience spectrum. Can I give him my virginity and not get anymore attached to him than I already am? Can we be intimate and then still work together without issues? I can't afford to lose this job. If I do, I might cost Tessie and me our freedom. I want to say yes to him so bad, but I'm trying to think logically. My mind's still whirling when I feel his hands tighten on my hips. Looking down, our eyes meet and hold.

"Give me your mouth, Taja."

Without thought, I do as he asks. He pulls me tighter to his body as our mouths meld. He tastes of smooth, aged whiskey and all man. My hands instinctively slide into his hair, and I take hold of it. A simple kiss and I'm soaring. This man's pure magic, and I want my fill. I take the initiative and deepen our connection. It does funny things to my belly when Vex groans his approval. I feel powerful and wanted. My lack of experience doesn't seem like a bad thing when I feel the changes in his body. Vex doesn't make me feel young and small. He makes me feel bold and alive for the first time in a long time.

After a few moments of enjoying each other, Vex gently nips my bottom lip and pulls back a bit. I slowly open my eyes to see his heated ones staring into mine.

"It's not if, it's when, Taja. Get your head wrapped around that. Because when it happens, I'm taking my time. I want every inch of you. I want every fucking thing you have to give, and I'll be greedy about taking it."

"Okay, Vex," I whisper in agreement. At that moment, I'd have agreed to anything with him.

"Let's get you home before I make good on that promise right here in the parking lot," Vex says with a small grin.

I release his hair and take a step back. Vex stands up and mounts the bike. I climb on behind him and place my hands around his waist. I drop my forehead to the back of his shoulders and release a shaky breath.

It's not long before we pull to a stop in my driveway, and I dismount the bike. Vex snakes his left arm around my waist and pulls me tight to his side. I can barely make out his features in the darkness, but I can feel his intensity.

"Mouth, Taja," he rumbles out.

I instantly comply, and things heat up instantly. I no more than place my hand against his jaw when the porch light flips on, and I hear the house door open. Before I can pull away, Tessie interrupts our moment completely.

"Hey, Taj! When you're done making out with the hot biker dude, can I tell you how flippin' awesome my day was?" Tessie's voice is a loud, excited screech that most likely scared every cat in the neighborhood. I step back from Vex quickly while listening to him chuckle.

"I take it you enjoyed your day at the garage, Tessie," Vex says to her in an amused voice.

My adorable, excited younger sister comes bounding down the steps and rushes up to the bike. She slides to a quick halt, throws both arms out wide, and hollers in response, "Best day ever!"

I look at her smiling face and feel a whoosh in my belly. It's been a long time since she was this happy about anything. Tessie needed something like this to pull her out of her funk. My gratitude to Vex and Chubs knows no bounds.

"I met all the guys, and everyone was great, but Chubs, Petey, and Trigger are the freakin' best! They showed me things I didn't know, and Petey let me use his tools since he mostly works the front of the store now. And he has every tool imaginable! How cool is that? No one even cared that a girl wanted to work on cars. They just helped me out like I belonged there. They said I can come back tomorrow and finish up on your car. And Chubs introduced me to his girlfriend, Lucy, and they took me out to dinner. It was so cool! Lucy's so nice, and I really like her. But, Taj, seriously, you've never seen someone who can eat like Chubs! It was un-frickin-believable!" Tessie shouts most of this and then stops long enough to take a long, much-needed breath.

I can't help the huge smile that spreads across my face, and I notice that Vex is sporting one too. Tessie's excitement is contagious and endearing to see. I send up a silent message to Mom, thanking her for placing Tessie in my life.

"So, can I go? Can I? Please? I have to finish up the car, and Trigger said he'd come in on his day off just to help me," Tessie asks while turning pleading eyes my direction.

"Of course, honey. We'll call for an Uber…"

"No need. Chubs said he'd pick me up at 9am if you said yes. I just have to text him and let him know I can. Thanks!" Tessie interrupts to say before bolting back toward the house. Upon reaching the door, she turns back to us and proceeds to say, "Sorry for breaking up your moment earlier. Go back to sucking face. I got a text to send. Night, Vex."

"Night, Tessie," Vex answers with a laugh as she rushes inside and closes the door.

"She's not going to sleep at all tonight," I say with a smile.

"Not for a second," Vex agrees.

"I better get inside and let her talk herself out," I inform Vex with some regret.

"Yeah. I'll pick you up tomorrow for your shift. Plan on getting home very late tomorrow, Taja. We'll be spending some time together after your shift," Vex informs me in a serious voice.

"I'll see you tomorrow, Vex," I respond as I walk to the house.

Chapter 10

Vex

I have some time to kill today before I pick up Taja, so I take a run to the club's garage to see how Tessie's doing. Dismounting my bike, I walk in the front door and immediately see Petey behind the parts counter. Mac's perched on one end of the counter, humming to himself.

"Hey, Vex. How's it going?" Petey asks.

"All good, Petey. Hey, Mac."

"Hey, Pretty Boy," Mac shouts as he approaches with his wing extended.

I chuckle at the feathered little menace as I fist-bump his wing.

"Need something, Vex?" Petey questions.

"No. Just thought I'd stop and see how Tessie's doing. I saw her last night, and she was pretty excited about coming back here today."

Petey's smile instantly drops, and so does my stomach. What the hell's up with his expression?

"Jesus, Vex. She's only 15 years old!" he half-shouts at me.

"Perv! Kickass, Gramps!" Mac adds his two cents worth.

"What the fuck, Petey? I know that shit. I'm not here to hit on her for fuck sake," I say, chuckling at him as his expression slowly changes back to friendly. "Her sister bartends at the club. Met Tessie when I gave her sister a ride to and from work. Tessie was excited about coming back here today, so I thought I'd stop and check on her. Her sister, Taja, worries about her."

"So, it's the sister you're after. Got it now. Sorry about that, brother," Petey states with a grin.

"Not after anyone. Not looking to settle down. Ever. I'm not that guy. Not happening," I insist while watching Petey's grin get bigger. Fuck me. I said too much, and Petey's not one to miss anything.

I shake my head in disgust at myself and walk off before I say anything else. I hear Mac cackling as I walk away. Entering the garage's workspace, I spot Tessie by Taja's car. She's listening intently to Trigger as he explains something. Looking closely at her expression, I can easily tell how much she's in love with being here. I find myself liking the fact that she'd prefer to be here learning a trade than hanging out at the mall. She may be young, but she knows who she is and what she wants. Someone's done a great job at raising her. Tessie looks up and spots me walking in her direction. Her face lights up, and I know she's going to be a heartbreaker in the near future. The girl's gorgeous.

"Hi, Vex!"

"Hey, brother," Trigger adds to her enthusiastic greeting.

"Hi, Tessie. Trigger. How's it going?" I ask.

"The starter's in and works perfectly. Trigger showed me how to run diagnostics on Taja's car, and it showed a few issues that should get fixed. If she'll okay the repairs, he promised he'd show me how to fix all of them. If it wasn't for the cost, I'd wish the engine would die, so I could learn how to put in a new one," Tessie finishes with a snicker.

"Pretty sure that'd make you happier than it would Taja," I reply.

"That's what I told her too," Trigger adds with a grin aimed at Tessie. "Girl's a fast learner and a hard worker. She's welcome to come here anytime she wants."

"Sounds like you've got yourself a great mentor, Tessie. If it's got a motor, Trigger can fix it. I'd take advantage of that offer. Is working on cars something you want to do for a living?" I ask her. I'm curious about all things Taja, and that includes her sister. Taja's tight-lipped when it comes to talking about herself and her life, and I still know very little about her.

"Mom and Taja have always wanted me to go to college and get a degree. Taja's worked a lot of extra hours to put money away for my college education. But that's never been my dream. I want to go to a trade school instead. I want to be a mechanic. I love working with my hands and fixing things. But I don't want to disappoint Taja after all she's done," Tessie quietly tells us.

It's obvious she's torn between following her dream and the fear of disappointing her family. That's a lot of weight for a young person to carry. I know exactly how she feels due to my own family issues. Family expectations can easily break family connections. I don't want that for Tessie and Taja.

"Does Taja know this? Have you told her what you want?" I ask carefully.

"No, not exactly. Not in so many words. She knows I love fixing cars, but I've been afraid to tell her I don't want to go to college. I just wish she'd use my college fund for her own education. She quit after Mom died, and she's so close to graduating."

"Sorry about your mom, Tessie. When did she pass?" Trigger softly asks.

"Late winter. Cancer. She fought hard for a long time, right up to the end. Now it's just Taja and me."

Tessie's eyes are a little wet and a lot sad, but she's holding herself together in a manner way beyond her years. I look closely at her and see a strength I'm sure she inherited from her mother.

"Damn, Tessie. I'm so sorry about your mom," I tell her sincerely.

"Yeah, me too. Thanks, though. She was the best mom ever. We miss her every day. It sucks."

"Where's your dad? Is he in the picture?" questions Trigger.

"No, he's not. Best thing he ever did was leave us. I just hope he stays gone," Tessie spits angrily.

"You said Taja quit college when your mom died. Why?" I ask.

"Money. She only has a semester left. That's why I wish she'd use my college fund and finish up her degree. But she's stubborn and said she'd finish up later when we can afford it. She's going to become a nurse, maybe a doctor someday. She took great care of Mom. She loves nursing and the whole medical field. She's always been a straight-A student. She's super smart, and she loves school."

Pride glows on her face and in her voice. The sisters are close, and it's obvious. I feel a tug low in my gut, but I ignore it. That's one of my skills—ignoring things.

"You need to talk with your sister, Tessie. I'm sure she only wants the best for you, and that includes you being happy. If she knows you're serious about a trade school instead of college, maybe you can convince her to finish up her degree. She'd be in a better position financially to help you with trade schools," I tell her.

"Yeah, I know I should. But she's done so much for me and so little for herself. I don't want to let her down."

"Here's a thought. You like working here. I like having someone to teach. Would your sister be okay with you coming here a few hours each week to learn the trade? That way, you'd know by the time you graduate if you really want to go to a trade school or not. I'm sure I can talk the club into paying you a small wage to help out around here. That money could be put away toward your trade school. Is that something you and her would be okay trying?" Trigger offers.

"Oh my God! Are you serious? I'd love that! Holy crap, that'd be perfect! Well, perfect if I can talk Taja into letting me do that. Are you sure you want to do that? I don't know much, but I'll work hard," Tessie exclaims.

The look on her face when Trigger made his offer was worth more than any work she ever accomplishes. I'm watching Trigger's face and note that it softened immediately when Tessie's lit up. I'm sure mine's looking similar to his. I've never felt the urge to hug Trigger before, but he's close to getting one right now.

"I offered and I meant it. I'll speak with Petey and Gunner today about it. What would keep your sister from agreeing to this? What're her concerns?" Trigger asks.

"Safety. She always worries about where I am and who I'm around. And she'll worry about me doing this and keeping my grades up," Tessie responds.

"Then maybe she'll feel better if Vex and Freddy speak with her about your safety here and how serious we'd take it. And she should meet me and Petey. She's met Chubs, and they don't get any better than him. You go home today and talk with her. If she's agreeable, she's welcome to come here and meet the rest of us. That work for you?"

"Yeah, that'd make her feel better, I think. As long as she knows I'm safe, she'll probably agree. Oh my

God, I can't wait to talk to her!" Tessie shouts the last part.

Trigger and I both grin at her enthusiasm. I hold out my fist, and she bumps hers against it with a blinding smile.

Pulling into Taja's driveway, I watch as she approaches the bike. She's in her work uniform and carrying a huge ass purse. You could hide a small child in that thing. She stops next to the bike, eyes still not meeting mine, and stows the purse in the saddlebag before settling in behind me. I turn my head so I can see her and the small smile gracing her face.

"Kiss."

Taja leans closer to my face and asks, "What?" over the rumbling of my bike.

"Kiss."

She leans close enough to place a soft kiss on my mouth. I turn more her direction, reach up and pull her mouth firmly against mine. Then I kiss her the way she should always be kissed. When I'm done, I pull back and watch as her eyes slowly open and meet mine.

"That's what I want when I ask for a kiss, Taja. I want all of you each time. Let's get to work before I have you naked here in your driveway. Yeah?"

"Yeah, Vex," she replies with a saucy grin.

It's annoying the fuck out of me how all these customers eye fuck Taja. I'm not sure she even realizes all the filthy thoughts these asswipes are having while looking at her. She's not encouraging them. She's just doing her job, but it's still setting my teeth on edge. I've never experienced a shift this fucking long before. I just want it to end so I can have Taja to myself.

I make my way over to the end of the bar and take a seat. As soon as she sees me, she grabs a beer and heads my way. Setting it down in front of me, I'm graced with a beautiful smile. Suki, on the other hand, is obviously trying to shoot death rays at me. I grin, tip my bottle toward her, and then take a healthy swig.

"Why's Suki upset with you?" Taja asks, apparently having noticed Suki's look too.

"She's being a good friend to you. She's hoping to scare me away."

"Is she going to succeed?" Taja asks with a slight tilt of her head.

"Nope. Not scared of much, Taja. If you decide you don't want to spend time with me, I'd understand. I wouldn't bother you in any way. But it's your call, not Suki's or Freddy's. You decide anything yet?"

"I should be saying no to you, but I'm not sure that word's possible where you're concerned. The smart move would be to keep my distance, but distance is the last thing I want. I know this is a mistake, and I'm going to regret it. But I've lived with narrow boundaries my whole life. I've done that to myself because I chose it that way, but I need to step outside of those boundaries and live a little. Even if it's just for a night. I have zero experience with men like you. Zero experience outside of always doing the right thing. The proper, expected, acceptable thing. I know what I want, and it's time with you. Question is, are you okay with knowing I'm not the 'pro' you're accustomed to?" Taja answers me in a quiet voice. I had to lean close to hear her, and her warm breath on my neck is doing things to me. Pro or not, I want her.

"Sounds like we're on the same page."

Taja pulls her phone out of her apron pocket and looks at it with a smile. Showing the screen to me, I see a text from Tessie.

Tessie: Spending the night at Megan's. Be home around 10am. We need to have a talk about something VERY important. Luv you!

Taja texts something back before placing her phone back in her apron. Eyes on me, she asks, "Any idea what's so important?"

"That's between you sisters. But listen to her, Taja. She's a smart kid and knows what she wants. After your chat, if you have questions or concerns, call me."

Taja stares at me for a few beats before nodding her head and walking off. I watch her for a few minutes before finishing my beer and getting back to work.

When I pull my bike into Taja's driveway, I park it next to her car. Chubs must have driven it home when he brought Tessie back. Taja dismounts the bike, grabs her purse out of the saddlebags, and then leans into my side. I shut off the bike and wrap my arm around her waist.

"Want to come in?" she asks. She sounds a little nervous but determined.

"If I come in, with Tessie gone tonight, shit's going to happen, Taja. You ready for that?" I ask, trying to give her an out if she wants it.

"Are you trying to warn me away from you?" she questions with a small smile.

"I'm trying to be a good guy. I don't want you to have regrets, Taja. But I'm not looking for a relationship, and I want you to be very clear about that before I have you naked. We're friends now, and I want to be friends after. If that's not something you can do, then I need to leave. Your choice."

Taja stares at me for a moment before grasping my hand and giving it a slight tug. I dismount my bike and follow her to the front door. Watching her ass as she mounts the steps and then through the door has me hardening quickly. I shut the door behind me, flip the lock and turn back to see Taja dropping her purse and apron on the couch. I move into her space and place both hands on the sides of her neck. I waste no time before I claim her mouth.

I adjust her head and deepen our kiss. I want to taste everything she has to give. I feel Taja's hands grab my hips and pull our bodies tight together. I know she can feel what she's doing to me because she stiffens for a split second before melting completely against my front. I drop one hand from her neck to her ass and rub my hand over its plumpness. Fuck, she's got a great ass, and that's always been a weakness of mine.

I move my mouth off of hers, glide my lips across her cheek, and down to her pulse point. The low sounds she's making are so genuine they're turning me into steel. It's been a while since I've been with someone who made real sounds and not the fake ones so many women think are a turn-on. For the record, they're not. But Taja's are amazing, and I'm looking forward to the ones she'll make when my mouth ends up on even better parts of her.

Sliding my other hand down to join the first one on her ass, I lift her. Taja automatically wraps her legs around my hips as I turn us to place her back against the door. Moving my mouth back to hers, I grind hard into her softness. My cock can feel the heat coming from her, and he knows what's coming. I listen closely to Taja's breath hitch for a second and then resumes when she slides herself up and down my length. Wrapping her arms around my neck, I feel her hands sliding into my hair. She pulls back on it, and I lose her mouth for a second before it lands on my neck. She's sucking and licking, and it feels unbelievable.

"Where's your room?" I ask, and even I can hear how husky my voice sounds.

"First door on the left at the top of the stairs," she replies in between tiny nips.

I waste zero time getting us to and in her room. There's just enough light from the living room lamp that I can see the way. I don't even set her on her feet before I drop us both on her bed. I brace so I don't crush her as I shift my weight slightly to the side.

"Light, Taja. I need to see you," I tell her.

A muted bedside lamp switches on, and I see the scarf draped over it. It's enough for now. I slide a hand down her stomach and start pulling her t-shirt up. Taja assists by leaning up slightly, and together we pull it off. I toss it toward the floor and then run the back of my fingers up her ribs to the bottom of her bra. I cup her breast and listen to her breath catch. Running my thumb across her nipple, I feel the shiver that runs her full length. I lean up more on my right forearm and slide my leg between hers. Looking down at her, I'm frozen for a moment by how pretty she is.

I continue thumbing her nipple while dropping my mouth to her other breast. That nipple hardens instantly, and I nip it lightly with my teeth. Taja's back arches, and that offer is all I need to know she's as into this as I am. I reach behind her and unclasp her bra. Pulling back slightly, I pull it off and toss it away. My greedy eyes take in her naked breasts. Round, firm, with nipples darker than I expected. Not large but absolutely perfect.

"I want to see you too, Vex. I need to feel your skin," Taja whispers.

She sounds almost shy, and I'm taken aback for a moment. Shrugging it off, I roll to my back, do an ab curl and remove my shirt. I move to my knees and straddle her hips. Taja's hands instantly land on my abs and glide up and down them. Her eyes are tracking her hand movements, and she is biting her lip slightly. It's a pretty fucking good look on her, and my jeans are beyond uncomfortable now.

Her fingers find the barbells in my nipples, and she gives them a slight pull. Fuck, I felt that everywhere. I move my hands to her breasts and cup both. Taja's eyes shoot to mine before they droop slightly. I lightly pinch and tweak her nipples before leaning down and taking one into my mouth. Again, I feel her back arch, and her hands land on the sides of my head.

"Oh God. Vex. That's amazing. Don't stop," she groans out.

I don't. I'll give her anything she asks for and more. I give her the best nipple play I know how to give and love the sounds coming from her throat. When I feel her bottom half-straining upwards, trying to make contact, I slide my mouth down her stomach to the top of her pants. I sit up on my knees and undo them while staring into her eyes. She lifts her bottom, enabling me to pull them below her ass. I feel her kick her shoes off, so I stand up at the foot of the bed and remove her socks, pants, and panties. She's gorgeous and my eyes can't get enough. While looking my fill, I remove the rest of my clothing. Before dropping my jeans, I remove a string of condoms from the pocket and toss them on the bed.

Still standing at the end of the bed, I reach down and give my cock a few tugs. Taja's eyes are no longer drooping but wide open and glued to my hand. I know I'm larger than normal, and I can't help but smirk a little at her expression. She looks a little scared, a little excited, and a little in awe. Yeah, all are good for my fragile male ego.

I walk to the side of the bed and stand facing it while I pull on Taja's hand, helping her to sit up. She swings her legs to the side of the bed, and I move in between them.

"Touch me," I order in a raspy tone. Yeah, she has that effect on me.

Taja slowly and carefully places both hands on my cock and runs a thumb over the head. I grit my teeth because I need her to use a firmer touch, and I need that shit right now.

"Harder," I bark.

Her hands tighten, and then one drops to my thigh while the other begins stroking. Heaven! I thrust lightly into her hand and watch her expression closely. I know she's not overly experienced, and I don't want to rush her. But, fuck me, I need this woman's touch.

Taja's grip tightens even more, and she's now stroking me exactly how I like it. Her other hand leaves my thigh, and I sigh in relief and ecstasy when it finds my balls. She's gently rolling them around in her hand, almost like this is completely new to her. My mind blanks out on that thought when I feel my balls start to tighten and draw upwards. I've never been this close, this soon, before. I pull her hands off of me, concentrate on not coming just yet, and push her onto her back. I slide in on top of her and start kissing and nipping my way down her body.

I pull my hair back out of my face and kiss her lightly right above the pubic bone. I'm pretty sure she's stopped breathing. Sliding further down the bed, I sit up, ass on calves, and push Taja's legs up until her feet are planted next to me. Everything she has to give is in view, and it's a beautiful sight. Running my fingers down her pubic bone until I feel heat and dampness, my eyes meet hers. I'm so fucking hard, it's painful. But I want her as ready and hot as I can get her before my cock gets his share.

I dip the tip of my finger into her wetness and feel her body jerk. I slide that finger up to her clit and rub it gently before gliding it back down and in slightly. Taja's whole bottom lifts off the bed, begging for more.

"You okay? This okay, Taja?" I ask, but at the same time, I'm praying she says yes.

She nods her head and takes a deep breath.

"Words, Taj. I need the words, babe."

"Yes, Vex. Don't stop, please," she barely utters.

I slide back and down, and my mouth finally finds what it's been wanting since I met her. Taja's body heaves as my tongue drives deep into her. She's tight. She's so unbelievably tight that my cock protests at the time my mouth's taking. Using lips, tongue, fingers, and every technique I know, I get to bringing her pleasure. It's not long, and Taja's writhing on the bed and nearly pulling my hair out. Taja's breathing is harsh, and her moans are cock-hardening. I continue until I know she's come hard a few times and is primed for the rest of me.

Quickly sliding up her body, I grab a condom and roll it on. I take a moment to slide my tongue across and around her nipples. I nip lightly at each of them before shifting my position. Balancing over her, I slide my hips between her thighs and line up my cock. I'm not positive I could stop now, even if she asked me to. I've never felt this much of a need to be inside of someone before. It's like it's out of my hands, and it's just got to happen.

I grasp her thigh, lift it slightly to get the best position, and push into her tight heat in one motion. Taja's body stiffens, her nails dig into my shoulders, and she gasps. She's so tight. I have to push hard to get seated all the way. When I do, I notice she's again not breathing. I pull my face out of her neck and look at hers. Her eyes are closed tightly, and her jaw is clenched. I don't move at all, giving her body time to accept all that is me.

"Okay?" I grunt while trying to hold still when my whole being is screaming at me to move.

"Yeah. Fine. You're just… big. Sorry, I'm fine now," Taja answers while taking a breath.

After another moment, I feel her body relax, and I start to move slowly. She tenses at first but before long is moving against me. Her hands relax and start moving through my hair and against my shoulders.

I bury my face in her neck, bite down slightly on it and start moving my hips harder. Readjusting her leg opens her up more to me, and I lose myself in the feeling of Taja. I use one arm to brace myself and use the other hand to reach down between us and find her clit. Stroking her softly while thrusting hard, I feel her start to tighten up again. Knowing she's about to come, I push deep into her while pinching her clit. She explodes, and I curse myself for not watching her face.

As her body's coming down, I grasp both of her hips and slam myself into her several times, groaning as I come into the condom. As my body starts to relax, I glide a few more times in and out of her. She feels so good, so tight. I want our bodies to stay connected. I stay planted deep and still for a few moments before rolling to my back, disengaging us.

I slide an arm under Taja's shoulders and curl her into my side. Her hand lands on my abs and starts lightly tracing them. Her leg lays across one of mine, and we're full-on front to side. I turn my head and lay a soft kiss on the top of her head. When she looks up at me, I lay another on her mouth.

We lay quietly for several minutes before I carefully pull my arm out from under her head. I reach down, remove the condom, and Taja takes it out of my hand and drops it in the wastebasket on her side of the bed. I don't hesitate in pulling her back to my side. I roll so we're facing each other and run my hand gently through her hair. It's long, soft and I like the feel of it.

Taja inches closer so we're touching from chest to toes and pushes her face into my pec. I feel a soft kiss laid there, and it tugs on something low in my gut. I instantly push that feeling aside and concentrate on just having a beautiful woman's body pressed to mine. That I can handle. Emotions—not so much.

Moments later, Taja slips from my arm, pulls her shirt and panties on, and walks out of the room. I know it's time for me to make my exit, but I'm not ready to call it a night. I need more of her sweet body before our time together is over. It's not long before she walks back in and settles next to me again. I give it a beat and then pounce. I grin when I hear her small squeak at having my body suddenly sprawled on hers, but it's not long before it's moans and gasps I'm hearing. My grin disappears, stripping her clothes back off of her, and I get down to business.

I wake slowly and am momentarily confused as to where I am. I look down and find myself curled around Taja's back with my arm wrapped around her waist. I'm stunned to realize I'm cuddling her and that I'm still in her bed. Unprecedented territory for me. I'm hit with an urgent need to get the fuck out of here. I need to make tracks and not look back. I need to get back to who I am and not this guy.

With that in mind, I carefully pull away from Taja's sleeping form. I carefully cover her nakedness with her comforter and exit the bed. As I'm quietly but hurriedly getting dressed, I notice something odd. The string of condoms I tossed on the bed earlier are now on the floor, and there's only one missing. What the hell? My stomach drops when I realize what that means. I never, and I mean never, have had sex without a condom. Ever. And the proof that I did this time, more than a few times, in fact, is staring back at me. I'm clean and I'm sure Taja is too. That's not my concern. I don't want kids, never have wanted them. How the hell did I forget to wear a condom tonight? Fuck me.

I pick the condoms up, shove them in my hip pocket and pull out my wallet. I toss a fifty-dollar bill on Taja's nightstand to pay for the morning-after pill and leave her room. I'm unsettled about this fuck up. I only have myself and my greed for Taja to blame. I have to chat with her about this, but right now, I need to get gone.

Chapter 11

Taja

I laid listening to Vex getting dressed and then leaving the house. I woke when he did and felt his entire body stiffen. I stayed still to avoid the awkwardness of watching him panic about still being here. I know the kind of man he is when it comes to women, so I'm not surprised at his rush to leave. A little hurt that he couldn't wait to be rid of me, but I knew what I was getting into from the start. He never lied about that. I respect him for that more than I respect myself at the moment. I tossed all my morals aside for half a night with a gorgeous guy. A guy I knew was going to walk away immediately after. And worse yet, I don't feel regret at my decision. Vex was amazing and being with him was more so. I toss my hand up behind me, switch my lamp off, and with a small smile on my face, drift back to sleep.

"Taja!" I hear at the same time as Tessie lands on my mattress with a bounce and a giggle.

"Go away, brat. We'll talk after I shower and have coffee," I tell her with my head still buried against my pillow.

"I'm going to bounce on your bed until you sit up and listen to me," Tessie threatens.

I realize I'm still naked, and I know she's not bluffing. Shit to hell and back.

"Go make coffee while I take a quick shower. Then we'll talk," I order her.

"Okay, but you have ten minutes, and I'll be back up here," she states as she jumps up and rushes out of the room.

I quickly scramble out of bed and grab my fuzzy robe. I waste no time in heading directly to the shower.

While showering, I notice a small amount of blood on my thigh. Instead of sadness, I grin a little at why it's there. I hurry through my shower and brush my teeth before heading back to my bedroom. I flip on the overhead light and make my way to my dresser. After getting dressed, I turn to exit the room when I spot something on the nightstand. Walking toward it, I feel my stomach plummet. No, please don't be what I already know that it is. I pick up the fifty-dollar bill like it's a hot piece of coal and toss it into the drawer. Hiding it isn't going to take away the cheapness I suddenly feel about last night, though. I feel heat and wet hit my eyes, but I shove that shit down hard. I swallow the lump in my throat the best I can and drop down hard on my bed. The bed that still smells like Vex, me, and sex.

Why would he think he needed to pay me for sex? I frantically think back over our conversations, and I can't remember anything I'd have said that would indicate I was for sale. Or that I'm a prostitute, for Christ sakes! Holy Mother of God, is that what he thinks of me? I wasn't much of a challenge for him. That's true. I doubt many women are. But I chose to be with Vex because I liked him. Not for money. I feel sick to my stomach, and I feel cheap. All the good thoughts about last night are gone, and I'm suddenly ashamed of myself and my actions. Anger burns deep in my gut, but it's only at myself. In my inexperience, I didn't know all the rules to the game. Vex didn't use me or steal my virginity. He paid for it with cold hard cash. Not sure I could hate myself more than I do in this moment.

"Taja! Coffee's on!" Tessie shouts, pulling me out of my thoughts.

I stand, square my shoulders, and plaster a smile on my face. Tessie must never know what happened and how far I fell. I'm supposed to be her role model now that Mom's gone. Oh my God—Mom.

"Please, don't be too disappointed in me, Mom. I'll do better. Promise," I whisper as I leave the room.

After giving me my coffee, Tessie lets me know she doesn't want to go to college and lays out the plan she and Trigger came up with. She was hesitant at first, but her excitement quickly took over. I never meant for her to feel like she had to go to college. I just want her to be happy and loving what she does for a living. As Tessie's explaining, her smile grows.

"So, see, it's the perfect solution to everything!" Tessie nearly bellows at me in her excitement.

While I love her enthusiasm and seeing her smile, I'm numb from top to toe. I'm not near as positive her idea's as good of one as she is. My first instinct was to scream no! My second was to scream hell no! But I need to be rational about this and not let my emotions concerning Vex interfere.

"You've explained everything, Tessie, but I need time and more coffee to process it. Let me think about it, okay?"

"What's there to think about? It's perfect! Trigger said you should come and meet him and Petey since they'll be the ones looking out for me. They're freaking fantastic guys, Taj! Ask Suki! And you already know Freddy and Vex. You met Chubs. Does he look like a serial killer? No! Please, Taj, puuulllleeeeeese!" she says while giving me her big eyes.

"I'm not saying yes or no. I'm saying let me think about it. And I will speak with Suki for sure."

"While you're thinking, remember this. School's still out for the summer, and next week I turn sixteen. A lot of the girls in my class are getting jobs," Tessie adds with a sly grin. There goes my argument about keeping her grades up. At least for now anyway.

"I just never wanted you to have to work so young," I tell her quietly.

"You did it. And I don't have to; I want to. Big difference. Please remember that," she replies just as quietly as she stands and walks out of the kitchen.

I drop my head into my hands, knowing I'm fucked. Tessie wants this, and I don't want to stand in her way. I'm hella proud of her. But one concern we didn't discuss is Rooster. He's not happy I'm working for The Devil's Angels MC but has somewhat accepted it since he's getting his money from me. I don't see him being okay, in any way, Tessie will be too. Bridge to cross later, I guess.

Tessie's nearly bouncing in the seat as we pull into the club's garage. I'd have loved to sit around and wallow in my misery today, but she called Trigger, and he said to come on over. So here we are with me about to meet and assess her possible coworkers and supervisors.

Walking in the parts store door, I see a large guy behind the counter while a younger, bald version of him leans against it. Both sets of blue eyes swing our way, and I watch while the older guy's face breaks into a huge grin.

"Hey, Tessie. You got her here. Now it's up to us to convince her, right?" he rumbles out.

"Yeah, Petey. Do your best," Tessie grins back.

"Hi, Taja. I'm Petey Taylor, and this ugly guy's my son, Axel. Nice to meet you."

"You're the new bartender at Dreams, right?" Axel asks.

"Yeah, I am. Nice to meet you both," I reply.

"Freddy's been singing your praises. He claims life's easier now that he has you and Suki behind the bar," chuckles Petey.

"Freddy's a great guy to work for," I state. "He makes it easy."

The door to the garage opens, and in walks a couple more men. One is slightly older, shorter than Petey and Axel, but built solid. The other man's the largest person I've ever seen up close before. Tall, dark, and drop-dead gorgeous doesn't even begin to cover this man. Oddly enough, he has a parrot on his shoulder. Yes, a real live parrot.

"What up, bitches?" the parrot screeches.

"Mac! What the fuck? Watch your fucking language! There's women here! And who're you calling bitches?" Axel shouts.

"You!" screams the bird.

Petey smacks Axel on the back of the head at the same time Tessie and I snort out a laugh. When we do this, the bird's head swings our way, and he lets out a long, low wolf whistle.

"Mac, behave! Axel, shut it! Taja's going to think we're all like you two nut jobs, and Tessie won't get to learn from me." This was hollered by the shorter, older guy before he calmly turns to me and holds out his hand.

I take it and instantly like this man. I like that he's concerned about Tessie getting to learn from him. That he's worried about our opinion of them. His face is honest, strong with kind eyes, and his handshake is firm. Mom once said that a weak man would have a weak handshake. I've always remembered that.

"You must be Trigger. Nice to meet you. I'm Taja."

"No one else you could be. You two are the spittin' image of each other," Trigger states with a grin while releasing my hand. Tossing his hand toward the huge man, he says, "Gunner, Club President. The bird's name is Mac. Obviously, you've already met Petey and Axel. If it helps with any concerns you may have, Axel doesn't work here."

Axel protests. Mac screams "Woop! Woop!" and the other guys chuckle at the last comment. Tessie giggles while I understand right away that this is a tight-knit group. I've noticed the same with the members that come into Dreams. They tease, joke, and harass each other, but their loyalty is a tangible thing.

"Who would be Tessie's direct supervisor?" I ask Trigger bluntly.

"Petey's the manager here, but Tessie would be working directly with me. I'll oversee anything she does and work with her on what hours work best for you two. She'll start out doing the grunt work. Cleaning around the garage and storefront, oil changes, tires, things like that. Depending on what I'm working on, she'll be assisting me. We do regular auto and body repair, along with custom jobs and bikes. Wide range of things she can learn," Trigger responds.

"We'll pay Tessie minimum wage to start out. When Trigger and Petey feel she's earned more, she'll get a raise. Axel's wife, Bailey, is our club accountant, and she's always willing to help set up savings accounts, college funds, things like that. Bailey suggested that Tessie and you call her, and she'll explain what she can do for you two financially," Gunner tells us.

"I'd work for free just to get to learn things," Tessie insists.

"You're young, Tessie. You have a lot to learn, but Trigger says you have skill and the desire to learn. But the club will pay you a wage. We'd never expect you to work for free. Maybe somewhere down the road, you could work your way up to being a full-time employee here," Gunner informs her.

"Thank you, both of you, for explaining things. Tessie will be turning sixteen very soon. She's mature and very responsible for her age. But I'm sure you can understand my concerns with her working with all men. Men that we don't really know. Her safety's my only real concern at this point, I guess," I tell the group while looking each guy in the eye.

"Smart and understandable, for sure. I have a daughter that's slightly younger than Tessie, and that would be my concern too, Taja," states Petey.

"I'll show you around the garage and shop. You can see where Tessie would be working and meet the rest of the guys here. Not much we can say to ease your mind, Taja, but I will say this. On my life, Tessie will be safe when she's here. I know Petey will say the same thing. Not saying she won't hear some colorful language, though," Trigger says in a serious tone.

I grin at him before going on our tour.

After returning home with Tessie, speaking with Suki at length, I finally get a moment to myself. I'm ready for work, and I'm trying to gear myself up to have to face Vex tonight. I blast music louder than usual on the drive to Dreams. No way am I going to let him know how hurt I am over the money he left. Offended, yes. He'll hear about that. Hurt, though, is for only me to know.

I arrive at the same time as Suki, and we walk in together. I don't look for Vex. I just get to work. It's busier than hell today in here, and the music is blaring. Suki has tossed a few searching looks my direction, but I pretend not to see them. I remind myself to smile more to stop any suspicions she may have.

Several hours into my shift, and I still haven't seen Vex. Since we always work the same hours, I'm starting to feel like I'm being avoided. Maybe he's worried I'll be all clingy and weird now. He couldn't be more wrong. I may want to be clingy and claim that man as mine, but I don't even allow myself to entertain that thought. I knew what was what before I ever lost my clothes with him. No going back on that now. But even though I dreaded having to put on an act in front of him today, I'm feeling this odd ache that he's so done with me that he doesn't even want to see me at work. I'm pretty sure I've lost my damn mind.

Things have been odd, to say the least, for the last few days. Vex still hasn't shown up for work. I wanted to get the satisfaction of seeing his face when I shoved his fifty at him, but now I'm so over it. I placed his money, along with an additional fifty dollars, into an envelope with a note and tossed it into his locker at work. He has a padlock hanging from his locker that's unlocked, so I used that to secure his locker. I wouldn't have bothered, but after seeing how many bras, thongs, and panties were tossed in there, I thought I'd better so nobody could find my note to him. Then I immediately washed my hands. Twice.

On my days off, I decide to clean the house like it's never been cleaned before. When my mind is stressed, my body has energy to burn. Tessie's avoiding me and my cleaning binge now that I gave the okay for her to work at the garage. She nearly strangled me when I broke the news to her, and she hasn't stopped smiling since. Today was her first full day, and I drove her there this morning. She packed a lunch, donned her oldest jeans and t-shirt, and off we went.

I prayed to every god I've ever heard of that we wouldn't run into Vex there, and someone was listening. I followed Tessie in and approached the counter to speak with Petey and Trigger before I left her in their care. I went back in to remind them of their promise to keep her safe, but I almost lost my will when I saw the smiles they had for her. And then Trigger held up a pair of coveralls with a patch with Tessie's name on it. She squealed, they grinned bigger, and my speech about safety faltered.

"Put your lunch in the breakroom and get these on. We have work to get to, girl," Trigger gruffly says to her.

Tessie sprints through the door to the back, and I turn to the men. Squaring my shoulders, I get ready to lecture two bikers.

"Here it comes, Trig. Pay up," Petey crows.

"She hasn't uttered a damn word yet, Petey!" sputters Trigger.

"Okay, we'll play this out. What's up, Taja?" Petey grins at me.

"Uh, well, I just wanted to remind you two about Tessie and your promise that she'll be safe here," I mumble.

"Hah! Put it in my hand, you short bastard!" Petey shouts while holding his open hand in Trigger's direction.

"Jesus H. Christ, Petey! Now I know why Axel's such a pain in the ass!" Trigger huffs out while slapping a wad of cash into Petey's waiting hand.

"Do I want to know what's going on?" I ask.

"I told Trigger you'd show today, worried about Tessie being here. He said he made himself clear about that, and you'd be fine," Petey explains with a grin while counting his money.

"Sorry, Trigger. You did make yourself clear, but I'm a worrier. She's all I have left in this world, and she's everything to me. I hope I didn't offend you," I reply softly.

"Not offended in the least. Glad she has someone like you in her life. Family's important. I'll have my eye on her at all times and so will Petey. When the rat bastard's done counting my money, that is," Trigger answers with a grin while holding a piece of paper out to me.

I take it and relax when I see several phone numbers, including Trigger's and Petey's.

"Thank you. I'll get out of here and let you guys get to work," I say, grinning back at them. I get a finger wave from Trigger and a chin lift from Petey.

With Tessie out for the day, Suki comes over, and we work on the plans for her sweet 16 birthday party. It's a surprise, one I'm hoping she'll love, and we have lots to do yet.

"How's things going with Rooster?" Suki asks while multi-tasking like a champ. She's painting her fingernails, surfing online for a new outfit, and eating the largest cookie I've ever seen. I'm serious. It's the size of her head.

"Okay, I guess. He gets his money, and I get a Rooster-free life. Win-win."

"Everything else okay with you? You've seemed off for a few days now," Suki questions while shooting a look my direction.

I carefully blank my face and nod.

"Things are fine. I've just been worried about Tessie working at the garage. I haven't said anything to her, but I'm not sure how Rooster's going to take the news. I'm praying he doesn't decide he wants some of her paycheck too."

"We really should come up with a plan to have that man offed," Suki tosses out casually.

I grin because great minds think alike. Rooster will continue to be a pain in our asses for years to come yet, though. I've wracked my brain trying to think up a way to get him out of our lives, and so far, I've come up short.

"Yeah, it's always fun to dream about, but the reality is, I'm stuck with him," I say.

We continue to chat while making plans for Tessie's party. I no more than get the table cleared of the evidence when I hear a vehicle pull in the drive. Glancing out the window, I see the wrecker with Chubs and Tessie in it.

A moment later, Tessie comes bounding into the house and hits the kitchen with a full beaming smile in place.

"Have fun today, Tess?" Suki asks.

"Yes! Trigger showed me a bunch of stuff and let me change the oil in a couple of cars. Chubs took me on a wrecker call, and then we stopped at Sweet Angel Treats Bakery, and I met the Prez's wife, Ava, and Petey's wife, Trudy. They're awesome! They loaded us up with treats, and we pigged out on the way back to the garage. Trigger gave Chubs hell for not saving much for them, and it was funny. The guys are great. You don't have to drive me tomorrow, Taja, because Chubs is going to pick me up on his way," Tessie responds in almost one breath.

I grin at her and know I made the right decision in letting her work there. She needed this with Mom's passing, and I like that she's finding her way back to being a normal teenager.

"When you do the inviting for my party, can you make sure that Trigger, Chubs, and Petey are invited too?" Tessie asks with a sly grin.

"Uh, what party?" Suki questions while trying to look innocent. Epic fail.

"For my 16th birthday. Not stupid, ladies. No way would Taja let that day pass without a party," Tessie responds as she walks out of the kitchen.

Nope, she's not stupid, and we're busted. I get down to the business of adding those names to the invitation list.

Chapter 12

Vex

Pooh, a club member, and my closest friend, has shit happening with him and his woman, Pippa. A child's involved, and they've needed my help the last few days. I'd always be there for any club member or their women, but that means I had to blow off work. I can only imagine how Taja's viewing my sudden absence. I hate that she probably thinks I'm avoiding her, but it can't be helped. I've wanted to text her a dozen times and explain, but that might give her the wrong idea too. We had our night, and it was spectacular, but that's all we're going to have. But I'm having a difficult time keeping her off my mind. Especially now that I suspect I was her first experience.

I was so wrapped up in her the night we were together that I didn't notice anything off with her. I did note that she seemed unsure of herself, but I put that down to her not having a lot of sexual encounters. I didn't suspect that she'd had none until I got back to the clubhouse and hit the shower. Blood on my thigh. My stomach dropped, and the guilt hit hard.

Every woman's first sexual encounter should be special and with someone that's capable of caring for her. I'm not that man. If I am Taja's first sexual partner, she got shortchanged and deserves better than I can ever offer her. Why she didn't tell me, I have no idea. But not knowing ahead of time doesn't ease the guilt.

I came into work early today, but I only see Marti's car in the lot. Marti's a club slut and bartends part-time at Dreams. Likable, nice, and a bit dense, but she has a good heart. I approach the bar and take a seat. When Marti stops in front of me, I ask, "Why are you working this shift?"

"Taja and I swapped a few shifts. She's planning a party of some sort and has a date tonight, I think.

Or some kind of date night thing. I'm not sure, but she's covered for me before, so I wanted to help her out," Marti informs me before setting a beer down and walking off.

I immediately squash down the rush of anger at hearing Taja has a date. Nope, don't care. Not one bit. *Fuck that,* I think as I swallow down a large portion of my beer. Leaving the bar and my beer behind, I head to the break room where our lockers are located. I find mine locked and that too sets off my anger. I don't know if I even have a fucking key for it since I can't remember the last time I used the lock.

I check my keychain and don't find a padlock key. I storm across the hall into the dancers dressing room and rummage around the makeup tables until I find a nail file and bobby pins. I ignore the whistles and the flashing of skin. Stomping back to the break room, I attempt to pick the lock. It's a no-go. There's never been a lock I couldn't pick. What the fuck? Temper rising, I lose my patience and punch the locker a few times, leaving dents behind. Running both hands over my head and through my hair, I stand staring at that fucking locker. I can't even remember now why I wanted it open. But now that I'm pissed off, it's going to get opened, one way or another.

I stride down the hall to the office and push through the door. Freddy looks up from his desk, and I see his eyes widen. I'm guessing I look as angry as I feel. I walk to the large toolbox in the corner, open it and pull out some bolt cutters. Without a word to Freddy, I head back out and down the hall to the break room. Bolt cutters are amazing tools. One hard squeeze on them, and the lock breaks. Tossing the bolt cutters down, I rip the lock off and hurl that across the room, leaving a large dent in the drywall. I rip open my locker and stand there, still not knowing why I wanted into it so bad. Guess I just didn't like being locked out.

"Everything alright, Vex?" Freddy asks from the doorway.

I glance his direction and notice he's not alone. Standing beside him is Pooh. With a shit-eating grin in place because he must want an ass-whooping today.

"Every fucking thing's just fucking fine," I spit while enunciating each word slowly and clearly. Freddy's eyebrows shoot upward while Pooh's grin gets wider.

"Either you're on the rag, or you've finally been told no by a female," Pooh states.

"Fuck you, Pooh. What're you doing here anyway?"

"Dropping off paychecks and watching you lose your shit. Be glad it's me and Freddy and not Axel that's here. He'd harass your ass until you spilled why you're having a temper tantrum," Pooh says calmly. He's not bothered in the least by my glowering face. Fucker has more guts than brains, apparently.

I watch Freddy turn and walk off. Pooh steps inside the room and closes the door behind him. His face loses the grin as he approaches me.

"You ready to talk yet?" he asks quietly.

Pooh and I are close. He's more than just a club brother to me. He's as close as a real brother. But I still very seldom share about myself with even him.

"Nothing to talk about. Just irritated that my locker was locked for the first time in forever," I answer.

Pooh stares me down for a long moment before turning for the door. When he reaches it, he turns back and says, "When you're ready, I'll listen. Love you, brother."

I nod but don't respond as Pooh waits a beat before opening the door and leaving.

Looking into the locker, I see a sealed envelope with my name on the front. I pick it up and stick it in my back pocket, not thinking much of it. It's not uncommon for the dancers to leave me notes, naked pictures of themselves, and lingerie in my locker. With that thought, I scoop up all the pieces of clothing and toss them across the room. It irritates me that they do this, thinking it'll bring me running to them. Jesus, there really is more to me than just my appearance, but they don't take the time to see that. Still angry at the world, I stalk out of the break room and get to work.

Still in a pissy mood after my shift, I go for a long bike ride. It's the wee hours of the morning, but the wind and the road calm me down. Not wanting to examine why I cruise past Taja's house on my way to the clubhouse. It's dark and quiet as it should be at this hour. It looks like a home, cared for and loved, and I realize how empty my life is always going to be.

Reaching the end of her street, I make the turn and twist the throttle. As I do this, I notice a bike with a rider parked near the curb. I only get a glimpse, but there's something familiar about him. Looking into my mirror as I release the throttle, I see his bike light up and pull away fast. He disappears at the first intersection, and I know I'll never find him by the time I get turned around. I pull my bike to a stop in the exact place he was parked and look down the side street. I have a perfect view of Taja's house. I leave headed for the clubhouse, but I leave with a pit in my stomach.

It's late afternoon when I finally hit the main room of the clubhouse. Ava's dog, Loki, is laying full-out on his side near a couch. Her bird, Mac, is strutting his feathery ass up and down the bar singing the theme song to *The Big Bang Theory* TV show that's playing on the flatscreen. Gotta give him props—I can't sing it with how fast the words are said.

I amble my way into the kitchen, make a bowl of cereal, and head back to the bar to eat it.

"Hey, Mac. How're you doing, dickhead?" I ask him.

"Pretty boy has jokes!" he screeches at me as he stops singing.

"Don't be a hater, Mac. If your head wasn't so out of proportion to your body size, the females might like you just as much," Axel says as he plops his ass down next to me.

"Ladies looooooove me!" Mac insists loudly.

"Nobody loooooves you," Axel replies.

"Mom does!" Mac comes back with.

"She has to. It's the law. So shut it, birdbrain!" Axel continues to argue. These two argue anytime they're in the same room together.

"You shut it!" Mac predictably says back.

"You!" shouts Axel.

"I've got to save more cashews," Mac states mournfully before giving us a wing-wave (possibly trying to flip Axel off) and walks away.

"Hah! I think I just won against that feathered menace," Axel laughs.

"You're proud that you won an argument with a fucking bird? Axel, brother, you need some kind of deep therapy. Seriously," I tell him while shaking my head sadly.

"I have no dignity. I'm counting it as a win," Axel states proudly.

Axel's a great club brother. He's the VP and very loyal to his club, family, and friends. The perfect person to have at your side when shit's going down. You want to have a good time and a lot of laughs? You call Axel. You plan on kicking some ass? You better call Axel to help, or he'll pout worse than any 13-year-old girl you've ever met. But I'm still convinced that he was oxygen-deprived at birth. Petey, his dad, says no, but I don't think any of us believe him.

Axel's the one who brought me to The Devil's Angels. I was in a bar drunk off my ass and wanting a fight. I wasn't in the condition to win a fight, and Axel recognized that. He got me to go outside with him, with me thinking I was going to get the fight I wanted so badly. Instead, he tried talking me down. When I swung on him, he knocked me on my ass. He helped me back to my feet before clocking me again. While I was flat out on my back, he made a call. I'm stubborn as hell, so while waiting for Petey to arrive in his truck, I got up and got knocked back down a few more times.

Next morning, I woke up in The Devil's Angels clubhouse with a pounding head and face. On the nightstand next to me were a couple bottles of water and ibuprofen. It wasn't long before Axel stuck his head in the door and told me to get my ass up and out to the main room. I started as a prospect that day and haven't looked back since.

"Known you for several years now, Vex. You've always been silent about your past life, and I've let you be on that. Your business unless you want to share. But you know if you need something—anything—you only need to ask, right? Not much I wouldn't do for you. You haven't been yourself lately, and it's been noticed. Is something wrong or going on with you?" Axel asks in a quiet, serious tone.

"Nothing serious, Axel. With everything happening with Pooh and Pippa, nothing going on in my life's as important as that. I'll deal," I answer him.

"You've been there every step with and for Pooh and Pippa. But that doesn't mean your shit isn't important too, Vex. You need anything, call me. I'll listen, kick some ass, or just give you the best advice I can if that's what you need. Just sayin', I'm on your side."

"Thanks, Ax. I mean that. Thanks."

I get a backslap as he stands up and leaves the clubhouse. I finish my cereal, thinking that I need a better poker face. I don't like everyone knowing that I've been unsettled. Mostly because I can't explain the reason for it even to myself. I know it involves Taja, and this draw to her. But it's more than that. Ever since Tessie asked if I had a brother, I've been thinking a lot about my family—my mom, my brother, even my dad, though not in good terms when it concerns him. I miss Waianae, Hawaii, where I spent the good times of my youth. It's a rough part of the island, but that's where Tutu, my grandmother, lived. I don't miss my dad and the expectations he had for me, my brother, and Mom. They were unattainable, but that never kept him from expecting them.

I shake myself out of my thoughts and head outside. Striding directly to my bike, I toss a leg over it, slam my helmet on, start the bike, and head out for a ride. This is the only way I know to clear the cobwebs from my head. This and a hot willing woman. Bike ride it is for today, though.

A few more days pass before I pull into work and see Taja's car in the lot. I feel my temperature rise, and it's not in a good way. I park my bike and stay seated for a few minutes trying to quell my anger. While lying in bed last night, I remembered the note I'd found in my locker. I pulled it out, opened it, and wanted to put my fist through the wall.

Vex,

Thanks for a great night. Practice makes perfect it seems. The dancers were right – you're a great lay. Not sure why you left the money behind. Unlike them, and you, I'm not a pro. I've returned your money along with a tip for services very well rendered.

T.

I texted but received no answer. I called her and again no answer. I'm angry as hell at the tall blond wench. We'll be having a discussion, and she's not going to like the topic. I'm a pretty easy-going guy, but she's found a way to set me off like few have ever done.

Entering the club, my eyes find Taja behind the bar with Suki. She's smiling and laughing, and I have to force my eyes not to go squinty. I also force myself to stop and speak with Rod before I head to Freddy's office.

After I get the lowdown from Freddy as to what's happening tonight at the club, I make a round then seat myself at the bar. Taja immediately sets a beer down in front of me.

"Hey, Vex. How's it going today?" she asks casually with a small smile.

"Been better, Taja. Your phone not working?" I snip back.

"It's working just fine," she replies before walking away.

I'm not used to women blowing me off. While I get sick and tired of women rubbing against me and grabbing my junk, I'm also finding I don't like being ignored by Taja. I drink my beer while watching her interact with the customers. Before that can annoy me too much, a fight breaks out by the stage, and I'm a little too happy to bust some skulls.

When the fight is broken up, and the troublemakers hauled out the door, I see Pigeon, Toes, and Horse Nuts chatting up Suki and Taja. Pigeon has never hidden his feelings toward Suki. I don't know how deep they run, but I do know he's always trying to get her to spend time with him. No idea where Suki's at with all that, but that's their deal. What's now pissing me off isn't Pigeon and Suki. It's Toes and where his eyes keep landing when he looks at Taja. God didn't give her that ass for his eyes to enjoy.

Striding to the bar, I lean in between Toes and Horse, facing Toes. Our faces are close, and his eyes widen at my sudden appearance. I glare at him without saying a word. I know I'm confusing him, but I don't care. He needs to get gone. Now would be a good time for that to happen.

"There a problem, Vex?" Pigeon asks quietly as he steps up to my side.

"No. Toes has decided he wants to drink some place different tonight. Right, Toes?" I growl while staring Toes down.

"I do?" Toes exclaims while proving why the club members have been hesitant to patch him in. He's not always the quickest on the uptake.

"We both do. Let's hit the road, Toes," Horse states while standing up. Horse catches on quickly and will make a great club member someday soon.

After Horse and Toes walk out the door, I turn around to find several pairs of eyes on me. I ignore the looks and sit my ass down on Horse's vacant stool. Suki plops a beer down within reach at the same time Pigeon and Freddy take the stools on each side of me. Taja and Suki move away to fill orders while Pigeon and Freddy sit quietly, waiting patiently.

"You two can stand down. Everything's fine," I bark.

"Never seen you so angry all the damn time before, Vex. Makes me nervous," Freddy says.

"What's going on, brother?" Pigeon questions.

"Not a fucking thing," I answer, calmer now that my anger is disappearing. I set my beer bottle down, stand up, and leave them sitting there.

"Did you really think you were going to slip out tonight without talking with me?" I ask Taja as she slides onto her car seat.

I grin a little evilly at the squeal of fear that leaves her perfect mouth. I also grasp her forearm before she can bolt back out of the car. I wait until she settles down and then take her keys from her hand. I pocket them and wait for her to speak.

"What the hell are you doing in my car?" she screeches at a level I'm sure only dogs can hear.

"I broke in. That's not important. Here's how this is going to go, Taj. I'm going to talk. You'll listen and answer appropriately when and if I ask you something. Nod your head if you understand," I say.

"You broke…" Taja starts to holler before I lean over and slam my mouth down on hers. My kiss is harsh, but it stops her from speaking.

I continue tasting her until I feel her body relax. I slowly pull my head back and enjoy the look on her face. It doesn't last near long enough, though, before her eyes narrow at me.

"I enjoyed our night a fuck of a lot more than I should have, Taja. No, be quiet. I'm talking right now," I say when her mouth opens to protest.

She closes her mouth, but her whole body glares at me as I continue.

"Every fucking second with you was spectacular. Never thought you were doing it for money. I know you don't roll that way. Maybe that's why I was so determined to spend time with you. You're real, and I like that. I've found I like that a lot. I left the money, not as payment, but to use for the morning-after pill," I state, watching her eyes grow larger when the last sentence sinks in.

"You used condoms!" Taja shouts, almost accusatory.

"Not every time we fucked Taja. And I'm sorry about that. I've never had sex without one, and I fucked up with you. I'm clean, so you don't need to worry about that. I'm assuming you are too. Correct?"

"Yes, of course, I am," she murmurs.

"Are you on birth control?" I ask while holding my breath.

"No," she barely whispers as I feel my stomach drop.

"Oh fuck, Taja. We might have a problem then," I groan out.

She's deathly silent for a few minutes while staring across the parking lot. I let her have her thoughts while my mind tries to sort through the mess we could now be in. Finally, her eyes swing my direction, and I can easily spot the steely determination in hers.

"*We* don't have a problem, Vex. *I* might have one, but I'll deal. We knew going into that night that we had an expiration date. We work together, and I have no problem with that continuing, but that's all the relationship we're going to have. Thank you for clearing up the money thing. You need to walk away now."

My anger comes rushing back, and I slam my fist on her dashboard. I instantly regret it when I see her flinch and lean further away from me.

"Don't do that! Don't flinch, and don't lean away from me in fear, Taja! Don't ever fucking do that! I would never lay a hand on a woman and especially not you! Jesus fucking Christ!" I rasp out in frustration.

"You need to get out of my car, Vex. I need to get home and process all of this," Taja says while holding her chin up at a determined angle.

Emotions are too high and the topic too heated, so I see the wisdom in her words. I open the door and step out. Tossing the keys to her, I lean my head into the opening and ask, "Were you a virgin?"

"Yeah, I was," Taja answers softly as she starts her car. She immediately puts it into gear and starts to pull away. I slam her door with enough force to rock the car and watch her leave the lot.

I spend the rest of the night riding my Fat Boy, but not because I need to clear my mind. I'm very clear on what to do. I'm not sure how I'm going to make

Taja understand, but I'll find a way. The game has changed. If there's a baby, I'm going to be in it and Taja's lives. That's non-negotiable. I think I may force my way into Taja's life whether there's a baby or not. She intrigues me. She challenges me and doesn't bow at my feet. I like her determination to give Tessie a good life. I simply flat-out like and admire her.

I turn my bike into the club's gym and park it. Walking inside, I spot Axel, Pooh, and Cash standing at the counter together. Axel's speaking, and the other two are laughing at him. Common occurrence when Axel's involved. I give a chin lift their direction but head for the locker room. After changing, I hit the weights. After a long workout, I'm feeling more like myself again. My muscles ache, and my lungs are burning. It's time to hit the shower, then head to the clubhouse for some sleep.

Wrapping a towel around my waist and using another to dry off with, I head to my locker. While sitting on the bench towel drying my hair, Pooh walks in and takes a seat on the bench across from me. We sit in silence for a few minutes before I break it.

"I fucked up. Bad. Like worse than anything even Axel has fucked up."

Pooh's eyebrows rise, but he stays silent.

Slinging the towel around my neck and pushing the hair out of my face, I drop my forearms to my knees and stare at the floor. Pooh won't judge me, that I know. I take a deep breath and start laying it out for him.

"I promised myself I'd stay away from fucking other employees of Dreams. Too messy. That idea went out the window when Taja started bartending there. I didn't act on it right away, mostly because Freddy asked me not to. So did Suki. I knew it would be a mistake, but fuck, God, I wanted her. We became good friends over the next few months, and I liked more and more about her. Things went sideways when I kissed her. No turning back for us."

I hesitate, trying to get my words straight when Pooh speaks for the first time.

"So, you two hooked up. Both consenting adults. Where's the problem? Is she wanting more than a hookup now?"

"She was a virgin and didn't tell me. I knew she didn't have a lot of experience, but I never expected that. Things were off the charts between us. I lost my common sense as soon as I touched her. We had sex several times that night. Only once with a condom. And I stayed the night, wrapped around her and liking it. A fuck of a lot."

"Holy shit, Vex! You've lost your damn mind!" Pooh sputters out. I'd laugh at the look of astonishment on his face, but I don't have it in me at the moment.

"It gets worse," I warn him. "I freaked the fuck out when I realized I had spent the night. I panicked even more when I realized the condoms were still lying there, unused. I bolted and left without waiting for her to wake up."

"Holy shit, Vex!" Pooh repeats. "Not even Axel's done something like that!"

"Still not done, Pooh," I say while watching him brace for the next stupid thing I did.

"Fuck me. Lay it out, brother," Pooh states lowly.

"I tossed a fifty on her nightstand before I left. I was thinking she would use it for the morning-after pill. She took it as I was paying her for the night.

She didn't realize that I didn't use a condom each time. Before I could talk to her about it, shit went down with you and Pippa. I didn't see her at work for several days. Let's just say she's angry and probably scared of what the future holds for her. I certainly didn't leave her that morning with the impression that I can be counted on."

I explain the rest of the mess, the note, and my current thoughts about her and the possible baby. By the end of it, Pooh's got a thoughtful look on his face. I half expected disgust or even anger, but I should've known better. That's not Pooh. He'll stand behind me no matter what I decide to do, but with the kind of man he is, he won't stand quietly if I didn't do the right thing.

"Do you care about her or just what happens if there's a baby?" he asks quietly.

"I like Taja. A baby will complicate things, but even if there isn't one, I want Taja. She's strong, fierce, and family's everything to her. Nothing matters more to her than her sister, Tessie. She would sacrifice anything for her little sister. Taja took care of her mom while she was sick and dying while working, paying the bills, and raising Tessie. She faced down Trigger and Petey to make sure Tessie would be safe working at the garage. How do you not admire and respect that? I think she's exactly what I need. But after all my mistakes with her, how do I convince her to give me a shot?"

"Don't let her push you away. She's going to try after all of this, especially if she's as independent as she sounds. Don't try to control her, though. Just be a steady presence in her life. But if you're going to go for Taja, remember she comes with a sister. Make friends with Tessie. You'll want her on your side. You need to be sure about this, Vex. She's not going to let you in easily. She'll be protective of herself, Tessie, and a baby if there is one."

"Yeah, I know they're a package deal. I'm good with that. I just don't know how to proceed at this point," I groan.

"You'll figure it out. Here if you need help with anything, brother," Pooh says.

"And you need to give up all the other women. Quickest way to get kicked to the curb, permanently, is if you're still dicking your way through Denver," Axel adds his advice while stepping around the lockers and into view.

"What the fuck, Axel? You being a creeper now?" I exclaim.

"You've been off for a while, Vex. Me, along with everyone else, has been wondering why. Came into the locker room, heard you talking. So, yes, I've become a creeper. Wanted to know what was wrong and if there's any way I could help. What? Don't give me that look! I have great ideas sometimes! Bailey's still with me, and I've done some stupid things, so I've learned some lessons along the way. And I won't tell anyone about how incredibly bad you fucked up. Way worse than me, I need to point out. Hey! I just thought of something! If your boys are good swimmers, our kids will be close in age!" Axel says excitedly.

"Axel, please, shut up now," Pooh states.

"Fine, I will. But if you need advice on how to get yourself out of a mess, I'm your man. Just sayin'," Axel spouts as he leaves the locker room.

"He's going to pout all day now," Pooh groans before laughing.

Chapter 13

Taja

I drive home with shaking hands. I can't believe I was so wrapped up in the feeling of Vex that I didn't notice we didn't always use a condom. What the hell's wrong with me? I know better, and he does too. What if there's a baby already growing inside of me? My thoughts are scattered about that. I've always known I wanted kids. I've always wanted a big family to love and care for but not by myself. Maybe God has a different plan for me than the one I wanted.

When I get to the turn for our street, I see a lone biker sitting on his bike near the curb. My first thought is Vex, but the tightness in my chest says different. When my headlights slide across his face, I recognize Popeye. I continue to my driveway but notice the bike following me. I shut my car off and step out just as Popeye comes to a stop behind me. I wait until his bike is off and walk over to him.

"Why are you here? I've paid the bastard on time each month. He's getting every fucking spare penny I have. Tessie and I don't have a dime to our name after he gets his share, Popeye," I spit angrily.

"Rooster wants you and Tessie at our club party next weekend. Wants to show off his two girls," Popeye answers, completely unaffected by my anger.

"To who? Prospective buyers?" I ask incredulously.

"Who knows. Maybe. Doesn't matter. Just have your asses there."

"You drove all the way here to tell me this? I'm not exposing Tessie to his club members. No way, no how. Not happening, and you need to let him know that. Next time, save yourself the trip and text me. I'd rather not have the visual reminder of your cut that I share blood with your Prez," I inform him before turning and walking toward the house.

"Be there, Taja, or you won't like the consequences," Popeye orders before starting his bike and leaving.

I don't get much sleep, and I wake up in a bad mood. I realized while I was trying to get to sleep that Rooster's club party is the same day as Tessie's birthday party. There's no way we could go even if we wanted to. Going to Santa Fe is a hard no and always will be.

When I get downstairs, I find that Tessie's gone already, so I'm guessing Chubs picked her up again. They're becoming good friends, and I know she thinks the world of him. It would be hard not to when the guy is always smiling, happy, and helpful. Tessie's told me how much he loves his food, so I decide to make him some treats today. I also need to run invitations up to the garage for the other guys.

I take a few minutes and enjoy a quiet cup of coffee before hitting the shower. I dress in some old cutoff jean shorts and a tank top, slip my feet into flip flops, and get to work making my almost famous chocolate chip and bacon cookies. Everyone gives me a weird look when they hear what's in them but love them once they've eaten one. I'm hoping Chubs is the same.

I try to keep my mind off the possibility of a baby, but it's hard to. I need to stop at the pharmacy and pick up a pregnancy test or two so there aren't any more questions if or not. There's a part of me that's scared about knowing, but I've always been the kind to feel knowledge is power. No matter what happens in my world, once I process and make a plan, I can deal with it. This won't be any different.

Before leaving for the garage, I throw together some roast beef sandwiches from leftovers we have, grab a few bottles of water and a bag of chips. I add more cookies to the bag for Petey and Trigger and head out.

"Hi, Petey. How're you doing?" I ask, walking up to the counter.

"Doing great, Taja. What'cha got there?" he asks, indicating the cooler in my hand.

"We had some leftovers from a roast, so I made some sandwiches for Tessie and you guys for lunch. Chips and water included. Also, some chocolate chip and bacon cookies…," I say. I no more than say the word cookies, and Petey is hustling out from behind the counter and waving his hands in the air at me.

Before I can ask what's going on, he places a very large hand over my mouth and whispers, "Shhhh! Don't say cookies out loud, or Chubs'll be all over you before any of us get one!"

"Who's got cookies?"

Petey rolls his eyes and removes his hand.

"See? Toss the cookies and run, girl! Save yourself," Petey says, laughing as Chubs appears next to him, smiling huge, hand lovingly rubbing the cooler.

"Hi, Chubs. You've been so nice to pick up Tessie. I thought I'd make lunch for you guys. And yes, I have cookies. They're chocolate chip and bacon. Hope you like them."

"Two of my favorite things! I'll love them, don't you worry!" Chubs answers while starting to pull the cooler away from me.

"Not so fast, Chubs. Release the cooler, and nobody gets hurt," Petey tells him. "It's for all of us, and I'll hand it out because you'd grab and go leaving us not even a crumb. This isn't my first rodeo with him," Petey informs me with a wink.

I let out a laugh when I see the look of disappointment on Chubs' face, but he complies with Petey's demand. I hand the cooler over to Petey just as Trigger and Tessie walk through the door leading to the garage.

"Hey T! What're you doing here?" Tessie asks as she rushes up and gives me a quick hug. I explain why I'm here again and then hand each of the guys their invitations.

I know in my heart that three bikers probably aren't big on the idea of attending a sweet 16 birthday party, but I promised Tessie I'd invite them. I'm very pleasantly surprised when Trigger asks if he can bring his woman. The fact that he's willing to spend his day off doing this for Tessie warms me toward him even more. Then Petey and Chubs ask the same thing.

"Of course, you can. We'd love to have them. It's not going to be a fancy thing at all. Just a cookout with Tessie's friends," I tell them.

"Cake?" Chubs asks.

"Yes, there'll be cake too."

"Petey, please bring Bella! Can she come too?" Tessie asks excitedly.

"Absolutely, Tess. She'd love to come. She's home schooled, so she doesn't have a lot of friends outside of the club, so thank you for thinking about her," Petey says, aiming soft eyes at Tessie.

Turning to me, Tessie explains that she met Bella a few days ago, and they hit it off right away. And that she's Petey's youngest daughter, Axel's youngest sister.

"Yes, please bring her, Petey. If she ever wants to come hang out with Tessie and me, she's welcome to. She'll meet some of Tessie's friends at the party, and they're at our house quite a bit. It may help increase her girl gang," I tell him.

"Thank you, Taja. That would be great for her to meet more people close to her age and have friends she can socialize with. We'll be there for sure," Petey responds.

Tessie squeals, the rest of us grin, and then Trigger swears loudly.

"Where in the hell is Chubs and the cooler?"

On my way home, I stop at a pharmacy. I sit in the parking lot for a few minutes, nervous to go inside. Not knowing seems easier, but I have to do this so I can make a plan if needed. I go in and buy a few tests that will determine my future. Hard to believe that something that fits in a small plastic bag will have the ability to change my whole life. A condom's even smaller. I'm such an idiot.

Pulling into my driveway, I see Vex's bike parked there and the man himself sitting on the porch steps. I can't catch a break. I need to take these tests and process whatever the results are, and I need to be alone to do that. I decide to get whatever Vex wants to talk about out of the way quickly. I leave my car and approach him.

"Why're you here, Vex?" I ask.

"Why do you think, Taja?" he asks.

I roll my eyes and step around him to climb the steps. He follows me to the door and steps inside, shutting it behind him. I walk through the living room and into the kitchen with Vex on my heels. I set my purse and shopping bag on a counter before grabbing two waters out of the fridge. I hand one off to Vex and crack mine open. I take a seat at the table and indicate with my hand that he should too.

"You bought pregnancy tests. Can you take one this soon?" Vex asks in a low rumble.

"It's best to wait and take one the day after a missed period. They can be taken one to two weeks after sex too. Not as accurate, though, as waiting," I answer him.

"Where's your head at with this?"

"Scared, nervous. A little hopeful that we might get lucky and get away with our mistake," I quietly tell him. I hesitate before finishing my thought. "Wondering what it would be like to be pregnant and have a baby. What he or she would look like. Be like. Grow up to become."

"You're not freaking out?"

"I had a few moments of panic last night, but it is what it is now. We can't go back and change things, so I have to look forward. Once I know for sure, I can start making plans. I'll be fine once I can do that," I explain. "What about you? What's your thoughts about this?"

"I'm good. My head's on straight about this. If you're pregnant, you're not doing it alone. Accept and know that now. It'll be our baby. Ours. Not yours. Not mine. Ours. As in ours together."

Vex's gaze on me is steady, and I can see the truth in his beautiful eyes. He's not going to disappear or brush me off. He's in this mess with me. As I'm sitting here digesting his words, his warm hand lands on mine on the table. He threads our fingers together and gives my hand a squeeze. My heart does a slow flip-flop, the same as it always does when I have Vex's attention or touch.

"I believe you mean that, Vex. Thank you. But we're probably worrying for nothing."

Without releasing my hand, Vex stands and steps to my side of the table. Using my hand, he pulls me to standing, and his other hand lands on my hip. We're touching from chest to thigh, and I'm finding it far from unpleasant.

Looking up to his face, I see that his eyes are heated. I press tighter to his body and allow myself to enjoy all that's Vex.

"Pregnant or not, we're going to be okay, Taj. If we are, I want you to understand that we'll be a family. Us three and Tessie too. We'll find the way that works for us. We'll make it work," Vex states firmly. No waver, no doubt in his voice.

"Okay, Vex. Thank you," I say while dropping the side of my face against his chest. He releases my hand, wraps both arms around me, and stands steady. After a moment of silence, Vex steps back. I start to turn back to my chair when I'm suddenly airborne and being cradled in his arms. My startled eyes shoot to his and see his whole face grinning wolfishly at me. Instinctively, I toss my arm around his neck and hang tight when Vex puts us into motion.

"What the hell?" I shout.

"It was dark and shadowed in your room the night we spent together. Today, it's light out. I'm now going to see what I missed last time, Taja. I want you naked and screaming my name, baby. You okay with that?" Vex rasps out.

Before I unscramble my thoughts and answer, we land on my bed, Vex on top. He immediately shifts his weight slightly to my side, and our mouths collide. Vex completely overwhelms my senses. His taste, touch, heat, and skill keep me enthralled while he explores my mouth. When his hand cups my breast, I come unstuck and roll him to his back. Sliding on top of him, I let my lips roam all the bare skin I can find. My hands slide under his shirt and discover his eight-pack abs. I lightly run my fingers over the defined muscle. There's nothing soft about Vex. He's hard everywhere, and my hands enjoy every inch of him.

Vex's hands cup my ass and start sliding my lower half against his. I push up so I'm sitting astride his hips and let him create wonderful friction with our bodies. I pull his t-shirt off and bare his muscled body to my eyes. He has several tats that only increase my desire for him. The tribal tats fit Vex's body like he was born with them. With his hair, eyes, and olive-brown skin tone, he has an untamed look. It all works beautifully together.

"What're we doing, Vex? Are we complicating things?" I quietly ask.

"Nothing's complicated with us. We may or may not be pregnant, and we'll get the answer together. We'll deal with it together. Today, we're just enjoying each other. Spending time together. Don't overthink this. There's nothing to be worried about. We're both adults, Taja. It's not wrong in any way for us to be together."

"Regardless of how things turn out, I don't regret being with you. I don't think being with you was wrong. But this is all new to me, and I don't know how to be casual about it. I don't want to let feelings get involved and then end up gutted. How do I protect myself from that? You're an overwhelming force, Vex. I know you're a good guy. I've seen that so many times at work. I like you as a person, as a man. I like who you are. But we're worlds apart in sexual and relationship experience. I want to be with you, but I need to know how to keep it straight in my head that physical is all this is," I explain.

"Take one day at a time, Taja. Don't decide what we are or aren't today. Neither of us knows what we are yet. Let's just be ourselves and see how things go," he responds while lifting me off of him and laying me flush against his side. I rest the side of my face on his pec and settle my hand on his abs.

"Okay, I can do that," I answer with some doubt evident in my voice.

Vex dislodges my hand and head when he rolls to face me. His hand finds my hair at the side of my face and burrows into it deep enough that he's cupping the back of my head.

"I didn't come here today to coax you into bed with me. I came because I wanted to know how you're doing with everything. I came to talk with you about not shutting me out. About letting me in a little more. But shit gets out of hand fast where we're concerned, and here we are. I want you, no doubt there. But I want you to be comfortable with the idea of us having sex again. I'm not trying to pressure you. The ball's in your court whether we do or not. Even if you say no, that's not going to change me from seeing this through with you. You understand what I'm saying?"

"Yeah, I do."

"Why didn't you tell me you were a virgin, Taj?" he asks with concern in his voice.

"I was going to, but things got out of hand so fast. I got so wrapped up in touching you and how you were making me feel, it was too late to say anything," I mumble in embarrassment while dipping my chin.

Using the hand in my hair, he tilts my chin back up until our eyes meet.

"Never be embarrassed with me. You and me? We're always going to be honest and open with each other. Anything you need or want to say is something I need or want to hear. There's nothing to be ashamed of when it comes to us having sex. It's natural, and it's explosive between us. It's not usually that way, the way it was with us. It's only the two of us in this room, and I'd never judge you for asking a question or having doubts. We'll talk out anything together. Yeah?" Vex orders in a low, firm voice.

"Yeah."

"And if at some point you want to try freaky things, I'm here for you. Use me any how you want," he adds with a grin and a wink.

I grin back as my whole body relaxes, and my mind calms.

"Another question for you. When's your period supposed to start?" Vex questions, face serious once again.

"End of next week," I answer after having thought about it for a few seconds.

"Maybe make a doctor's appointment for the week after that just to confirm whatever the home test tells us. You have health insurance through Dreams, but any out-of-pocket expenses, I'll pay. And I'll be going to the appointment with you."

"You're kind of bossy. You're aware of that, right?"

"Yup, well aware. Get used to it because you might have to deal with it for a very long time," he answers with a smug smile.

"I'm not going to let you steamroll over me," I warn.

"Hope not. I like your mouthy-ass ways."

Vex leans forward and nips at my bottom lip playfully before pulling back.

I let my eyes wander the planes of his face before surprising both of us.

"You bring a condom?"

Vex's face breaks into a pantie melting smile before he pulls one from his pocket and holds it up between us.

Again, I surprise both of us when I ask, "Will you show me how to put that on you?"

He does, and it was spectacular. Luckily for me, he brought three condoms and left with none.

Chapter 14

Vex

Driving my truck, I pull to a stop at the club's garage and auto body shop. I walk into the nearest garage bay and look around for Tessie. I see her, head close to Trigger's, listening intently to whatever he's explaining about the car they're both looking at. Stopping next to her, I grin when she glances my way quickly before turning back to Trigger. Guess I can't compete with Trigger and a motor. I patiently wait for Trigger to finish up his lesson and admire his dedication to teaching. Good guy to the core.

"Hey, Vex. Need something?" Trigger asks.

"Question for Tessie," I answer before turning to her. "Have you taken driver's ed yet?"

"Yeah, I have my permit. I just need more hours in the car to get my license," she replies, looking confused.

"What time do you get off work today?"

"If you're taking her driving, she can go now," Trigger answers for her.

"You're taking me driving?" Tessie asks with a hopeful look.

"Yep, if you call Taja and get the okay from her first," I answer.

Trigger chuckles when Tessie's phone appears in her hand faster than you can blink.

Quick conversation later, we're sitting in my truck, Tessie behind the wheel. I give her a few minutes to adjust the seat and mirrors and to familiarize herself with everything else. Blinding smile in place, she starts the truck, and we're off.

Less than five minutes later, and I'm saying prayers that I'm not even sure are correct. My fingers are surely leaving permanent marks in the dash, and

I'm surprised my feet haven't shoved through the floorboards yet. Tessie has one foot on the gas, one on the brake and uses them indiscriminately. It's not humanly possible to be this bad of a driver and smile so big while doing it.

Realizing this could turn out bad for us, I direct her to the lesser-used side roads. No way am I going to be strapped in this potential death mobile on the crowded freeways. Once we're out of town, I get her to use some dirt backroads to enter the club property from the backside of it. We accomplish this with a close call of bringing the gate post with us, a little less paint on the driver's door, and a girlie-sounding squeal that I will forever deny making. My balls have crawled as far up into me as they can get, and I doubt I'll be seeing them anytime soon.

Beautiful little Tessie has a lead foot, and I'm grateful my truck is large and built strong. I don't care about a few dents. I only care about breathing tomorrow.

When I point to Petey and Trudy's house, Tessie applies the brake hard enough to engage my seat belt and test its strength. It holds, and I remind myself that we're alive, and the vehicle is no longer in motion.

"That was flipping awesome!" Tessie gushes as she removes her seat belt and jumps out the door. She rushes to my side just as I open the door, and I get a quick hug.

"Can I go see if Bella's around?" Tessie asks.

"Yes! Please! I mean, yeah, she'd love to see you. I'll come get you when I'm ready to leave," I tell her with what I'm hoping is a steady voice while pointing with a shaky finger to which house Bella resides.

After Tessie disappears into Petey's house, I drop my head against the neck rest and sigh. How do I tell her she sucks at driving, and I'm a frightened little girl about ever riding with her again?

"What'cha doing, Vex?"

Opening my eyes, I see Craig's little face peering up at me curiously. As he usually is, the kid's covered in dirt, grass stains, and what I'm hoping is mud this time. You can never tell with him, though. Craig is Pooh's soon-to-be son. Pippa, Pooh's woman, has already adopted him, and Pooh will too when they marry. Standing next to Craig is Gee. Ironically enough, the pig's cleaner than the kid.

"Counting my blessings. Where's Pooh?"

"Right here. Why're you in the passenger seat?" Pooh asks as he steps next to Craig.

"He's counting his blessings. Whatever the hell that means," Craig states while flicking caked mud off his arm.

"Don't let Pippa hear you swearing again, little man. Unless you've suddenly developed a taste for dish soap," Pooh says with a laugh at the look on Craig's face. The kid is notorious for not only his bad language but his dislike for soap and water.

"It's just us men here. You said I can swear when the women aren't around," Craig reminds Pooh.

"That's not exactly what I said," Pooh replies with a grin.

"But it's what I heard. I gotta go before Trudy sees me. She's pretty quick on her feet when she's got a washcloth in her hands," Craig says with a wave as he and Gee head down the street.

"Passenger seat?" Pooh reminds me of his question.

I explain to him about Tessie's driving lesson. By the time I'm done, he's bent over laughing his stupid ass off at me.

"Not funny! How do I tell her she sucks big time?"

"Who sucks big time?" Axel asks as he and Gunner, with Mac on his shoulder, stop next to Pooh.

"You do!" Mac shouts.

"You know what, Mac? Your mommy isn't here to save your ass today. Maybe it's time the birdie goes bye-bye," Axel shouts back.

"Bring it on, girlfriend!" Mac responds.

Axel makes a mad grab for Mac but ends up jerking his hand back with beak marks on it.

"You bit me!" Axel accuses.

"Stop right now! I'm not listening to you two argue for one more second today," Gunner adds to the shouting match.

"He bit me!" Axel insists.

"And I don't give two shits about that!" Gunner says exasperatedly.

I see the perfect solution to my and Gunner's problems. Time to get cagey.

"I was giving Tessie a driving lesson. Made me a little nervous, to be honest. I'm not cut out for it. I really suck at teaching, I guess," I interrupt, adding in a mournful look.

It works to distract Axel from throttling Mac.

"How hard can it be to teach someone to drive? Losing your touch with the ladies, Vex?" Axel asks with a smug smile. "I taught Bailey how to drive a stick shift in no time flat."

"Would you be willing to try with Tessie? She's turning sixteen this week but still needs more in-car driving hours. She's such a great kid. I hate to see her be disappointed if she doesn't get those hours. You can use my truck. Maybe just keep her on the compound and put her through the paces?"

"Sure. Be happy to," Axel answers as we all watch Tessie and Bella walk in our direction.

"Hey, Tessie. Me and you are going for a ride. You're driving. I'm teaching," Axel tells her as I quickly get out of my truck so he can climb in.

"Can I go too?" asks Bella as Tessie hurries to the driver's side.

"No!" Pooh and I both shout at the same time.

Bella's eyes go wide in surprise at our tone, but Pooh smooths it over with a lie.

"I need you to help me find Craig, honey."

"Oh, okay. See you in a while, Tessie!"

As the truck's engine roars to life, Axel lowers his window and gives me a cocky grin.

"Watch and learn," he laughs.

His eyes go wide, and the grin and laughter leave his face when Tessie drops the truck into gear. She leaves us in a cloud of tire smoke as they screech their way down the street. Nice to know I'm not the only man Tessie has made squeal like a girl today.

"Have fun, Assman!" Mac bellows.

"He's going to kill you when and if he survives," Gunner chuckles.

"He has to survive first, though," I answer calmly.

"He'll never want to teach me to drive now," Bella moans.

"I'll teach you, sweetheart. But promise me now that you will never, ever get into a vehicle that Tessie's driving," Pooh commands.

"Not that stupid, Pooh. Holy crap! I think she just turned that corner on two wheels!" Bella says with a little awe in her voice.

Me: You ever ride with your sister?

Taja: Of course. Why?

Me: You didn't think to warn me?

Taja: About what?

Me: Never mind. I'll have her home in an hour. I'll bring dinner.

Taja: You don't have to do that but thank you.

Me: See you soon

There's no way Taja hasn't noticed how horrible Tessie's driving is. She's messing with me, and I like that. Means she's getting more comfortable with me. I chuckle to myself as Gunner, Mac, and Bella walk away. I turn to Pooh and see he's still laughing about Axel's predicament.

"You're a dead man walking when he gets back here," Pooh sputters.

"Yeah, I know. Worth it, though, just to see his face when she hit the accelerator. You going to stick around for the beat down?"

"You couldn't pay me enough to miss seeing Axel's face when they get back here," Pooh confirms what I already knew as we both listen to tires squealing in the distance.

A few minutes later, and I see my truck barreling down the road toward us. Even from a distance, I can hear Axel shouting. Pooh's bent over again, laughing his ass off. I can see that Axel has one hand on the dash and one on the oh-shit handle. That's all I notice before Pooh and I are both scrambling to get out of the way of the sliding truck. It comes to an abrupt stop, smoking tires and all, with one tire jumping the curb and landing on Petey's lawn.

Tessie calmly shuts the engine off and steps out, smile still in place. Axel stays sitting in the truck for another moment before he slowly gets out. His face is pale, but the glare he's aiming in my direction says there will be consequences. I make sure he sees the big-ass grin on my face.

"Rat bastard!" Axel rasps out in a much smaller voice than he usually uses. He clears his throat twice and stabs his finger at Tessie before continuing.

"That was some kind of fucked-up *Dukes of Hazzard* shit right there! What the fuck, girl?"

Pooh and I are laughing too hard to respond, but Tessie shares her thoughts instantly.

"I don't like Axel as my teacher. He hollers and screams a lot, and I'm sure I heard him giving himself the last rites. Who does that? That's just rude when I was just practicing my turns and stuff," she says with a small sniff.

Axel turns and starts walking slowly toward his house. I'm shocked that he's not rearranging my facial features already. He turns and continues walking backward while saying, "This isn't over. You'll be getting the ass-whooping you deserve, Vex."

We watch him disappear into his house, and I turn to Tessie, holding out my hand. She frowns but hands over my keys. Pooh walks away, still laughing.

"Where do you want to get food at? I told Taja I'd bring dinner when I take you home," I ask her.

"You like her, don't you?" Tessie questions.

"Well, yeah, I guess. We're friends. We work together. We, uh...," I fumble for words.

"Yeah. You like her," she replies with a grin.

"Whatever, kid, let's go."

Chapter 15

Taja

I'm weeding the flower bed in front of the house while laughing myself silly. I knew I'd be getting a call or text from Vex after he rode with Tessie. I'd do anything for that girl, but there's a reason she doesn't have enough training hours yet. She took five years off my life the last time I let her practice. Her driving literally caused me to piddle a little, not that I'd ever tell her that. I haven't worked up the courage yet to let her try again. For someone who knows and loves cars so much, she can't drive one worth a damn.

I try to hide my smile when I see Vex's truck turning into my drive but don't succeed much when I see a few scrapes of paint missing from his door. I can clearly see his glare as he comes to a stop, and Tessie bounces out of the truck. She's carrying take-out bags, and I rise, brushing the dirt from my hands. Tessie heads into the house while Vex emerges from his truck, slamming the door behind him and approaching me.

"You're an evil wench," he mutters as he stops in front of me.

"I've been called worse."

"You could've warned me that she thinks she's Dale Earnhardt, Jr. behind the wheel," Vex continues.

"Could've, but she needs the hours," I answer with a grin.

"And you're too scared to let her get them with you," he states while putting his hands on his hips.

"Too scared and too smart. I might be blonde, but I'm not dumb. Not suicidal either."

"I'm buying her a tank for her birthday. She'll be safe, at least. The world—not so much," Vex snorts while finally giving me a grin.

"I probably deserve a spanking for not warning you."

Vex raises one eyebrow, and the grin spreads.

"I like how you think. But you're going to get way more than just a spanking, woman."

Tomorrow's Tessie's birthday party, and I have everything ready for it. Suki's coming early to help me set up and to help with the grilling. Earlier in the week, Chubs called and asked if he could bring the cake. I readily agreed since it seemed important to him. Vex invited himself by informing us we owed him a meal and got a smile from both Tessie and me. He also promised Tessie he'd take her driving again, but before she could touch the keys, they had to have a talk about which pedal to use and when. She agreed, and they're going again on Sunday. I'm so relieved not to have to be a part of that. Having a man around is not such a bad thing, it seems.

I sent a text to Rooster explaining that we couldn't attend his club party. I didn't tell him why exactly, just that we had plans for that day. I've not received a reply as of yet. I'm dreading the one that I know will come, though. Until then, I'm going to make sure Tessie's birthday's a great one.

I'm putting groceries away when Tessie sits down in a kitchen chair. Looking in her direction, I know something's up. She's always been easy to read, and today's no different.

"What do you want?" I ask while trying to stuff a few more things in the overflowing fridge.

"You know I'm not really a kid anymore, right?" she asks softly.

I stop what I'm doing and face her, curious where this is headed.

"Yeah, honey, I know that. Why?"

She hesitates for a moment, then stares hard into my eyes. I brace.

"You like Vex. And you should like him. He's…" she holds up a hand when I start to interrupt her. "Great. He's a biker, but he's nothing like Rooster. I don't think anyone in his club's like Rooster. You've spent your whole teenage years and up until now taking care of Mom and me. You should be dating, having fun, and enjoying life, Taj. I guess what I'm trying to say is I think you should go for it with Vex. If it works out, great. If not, his loss. But I'm old enough to take care of myself, and you don't need to be here every minute when you're not working. I'm not going to freak out or think you're a bad sister if a guy spends the night here. I know who you are and how Mom raised us to be, but I don't think she ever wanted you to set a perfect example for me. Just a real one."

I take a seat across the table from Tessie and look at her. Really look at her. She's beautiful and close to being an adult. Legally I mean, because she's mature for her age already. We've always been close, and we've never kept secrets from one another. Guilt hits me because I'm possibly keeping a huge one from her right now.

"I know you're mature enough to handle it if a guy spent the night here. You're all I have left in this world, so I never wanted to expose you to just anyone. I'm not the type to be bringing home random guys anyway. Yeah, I do like Vex. But Vex isn't looking for a long-term relationship, and I respect that. I don't want a guy around just to have one in my life. I'm okay with running solo until I find the right guy."

"What if you already have, and neither of you realize it yet?" Tessie questions.

"I don't think Vex is that guy, Tessie," I tell her gently because I now know she likes him for me.

"Time will tell. Just don't push him away because you think you should in some misguided attempt to set a good example for me," she replies with an impish smile.

"Okay, brat, I won't. We'll see where things go," I respond.

I know now's a good time to tell her about Vex and our possible predicament, but no sense in that until we know for sure ourselves. The guilt's still there, but it's manageable.

Dawn brings a beautiful Colorado morning with it. It's going to be a warm day and perfect for a cookout. I take a quiet moment to enjoy a cup of coffee before the day brings on chaos. It'll be a loud and boisterous day with Tessie and her girl posse. I'm looking forward to it.

I hit the shower early so I can get started prepping the food and drinks. It's not long, and Tessie's up and helping me in the kitchen. We work side by side for about an hour when I hear a vehicle pull into the drive. Looking out the kitchen window, I see an unfamiliar truck. My first thought's that Rooster sent someone to force us to his party, but that goes out the window when I see Toes and Horse Nuts step out.

"Who's here?" Tessie asks.

"A couple of the club members," I answer as I open the door for them.

Both guys come in carrying several bags of ice and set them on the counters and table. Toes immediately walks back outside without so much as a glance in our direction.

"Vex said to drop some things off for the party," Horse Nuts informs us in his deep, raspy tone.

I watch his eyes bounce from mine and land on Tessie for a few seconds longer than I like. After a long hesitation, he walks back out the door.

"Who the frig was that?" Tessie whisper-shouts.

"Toes and Horse Nuts," I tell her with a frown hitting my face.

"Is the hot one Horse Nuts?" she again whisper-shouts at me.

"I guess. Why?" I clip.

Before she can answer, the two guys re-enter with full arms. This time it's with beer and soft drinks. Another look at Tessie and Horse follows Toes back out the door.

"You're so blinded by Vex's off-the-charts hotness factor that you haven't even noticed this guy? Seriously?" Tessie questions while shooting me big eyes.

Another trip in, and both guys set down a few large coolers for the items they brought. Horse's eyes immediately find my sister. My sixteen-year-old sister! I shoot death rays with my eyes at him, but he doesn't notice. Toes does, though, and with a grin exits the house.

"Thank you for dropping this stuff off," I say while opening the door, hoping he'll catch the huge-ass hint I'm giving him.

"Yes, thank you. I'm Tessie, Taja's sister," Tessie says while walking forward with her hand out.

"Nice to meet you, Tessie. I'm Horse. What's the party for?" he asks while gently shaking her hand.

"My birthday's today."

"And I didn't get an invite?" he responds with a charming smile. Fuck, now that I'm looking closely at him, he is hot. Damn!

"Nope, sorry. Close friends and family only. Thanks for coming, Horse," I interject quickly. And not so politely.

Horse's head snaps my direction as he finally releases Tessie's hand. His smile broadens as he walks to the door. Turning in it, he says, "Hope you have a great birthday, Tessie. Every beautiful woman deserves that."

"Thank you. You can come back at 2pm if you'd like. Petey, Trigger, Chubs, and Vex will be here," Tessie offers.

"I just might do that," Horse answers, and with a wink at Tessie, he strolls out the door.

I hear Tessie's squeal of delight as I follow Horse outside and down the steps. When we're a short way from the house, he turns with a wicked grin. Before he can say whatever he's thinking, I get there first.

"I will eliminate you and your boy parts from this earth if you even think of hitting on my sister. Slowly, painfully and I'll smile the whole fucking time I'm doing it. My sixteen-year-old sister! Six-fucking-teen! Then, if there's anything left of you, I'll sit back enjoying the view while Suki finishes you off. And just because I'm a bit demented, I'll ask Trigger, Petey, Chubs, and Vex what they think I should do with your pedophile remains," I warn, meaning every single word.

I watch his eyebrows slowly climb and his mouth slowly drop during my tirade.

"Sixteen? Are you sure?" he asks in shock.

"Yes, I'm sure," I say, rolling my eyes so hard I'm surprised they don't land on the ground.

"Holy fuck. She looks older than that. Sorry, Taja, didn't know. Thought she was close to my age," he answers while shaking his head and walking toward the truck Toes is waiting in.

I'm somewhat appeased. Horse is a nice guy, and I can't blame him since he didn't know she was that young. She does look and act older, and it's fooled people before. Gah! The poor guy probably thinks I'm certifiably unbalanced now since I went all Terminator on him. *I'm off to a great start today,* I think as the truck backs out and leaves. Unbalanced or not, he's been put on notice.

Stepping back inside, I cringe at Tessie's glare. I admit I could've handled it better, but no way I'm going to allow a grown-ass man to check out my little sister.

"Cockblocker," Tessie calmly states.

"Tessie! Oh my God!" I screech.

"I get why you did that. He's too old for me. At least right now he is. But I've been raised right by good women, and I'm not likely to jump into bed with the first hot biker I see. I know my worth as a female, and no man's going to change that. It's harmless to look and flirt, though. I'm not like you. I have no intentions of dying a virgin. I'm going to live my life and enjoy the heck out of it. There will be no cobwebs for my lady bits. I'm sixteen now, and it's okay if I do stupid things or make mistakes. I'll learn from them and do better the next time. I love you, Taja, but it's time you start to live a little too. And you need to ease up and put some trust in me," Tessie says with a small grin.

"Do we need to have a chat about birth control?" I ask, grinning back at her.

"Only if you're confused by the subject," she responds saucily as she struts out of the room.

People have started showing up, and Tessie's smile has never been bigger. Her girl gang's all here, and true to their word, Petey, Trigger, and Chubs have arrived and brought their women. Petey introduced me to his wife, Trudy, and I instantly liked her. She's got a smile that just draws you to her. I can see the love and commitment between them, and I want that for myself someday. I met Bella, and she's so damn cute. She's confident, outgoing, and clearly loves her parents. I can see why Tessie likes her so much, even with a few years between them in age. Bella's fitting right in with Tessie's friends, and I hope to see her around more after today.

Trigger's lovely lady, Tammy, is very classy. They look like an odd couple on the surface. A biker through and through and a lady that looks like she just walked out of Vogue magazine. Tammy's charming and appears right at home at a teenage girl's backyard birthday party, though. Both Tammy and Trudy are mingling and chatting up the other guests while their men stand together drinking beers.

The day only improves when Chubs and Lucy arrive. He waves me over to him to ask where to put the cake. I point to a patio table that's on the deck, under the roof, and out of the sun. Chubs grins and disappears back around the corner of the house.

Lucy's cute and very tiny. I feel like a giant standing next to her. She's quiet and shy but friendly. But she wins my loyalty when she spots Tessie, and her face softens into a smile. She hugs Tessie and wishes her a happy birthday just as Chubs comes back around the corner carrying the cake that causes Tessie to gasp in joy.

Everyone walks over to get a better look at it, and I have to say I'm very impressed. It looks just like a toolbox with the lid open. A bright pink toolbox with Tessie's name painted on it. Inside it are numerous tools, all made from chocolate fondant, gum paste, and cake, and are true to size and shape. The whole thing looks so real I hate to cut into it. Tessie's got her mouth open, but no words are escaping. I'm so glad I thought to hit record on my phone. Her face is priceless.

"Oh God, Chubs! It's freaking awesome! I love it," Tessie whispers to him.

"Ava, our club president's wife, owns Sweet Angel Treats Bakery, and she made it. She also said to tell you happy birthday. I especially like the little touches she did like the grease rag hanging out of the drawer. And it's a huge cake, so there's enough for everyone," Chubs answers with his ever-present grin.

"Wow, Chubs, thank you! That's the coolest cake ever," I tell him with feeling.

"It matches my toolbox at the shop. Thank you, Chubs!" Tessie tells him before hugging the hell out of him.

"You have a toolbox like this at the shop?" I ask, surprised.

"Yeah. Trigger and Petey got it for me and had Gary paint it pink and put my name on it. It's my gift from them. It's friggin' awesome!" Tessie replies.

"Sweet Angel Treats Bakery's where I buy those cookies from, Taja. The giant ones you're always teasing me about. I'll take you there. Wait until you see everything else she makes," Suki adds.

Everyone eventually drifts away to get drinks or grab some chips, but I stand by the table looking at that cake. I'm missing Mom today, and I know Tessie is too, but it's made it easier to see the people we've gained in our lives. Mom would be happy and proud to see her two girls are not only surviving but doing well.

Chapter 16

Vex

I'm supposed to be at Taja's by now for the party, but I'd promised Pooh to help him seal his driveway today. We're nearly done, so I'll be on the road right after I shower and change.

"You mentioned nomad a while back. You still thinking about that?" Pooh asks as we work side by side.

"No. I'm not going anywhere."

"Glad to hear that, Vex. I would've hated to see you go. You deciding to stay have anything to do with Taja?"

"Yeah, it does. Before we hooked up, I was frustrated with being hung up on her. It wasn't like me, and I didn't like the change. Made me angry. We worked together almost every day, became friends, but that was it. I wanted more, but I didn't too. I thought leaving would solve the problem for me. Sucked having to sort my head out, but I have," I answer him honestly.

"She speaking to you after the money thing went down?" Pooh asks while aiming a grin at me.

"Yeah, we talked it out. Waiting to see if our fuck-up will have consequences or not," I reply with a glare at his grin.

"And if it does?"

"I'm okay with it. I'm not as scared about being a dad as I thought I would be. I might suck at it, though. Didn't have much of an example growing up," I explain while giving a rare glimpse into my childhood.

"Me neither, but I love Craig like he's my own, and I can't wait to have more with Pippa. If it helps, I look to Petey when I need advice or a great example. And Gunner now that he has his girls. The jury's still out on Axel. Alexia might become the poster child for psychotherapy with him as her father," Pooh says with a snort of laughter.

"Fuck you, Pooh! I heard that," Axel sputters indignantly.

"I meant for you to hear it, you eavesdropping bastard," Pooh admits freely.

I look up to see Axel standing by the edge of Pooh's driveway, holding his tiny, newborn daughter Alexia. She's swaddled in a Harley Davidson baby blanket and is wearing a pink stocking hat with cat ears attached. I set down my broom and walk over to peer at her sleeping face. Brushing my hands off on my jeans, I reach out and take her miniature form carefully from Axel and rest her against my shoulder. I love her baby smell and brush my lips across the fine hair peeking out from her cap. Looking down, I see her tiny mouth pucker for a moment before relaxing again. I feel a tug on my heart and know this little one will always be surrounded by love.

"Looks like you have another female admirer, Vex," Bailey says as she comes to a stop next to me.

"Like he needs another," Axel says, rolling his eyes.

"How come Gunner could produce twins, and you couldn't, Axel? Your swimmers take the slow bus?" I taunt.

"My swimmers are superstars. Gunner's just a show-off," Axel states.

"How much maternity leave are you taking, Axel?" questions Pooh.

Axel snorts before answering. "Paternity leave. Starts with a 'P.' Paaaaaa-tern-ity. Say it with me, Pooh."

"She's beautiful, Bailey. You've done good, woman," I tell her while ignoring Axel. "How're you doing, honey? You're a new mom and have Axel to deal with. Must be tough."

"Let's just say that little Alex is less work than Axel," Bailey replies while wrapping her arm around Axel's waist and grinning up at him.

"Not true. And how come no one asks me how I'm doing? Dads matter too, you know," Axel complains.

"How're you doing, Princess A?" Pooh asks in a polite, concerned voice.

"It's too late to care now, you bastards. But since you asked, I'm exhausted. The pregnancy was long, and Alex gets me up several times a night. It's worth every second, though, and I'm rocking this fatherhood shit," Axel tells us before reclaiming his daughter and stalking toward Ava and Gunner's house.

"Postpartum hitting him hard?" I ask Bailey with a laugh.

"Yeah, I think so. He's exhausted. Other than breastfeeding her, I never get to hold my own damn daughter. I've changed one diaper so far, and Axel stood over my shoulder, coaching me on technique. At this rate, she's going to grow up thinking he's both mom and dad," Bailey tells us with a huge grin.

"She's gonna be a daddy's girl, and that's not a bad thing," Pooh states.

"No, it's not. Especially when she has a dad that loves her as much as he does," Bailey responds softly.

After finishing Pooh's driveway, I shower and speed off to Taja's house. Walking around the corner of the house, I see a lot of people of all ages enjoying the day. I spot Taja standing near the grill with Suki and head that way.

I can't explain why I do what I do next, but it just feels right. Maybe it's from having just held Axel's little one. Maybe it's because I care about Taja more than I want to admit. But when I reach her side, and she looks up at me, I just act.

Gently grasping both sides of her face, I slide my hands so I'm cupping her neck and use my thumbs on her jaw to tilt her face up to mine. I stare down at her shocked eyes for a moment before claiming her mouth. It's a slow and sensual kiss. A claiming kiss. I ignore the dead silence that falls around us and sink myself into the connection with Taja. After a perfect moment, I slowly pull my head back and watch her eyes open. I know by the look in them that she's here with me, uncaring also about our audience. I give her another brief, hard kiss and then place my forehead against hers, still gripping her neck.

"Hey, baby, sorry I'm late. Had to help Pooh first. What do you need me to do now that I'm here?" I question in a low voice.

Taja places a quick kiss on the underside of my jaw before pulling out of my grip. She doesn't go far, though. She leans back in, placing her head against my upper chest, and wraps her arms around my torso. I pull her tight to me and just hold on for a moment. I enjoy the hell out of it too.

Pulling away again, she answers, "Just glad you're here. Thanks for sending over the drinks, ice, and coolers. That helped a lot. Want a beer?"

Before I can answer, a loud, long whistle splits the air, and I swing my head in the direction it came from. I see Tessie sitting on top of a picnic table with Bella and several other girls around her age. She's grinning from ear to ear and holding both thumbs up. I wink and return her smile.

"Holy crap! When did this happen, and why didn't someone tell me?" hollers Suki from beside us. Suki's not happy with either of us.

Looking around the yard, I enjoy the look of shock on my club family's faces. Trigger's got his forgotten beer bottle halfway to his mouth, and Tammy's jaw is near the ground. Trudy's got the biggest eyes I've ever seen while Petey's grinning before giving me a chin lift. Chubs has even stopped eating for a moment to gawk. Lucy, like Petey, is simply smiling. Those two always seem to know what's going on before anyone else does.

"We've caused some eyebrows to raise," Taja informs me. "Why's everyone looking so shocked?"

I chuckle because it's true, and I don't care. I drop a light kiss on Taja's mouth before answering.

"I guess they never thought they'd see me in a relationship."

"Is that what this is?" Taja asks in a soft voice.

"I think so. You okay with that?"

"Maybe. Depends on why you suddenly want that with me," she replies suspiciously.

I'm aware that Suki's standing close enough to hear us, so I drop my mouth next to Taja's ear to whisper quietly.

"Because of you. It's all you. It's not what you're thinking, so forget that right now. Let's go blow what's left of their minds, and we'll talk later. Yeah?"

Pulling back, I get a blinding smile from Taja along with a nod.

"No, no, no, no! No whispering, you two! What the hell? Didn't we have a chat, Vex? Taj, girl, really?"

Suki grumbles from beside us, but neither of us pay her any attention. We get busy. Working beside Taja, we get everyone fed, and the day goes off without a hitch.

"You let me preach to you this morning and never said a word, Taja. What the heck?" I overhear Tessie saying while I'm sitting on the couch enjoying a beer.

"I didn't know what to say. I like Vex a lot, but I wasn't sure it was returned," Taja responds.

"It looks returned to me," snorts Tessie.

"Well, yeah, now it does."

"I should have realized before when I caught you two swapping spit in the driveway. I was so excited about working at the garage that I kind of skipped over that. Oh my God! Did you do him then?"

"Tessie! Hush your face! No, I didn't do him then. We are not having this conversation," Taja exclaims in an exasperated voice.

"You've given up your V-card to God's hottest creation yet failed to mention it to me? What's wrong with you?" Tessie continues berating Taja.

"He kissed me at your party! Who said anything about sex?"

"That wasn't a kiss between two people who haven't seen each other naked. That kiss was like public sex. You can say what you want, but you've gotten down and dirty with that Hawaiian God."

"Tessie, stop! I'm not giving you details, for Christ sake."

"So, tell me, big sister of mine, what's it like to have your hands all over that…"

"You both know I can hear every word, right?" I interject then grin when I hear one of them squeak. I grin even bigger when I hear a door slam.

I finish my beer, kick off my boots, and stretch out on my back. Flipping on the TV, I find a ball game to watch. A few minutes later, I hear footsteps on the stairs. Tessie sits herself on the coffee table between my position and the TV. I raise my eyes to meet hers.

"I'm glad Taja's living a little. Glad it's with you because you seem like a good guy. We could use a man in our lives, but neither of us know how that works since we've never had one. Taja's never wanted one around because she believes all men are like our dad. Prove her wrong, not right. Don't eff this up. I'm cool with you staying over. Taja's more uptight about it because of me. My bedroom's a few rooms away from hers, so we're good there. And I sleep with my earbuds in most nights anyway. So, what I'm saying is that your monkey sex sounds won't bother my sleep. But here's some house rules so we all get along. And before you ask, Taja hasn't discussed or agreed to these, but I think you and I should. Ready?"

"Lay them on me, little one," I tell her settling a little more comfortably on the couch. This should be good stuff. Little Tessie reminds me a little of Axel. She thinks it—she says it.

"No sex on the couch. It's a communal couch, and I don't want to be sitting where some demon child from hell might have been conceived. No running around the house naked. I'm sixteen, and my hormones can only take so much on any given day. And frankly, you're a hotness overload, so be kind to me by keeping your clothes on. Boxers are okay, but not boxer briefs. Too tight and um, revealing, you know? I don't ever want to know what you're packing because that might make me want to hate my sister. Next, our hot water has a limit, and I'm not big on cold shower,s so take quick ones, please. If I get a cold shower in the morning, it sets me up for some mood swings all day, and you won't like me very much when that happens. Bella's been telling me how cool her brother is and how lucky she is to have him. I want that too. Taja's the best at being my sister, and I love her to death. And I never told her this because I didn't want to hurt her feelings, but I've always wanted a big brother. If you're with Taja, then that makes you my big-brother-like person. I have high expectations, so you'll need to step up and meet them. Bella and Axel have set the bar high. Don't let me down."

"Is that all?" I ask while fighting a laugh.

"Not quite. This one's important, so listen close. The toilet seat's to be kept in the down position. I'm not taking a late-night swim because you forget that rule. We've always been a house of women, so an up-toilet seat isn't something we think about."

"Anything else?" I ask while still fighting a laugh.

"Probably, but that's all I can think of right now. I'll get back to you later if I come up with any others," she answers with a careless flip of her hair.

"I can agree to those," I tell her solemnly. I'm a little worried about the toilet seat rule, though. I don't remember the last time I thought to put one back down, and I can see why that's important to her. I'll do my best.

"Good chat," Tessie says with a wide smile as she stands to walk away.

"Tessie," I say, stopping her. "I have no fucking idea what a sixteen-year-old female wants for her birthday, so how about I give you cash, and you can buy whatever you want or need?"

"Cash is good," she says with a wicked smile and an outstretched palm.

I reach into my hip pocket, pull out my wallet and open it. I withdraw several twenties and hold them up to her. She takes them with one hand while snatching my wallet from me with her other. She turns, sits herself on my gut, and proceeds to pull out my driver's license.

"Vex Dagen. Age 29. 6'3" 208 pounds."

"That's me," I say while chuckling at her audacity.

Tessie takes all but two of the twenties I handed her and places them back into my wallet along with my license.

"Forty bucks is plenty for my birthday. It's more than generous, and I appreciate it. Thank you, Vex Dagen," she says while standing, dropping my wallet on my stomach, and walking away.

I like that girl.

I spent the night at Taja's, and it's now one of the best nights of my life. Yes, the sex was spectacular, but that wasn't what made it meaningful. We laid in bed and talked. About ourselves, our families, our hopes, our futures. I've never done that before, never wanted to, yet I'm looking forward to more nights like that with Taja. I noticed she said very little about their father, but we have a lot of time to finish that conversation. Waking up next to her, this time without the panic attack, is an experience I plan on getting more of.

We're both working tonight at Dreams, but before that shift, I promised to help out at the gym since Axel's off still. We've been calling it maternity leave, even though he insists it's paternity leave. It's the quickest way to get him to hang up on you when he calls to micromanage something to do with the gym. Cash has perfected the technique.

Walking into the gym, I head to the check-in desk where Pooh, Pigeon, and Cash are standing. I know

I'm about to catch shit from them, but I'm smiling anyway.

"Hi, Brother Vex. Let me help carry that ball and chain you're dragging behind you," Cash starts off with a grin.

"Gossip travels fast," I answer. "Jealous much?"

"Fuck yeah, I am. Taja's hot as hell," Pigeon adds. "Tall, great ass, a mouth that…"

"Finish that sentence, and I'm gonna have to kill you," I interject before Pigeon gets himself somewhere he can't get out of. My smile's now vanished, and my blood pressure is instantly rising.

"I'd shut the fuck up, Pigeon," Pooh advises with a smirk.

"Gets a woman and loses his sense of humor. How's that keep happening? What the hell is it with you guys?" Pigeon asks in a confused voice.

"Someday, some unlucky woman will help you figure that out," Cash answers.

Lola Wright

Chapter 17

Taja

I know I should've told Vex about Rooster and his money demands. I also know Vex will lose his shit about that. I'm going to have to answer to Rooster soon about not showing for his club party, and I'm dreading it immensely. It seems strange to be so happy with Vex now in my life and yet so displeased at having Rooster back in it. I have no clue how to balance all that. So, I do what most women do, and I call my best friend.

"What's up, Chicklette?" Suki says, answering her phone.

"Need advice."

"You don't even tell me you're hooking up with Vex, but now you want my advice? My advice is to keep hooking up with Vex and give me all the dirty details about it," Suki says, laughing.

"I haven't told Vex about Rooster or even that my dad's an MC President. And I haven't mentioned that Rooster's charging me to keep Tessie. Do I tell him, or is it too soon to get into the gory details of my life?" I ask, cutting right to the heart of my problem.

"You tell him everything, and you do that shit ASAP. MCs don't like secrets kept from them, especially when it concerns other MCs. Vex needs to know exactly what you're dealing with, and he needed to know that yesterday," Suki tells me in a suddenly serious voice.

"Oh God, I know you're right. But what if he decides I'm too much trouble and bolts?"

"Vex isn't one to bolt because things are difficult. But if he was and did that? You're better off without him. Nobody wants a weak man. I know you're all Little Miss Independence and have had reason to be that way, but let him in. There's no shame in letting others help carry your burdens, and Rooster's a large-ass burden. Better if you two have a united front than to give Rooster something he thinks he can exploit," Suki advises.

"You're right. I'll talk with Vex tonight after our shift. Thanks, Suki. Love you."

"Love you too. See you at work."

The music seems louder tonight than ever before. It's thumping throughout the club and inside my skull. It's busy, and I haven't had a second to catch my breath yet. I've seen Vex from a distance a few times tonight, but he's been busy too. Out of the corner of my eye, I see a few guys sit down at the bar at my end. Heading toward them, I notice their cuts have Devil's Angels patches on them.

"What can I get you guys?" I ask politely while making eye contact with each.

"You Taja?" one of the dark-haired men shouts over the music.

"Yes, I'm Taja."

A large hand reaches my direction, and I shake it while looking at the face that it belongs to. It's a beautiful face in raw masculinity. Nothing pretty about the hard planes and bone structure, but it's striking. Broad forehead, high cheekbones, square jaw. Short blond hair, almost spikey looking, tanned skin, and blue eyes so light they almost look gray. I see the slight lip tilt and know he's patiently watching me check him out. I pull my hand back and tuck my hair behind my ear in an embarrassed, nervous gesture.

"Cash," the blond Adonis rumbles out in a deep voice. Tipping his chin in the direction of the other two men, he says, "Rex and Reeves. Nice to meet you, Taja."

"You the one whose sister works with Trigger?" asks the one indicated as being Rex.

"Yes. Tessie's my younger sister," I reply.

"Heard about her. Trigger loves having someone to teach and boss around. Petey said she hangs on every word Trigger says, so that's a match made in heaven. She'll learn a lot from him about cars and about being bossy," Rex tells me with a grin.

"She's already bossy, so no worries there," I answer, grinning back.

"Heard she's in need of some driving tips too," adds Reeves with a chuckle. "Axel swears she was possessed when he rode with her."

"Oh shit! She drove with Axel, too? I only knew about Vex riding with her," I tell them with a cringe of embarrassment.

The men are all laughing when Vex steps up next to me behind the bar and casually tosses his arm around my shoulders. When I look up in surprise at him being there, he pulls my front to his side possessively. I wrap one arm around his waist and rest my other hand on his abs. His eyes stare into mine for a moment before he levels them at his club brothers.

I watch as Cash holds his palm out toward the other two guys and watch in dismay as they each place money into it. I'm confused, but it doesn't last long.

"Seriously? What the fuck, Vex? I thought Pigeon was talking out his ass," Rex grumbles as Cash counts his money and then places half of it in my tip jar.

"Is there anything you guys don't bet on?" I ask, exasperated as I feel Vex's body moving with his laugh.

"Nothing's sacred, Taja. It won't be long, and you'll be betting against someone too," Reeves tells me.

"I'm her best friend, and I would've lost money on her. I never thought she'd be that stupid," Suki says with a frown as she joins our group.

"Hey!" Vex and I both shout at the same time.

"I didn't mean that the way it came out!" Suki hurries to explain. "I just meant that usually I can tell when something's up with Taja. I'd warned Vex about even thinking about going after her, and I thought he understood why. And I never thought she'd choose Denver's biggest man whore…"

"Hey!" Vex and I repeat.

"I might wanna just walk away now before I choke on my foot," Suki mumbles as she walks off amid the guy's laughter.

"I better get back to work before I start questioning the man whore comment," I tell Vex and watch as his face suddenly shutters his thoughts. Unease hits my stomach as he releases me, and I leave him with his friends.

After our shift, Vex follows me back to my house. I wanted to get home right away because Tessie's been radio silent all evening, and that's not like her. She usually texts me dozens of times, and I've heard nothing from her since around 8pm.

Pulling into my drive, I get a bad feeling when I see the house is completely dark. It's not unusual for Tessie to wait up for me, but even when she doesn't, she leaves a few lights on. She won't admit it, but she's always been a little afraid of the dark.

I'm walking quickly to the porch when Vex appears at my side and uses his hand to pull me behind him. Looking at his face, I see concern. I grip his bicep and feel my stomach drop.

"Something's wrong," Vex says before stopping and turning to face me. "Go wait in your car. I'll go in and check things out."

"No way! I'm staying with you. Oh God, Tessie," I say as I start to push past Vex.

"Stay behind me then. Get your phone out and pull up Freddy's number just in case you need to make a quick call. I mean it, Taja. Stay behind me."

Once we're at the door, I know she's no longer in our home. There are a few spots of what looks like blood on the door jam, and the door isn't closed all the way. Vex slowly pushes the door open, and we see Tessie's cell phone on the floor just inside. Stepping into the living room, Vex flips on the light. It's obvious there was a struggle. A few things are knocked over, and there's more blood, like a handprint, on the wall next to the door.

"Call Freddy and Trigger now. Cash too if you have his number. I'm gonna check out the rest of the house," Vex orders before walking off.

I'm trying not to flip out and to stay calm and rational. Not easy when your little sister is missing and someone left blood behind. I make the calls and then scurry through the house until I catch up with Vex.

After we've determined that Tessie is definitely missing and that no one else is in the house, I collapse on a kitchen chair, shaking.

I make several calls to Tessie's friends hoping this isn't what it looks like and that one of them knows where she's at. I call a few neighbors too, but most don't know anything. One neighbor, Mr. Shegan, said he'd seen a ratty-looking black van turning out of our street around 8:30pm when he was walking his dog. He didn't recognize it as one from our neighborhood and that it had New Mexico plates. I feel the panic start to rise, but I beat that down the best I can. Vex grabs a chair and pulls it over so we're facing one another and sits.

"Any idea who could've taken her?" he questions quietly.

"Rooster."

"Who's that?" he asks.

"Our dad. President of the Spirit Skulls MC out of Santa Fe. They're all lowlifes and dirtbags. I should've known he'd do something when we didn't come to their club party. I didn't think he'd do this, though," I explain while trying to surface from the crushing guilt. I didn't do my job and keep her safe. I then tell him what Mr. Shegan had told me.

Before Vex can say anything, we hear a bike coming down the street. Not long after Cash walks inside, we hear more. Soon, the house is crawling with bikers.

"What do we know?" Trigger barks at no one in particular.

Vex explains what I've told him so far and what we've found. I watch as Trigger's face changes from concern to rage.

"I remember Rooster. The Skulls were a Denver club before most of you guys were old enough to ride. His club's as dirty as they get. How the fuck are you two his daughters?" Trigger spits.

"It wasn't by choice!" I holler back.

"Shit! Sorry, girl. I wasn't blaming you. I didn't know that asswipe even had kids," Trigger says in a much calmer voice.

"I remember him too. Gunner's dad and I had several run-ins with Rooster and that club until they left town," Petey adds.

"I remember the name, and Dad talking about problems with them. Don't remember much else, though. How'd we not know we have another club's president's daughter working for us?" Gunner asks while prowling the kitchen.

"That's on me, Gunner. Taja was just working for us for three days as a fill-in. I didn't have Rex run a background check for that short of time. Then things changed, and she stayed on full-time. I forgot to get with Rex and have it done," Freddy states.

"You said something about a club party, Taja. What was that about? Tell us everything you can because it could help," Vex asks me.

I tell them everything. I don't hold back out of embarrassment. I have no reason to be embarrassed about Rooster's behavior. That's all on him. As I'm talking, I can feel the room start to vibrate with anger. It's a tangible thing, and it would be frightening if I was the cause of it. I keep my eyes on Vex's as I spill my guts about our family's dirty secret. Rooster.

"It was your dad that gave you the black eye when you first started at Dreams?" Freddy asks.

"One of his men. He watched and was okay with it."

"And he's been charging you rent on your own house and payment to keep Tessie?" Gunner rumbles out.

"Yeah. Said if I didn't, we'd have to earn the money for the club in other ways," I tell him. The oxygen in the room disappears. I pull my eyes off of Vex's, meet Trigger's, and then pass through the rest of the guys before stopping on Gunner's.

"Please. I need her back. Please help her. He'll do what he threatened to do. I don't have much, but I can sell the house. I'll work for free. I'll trade places…"

"You won't do any of those things. Grab some clothes and whatever you need for a few days. Toes will take you to the clubhouse. You stay there until we get her back. Don't leave the compound unless it's with one of us," Vex orders while standing up. He pulls me up and into his arms. Cupping the back of my head, he pulls me tight. I cling to his strength and pray they can bring my little sister home.

Chapter 18

Vex

After some discussion, Cash, Pooh, and I are headed toward Santa Fe. Cash is on his bike, Pooh and I in Pooh's truck. Too many bikes coming into town would alert Rooster's club. No cuts on any of us. Our plan is recon at this point. Find their clubhouse and see if we can get eyes on Tessie. Rex is working his magic on his computer, getting us intel on the Skulls. The rest of the guys are on standby, waiting to hear from us. We'll make further plans once we find her location.

To have raised two girls that turned out like Taja and Tessie, their mother must've been a hell of a woman. I wish I'd have met her because I'm sure I would've liked her. How someone like that ended up with Rooster is beyond my comprehension, but it happens all the time. My own mother married someone not so different from Rooster. A tyrant that's kept her cowed most of their time together. To this day, she won't listen to a single word against him. I was a rebel from a young age and a disappointment to my dad and his plans for my life. I refused to bend to his will and be what he wanted me to be. When I couldn't take his constant pressure anymore, I left my home state of Hawaii and have never been back. I begged my mom and younger brother, Max, to leave with me, but she refused. I call, keep in touch with her and Max, but she's been angry at me since I left. Our conversations are hard and stilted. Max is an adult now, but he's always been under Dad's thumb. I haven't spoken to my dad in almost a decade, and I like it that way.

Santa Fe's about a six-hour car ride from our clubhouse outside of Denver. It doesn't take near that long before we hit the outskirts and stop at a gas station. Cash pulls up next to my window, and we go over the intel Rex has given us so far. The Spirit Skulls' clubhouse is a rundown two-story house about two miles out of Santa Fe. An aerial shot of it shows a large hip-roof barn off to the side and fields surrounding the property. It's not going to be easy to approach without being seen.

We drive most of the way there before hiding the bike and truck behind a small hill along the road. We split up and approach the property from different directions. We can't get too close since it's now daylight, but we all scout out what we can from our directions. I'm lying belly down on a small rise a few hundred yards from the barn, scoping the landscape and buildings with binoculars. There are about a dozen bikes and a few vehicles parked around the house, but no movement anywhere that I can see. The windows on my side of the house are all covered with either blinds or sheets, so I can't see in any of them. I feel my phone vibrate, and I carefully pull it out to read the text.

Pooh: Can't see inside house. Hay mow northside guy on lookout.

Me: Armed?

Pooh: Yeah. Rifle with scope.

Cash: One on southside too. Armed. Double doors on bottom of barn.

Me: No movement anywhere that I can see

Cash: We wait for now. Stay low and still.

About an hour goes by, and someone walks outside from the front of the house. Another man joins him, and they stand around talking and smoking. After a few minutes, they walk to the barn and disappear inside. Two other men walk out of the barn and head directly into the house. Shift change.

Pooh: Either they're always careful or they're expecting blow back

Me: Maybe both

Cash: Bikes coming

I hear several bikes at the same time I read Cash's text. I hug the ground a little harder, glad Pooh double-checked us for anything shiny that might give off a reflection. His military experience makes him perfect for this kind of shit.

I watch four bikes pull up to the house, and the riders enter it as a group. Not an impressive-looking group of men. Out of shape, greasy hair, dirty clothes, bikes not taken care of. Unfortunately, they're what most people think of as bikers, and it couldn't be further from the truth.

Rex: Bar in town named Ike's. Skulls hangout. Apts above it are used for pimping their girls. Trigger, Prez and others coming your way. ETA 2 hours.

Pooh: LEO's?

Rex: Skulls control the town. Police Chief is tight with Rooster. Kickbacks most likely. Don't count on them for help.

Cash: Support clubs? Friends?

Rex: Not that I can find. They're not liked.

Me: Rooster own a home, property?

Rex: Haven't found anything yet. I'll keep digging.

Rex forwards photos of Rooster and several of the club members. I can't see Taja or Tessie in Rooster's face, and I'm grateful for that. Hard, dirty living has taken its toll on him, and he looks old and tired. Eyes have an evil glint, and they match what we already know about him. I'm finding it hard to understand how he produced the young women that I've met and gotten to know. It makes me realize how powerful of an influence their mom really was on them. I thank God that she survived long enough to be that.

Lola Wright

Chapter 19

Taja

After grabbing some clothes, I ride with Toes to The Devil's Angels clubhouse. Vex got to hold me for a quick moment before we left, and it helped slow the shakes I had. I'm not ashamed to admit I needed his strength because mine had vanished. I feel like I'm missing a limb, and my mind is numb.

"We'll get her back, Taja," Vex vowed before giving me a hard kiss and walking back into the house to help make plans.

It's dark and silent when Toes guides me into the clubhouse. I follow him to the bar area and take a seat. Toes sets a beer and a shot of something in front of me. I'm not a drinker to speak of, but I shoot the shot and then chase it with a large chug of beer. My eyes water, and my throat burns, but I still feel numb inside. Instant regret swamps me when I remember I could be pregnant. I'll never make that mistake again.

"Follow me. I'll show you to Vex's room," Toes mumbles as he turns to walk off.

"Is there a reason why this is the first you've spoken to me tonight?" I ask him.

Toes hesitates before turning back to face me.

"Vex has made it very clear you're his. He's never done that before, as far as I know. He's a great guy but not someone to cross. Not if breathing's important to you. And if you get on the wrong side of Vex, you're on the wrong side of Pooh. Another great guy, but he can be fucking deadly when crossed. I'm a prospect hoping to get voted into the club, so I can't have those two against me if that's ever going to happen."

"I'm pretty sure Vex wouldn't be upset with you for speaking to me," I tell him confidently.

"Vex saw me checking out your ass at Dreams. Yes, I'm guilty of it. I'm a guy, so, yeah, I do that shit. Since that night, I've been placed on shit duty. Literally, shit duty. My new job is to make sure the compound has no animal shit anywhere, and Ava has a bunch of pets. Craig even has a skunk. Have you ever had to clean up skunk shit? Vex handed me latex gloves to use to pick up the bird shit. Like, with my fucking fingers! I now spend my days walking the compound on fucking Poo-Poo Patrol. Horse said it's no coincidence that my new duties took effect the morning after I looked at your ass. So, please, Taja, understand I'm not angry with you. It's not that I dislike you. It's that I fucking hate spending my days dealing with shit. No ass is worth that!" he explains before turning away again. I silently follow him to Vex's room, having absolutely no clue what to say to all of that.

After Toes leaves me in Vex's room, I take a seat on the unmade bed, exhausted in mind and body. After a moment, I get back up and make my way into his bathroom. I wash my makeup off, brush my teeth, and return to the bedroom. I rummage in his dresser until I find a t-shirt to sleep in. I have this urge, this need, to have Vex close, but this is the best I'm going to get tonight.

Looking around, I see a set of folded sheets in a laundry basket next to the dresser. I strip the bed, remake it, and climb in. My mind is whirling, and I doubt sleep's going to come, but I need to try. I toss and turn for what seems like hours before giving up. Sitting up, I place my back against the headboard and pull my knees to my chest. I pick up my phone and send off a text.

Me: Any news?

Vex: Not yet. You at the clubhouse?

Me: Yeah, in your room

Vex: If it smells bad, it's Pooh's fault.

Me: It does. He needs cologne or soap/water

Vex: I'll let him know. Miss you baby

Me: Missing you too. I want you and Tessie back here with me

Vex: Working on that. I'll bring her back

Me: Please do that but be safe. I can't lose anyone else, Vex. I really can't

Vex: You're not going to. Kitchen is stocked. Eat/drink anything you want. Get some sleep. I like knowing you're in my bed. Take care of yourself and our little one

Me: Possible little one but I will. Promise

Vex: Gotta go. I'll keep you posted

Me: Thx

I pull on a pair of yoga pants under Vex's shirt and leave the room. I find the kitchen and get to making coffee. I fill a mug, planning on returning to Vex's room, but find Toes in the doorway.

"Vex said to make sure you eat something. Cupboards are stocked, and the fridges are full."

I stop myself from smiling at the latex gloves he's wearing, along with a frown, and nod my head. I set my cup down and rummage up a light breakfast. Taking everything back to Vex's room, I climb back into bed and start eating a bowl of fresh berries and yogurt.

It's only a few minutes, and I hear a scratching at the door. Curious, I walk to the door and pull it slightly open to peer through. An extremely large ball of fur pushes itself through the door with an angry meow, and I realize it's a cat. A very fat cat. I watch in awe as he struts across the room and jumps onto the bed. The bed actually bounces a little before the cat settles down. I find myself facing one large, pissed-off kitty. I'd just leave him be, but he's between me and my coffee. That's a no-no. I approach slowly and hold the back of my hand out to him. He stares balefully at me without so much as a blink.

"Who's a pretty kitty?" I murmur.

"Meow."

"Can I pet you?"

"Meow."

I take that as a yes, even though I don't speak cat, and slowly run my finger down the back of his head. I don't get attacked or bitten, so I bravely start petting him from head to tail. When I hear his motor start purring, I prop half my ass onto the bed next to him and continue stroking. He stretches out, and before long, I feel a paw land on my thigh. I realize he's not so much an angry cat as he just wants things his way as soon as he wants them. Typical cat, but he has a lot more weight to throw around than most. The fat bastard falls asleep, snoring and all while leaning against my leg. I lean back against the wall and get back to breakfast. When finished, I stretch out on my side, curl up with the cat and fall asleep.

I wake suddenly and bolt for the bathroom. I barely make it to the toilet before my breakfast reappears. As I'm hugging the toilet, the cat stands on his hind feet, placing his front paws on the toilet seat, and stares at me. Nothing like having an audience at the worst time.

"Please, go away," I mutter miserably.

"Meow."

"Please. I'm begging you to leave," I say as my stomach decides it's time for round two.

"Meow."

I hear knocking on the bedroom door, but I'm in no shape to answer it. My arms are shaky at this point, and I have sweat running off the tip of my nose. Round three commences.

"Taja? It's Axel. I'm coming in," I hear before the door opens, and in walks Axel. He has a teal-colored baby sling across his chest, but I don't even have the energy to do a double-take at the bizarre sight. I give a half-wave and rest my head on my arm.

"I know all about this. I'll be right back with ginger ale and some crackers," Axel says softly before patting me once on the back.

"Oh God! Don't mention food," I whine.

"It'll help. Trust me. I know all about morning sickness," he explains.

"This isn't morning sickness. This is stress," I tell him, probably out of denial.

"Yeah, right. Whatever, the ginger ale will help. Need help back to the bed?"

"No, thanks. I'm fine dying right here," I groan as he gives a short chuckle and disappears.

"Meow."

I slowly pull myself up, flush the toilet, and lean against the vanity. Looking around, I see mouthwash and use it. I shakily make my way back to the bedroom and retrieve my toothbrush. After taking care of business in the bathroom, I hit the bed in relief. Just as I'm relaxing my muscles, the cat lands next to me and stretches out. I place a hand on his back and enjoy the softness of his fur.

"Yo!"

Turning my head, I see Mac standing next to the bed in all his glorious colors.

"Hi, Mac. How're you?"

"Mac's good. Mac's a hottie. You got cashews?" Mac says in a too loud voice.

"No, sorry, Mac. No cashews," I inform him.

He flutters himself onto the bed next to me and tilts his head comically while eyeing the cat.

"Don't piss off the cat," he warns me.

"What's its name?"

"Duffy. Pretty kitty. Pretty kitty. Prettyyyyy kittyyyyyy," Mac answers.

"You call him pretty kitty so he doesn't eat you?" I ask, not even realizing I'm carrying on a conversation with a bird.

"Yep. He likes it."

"Mac! Get the hell out of here and leave her alone," Axel commands as he enters the room, baby sling still attached. He sets a full glass and a sleeve of crackers on the nightstand next to me.

"You get out!" Mac returns.

"Taja doesn't need to deal with you right now. She's sick," Axel barks back.

"Cooking a kid?" Mac inquires with another head tilt.

"Not cooking a kid, you moron. It's called a bun in the oven," Axel retorts.

"Same thing," Mac cackles.

"Stop saying I'm pregnant!" I shout. "I threw up out of stress. Why do you assume I'm pregnant?"

"Vex told me it's a possibility. Forgotten condom and all that," Axel states while cradling the sleeping infant in the sling.

"Vex told you?" I ask incredulously.

"I overheard him talking to Pooh."

"Overheard?"

"Eavesdropping. It's one of my many skills," he answers with a grin.

"Oh my God! I don't even know yet myself. You haven't told anyone, have you?"

"I'm an eavesdropper, not a gossip," he says in an offended tone.

"Sorry. I didn't mean to bark at you, Axel. Thank you for the pop and crackers. Who's in the sling?"

"The cutest thing you will ever see. This is Alexia. We call her Alex, and she's my best creation. Bailey helped a little, but little Alex is all me," Axel says with pride as he dips down enough for me to see the baby.

She's beautiful! Miniature sized fingers curled into tiny fists near her face and a cupid's bow mouth. A light dusting of blond hair completes this sleeping angel. You can easily see Axel stamped all over her features. She's going to be a stunning beauty.

I sit up, lean against the headboard, and hold my hands out. Axel immediately takes a step back and raises an eyebrow at me.

"Can I hold her?" I ask.

"No! Sorry, but I just got her back from her mom, and it's daddy time," Axel says.

"Oink! Oink! Oink!" Mac screams.

"I'm not being a pig! Bailey had to breastfeed, and I just got her back!" Axel shouts back.

"I think Mac was announcing Gee's arrival," I tell Axel with a laugh as Gee stops next to him.

"Oh. Hey, Gee," Axel says to the pig.

"Was not," Mac adds as Axel turns a glare in his direction.

"Whatever. Sip the pop, eat a few crackers. When you're feeling better, come out to the main room, and we'll talk about what's going on. Yeah?" Axel tells me.

"Okay, I will. Thanks again. I'll be out in a few minutes."

Walking into the main room, I see a lot of people I don't know. I hesitate for a moment, looking around, when I hear my name called. Turning toward the voice, I see Freddy coming at me. He doesn't stop until I'm engulfed in his arms, and I have to admit it feels nice. After the bear hug, he guides me to a table, and we both sit. Duffy immediately starts pawing at my leg, so I bend down, pick him up, and set him in my lap. He's been a comfort for me, whether he intended to be or not. I softly stroke him, and he starts loudly purring.

"How you holding up?" Freddy asks.

"I'm okay. I'm scared for Tessie. I just want her home," I answer quietly.

"They'll bring her home, Taja. You both work for the club, so you're both family to us. Vex won't let you down. He's got Cash and Pooh with him, and the three together can be hell on wheels for anyone. Several other members left a while ago to assist."

"That makes me feel better. I'm glad Vex has good men with him."

"He does. No worries there. If you want to come stay at my house with me, you're welcome to. Vex just doesn't want you at your house or alone at any time," Freddy offers with sincerity.

"Thank you, Freddy. That's so nice of you to offer. Where will they bring Tessie when they get back?"

"Here to the clubhouse, I'm sure."

"Then I think I want to stay here for now. Thank you for the offer, but I want to be here for her," I explain.

"I get that. The offer stands, though, if you change your mind."

"Taja? I'm Rex. We met at Dreams. You doing okay?"

"Hi, Rex. Yes, I remember. I'm hanging in there," I answer as he takes a seat across from me.

"Is there anything you can tell me about Rooster and his club members that I can use? Even some small piece of info might give me something we can use to find Tessie," Rex questions.

"I don't know much. Rooster's woman's called Kiki. Don't know if they're married or not. She used to be a hairstylist with her own shop in Santa Fe. I don't know if she still owns it or not. It was called Kiki's Kut and Kurl, all starting with Ks," I say, rolling my eyes at the name.

"Okay, I can look for that. Anything else?"

"His go-to guy is Popeye if he wants something done right. Bear and Tats are the two he uses for dirty work. I don't even know most of the members. I just remember some of them from when I was a kid and from the few times he's been around since then. None are upstanding-type citizens," I tell him.

"If you think of anything else, come find me," Rex says as he stands up and walks off.

As soon as Rex exits, a gorgeous blond woman takes his seat and introduces herself as Ava, Gunner's wife.

"Hi, it's nice to meet you. Thank you for the beautiful cake for Tessie's party. She loved it," I say.

"You're very welcome. It's kind of my thing. I feed people and make cool cakes," she answers with an impish grin. I like her already.

"You're Petey's daughter and Bella and Axel's sister, correct?" I ask.

"Yes, and Mom to Mia, Zoe, Loki, Gee, Mac, and Duffy. I don't always claim Axel and Mac. Depends on what havoc they're wreaking," she answers with a laugh. "Has Duffy been a problem yet?"

"No! Not at all. He's been my sidekick all morning. He's even stretched out in bed and napped with me."

"Napping's his thing. If it were an Olympic sport, he'd win gold," Ava tells me with another grin.

"I've met Mac. He's hilarious. He must really like cashews because he asked me for some right away."

"He's saving them. He's got it in his head that he can take a bounty out on Axel's life if he has enough of them to use as payment," Freddy interjects with a chuckle.

"Damn bird needs to come up missing," Axel states as he and little Alex take the last chair at our table.

"You're as much the problem as Mac is," Ava replies while giving Axel that special mom-look we all know about. "Let me hold my niece."

"Nope. Just got her back a while ago. It's still daddy time. Besides, the guys wouldn't let me go with them to Santa Fe, so Alex is my reward for staying here," Axel answers while once again leaning away and cradling his girl.

"Pops is getting tired of you not letting the rest of us hold her. He said when they get back, you and him are going to have a come to Jesus moment," Ava informs Axel with a wide and slightly evil grin. "Trudy said she's not waiting that long. Good luck telling her no again."

"That woman's like a pitbull about holding my child!" Axel exclaims.

"And that pitbull's standing right behind you," Trudy says softly in Axel's ear.

Even with everything that's going on with Tessie, I can't help the smile I get from seeing Axel's expression of fear. He's lost this round, and he knows it.

Trudy steps to the side of Axel and holds her hands out. With the biggest pout I've ever seen, Axel carefully removes Alex from her sling and hands her over. Trudy places the baby against her chest and instantly starts cooing to her. Axel aims his pout in my direction, and I brace for whatever he's about to say.

"When you and Vex's baby's born, take my advice and keep it away from these two baby hounds."

I freeze and hold my breath hoping nobody else is paying attention to him, but it's all in vain.

"You're pregnant?" shouts Freddy.

The entire room goes quiet, and I can feel every eye looking my way. I use my eyes to shoot daggers at Axel, but he just shrugs his shoulders, pout still in place.

"I don't know yet, Freddy. It's possible. What I do know is that Axel has a big mouth! And you told me you weren't a gossip!" I spit in Axel's direction.

"I'm not a gossip. I was just giving you sound advice. You can't hold this against me. I'm under duress from having my only child stolen from me!"

"Does Vex know it's a possibility?" Ava asks with both eyebrows raised.

"Yes, he does, and he said he's fine with it if she's knocked up. He actually sounded kind of excited about the possibility," Axel answers before I can.

"Wow! Really? Vex?" questions Trudy.

"You know how he's been acting kind of off for a while now? Sitting in front of you is the reason. I think Vex has decided to join the land of grownups and calm down his old lifestyle. Gunner did. I did. Pooh did. It was inevitable that Vex would at some point too. He's seen how good Bailey has it now and wants that for himself, I think," Axel continues spewing his thoughts.

"Oh my God, shoot me now," I mumble.

"I have noticed he's not chasing skirts at Dreams anymore," Freddy muses out loud. "Maybe he has decided it's time to settle."

"That, or he's run out of women to f..." Axel starts to say.

"Finish that sentence, and you'll never get your daughter back, Axel!" bellows Trudy. Turning her eyes my direction, she goes on to say, "Don't listen to anyone but Vex. He isn't going to lie to you, that I do know. And he'd make a great dad because he's a great guy to begin with. We're just a little shocked because none of us knew he'd found someone he might be serious about."

"Look, I don't know where this is going with Vex or if it's going anywhere. We became friends, and things grew from there. He's perfect. Of course, I'm attracted to him, but time will tell how this is going to end. He may not even realize it himself, but his only interest in me could simply be that there's a possibility of a child. A sense of responsibility that he's misinterpreting as feelings. I don't know. In a few days, I'll know for sure about a baby, and we'll have to figure things out at that time," I explain.

"If there isn't a baby, would you want to continue a relationship with Vex?" Ava asks quietly.

"Yeah, I definitely would," I answer just as quietly as I watch Ava's eyes light with warmth.

"And if there is a baby? Then what?" questions Trudy.

"Then, together as a couple or not, we'll raise the child. He's not going to bolt or leave me hanging. Worst case scenario, we co-parent."

"Sounds like your head's on straight either way this turns out. No matter which way this falls, you have a job for as long as you want it with me. I have no one left in this world other than the club, so I'm claiming you and Tessie as family. You two need something? I'm your first call," Freddy states emphatically.

"Thank you, Freddy. That means the world to me."

"Can I have my daughter back now?" Axel interrupts while standing up next to Trudy.

"No. It's Ava's turn to hold her," Trudy says nonchalantly as she carefully hands the sleeping baby to Ava. Ava's face breaks out in a huge smile before she sticks her tongue out at Axel.

Sitting in a lawn chair outside the main door enjoying the feeble sun, I'm trying to keep my mind calm. My stomach has finally settled, but I'm sticking to only crackers to nibble on and hot tea to sip. I smile to myself, thinking back to earlier when I had the pleasure of meeting Bailey. She came looking for Axel and her baby but found me first. We had a nice chat with her explaining how Chubs delivered little Alex and how Axel declared Chubs his hero. When Axel entered the room and spotted Bailey, he tried sneaking away but was spotted. Bailey took off after him, and I knew who was going to win that race. I listened to Axel hollering that Alex wasn't hungry yet, and Bailey responding that her boobs were ready, though. Between pets and humans, this place is never quiet.

"Taja?"

Looking up, I see Bella approaching. She takes the chair next to me and sits on the edge, turning to face me.

"Hi, Bella. Nice to see you again."

"I wanted to come talk with you about Tessie missing. I can only imagine how you must be worried. I'm so sorry this has happened," Bella says softly.

"Thank you, Bella. Yeah, I'm worried. Scared to death, actually."

"Can I tell you how I came to live here?" she asks.

"Yes, please do," I answer, knowing already that she's adopted but not knowing the story behind it.

"My real mom's a bad woman. She sold me for drugs. Sold me to a sex trafficker, and I was on my way to a buyer when the Devil's stepped in. They saved me and brought me here instead. Several members offered to adopt me, but Petey and Trudy got the vote. That day, I gained a mom, dad, brother, sister, uncles, aunts, and every other relative there is. My life now isn't scary. It's great. I love it here, and I love my family. I'm loved, cared for, and safe."

"Oh my God, Bella. I'm so sorry you went through all of that," I tell her.

"It's okay, Taja. It ended well. But that's not why I'm telling you this. I want you to know the lengths the Devil's went to for me and for others in the same position. They didn't stop until they broke that trafficking ring up. They risked themselves to make others safe. They'll do the same for Tessie. They WILL get her back because to them, there's no other option. But when they do, give Tessie some space. I know from what happened with me I needed people to care and to be close but not push for details. I still haven't talked about everything that happened, but I'm doing it at a pace I'm comfortable with. I think that's the best thing everyone has given to me. They're there to listen when I need it, but nobody insists on anything I'm not ready to say."

"I get it, Bella. Thank you, I'll do that. I know you have a lot of people willing to listen, but you have another one now too. Here if you ever need anything, honey," I tell her sincerely.

"I'll remember that. I hope Tessie gets back soon."

Lola Wright

Chapter 20

Vex

It's been two days, and none of us have spotted Tessie yet. I've texted often with Taja, and I can feel her terror through the phone. I want to get Tessie back with us safely and then get both of us back to her sister. I'm worried about Taja and how she's holding up, but Freddy's sticking close to her, and that helps keep me calm. I know he cares about her and will do all he can to help her through this. Suki's been there for her too. But I want to be the one she's leaning on, and I know that's just being selfish. I need to be here because Tessie and Taja both are counting on me to make this right.

We're meeting with the rest of the club members in a few minutes to decide our next move. Rex found us an isolated roadside park where we won't draw attention to ourselves, and I'm impatiently waiting for the others to arrive. Planting my ass on a picnic table, I pull out my smokes and light one. Pooh sits down next to me, Cash standing nearby when I hear a bike in the distance. We watch as Trigger rides in and parks next to Cash's bike. He dismounts, walks to us, and stops directly in front of me.

"Any eyes on Tessie yet?" he rumbles.

"No. Rex located Rooster's woman's shop, though. She lives above it, so someone needs to sit on it," I reply.

"Others will be here soon. We'll figure out who's doing what then," Pooh adds.

Over the next ten minutes, we watch as club members pull in and park. Some in trucks, a van, and a couple more bikes. Everyone gathers around the table and waits for Gunner to speak.

"I've spoken with a few of our support clubs, and they're willing to help. We have a few options. We can increase our numbers and take down each location we think she might be in. If we do that, we need to effectively end all of them. We can wait another day or two, hoping to find where she's at exactly and only hit that place. Or, we can find ways to see into the buildings or get eyes and ears into them to locate her. Rex sent some electronic things we can plant near or in the different locations. We just have to get close enough to do it, and that's not easy considering the lay of the land around their compound. Also, word of warning. I've been told the last biker Rooster's club had a beef with ended up dead. Skinned alive and left in the desert. They don't play around, so everyone needs to be fucking careful."

"I've located a house a couple of the members share by following them when they left the clubhouse. It's a few miles from there. I can get inside and plant those devices. Maybe we'll hear them talking about Tessie or Rooster's plans for her," Cash adds.

"I can do the same with the barn at the clubhouse. Get in, get out. Someone in there has to be talking about this," Pooh states.

"Let me do the one at the barn. You cover me. You're a better shot than most of us anyway, especially at distance," I tell Pooh.

I watch as Pooh struggles to agree with me. He wants to be the one at risk, not me. That's just who he is, and that's why he's so valuable to our club. But he also knows me better than anyone, and he knows I need to do this for a young lady I hope to have as my family. I need to do this for Taja, Tessie, and myself. Pooh gives one quick nod, agreeing with me.

Gunner leads the rest of the conversation and hands out everyone's duties. Looking around the group of brothers we've become, I see a lot of angry faces. Not one of us can wrap our head around a father using his daughter as a bargaining chip. There's not a man standing here that Rooster should be unafraid to face.

Talking is done, and we're all on the move. Grabbing something to eat on the way, Pooh and I drive back to the clubhouse to await darkness. After eating, Pooh pulls out his M40A1 rifle with its 10 power, mil-dot crosshair Unertl scope. It's a beautiful piece of workmanship with deadly consequences for who or what ends up in those crosshairs. After checking it over, Pooh looks my direction.

"I know we need to get Tessie back, no question. But we need you whole, too. Don't take unnecessary risks. If you can't get the bug in place, we'll find another way. Taja doesn't need both of you hurt or MIA."

"Heard. Something I need to say in case shit goes south. You know I have family in Hawaii. A mom and a younger brother. I don't count my dad as family. Anything ever happens to me, contact my mom. My family's been into real estate development for generations now. Dad married into the wealth but controls my mom and brother with an iron fist. I rebelled and left when nothing I did was good enough for him. I'm not the kind of person to sit behind a desk in a high rise. I was more comfortable with a hard hat on, but that was beneath us, according to my dad. Point I'm trying to make is to contact my mom and have her sign my trust fund, company shares, property, and investments over to Taja. Only speak with her and no one else. In the safe in Gunner's office is paperwork I had drawn up a few years ago, giving you rights to handle my affairs if needed. Mom's name and contact info is included," I tell him, saying more about my history than I ever have in one sitting.

"So, what you're saying is you're pretty AND rich? Like Ivanka Trump but with a dick?" Pooh questions with his usual smirk.

"You're jealous now, right?" I smirk back.

"Not quite yet. You're filthy rich yet live in a room at the clubhouse that still smells like pig shit. What the fuck, Vex?" Pooh says, laughing his ass off.

"It only smells like that because of you and Craig, you worthless fuck."

"This is how this is going to go down. You're going to get back here in one piece. We're going to get Tessie back. Then I'm going to pull you into the adult world and help build a house for you, Tessie, and your baby momma."

After slugging Pooh's laughing self in the shoulder, I get out of the truck and prepare myself and weapons to get our job done. After another minute of enjoying his own joke, Pooh steps out to do the same.

Now that it's completely dark outside, I have my back pressed against the side of the barn. I have an earbud in, phone in my pocket, listening to Pooh keeping me updated on the men's movements. Moving cautiously and silently, I slip around the corner and enter the barn. I freeze in place and listen for movement. It's pitch-black inside, so using my phone, I make my way to the mow steps.

Once there, I can hear the men above talking with each other.

"One incoming from the house. Get out of sight," Pooh tells me.

I duck behind a large toolbox not a second too soon when the overhead light flips on. I listen to booted feet make their way to the steps and climb them. I pull my knife from its sheath and hold it in one hand while placing my other palm on my holstered handgun. I'm ready for whatever's about to happen. But instead of a fight, I want to fist pump when I hear the conversation taking place above me.

"Rooster's brat's a pain in the ass. The little bitch bit my fucking leg when I let her use the bathroom a few minutes ago. Fuck this shit. He needs to decide what he's going to use her for because she's more trouble than she's worth."

"You let a teenage girl get the best of you?" another voice questions amid laughter.

"Fucker has us grab her up, then he goes into hiding in case those assholes she's associated with decide they want her back. We can't even break her in because he's worried that'd lower her value. Can't mark her pretty face up, he tells me. Fuck that. He didn't say anything about marking her body, though. Bitch won't be breathing easy for a while," the original voice spews.

No longer wanting to fist pump, I fight the urge to storm the steps and put a hole in each of their skulls. Instead, I pull my phone and send a group text letting everyone know Tessie's in the house. Immediately, I hear Pooh's voice telling me to stay calm and stay hidden.

"Rooster's being sketchy as usual. I don't understand how this is a club problem when only he's going to earn from it," complains a voice I haven't heard yet.

"We need to consider that Rooster might have to be replaced as Prez. He's the only one that seems able to sock money away while the rest of us are scraping by."

"Club's not been in the black in years regardless of all the shit we do to earn."

I continue listening to them complain while hoping to hear something we can use. It's not long before I get what I'm waiting for.

"Better get back inside before Shorty gets us all killed by Rooster and Popeye. He hasn't taken his eyes off that girl yet, but if he doesn't keep his dick to himself, we'll be dead alongside him. I'll be glad tomorrow when us four get relieved, and this shit show becomes their problem and not ours. Catch you later."

I listen to him clomp back down the stairs. I get a good look at what he's wearing before he kills the light and exits the barn. Moving to the stairs, I reach up and attach the bug as high up as I can reach on the steps. Activating it, I move silently toward the door. I listen as Pooh tells me Rex said it's working. Not sure it's needed at this point, but it may come in handy later. I slip out the door, seeing someone's legs dangling out of the hay mow door above me, and make my way to the side of the barn. Out of everyone but Pooh's sight, I shoot off a text explaining what I've heard.

"It's clear around you to make your way back here. I can't see in the windows, but no one's looking out of them," Pooh says.

Me: I'm going closer to the house to see what room she's in

"Wait for the others. They're on their way, Vex. They're only minutes out. We know where she is now, and we'll get her back tonight," Pooh argues. When I don't answer, I hear Pooh sigh. He'd do the same damn thing in my position. I'm not waiting to see if Shorty can keep his dick to himself or not.

I start inching my way to the other side of the barn, the side closest to the house. I pass under the dangling legs and inch around the other corner. No lights are on upstairs in the house. Downstairs, I see two windows lit up. Not having a full moon tonight's a plus, but there's still a fair amount of ground to cover that's wide open.

"Since you're being a stubborn ass, I'm moving positions to cover you better. Fucking barn's in my way now. You're buying me a steak dinner for this," Pooh bitches in my ear.

Taking the chance that no one can see me while wearing all black, I make my way across the yard, hoping not to trip over some unseen object. I make it to the house and slide along it until I'm next to one of the lit windows. There's a curtain, but it's threadbare, and I can see one guy sitting at a table scarfing down a sandwich. It's the guy from the barn. Ducking under that window, I keep moving until I'm nearly to the front of the house and the next window. I wait a beat and can hear a TV playing. Hoping the second guy's watching it and not the window, I lean up and look in. My heart stops for a second when I realize the second guy's sitting in a chair right by the window. Our faces aren't two feet apart, but he's looking the other direction. He's looking at a bound Tessie, propped up on the end of a couch. She's staring directly at me, and I see it in her face, briefly, when she realizes what she's looking at. Her face goes blank, and she shifts her eyes to her captor. Good girl. She's smart and knows not to give me away. When the man glances toward the TV, Tessie casually holds up four fingers before folding her hand closed. When the man doesn't look her direction, she gives me the universal sign for gun—index finger and thumb pointed out before closing her hand again. I nod once and duck down again. Inching forward, I'm next to the beaten-down porch and can see the front door.

"Everyone's here. Cash is coming in from the other side of the house. He should be on the opposite side of the porch by now. Where you at?" Pooh questions just as Cash appears in my line of sight. He gives me a chin lift and leans back around the side of the house. He can text our locations without being spotted. He's in a blind spot for Rooster's men. I make my way around the porch to meet up with Cash.

"Petey, Trigger, and Reno are in the barn. They'll deal with those two. Gunner, Horse, and Reeves are at the back door of the house. Me and you have the front. Pooh's worked his way close and will take out any strays if needed. Where's Tessie?" Cash questions.

I explain what I know, and he passes the info to the others. Gunner answers that everyone's in place, and we're moving in twenty seconds. I pull my handgun and step onto the porch to the side of the front door. Cash takes the opposite side, and we wait the few seconds until go time.

Cash points to me and mouths "Tessie," and I know that means she's mine to get to, and he'll deal with the man first. I nod.

Stepping back, I lift my foot and kick the door in. Tessie immediately throws her body to the floor and stays low as I rush to her. No hesitation, she does the right thing. Before I even make it the few steps to her, I hear a gunshot as Cash does his job. I hear another and know the man in the kitchen is no more. Dropping down on my knees beside Tessie, I scoop her up and stand. Her bound wrists drop over my head, and she buries her face in my chest, holding on tight. Gunner and Horse enter from the back of the house and come to a stop when they see we're not the one bleeding.

"She okay?" Gunner barks.

"She's in one piece," I answer as Tessie nods her head without looking up.

"Get her out of here, and we'll meet you and Pooh back at the roadside park. We'll finish what needs to be done," Gunner orders.

I don't waste a second before stalking out the door with my cargo. I can feel her shaking, but she's not making a sound. The barn's lit up. I can see Petey in the doorway, so I walk that direction. Pooh pops up out of the darkness to walk beside me. When Petey spots us, he holds his hand up, and I realize he doesn't want Tessie in that barn, and I know why. She doesn't need to see what's most likely a bloodbath. I stop, and Petey hollers to Trigger that I have Tessie. Both men hurry our direction, and both are wearing relieved faces.

"She injured?" Trigger rasps out as he comes to a stop, laying a hand on Tessie's back.

"I'm mostly okay, I think," Tessie mumbles out against my chest.

"Thank fuck," Petey whispers as he uses his knife to cut the zip ties binding her wrists and ankles. Tessie doesn't lift her head nor loosen her hold on my neck.

"Meeting everyone back at the park. See you then," I tell them before Pooh and I start toward where we left his truck.

Waiting at the park for the others, I finally get Tessie to let go so we can check her over for injuries. Her ribs took a beating, but I don't think any are broken. She's battered and bruised, but that appears to be the worst of it. I get her to drink some water, and Pooh insists she eats a candy bar. Neither should have been hard to convince her to do since she said they hadn't fed or given her water, but she's still shaking like a leaf and trying hard to cover it. The girl's got a steel backbone, but the shaking's understandable. No tears, no hysterics. I'm proud as fuck of her. I pull out my phone and hand it to her. She's sitting in the passenger seat, me standing outside the open door. Her eyes meet mine, and she hands it back.

"Honey, you need to call Taja. Let her know you're okay," I tell her.

"I need you to do it for me, Vex. I'll start crying, and she'll start crying. I don't want to do that," she says very softly.

"Tears are okay, Tessie," Pooh tells her gently.

"I'm not sure if I can stop them once they start. I need to get my head on straight before that happens. Taja has always been the strong one, the dependable one. I need to be that this time too. Please, Vex? She needs to know you got me, and I'm okay, but I need some time first," she implores.

"I get that, honey. I'll make the call," I answer.

"Maybe we should wait until a decent hour. She's probably sleeping and…" Tessie starts to say.

"Taja finds out you've been found and are safe, and she's not been told for hours? Do you think either of us would survive that? No, honey, we can't wait. I promised her, and I'm not breaking any promise I make to either of you," I tell her.

"She'd kill us both. Dead. Very dead. Better make that call," Tessie agrees with the beginnings of a grin.

While speaking with a very relieved and tearful Taja, the others pull into the park. I watch as

Trigger gently pulls Tessie to his chest and drops a kiss on her forehead. Petey waits for his turn, and after it, I hear Tessie quietly thanking everyone for what they did for her. My attention had drifted for a moment, watching the guys with Tessie, but it snaps back to Taja when I hear what sounds like the phone falling to the floor.

"Taj? You there?" I ask.

No answer except for a fucking meow. Duffy must be in my room, and now I'm worried Taja's going to get chased out of it.

"Taja?" I repeat. I can hear sounds, so I know the call hasn't dropped, but I don't know what I'm hearing exactly. I wait for another minute before disconnecting and calling Toes. After a few rings, his sleepy voice answers.

"What?"

"You at the clubhouse?"

"Yeah. Who's this?" he asks, sounding like he's actually falling back to sleep.

"It's fucking Vex, you dickwad. Wake the fuck up! I called Taja, and I think she dropped the phone. Go check on her and make sure Duffy doesn't have her cornered somewhere," I shout.

"On my way," Toes answers, sounding much more alert.

"Keep me on the line," I order.

"Uh, Vex? She's fine, I think," Toes says.

"What the fuck do you mean, you think? Is she, or isn't she?" I bark.

"She's throwing up, like big time, but she's also waving for me to leave. So, I'm not sure if she's okay or not, but she's breathing. Ouch! Fuck! Stop that, you fat bastard! Stop! Get away!"

"I don't care if that cat shreds you to tiny pieces. You stand there until Taja can tell you herself if she's okay. You got me?"

I now know what the sounds were that I was hearing before but at a distance. I wince as Taja's body rejects whatever she put into it recently. This goes on for a while, and during it, a battle's ensuing between cat and man. Finally, there's an unholy scream, a slamming door, and then silence.

"Toes? What the fuck's going on?"

"Hey, Vex. Sorry, it's me. Toes dropped his phone and ran. He may be bleeding out somewhere. Possibly terminal. I'm okay now. Everything's okay. Bring Tessie home, and all will be well. I want to speak with her, but maybe now's not a good time," Taja says in a hoarse, weak voice. She sounds exhausted, and I'm worried. "Tell her I miss her and will see her soon, yeah? And thanks, Vex. Please tell the others I said thank you so much. I have to go now." I hear the last sentence and then more vomiting before the line goes dead.

Looking up, I find every head turned my direction and a few with phones in their hand, making a call.

"What the fuck's going on there?" Gunner barks.

"Taja's puking her insides out. Duffy's apparently looking for a place to hide Toes' body, and other than that, I have no fucking clue," I answer.

"Axel? Get your ass to the clubhouse and check on Taja. She's sick, and that fat fucking cat won't let Toes near her. Trudy and Ava should be getting ready for work, so see if one of them can go to the clubhouse with you," I hear Petey say into his phone. "Yes, we found her. She's safe, and we'll be heading for home shortly. Taja knows. Thanks, Son. See you soon."

Petey looks at me first with a grin, then turns his eyes to Tessie.

"Axel said to tell you welcome home and warned me not to let you drive us there."

"Your son's just a big girl," Tessie says, managing a small grin.

"Been told that before, darlin'. Don't mean it ain't true," Petey responds.

"Let's get on the road. Need to get Tessie back to her sister, and we need to have Church. There's going to be fallout, and we need to be ready for that," Gunner orders as he gently cups Tessie's face with one giant hand for a quick second on his way past her.

Lola Wright

Chapter 21

Taja

After another round of vomiting, I flop onto the cool tile of the floor, exhausted. A part of my brain's hoping the floor's been cleaned recently, but the rest of me doesn't really care at this point.

"Meow."

I open my eyes long enough to see Duffy sitting next to my head, staring at me again. He hasn't left my side for long over the last few days, and I've enjoyed his company. But the staring? I could do without that.

"Taja? Coming in," shouts Axel before I hear him walking through the bedroom. When he enters the bathroom, he stops, crosses his massive arms, and smirks down at me.

"Hey, Axel."

"You look like hell, woman."

"Axel! Don't tell her that, you jackass!" Trudy admonishes as she pushes her way in to stand next to Axel.

"Truth."

"Oh, honey. Let's get you up and into the shower. You'll feel better after. Axel, go make some tea and grab some crackers. I've got her," Trudy says while helping me to sit and then stand shakily.

Axel exits, and Trudy helps me strip and get into the warm water. It does help, and my stomach settles. I feel even better after I towel off, get into clean clothes, and sit on the bed. Axel returns with hot tea and crackers.

"Still think this is just stress?" Axel smirks.

"Are you gloating?" I ask.

"It's one of my many skills, so, yes, I am."

"While you're doing that, someone else is bonding with your daughter," I reply, raising an eyebrow at him. The smirk disappears as quickly as Axel does.

"Well played, Taja. You're going to fit in perfectly here," Trudy says while grinning huge.

This is the kind of MC I wish I'd grown up in. I didn't, and I feel the loss of what could have been. If I am pregnant, this is what I want my child to have. A large family, unconditional love, and taking care of each other. I had that with mom and Tessie, but this is bigger. Tessie's going to eat this up. I drift back to sleep with a smile.

Standing in front of the clubhouse, I can hear the bikes and vehicles coming up the road. A few seconds later, I can see them cruising through the main gate. The second truck has barely stopped when the back door flies open, and I finally see my little sister. Wet hits my eyes, and my feet start moving toward her. She looks a mess. Wild hair, pale face, rumpled clothes, but she's never looked more beautiful to me. When I get close, I throw my arms wide and wrap them around her with care. We stand silently, holding tight, and savoring the moment of being back together.

"Oh my God, Tessie. I'm so sorry, honey. I'm so fucking sorry," I whisper to her.

"No! This wasn't your fault. This wasn't mine. Don't take this on yourself, sis. I'm okay. Bruises, that's all. Love you so much," Tessie replies fiercely.

"We got dealt a shit hand in the father department," I say while still holding her tight to me.

"But we struck gold in the mom department. I struck gold in the sister department," she whispers back.

Pulling back a little, I look her over from top to toe. She does the same.

"I've only been gone a few days, and you've lost weight. No offense, but you look like shit," Tessie states with a watery laugh.

"You look worse," I shoot back. We both grin, and I know we're going to be okay.

Looking over Tessie's shoulder, I see Vex standing back, allowing us this moment. His eyes are soft and radiating warmth toward us sisters. I squeeze Tessie one last time, release her, and start walking to Vex. After a few steps, I break into a run and leap at the last second, knowing he'll catch me. He does with a laugh as I wrap arms and legs around him and hold tight. Leaning back, I look down to view his gorgeous face but change my mind and drop my mouth to his instead. As I knew he would, Vex responds beautifully. Forgetting about our audience, I lose myself in him. The world's perfect for a few seconds before it gets interrupted.

"Who are you? Hey, what's going on?"

I pull my head back, look down, and see the dirtiest child I've ever seen. Gee's standing next to him wearing a shirt that reads "Eat More Chicken," and that's not even the strangest part of this encounter. There's a skunk on the other side of the kid staring up at me.

"Hello. I'm Taja. And you are?" I ask while still clinging like a monkey to Vex's laughing body.

"Craig. This is Gee and Bart. He doesn't stink, and he's friendly. You're really pretty. Why's Vex holding you? Can't you walk?"

Vex lets me slide down his body until my feet hit the ground, but he keeps an arm around my shoulders, keeping me close.

"Nice to meet you, Craig," I reply.

"You wanna pet my skunk?" Craig inquires.

"Worst pick-up line ever," Vex mutters.

"Can I?" Tessie asks from beside me.

"Hi, Tessie. Yeah, you can too. You're not taking him driving, though," Craig answers in a serious tone.

Tessie and I bend down and give Bart and Gee some love while listening to the guys chuckling.

"You're really pretty. Want to have lunch with me?" Craig asks while looking at me.

"He's getting better at this. Vex finally has some competition," Trigger says with a laugh.

"How about we have a snack together later? I need to speak with Tessie and Vex for a while first, though. Is that okay with you?" I ask.

"Yeah, that's good. I have to learn things first, then I'll come find you," Craig states before walking away with his little friends.

"He's adorable," I tell Vex.

"Not always, but he's usually amusing as hell," Vex replies. "Looks like I'm going to have to watch my back. You have another admirer."

After Tessie takes a shower, and we've spent some time together, she crashes and is sleeping like the dead. I made a point to thank each and every one of the members for what they did, but all just waved me off with a smile or a hug. And while I shouldn't have liked it as much as I did, Vex growled a little with each hug I received.

I'm sitting in the main room while the guys are in Church. I'm anxious for Vex to get a few minutes to tell me what happened and what the plan is for the future. I know this isn't over with Rooster. He needs to be six feet under before he'd give up when money's involved.

I watch as a stunning black-haired woman rushes across the room toward me. I have no clue who she is, but she's smiling and appears friendly as she takes the seat across from me.

"Hi, Taja. I'm Pippa, Pooh's woman. Sorry we haven't met until now. Things have been hectic as all hell lately. Anyway, I wanted to speak with you before Craig gets here."

"Hi, Pippa. Sorry, I don't know which one Pooh is, but I did meet Craig. He's adorable."

"It can get confusing around here, but Pooh's my guy. We live here on the compound next to Axel and Bailey. We're engaged. I recently adopted Craig. Tammy is my mom. I consider Trigger as my second dad and one of the best men ever. Have I confused you yet?" Pippa asks, quirking an eyebrow at me.

"Almost. I've met most of those people, and I'm sure Pooh was one of the guys I thanked this morning," I answer.

"I'll properly introduce you two later. Pooh and Vex are tight, so you'll see a lot of us. But the reason I wanted to speak with you is I wanted to tell you what Craig did. I'm still blown away," Pippa rushes out before stopping to laugh.

I already know her and I could be good friends. You can clearly see her love for the people she considers family when she says their names. Her whole face lights up, and she practically glows.

"Okay, so you need to know that Craig hates soap and water like it's out to kill him. Say the word bath, and you won't find him for hours. No lie! Everyone here can tell you how fast that little shit can run when he thinks he's going to get cleaned up. Anyway, he just came to the house after meeting you and told me he needed a bath because he had a date. Needless to say, I about passed out. First, because he asked for a bath. That's never happened. Second, because he's barely five years old and talking about having a date. After he took his bath, which means the bathroom got a bath too, he strolls into the kitchen in his Aqua-man underwear and asked me where his romantic shirts were."

Pippa stops again to laugh to the point of tears in her eyes before finishing.

"I look at him like he's lost his mind. I said, 'Craig, I don't know what you mean by romantic shirts. You only like wearing your t-shirts and hoodies. What's a romantic shirt?' He gives me that look that a child gives an adult when they think we're being idiots. You know the look? Yeah, it's always fun being on the end of one. So, he tells me that romantic shirts are the ones with buttons. I'm confused as hell at this point and ask him why they're the romantic ones. Again, I get the look before he explains that shirts with buttons are the ones Pooh wears when he's taking me on a date. T-shirts and hoodies are for getting dirty in, not dates. Oh my God, Taja, you should have seen the look on his face as he explains this, slowly, to the simple adult. I about peed myself!"

At this point, I'm laughing along with her and picturing that muddy little face again. I definitely have an admirer if he was willing to get clean and dress up for me.

"Please don't tell him I told you. I just had to share, so you'd know how serious he's being about your date," Pippa says after gaining control of herself. "I may have to hire you to date him every time he needs a bath."

"Awww! I'll treat our date with the utmost respect, Pippa. Thank you for telling me."

"He was stopping to tell Bella about his date and to ask her about his outfit on his way here, so I better get going before he sees me. Thanks, Taja. Nice meeting you. Why don't you, Tessie, and Vex come for dinner tonight? We'll grill something and relax on the deck."

"Thank you. I'd like that, but I need to talk with Vex and Tessie first. We'll let you know, though."

"Cool! Gotta scoot!"

"What kind of snack should I get ready for him? What's he like?" I shout out just before she exits the doorway.

"He asked Chubs to help him pack some snacks for you two before Church started, so he has it covered. But don't let him talk you into any more than one root beer," Pippa hollers over her shoulder as she disappears.

Within seconds of Pippa leaving, Craig comes walking in from the kitchen. Now that he's devoid of mud, I can see how cute this little boy really is. Dirty blond hair, combed neatly, and a big smile, he's all clean and shiny. He's got a backpack on and is being trailed by a pig, skunk, and a large-ass dog with Mac perched on its back. I smother a laugh when I realize there has got to be a joke in all of that somewhere.

"Hi, Craig. Who's your big friend here?"

"That's Loki. Miss Ava let him outside to go potty, so I asked him to come too. Have you met Mac?" Craig explains as he sets his backpack on the table and takes a seat.

"Yes, I have. Hi, Mac. Is Loki friendly?" I ask nervously as the dog starts sniffing my leg.

"Yeah, he's cool. Unless one of the twins cry. Or Bella gets upset about something. He's only bit a few people, I think, and I heard they were bad men. So, I don't think that counts. I heard Gunner say once that Loki lit some guy's ass up good, but I wasn't here for that. Oh shit! Sorry, Taja. I'm not supposed to use those words in front of women, but I forget sometimes."

"I won't tell," I promise him with a wink.

"I'm telling," Mac screeches while flying from Loki's back to the tabletop.

"I'll tell Axel where you're hiding the cashews," Craig threatens.

"I'm zippin' it!" Mac concedes.

"You look very nice, Craig. What kind of snacks did you bring us? Why don't you get them out, and I'll grab us a drink. Root beer?"

"How'd you know that's my drink?" Craig asks with a confused look.

"A little birdie told me," I joke as I walk behind the bar to retrieve his root beer and a water for myself.

"Mac? He's the only bird I know," Craig responds in a serious voice.

"It's just an expression," I tell him as I set our drinks down and take my seat again. When he continues to look at me in confusion, I explain what I mean by an expression. Craig listens closely and nods when I'm done.

"Okay, I get it. Chubs teaches me my important stuff, but we haven't gotten to expressions yet," Craig tells me as he starts setting out enough snacks to feed the entire MC.

He picks up a bag of licorice, opens it, and holds it out to me first. It's black licorice, which I hate with a passion, but I take a stick anyway. He pulls out one for himself and starts munching on it while I tentatively take a bite of my own. Surprisingly, it's good. When I finish mine, Craig immediately holds out another one, and I scarf that down as well. While I'm enjoying my treat, Craig takes the lid off a plastic storage container and sits it in front of Mac. I see it's full of various nuts and some cut up pieces of fruit. He then opens the next container, which also has fruit, and sets it on the table before picking Bart up and setting him in a chair. Bart places his front paws on the table and digs in. I continue watching with a smile while Craig sets down a container for Gee and Loki. The little guy takes good care of his friends.

We chat and snack for a few minutes before the guys start entering the room. Church is over. Vex takes the last seat at our table and gives Craig a fist bump. Another guy walks up and tousles Craigs hair and earns a grin for his effort.

"Are you Pooh?" I ask.

"The one and only," the man says with a sexy smirk.

Damn! Pippa's done well for herself. Now I understand the constant smile on her face. I'm thinking this when a hand is waved in front of my own smiling face, and I jerk my eyes to Vex's.

"When you're done pissing me off, you want to talk?" Vex asks with a frown. I listen, but I don't look when Pooh starts laughing his ass off.

"Uh, yeah, sure. That works," I mumble out.

"Hi, Taja! Good to see you again. You go talk with Vex, and I'll help Craig with these snacks," Chubs says from next to me.

"Thank you for the snacks, Craig. Maybe we can do this again someday if you'd like," I tell the little guy.

"Sure. I'll show you my fort if you'd like," Craig offers.

"Sounds good. Bye," I say as Vex stands, pulls me up, and guides me out of the clubhouse.

"Tessie in my room sleeping?" Vex asks as we walk toward the vehicles.

"Yeah, she's exhausted."

Reaching Vex's truck, he opens the door, waits for me to get seated, and then closes it. He walks to the other side and climbs in. Turning to me, I see his eyes are serious.

"Did Tessie talk to you about what all happened?" he asks.

"Yeah, some. I don't think she told me everything, though. She didn't want to talk about the bruised ribs, and I didn't push. Just told her we could talk about it whenever she's ready. Other than some bruises, they didn't touch her. I mean, they didn't sexually assault her," I softly say.

"From what I overheard from the men there, they weren't allowed to on orders from Rooster. Not out of any fatherly concern, but because it would lower her value," Vex spits out in anger.

I'm not surprised because I suspected as much. Money's all that matters to Rooster. The Devil's Angels getting her back when they did saved her from a fate worse than death. I couldn't be more grateful to them for that.

"What do I do now, Vex? Rooster isn't going to let this end. He doesn't like to lose to anyone. Should I take Tessie and leave? Where do…"

"No, neither of you are leaving. We made it clear that his beef's with the Devil's now. I don't think he ever really wanted Tessie to begin with. He was making a point that he gets his way every time, and you had defied his orders. There's history between the two clubs that dates back to before Gunner was Prez. Petey, Reno, Trigger—they all remember the Skulls and the issues between the clubs. We'll handle Rooster. In the meantime, we need to keep you and Tessie out of his reach. You'd be nothing but a bargaining chip for him."

"We can stay with Suki. She came to the clubhouse to see me while you were gone, and I know we can count on her."

"Not safe enough, Taja. Rooster won't care about collateral damage to get what he wants. And Suki would be nothing but that to him. I think it's best if you let Tessie stay with Petey, Trudy, and Bella. Petey offered, and he wouldn't have if he didn't mean it. The girls are friends, and Tessie can still go to the garage because she'd be riding with Petey. It's not going to be forever, just until things are safe again. Would you go along with that?" Vex asks.

"Yeah, I will. I know she's safer with Petey and on the compound than anywhere else right now," I answer after thinking it over for a moment. "I'll talk to her tonight and explain that this is just how it's got to be for now. God, I hate being separated from her again. How's it possible to hate one's own father as much as I do?"

Vex reaches over and cups the side of my face. I lean into it and allow his comfort to soak into my soul for a moment. I've liked Vex from the start, but he's becoming more to me with each passing day. That scares me because I don't think it's going to last, and I'll have to find a way to move on when the time comes.

Vex pulls his hand back and starts the truck. I look at him bewildered because I thought we were just sitting out here to have some privacy, but he throws it into gear, and off we go. I scramble for my seat belt, get it on, and turn my head his direction.

"Where we going?" I ask.

"To your place to get Tessie some things," Vex answers as he reaches over and grasps my hand. He pulls it his direction until our joined hands are resting on the console between us. I stare at our fingers intertwined and feel my heart give a slow thump.

"You got everything she might need?" Vex questions as he lifts the suitcase and backpack off the floor.

"Yeah, I think so. If not, I'll bring whatever I missed to her tomorrow," I answer.

"Taja?"

"What?"

"Grab the pregnancy tests too. It's time to find out, doll."

My eyes shoot to Vex's, and I realize he's right. I also realize this could be the beginning of the end for us. Regardless, we need to know for sure, and I'll deal with the fallout as it happens. I turn to my room, grab the bag with the tests, and follow Vex down the stairs.

"Wait. I don't need to bring these too. I'm just dropping off Tessie's stuff and explaining everything to her. I'll take a test in the morning," I tell him while setting the tests on the nearest end table.

"Where do you think you'll be in the morning, Taja?"

"I thought I was following you back to the clubhouse to speak with Tessie. Then I'd be coming back here, I guess. Or Freddy's place. He said I could stay with…"

"No. You'll be with me at the clubhouse, and we'll take the test in the morning. Together," Vex rudely interrupts.

"Are you worried I'd lie to you about the results?" I ask, shocked.

Vex sets the suitcase and backpack on the floor and moves in close to my front. Using his thumbs, he tips my head back and drops a quick kiss on my mouth. Still holding my head in his hands, he explains further.

"Fuck no, Taj. Never crossed my mind, baby. I promised you that we'd do this shit together. We'd find out. We'd decide how things are going to go, and we'd deal either way, but we'd do it together. And no fucking way am I letting you stay anywhere but with me. Not happening. You're not picking up what I'm laying down yet, but you will. Pregnant or not, we're together. We're seeing where this goes. Us, Tessie, and possibly a beautiful little girl with your eyes and big heart. Maybe a boy with my bossy ways. Who knows? Maybe just me, you, and Tessie for now. You get it yet?" Vex ends with a soft smile.

"I think so. Yeah, I do. I may need you to keep reminding me sometimes, though. And you are bossy," I reply while fighting my own smile.

"Good thing to know from the start, I guess," Vex says before capturing my mouth with his and kissing the hell out of me. Vex wraps his arms around me and holds tight.

Chapter 22

Vex

Laying in bed, Taja sleeping and tucked close, my mind's at peace. I don't really know when I went from wanting a night with her to wanting more than that, but that's how this has turned out. Not sure if it's shocked me more than my club family, though, judging by some of the skeptical looks I've seen. I'm well aware that I'm taking on not one but two women. Two women that are practically joined at the hip and will always be that way. I grin in the darkness, knowing I'm ready for both.

I've never had much interest in the inheritance my grandmother left me. It's been sitting for years, growing by leaps and bounds, but I have everything I've ever really needed. Club family, roof over my head, a new truck whenever I wanted one, and several bikes. But now I'm thinking I need something more permanent for our future. These women have struggled their whole lives to make ends meet and have no idea they'll never have to do that again. I'm also aware that neither are going to lose their independent streak, and I like that about them. There're going to be battles ahead, but I have no qualms about not fighting fair. Having money, lots of it, finally has some appeal to me.

At Church, Gunner announced that he reached out to Rooster and hasn't received a reply yet. Not surprising, really. Gunner wasn't trying to come to a truce but rather letting him know that we're his biggest threat now. Rooster's smart enough to know that since he lost four men and his clubhouse is now a smoldering ash pile. We know this isn't over, but we'll keep Tessie and Taja safe until it is. That was, of course, a unanimous vote. Numerous members offered up their homes as a safe place for the sisters since I live at the clubhouse. I need to have a discussion with Taja about that, but for now, at least Tessie's settled in with Petey.

Taja shifts slightly and then freezes. Tilting my head her direction, I see her squeezing her eyes shut tight and panting through her mouth. Before I can say anything, she bounds up, jumps over me, and hits the floor running. I scramble out after her and follow her to the bathroom. She's already on the floor in front of the toilet and making some gruesome sounds. I grab a washcloth, run cool water over it, and wring it out. I wait until she rests her head on her arms, then crouch down next to her and place the washcloth against her neck under her hair. I grab a hair tie off the counter, pull her hair back and use it to secure her hair out of the way. Reaching over her, I flush the toilet.

"Stay here, baby. I'll be right back," I tell her.

All I get is a nod, but that's enough. Walking into the kitchen, I make toast, grab the crackers, and then make a hot tea. Taking them with me, I return to my room and find Taja laying across the bed, belly down.

"Thought I told you to stay where you were," I say as I set my items down and take a seat next to her.

"Don't be bossy when I don't feel well enough to kick your ass for it," she mumbles back.

I grin as I wrap my hands around her torso and pull her up to sit against the headboard. I swing my feet onto the bed, so we're sitting beside each other, and hand her the tea. When she takes it, I notice her hands are still shaking. I don't think she's done with the bathroom yet.

"Do we even need you to piss on a stick at this point, Taj?" I ask, knowing she's going to argue.

"We need to know, Vex. One way or the other. And this could be a touch of the flu or stress."

"Think we already do know, honey. When you're done eating and drinking your tea, we'll get the test out and confirm it. Eat, drink. Then after the stick says positive, we'll make a doctor's appointment to get you started on prenatal care."

"Being bossy again."

"Get used to it," I say while laughing at the disgruntled look on her face.

Leaning our backs against the bathroom wall, sitting on the floor, we both stare at the plus sign on the pregnancy test. I thought when I saw the proof, there'd be some anger or disgust for myself and my carelessness. Instead, it feels right. Pride maybe? Definite happiness, no regret. Glancing at Taja's face, I see nothing. No expression whatsoever, and I don't know what to make of that. Is she mad, sad, scared, happy?

"This doesn't have to seem like a bad thing, Taja. It's a good thing. We're together. We'll be staying that way. With time, we'll be on solid ground, and things with Rooster will end. We can make this work between us. I think this is the result I was hoping for," I admit to her.

"I think it is for me too," Taja whispers. "I just don't know if it's because I want a baby, your baby, or to keep you in my life."

"Doesn't matter which, Taja. You've got me and our baby no matter what. You might not always think that's a good thing, but I'll do my best to make sure it is. I want this more than I realized. Holy fuck, we're going to be parents. I'm going to be someone's dad. Oh, fuck me, please, don't be a girl!" I say in a bit of a panic when I realize this could be a baby girl.

"What's wrong with a girl?" Taja demands to know in a pissy tone.

"I'll kill any guy that ever looks in her direction! If she looks like you, do you have any idea how many men that could be?" I shout back.

Suddenly, Taja dissolves into laughter. She's leaning against my shoulder, and her entire body's shaking with the giggles. What the fuck? I wasn't trying to be funny. I'm dead serious about the body count that will occur if we have a girl. This baby has got to be a boy if I have any hope of staying out of prison.

"I can't wait to ask Axel how he's going to handle it when Alex is a teenager and boys come sniffing around her! That should make his gossipy little ass disappear for a day or two. What if our baby's a boy and has the hots for Alex? I can throw that at Axel for months now," Taja gasps out between bouts of laughter. "With you being such a man whore, Axel's going to be scared that your son will be one too. And going to go after his daughter! Axel's going to have a mental breakdown!"

"Former man whore, thank you very much!" I inform Taja, irritated with that title even though it's been well earned.

"That's yet to be seen."

"You might not have noticed, but every fucking club member has," I mutter.

"Whoa! Wait a minute. Axel said something about you acting kind of off for a while and blamed me for it. How am I to blame?"

"First off, don't listen to much that Axel spouts off about. For Christ sakes, the man has a bird trying to take a hit out on him. I don't think either of them are mentally stable. But to answer your question, here are some truths you need to know. I wanted you as soon as I spotted you. For a night, for some hot sex, and that was it. That's how I'd always lived and what I thought I still wanted. I knew you weren't very experienced, and that was a huge draw for me. I was born with a dick so that inherently makes me selfish in the respect that I didn't want to go where a lot of others have been. That was new for me too. I'd never cared about that before. But Suki and Freddy both asked me not to go after you. That you'd been through enough, and I was a complication you didn't need. I agreed and backed off. During that time, we became more than just co-workers. We became friends, and I got to know you as a person instead of just a conquest. I found myself not wanting anything less or easy anymore."

"Are you saying you quit fucking around way back then?" Taja asks quietly while reaching for my hand.

"I tried to still be a whore, but nothing felt right. So, yeah, I quit fucking around and started thinking about what I really wanted. You. I wanted something real. I wanted a relationship, not just a night. And every thought came back to you. Maybe a part of me's happy about the baby because that keeps you in my life too. I don't know for sure, but I am positive that I'm happy as fuck that you're sitting here with me figuring this shit out together. I have to tell you, though, that there's a good chance I'm going to fuck this up. I don't want to, but I might."

"What if you make a mistake, and I call you on it? Will you talk it out or bolt? I'm willing to work with you on any differences we have, but not if you're going to run each time things get rocky. Mom gave Tessie and me stability. She was always there for us regardless of her health issues. No matter how mad, sad, depressed, happy, or sick she got, she kept our lives as stable as possible. I'm not saying our lives were easy, but we always knew she loved us, and we'd power through whatever life threw at us together. I need that from you. Especially now, Vex. Shit gets bad, I need to know you'll be there for me, Tessie, and our baby. If you can't do that, please tell me now," Taja says.

"No need to worry about that, honey. I'm all in. I'm just sayin' I'm positive I'll fuck something up. Call me on it, holler at me—whatever you need to do, but I need you to not bolt too. In my upbringing, when someone didn't conform to my dad's ideas, you became a cast-off. A throwaway. I need you to care enough to work through shit with me and not just walk away."

"What if I tell you I'm not going to let you fuck this up?" Taja asks softly.

"That'd be good," I say while smiling for the first time in several minutes. Relief hits me, and I know in my gut she means it.

Hand in hand, Taja and I walk into the main room of the clubhouse and spot Axel with the twins. In a neon pink baby sling around Axel's body is little Alex. We take seats at their table as Mac struts nearby up and down the bar. He's stopping every few steps to wiggle his tail feathers and bob his head to the beat boxing he's doing. He's good. I'll give him that.

"Who are these lovelies? Taja asks.

"Mia and Zoe. Gunner and Ava's twins. My nieces and my biggest fans," Axel replies while making funny faces at the giggling twins.

"Which is which?" Taja questions.

"Fuck if I know. I can never tell them apart. Only Gunner, Trudy, and Ava can. And I think Gunner just guesses most of the time," Axel answers.

Mac stops what he's doing and lands on the table in front of us in a flurry of feathers. It sets the twins off, and I have to smile at their laughter. They're beautiful little girls with black hair, green eyes, and chubby cheeks.

"Mia!" Mac states while standing in front of one of the twins. He moves to stand in front of the other twin and states, "Zoe!"

"Get out of here, Mac. You don't know which is which either," Axel sputters.

"Do too."

"Move yourself, Mac. I'm teaching the twins to say my name, and you're in the way," Axel orders. "I want to piss Gunner off and have them learn my name before they can say daddy."

"Dad'll be mad!" Mac screeches.

"Say Axel. Uncle Axel. Axxxxel!" Axel says repeatedly to the twins.

Nothing but big smiles from each of the girls, but Axel's determined.

"Say Axel! Uncle Axel! Come on, sweethearts, you can say it. Axel!" he continues.

"Mac," says the twin on the right, followed closely by the other with "Mac."

Clear as day, their first word that I know of is Mac. That's definitely going to put a few feathers up Axel's ass. I snort out a laugh at the look on his face, and Taja follows suit when Mac mimics the girls giggle.

"No, no, no, no, no, no, no, no, no!" Axel exclaims loudly. "Axel! Say Uncle Axel. Axel! Axel!"

"Mac," the twins say together.

"Both of you take that back! No, no, no, no! Axel! Axel! It's easy to say! Spit it out, girls—Axel!"

"Assssssss," says the twin on the left.

"Assssssss," says the other twin immediately after.

"Got that right!" Mac bellows while Taja and I lose our shit at Axel's dismay with his nieces.

"Fuck me sideways. Mac's brainwashed my nieces!" Axel whines.

"Wuck me. Wuck me," the right twin spouts loudly.

"Stop right now! No! Don't say that ever again!" Axel shouts.

"Wuck me. Wuck me. Wuck meeeeeeee," the left twin giggles while pointing her tiny, chubby little finger at Axel.

"Mom's gonna kill you," Mac says in a gleeful voice.

He's loving this. He may not need his cashews after all when Ava finds out what words Axel taught her daughters. I want to be around for that showdown.

"Just say Mac. It's okay. Stick with Mac," Axel implores the girls.

"Wuck meeeeee!"

"No! Stop that right now! Say Mac! Hell, say daddy! I don't care what you say, just don't say that again! Please, girls, save your uncle!" Axel says in a desperate voice.

Taja and I are definitely enjoying the shit show that Axel got rolling. Watching him panic gives me a warm, fuzzy feeling. He hands out so much shit to the rest of us, and it's nice watching him get some back.

"Wuck me!" hollers the right twin again.

"Axel! My office, right now!" roars Gunner.

Axel's head drops, chin to chest, in resignation of what's about to happen. He heaves a big sigh before he stands slowly and removes little Alex from her sling and kisses her forehead. He carefully hands her over to Taja then removes the sling to set on the table. Turning to each of the twins, he gives them a kiss on the head before turning to me.

"Please tell my daughter how much I loved her while I was on this earth. Bailey too. Take care of them for me and make sure I live on in their memories," Axel requests in a quiet tone before trudging slowly toward Gunner and the office.

"Last words?" Mac squawks.

"Yeah. Wuck me," Axel replies.

Taja and I hang with the little ones while waiting to find out Axel's fate. I know my grin's a little evil when I hear Gunner's voice at a booming level. I'm positive the walls have shaken a few times. I do kind of feel bad for Axel, but I'm also getting enjoyment out of this too.

Watching Taja, I know she's going to be a great mom. She's good with the twins and hasn't stopped cuddling Alex since she got her. She's also saying the word "daddy" and "dada" over and over again, probably hoping that might calm the beast if his little angels were to say that to him.

Mac has positioned himself near the office and is clearly trying to overhear what's going on in there. Occasionally, Mac chuckles and lets out a loud "Muuuaaahhaaaaa," so I know things aren't going in Axel's favor. If he doesn't survive Gunner's wrath, I'm nominating Pooh for the VP position. He'd be awesome at it, but I would miss Axel and his antics.

Toes walks into the room, glances our direction, and hurries behind the bar. Within a minute, he has a beer sitting in front of me and a Coke in front of Taja. I give him a chin lift and reach for my beer. When Toes walks away, I notice Taja grinning at me.

"What?" I ask.

"Is Toes really on Poo-Poo Patrol every day because he checked out my ass?" she whispers.

"Yup. He won't make that mistake again. I promise you," I respond.

"Seriously, Vex? Just for that, you're making him pick up shit with his hands?" she asks incredulously.

"I'm not a jerk. I gave him gloves," I smirk.

"So, what am I allowed to do when the dancers are rubbing all up on you and grabbing your junk? Firing squad? Stoning in the town square? Don't give me that look. I've seen them in action."

"Tell them I'm yours, and you don't share. Bitch slap them. Do whatever makes you feel better. If you can get that shit to stop, I'm all for whatever methods you use," I answer truthfully.

"You may regret saying that when there's no uninjured dancers on the stage," Taja says with a wicked grin.

"I won't. Freddy might not enjoy it as much as I do, though. But then again, he's claimed you as family, so he may be all for it. But until the baby's born, make the smackdowns verbal."

"Hey, Vex. Hi, Taja. What's got Gunner mad?" Chubs asks as he plops down on a chair. He tweaks each twin on the nose before holding his hands out for little Alex.

"Axel," I answer with a grin as I watch Taja begrudgingly hand over the infant to Chubs.

"Hi. There's my child," says Bailey as she stops next to us.

"Your child's here, but your man's in the office with Gunner," I tell her.

"I figured it might be Axel that Gunner's hollering at," Bailey responds with a grin. "What'd he do this time?"

"Accidentally taught the twins to swear," I reply.

"Oh God! That's not good," Bailey says with a cringe.

"It was totally an accident. He's so good with the girls, I know he didn't mean for that to happen," Taja adds.

"I didn't, but it did, and I'm now on LOTT according to their oversized father," Axel grumbles as he stops next to Bailey. "For years, the ass said."

"Asssssssss!" the twin on the right repeats.

Bailey and Chubs both turn their heads away from the twins while laughing silently. Axel stares down at the twin like she's trying to get him killed.

"Please don't say that around your mother! I survived your dad, but your mom has a mean-ass right hook. I like my face the way it is!" Axel exclaims.

"What's LOTT?" Taja asks.

"Loss of Twin Time," Axel answers dejectedly. "In prison, it's called LOP—loss of privileges. Gunner's probably spent a year thinking that up, just waiting to use it against me."

"Wuck me!" the twin on the left screams and then giggles.

"Give me my child, please. I'm going home to figure out ways around Gunner and his orders," Axel says while putting the sling back on and placing Alex in it.

After Bailey, Axel, and daughter walk out of the clubhouse, Mac lands on the table in front of the twins. They each reach their hands out to him, and it's cute to watch them interact.

"Axel," Mac states.

"Axel," each twin promptly repeats. This is clearly not the first time they've said it because it's said so perfectly. Maybe Axel was right, and Mac has brainwashed the twins.

Chapter 23

Taja

We're waiting at the clubhouse for Tessie. Vex and I decided to let her know about the baby, and I'm nervous about the upcoming conversation. I texted her earlier, and she said she'd be here soon. After this tough conversation, Vex and I need to decide where we're going to be staying for a while. The club doesn't want me back at my home because of Rooster. I agree with their logic, but Vex said we have other options than just his room here.

We've been chatting with Chubs and entertaining the girls. Not long after Axel left, Gunner made an appearance, grumpy face and all, and took his daughters to his office. Didn't speak, just picked the twins up and turned to leave when Vex stopped him.

"Axel didn't mean for the girls to say what they did. He wasn't teaching them swear words, but that's what they picked up on."

"I get that. But they're learning things rapidly now, and he should've known better," Gunner barks.

He's definitely not a happy daddy at the moment.

"He loves those girls like they're his own. And every little girl should have a guy like Axel in her life. Protective, loving. Nobody will ever get past him to hurt either of your daughters or his own. Don't punish your girls by keeping their uncle away from them. His heart's in the right place," Chubs adds in a quiet but firm voice while staring Gunner in the eye.

I'm a little shocked to hear Chubs speak up because he's always so easy-going, happy, and smiling. His comments in defense of Axel proves his loyalty because not many would risk irritating a man like Gunner. Gunner pauses, nods once, and walks off. I get the feeling that Chubs' comments struck a chord within Gunner. Gunner may be a hard man, but he's also a fair one. I have mad respect for Chubs' kind of loyalty but also for a man that's fair.

"Vex!" Toes hollers from across the room.

"Yeah?" Vex answers.

"Know anyone by the name of Brock Cooper?" Toes asks.

I have no idea what's going on, but one of the men sitting with me freezes in place for a quick moment.

"Who's asking?" Chubs questions.

"Horse Nuts is on the phone. Said there's a couple of suits at the gate asking to speak with a Brock Cooper," Toes replies.

"Tell him I'll handle it. Be there in a minute," Chubs responds while standing up.

"Chubs? Need a hand?" Vex asks quietly while also standing up.

"Nah, I got this. Stay with your woman. I'll call if I need anything. Thanks, Vex," Chubs answers as he walks away.

I don't know who Brock Cooper is, but I know enough about club life to not ask too many questions. If I need to know, someone will tell me. But I do know that Vex is tense and concerned about suits at the gate.

"Let me get this straight. You had unprotected sex, even though you both know better, and now you're pregnant. And I know you know better because you've been the one that's lectured me several times about that very subject. 'Condoms are cheap, Tessie. Babies are not.' I've heard that so many times coming straight from your mouth, Taja," Tessie declares.

"That sums it up," I mumble.

"One look at this hot Hawaiian and…"

"Tessie, we…" Vex starts to say before Tessie interrupts.

"Your ass-chewing will commence in a minute, biker boy. I'm not done with Taj, yet. I love you to the moon and back, Taja. And when I said you needed to live a little, I meant it. I'm glad you chose Vex to do that with, to give up that rusty old V-card to. Perfect choice for some fun. But a baby? You know I'll love that child and you forever. I'll be the best aunt any child could ever have. I'll rock the hell out of being an aunt. And we'll figure things out money-wise too so the baby never needs anything we can't provide. I can work more hours at the garage. I'd like that anyway. But Vex as a father?"

"Hey! I'll be a great dad," Vex protests.

"Hey! Your turn now, daddy-o!" Tessie shoots back before laying some truth on Vex.

"Taja's inexperienced, and from everything I've heard, you are far from that. You should've been the careful one. This wasn't your first time up to bat. Are you always that careless, and if so, how many brothers and sisters does this child have?"

"Zero. I've always been careful, and yes, I did fuck it up this time. I own that shit," Vex barks back while placing his hands on his hips and widening his stance.

Tessie mimics his pose and stands as close to nose-to-nose as she can get. The girl's got guts.

"What's done is done. Thank you for giving me a niece or nephew to love. Taja has always wanted kids, and she'll get her wish. But here's how this is going to play out. You're either in our lives, or you're all the way the hell out of them. We've spent a lifetime dealing with a deadbeat, useless father, and this baby isn't going to go through that too. You don't get the choice to play part-time daddy. Taja and I will be this kid's parents if you want out. Either all in or all out, Vex. I like you. I really do. But I know what it's like to have a dad that's lurking around the edges of your life waiting to exploit you in some way. Not saying you would do that. But my job now is to protect this baby from everything bad for it, even if that includes its dad."

"Holy fuck. You're going to be as much of a nutjob about this baby as Axel is with his, aren't you?" Vex questions with a grin.

"Damn straight, pretty boy," Tessie answers with her own grin.

My shoulders drop in relief that the worst is over. Tessie said her piece, has taken her stand, and I know there's no wiggle room in it. God, I love that girl. My baby's going to have a fierce aunt and protector.

"You've said what you needed to say. Now it's my turn. I'm going to be in your lives, like it or not. I'm not bailing on Taja or our child. I don't do things part-way, so prepare to see a lot of me. This is my child too. Taja's also mine, and along with her comes your pain in the ass self. I'm glad my kid's going to have you as her or his aunt. And, I'm only half-Hawaiian, as you put it. Before you ask, no, I don't surf, and I don't like Spam. But rule number one is that you will never drive anything with my child or Taja in it. You're a menace to society when you're behind the wheel. Sorry, Tessie, but you suck as a driver. I'll be working on that with you because I'm basically your big brother now, and that's my job. But I'm buying you a car of some sort so my truck doesn't pay the price for your lack of understanding brake versus accelerator."

Tessie squeals and throws her arms around Vex while my mouth falls open in dismay. I can't let him buy her a car. We can't accept gifts of that magnitude.

"Vex, no. You aren't buying her a car. That's too much," I protest.

"No, it's not, Taja! He got my sister pregnant, and I'll be helping to raise that baby. I'd say it's a fair deal," Tessie shouts at me.

"It'll be more like a tank, Taj. That only goes about 35 miles per hour, so she can't take out half of Denver. I'll figure it out, baby. Don't worry about her safety. I won't turn over the keys until I'm sure she won't get herself killed," Vex insists from beside a grinning Tessie.

Both are looking at me like I'm the bad guy here. I sigh, knowing when I'm beat. But Vex and I will be discussing this at a later date. I agree she needs a car, but not that he'll be paying for one.

There's a huge benefit in dating a man whore. He knows the female form and what brings it pleasure like no other. Vex is currently demonstrating his knowledge in all the best ways. My body is his toy, and this guy knows how to handle it.

"Oh God, baby. Right there, yesssss!" I moan as his mouth reacquaints itself with my clit.

I have one hand wrapped in his hair while the other is gripping the headboard above my head. Eyes closed, head thrown back, I'm lost in sensation. I feel a finger slide into me and pump while his tongue glides ruthlessly up and down my clit. I come, and I come hard. Stomach muscles contracting, body tensing before I relax into the orgasm and just enjoy. Before my mind has caught up to my body, Vex is on the move. He grabs my hips and pulls me down the bed a little, then grabs both calves and raises them straight up, so I'm looking at the tops of my feet. He shifts his body close so my legs are against his chest, and he slides into my body. He only enters part of the way before easing out and back in again. He does this a few times, each time going deeper until he's fully seated deep in my body. Vex stays still, giving a gentle squeeze to my calves. I open my eyes and see his heated ones staring down at me. Fuck, he's beautiful in all his wild glory.

"Play with your nipples. I want to watch you do it," Vex demands in a low, sexy voice.

I don't think. I just act. He hasn't guided me wrong yet. My hands find my breasts and squeeze gently before thumb and forefinger grasp each nipple.

"Fuck yeah. Don't stop, and keep your eyes open. I'm gonna fuck you now," he says.

"Condom?" I say, smiling impishly up at him.

"Not ever again. Not even after the baby's born. We'll figure it out, but I like feeling you wrapped around my cock, not latex. Now hush because the next word out of your mouth better be my name. You say it, moan it, scream it—I don't care. But when you're coming, I want to hear my name come from that mouth," he orders.

Vex starts using his hips, thrusting hard. God, he feels good. I pinch and roll my nipples, and it feels better than anytime I tried it on my own. I've never been able to make myself come before either. Guess my body only likes it when Vex is close.

After a couple of minutes, Vex bends my legs until my knees are interfering with my hands. I pull them out from between us and do enough of an ab curl to slide my fingers down his eight-pack abs. Relaxing back, I visually admire the body on its knees in front of me. Pure beauty, from the long, wild hair to the perfect V shape torso.

"Clit. Touch yourself, Taj. Touch me while I'm inside of you," Vex rasps out.

I reach down and slide my finger up and down his length as he slowly thrusts into me. Vex's hand grabs mine and places it on my clit. Using his hand, he teaches me the best ways to bring on the orgasm that's so close. I watch him watching my hand, and that's a turn on all by itself.

"Vex, baby, I'm going to come," I moan.

"Not yet, but soon."

Vex no more than says those words, and I lose him. He pulls out, flips onto his back next to me, and pulls on my hand. I roll his direction, wanting nothing more than for him to help me over the edge.

"On me, Taj. You're going to ride me until you come."

I swing my leg over his hips and watch his hand guide his cock until it's nudging at my entrance. Using his other hand on my hip, he guides me slowly down on his length. He feels so much deeper in this position that I gasp a little.

Vex pumps up into me each time I move my hips. This is amazing. I'm in control, and I'm loving it. I place my hands on his chest and slide myself forward and back, hitting my clit against his body each time. I watch as he licks his thumb, wondering why but not really caring because I'm caught up in feeling. I suddenly do care, and care a lot, when he pushes his thumb up against my clit at the perfect moment. I sit up straight to give him better access, and it's only seconds before I'm moaning his name non-stop.

"Vex. Vex. Please, baby. Vex!"

"Give it all to me, Taj. Don't stop yet. I want every fucking thing you have to give."

Vex moves his hand to my hip and uses both to hold my body still while he thrusts hard up into me. He slams my body down on his, and I come again. Or still. I'm not sure which. I just know the orgasm's raging inside of me. Vex comes, and even I can tell it's spectacular for him too. It's not long, and I'm collapsing against his chest, still connected.

Vex huffs out a laugh while pulling my hair out of our faces and holding it behind my head. I raise my head high enough to connect with his mouth, and he doesn't disappoint. He never does. We kiss for a moment, letting it tell the other how great it is to be alone together.

We lay in the same position until I feel him soften. He gently rolls me to his side while keeping his arm wrapped around my shoulders. I tuck my face against his chest and use my finger to trace one of the many tattoos painted into his skin. I know I need to get cleaned up, I can feel sperm sliding out, but there's something comforting in feeling it too. It's a part of him, and I like having it in and on me.

"You aren't buying Tessie a car. Without having to pay Rooster each month, we can afford to get her something," I tell him quietly.

"Am."

"No, you're not."

"Am."

"We have a baby coming. Spend that money helping me set up a nursery and buying all the essentials. Tessie can use my car until her and I get her one of her own," I say a little louder.

"Promised her. Not going back on a promise, Taja. Not to either of you. Won't happen, so you might as well accept that I'm buying her a car," Vex says firmly.

"We just had the best sex of my life, and now you're annoying me," I inform him.

"Baby, you haven't seen anything yet. My goal's to make each time the best sex you've ever had. Lots to learn, and I love teaching you, so prepare. As for annoying you? It's about to get worse, so brace."

Maybe I should have continued to enjoy the post-coital bliss instead of poking the bear. I take his advice and brace. Unfortunately, I didn't brace enough.

"I can easily afford Tessie's car. I can also easily afford to take over your bills so you can quit work, go back to college, and finish up your degree. You won't need that degree if you choose not to do that, though. Because, once again, I can easily afford to cover any expenses you have. I want you safe, healthy, and growing our child. Everything else, I'll deal with. Tomorrow, after the doctor's appointment, we'll stop at the bank. I'll transfer money to your account and get you a debit and credit card linked to mine. Buy anything you want or need for you, Tessie, and the baby."

I would have interrupted him, but I couldn't form the words properly. I sit up and twist to see his face. It's dead serious and not joking like I was hoping it would be.

"Are you out of your mind? I'm not going to live off you! I take care of Tessie and myself, Vex. That's my job and my responsibility. You wanting to help with the baby is great. I appreciate it, and it's the right thing to do. But you paying for me and Tessie too? No! Not going to happen," I inform him.

"It's going to happen. Exactly like I just told you it would. Accept it and save your arguments for something you have a chance at winning. And FYI—it's hard to take your argument serious when your tits are in my face. Not that I mind—ever—but now I don't want to argue with you. I want to fuck you again," Vex tells me with a smirk while stretching his arms up and placing his linked hands under his head.

His movement has made the sheets slip low on his hips, and unwillingly my eyes slip up and down all that's showing. I lose my train of thought and forget what we were talking about when he takes one hand, pushes the sheet lower, and grasps his cock. He gives it a slow tug, and my eyes are glued to it as I watch his cock lengthen and harden. With one hand behind his head, one on his cock, there's a lot for my eyes to worship.

Vex continues stroking himself, harder than I would've ever done, until a small droplet of moisture beads on the tip. Without thought, I swipe it up and suck it off my finger. When I hear Vex's long, low groan, I realize how much he liked what I just did. I move so I'm sitting on my knees next to his hips and wrap my hand around his cock. After a few strokes, I let my hand drift down until I'm cupping his sack. Another low moan and I'm licking my lips without conscious thought. I roll his balls gently in my hand and familiarize myself with the feel of him.

"Need your mouth, baby," Vex rasps.

"I don't know what I'm doing, Vex. I've never done this but, fuck, I want you in my mouth."

"Don't want technique. I want you," Vex replies.

I lean down and lick his tip. I taste him and me from our first round. When Vex removes his hand, I replace it with my other hand so now I'm holding all of him in my palms. Sliding my hand up and down his length, I slide my tongue across the slit and then around the head. The sounds coming from Vex make me bolder, so I wrap my mouth around his length and take him in as far as I can.

"I'm not going to move, baby. The control and pace are all yours. Do whatever you want to me because your fucking mouth is perfection," Vex says in a strained voice.

I take him at his words, and using my hands, tongue, and lips, I explore every inch of him. I don't worry about what's right or wrong. I just let my curiosity guide me. There's a lot of inches to enjoy, and I make sure to get my fill. I must be doing something right because I can feel Vex getting even harder. I get free rein for several moments before Vex's hand cups the back of my head, twisted in my hair.

"Baby, you need to pull back. I'm going to come," Vex tells me.

I'm not sure I'm ready for that experience yet, so I pull my head back but continue pumping him with my hand. My other hand feels his balls pull up and tighten. I know he's close. I ramp up my pumping and watch in fascination when he explodes. It's spectacular. When I feel Vex slowly relax his body, I take my hands off him. Looking into his almost golden eyes, I lick my hand clean.

"Fuck, Taj, you're killing me. Now, I wanna fuck you again."

Vex does an ab curl until we're nose to nose. Giving me a gentle kiss, he pulls me down on the bed next to him again. I snuggle close, and my heart stops for a second when he laces our fingers together and rests them on his chest.

"You need to come?" Vex asks.

"No, I'm good for now. Later on, the answer will be yes," I answer on a yawn.

"Get some sleep. I'll be right here when your answer changes."

It's morning, and I'm beyond irritated. We showered together, and the experience of running soapy hands all over Vex is one I'll never forget. Feeling him do the same to me was unbelievably hot. It wasn't long before I was pressed up against the shower wall, and Vex was deep inside me. After the best shower sex ever, we dried off, got dressed, and Vex got on my bad side.

"I adore you for wanting to take care of us, but it's not right, and I'm not going to go along with that. I'm pregnant, not disabled. I can and will continue working for as long as I can," I snap at him. Again, since he ignored me the first time.

"You're fucking adorable when you're mad, Taj. But the mother of my child isn't going to be on her feet all night in a strip club. You're not going to be serving drunks and perverts while growing our child. For that to happen, I'm going to pay your bills and every other fucking thing I choose to pay for," Vex calmly says. Again, since I ignored him the first time, he said it.

"You're so fucking annoying! You can't just decide these things and demand I go along with them," I shout.

He grins. Yes, he grins at me. That's like waving a red cape in front of a bull. I'm so pissed at him I can barely articulate my thoughts.

"Don't smile at me, you ass! I'm not…"

I get half of my thought out before running for the bathroom. Before my stomach contents even hit the toilet, Vex is pulling my hair back and holding it out of the way. I try to wave him out of the room, but he ignores that too. After I think I'm finished, I reach up and flush the toilet before resting my head on my arms.

"Would now be a bad time for me to sing that old song?" Vex asks.

I think I hear a smile in his voice, but he's got to be smart enough to know that could cause his death.

"What are you talking about?" I ask while staring into the toilet bowl.

"That old song by Paul Anka. "Having my Baby." If I was to start singing that, would it be amusing and lighten the mood? Or would that be an Axel kind of mistake that could cause great bodily harm?"

"Do it and die, biker boy," I growl.

"I'll just let the song run through my brain. Silently, so I don't have to pull another Axel trick and buy you flowers until you forgive me," he mutters.

I can clearly hear the smile and quiet laughter in his voice, and I want to snarl and snap, but he's kind of being funny too. He hasn't left me to suffer alone, and I know he never would. Point to the biker.

"Advice, Vex. Don't take relationship cues from Axel. The man's on LOTT, for Christ sake," I answer.

"Heard."

"You're pregnant," my family doctor says with a smile. "I'll have the nurse get you set up with an OB-GYN. I recommend Dr. Spitz. She's good, one of the best in the area, and I think you'll like her. In the meantime, here's a prescription for prenatal vitamins. Start them immediately."

"Thank you, Doc," I say as he exits the room.

Turning to Vex, I see the biggest smile ever. He's clearly okay with this baby regardless that we didn't plan for one. He stood tall beside me during the entire appointment. I even had to push him out the bathroom door when I needed to give a urine sample.

"Let's go. We have things to do and people to tell," Vex says while still grinning.

On the way out, we stop at the desk and collect the information the nurse has ready for us. While putting it into my purse, I hear Vex sharing the news.

"We're fucking pregnant!" he shouts to the waiting room full of people.

I hear a couple of gasps, but most laugh and congratulate us as we leave. Arm around my shoulders, Vex drops a hard kiss on my temple before leading me to his truck. I knew what answer the doctor was going to give us, but I'm still a little stunned. Vex is not.

We had another argument when he pulled into his bank's parking lot. He ignored me, and after he was done, we left with me still brooding. We made some other stops, including my home to pick up more things for Tessie and me. I stopped in front of a picture of Tessie, me, and Mom. She would be excited about the baby. I know she'd never be disappointed in me for letting this happen. She always saw the good side of everything. And she'd love Vex for many reasons.

"Bring it, baby. We should have your mom with us. Maybe grab a picture or two for Tessie too. Anything that means something, bring it. Until this is settled with Rooster, we won't be staying here. You won't be alone. You'll always have protection, as will Tessie. But you both need your mom with you," Vex says quietly from behind me.

He's right, so I gather up photo albums and Mom's jewelry box. She didn't have anything expensive, but what she had meant something to her and now us. Tessie will be thrilled to have her favorite picture of the three of us. I am too.

Walking into the clubhouse, I see Axel sitting alone on a couch in the corner. Leaving Vex's side, I approach the couch and take a seat next to Axel.

"Everything okay, Axel?" I ask.

"Yeah. Just waiting for Bailey to finish feeding Alex," he answers in a quiet tone.

"Where are they?"

"In the office. Bailey doesn't like an audience, and you never know who's going to walk in here. I thought I'd give them some mommy-daughter time."

Vex comes to a stop in front of me and uses his fingers to brush my hair back over my shoulder. I like that he's a touchy kind of guy. If I'm within reach, he's usually touching me. Sitting at a table, he'll scoot close enough that our thighs are touching. An arm around my shoulders or a hand on my knee. He's open about it, and I like that about him. A lot.

I watch with a smile as Gee comes skidding into the room, t-shirt and muck boots on. I swear that pig's always smiling. When he's close enough, I can read the writing on his shirt, "Bootilicious Bacon Maker."

I can't stop the laugh I let out while hearing Axel and Vex both snort-laugh at Gee too.

"Who dresses him?" I ask.

"Gee loves clothes. Pooh buys all the t-shirts that have sayings on them. Some, Ava loves. Some, not so much. Have you seen him skateboard yet?" Axel asks.

"No! He can skateboard?" I ask, surprised.

"Yeah, he can. Pretty good at it too. You'll see it eventually," Vex says.

"What're you two doing today?" Axel questions.

"Finding out we're pregnant," Vex answers with his big smile firmly in place.

"Knew that. Told you that before," Axel dismisses with a wave of his hand.

"Yeah, yeah, yeah, Dr. Axel, I know you did. Had it confirmed today by a doctor with an actual degree," Vex says, still smiling.

"Congratulations. Happy for both of you. Nothing like being a parent. Best job ever. Don't let Gunner scare you into keeping your child away from me, though. Regardless what that big cocksucker thinks, I'm the best dad and uncle ever. I'm the fucking O.G. of fatherhood. Need advice, I'm your man. Here for both of you if you need anything," Axel declares.

I stand up, as does Axel, and impulsively I reach out and give him a hug. He looks like he needs one today, and I like the guy. Axel doesn't hesitate before returning the hug. I grin as I hear Vex growl from behind me.

"I'd love to have you in our baby's life, Axel. And thank you for everything you've done for me. Not sure I've ever thanked you before."

"No thanks needed, Amazonian Lady. But you're welcome. Glad I could help," Axel responds.

"Amazonian Lady?" I ask while releasing him and stepping back. I find Vex's body and lean into it as he wraps his arms around me from behind, placing a palm on my stomach. It feels like an unconscious protective gesture.

"Bailey is Thumbelina because she's so short. You're very tall, so yeah, Amazonian Lady," Axel says with a smirk while crossing his massive arms.

"Thumbelina? Really, Axel? I'm not that short!" Bailey states loudly from behind him.

"Not nice. You could have warned me," Axel says, giving me his famous pout.

"And ruin our fun? I think not," I answer.

"Whatever. You guys can argue out the nicknames later. We're pregnant, Bailey," Vex interjects while giving my body a gentle squeeze.

"Congratulations! But I thought you already knew that?" Bailey says. "Axel told me a few days ago that Taja was pregnant."

"We had it confirmed this morning," Vex says with another squeeze.

"Worst kept secret ever. If Axel knows, the world knows. He's a gossip," Bailey tells us with a wink.

"I'm not a gossip! Give me my child, woman. You've had your time, and you're infringing on daddy time now."

Axel swoops up Alex and stomps away in a huff.

"He's a great dad," Bailey says softly, watching him walk away.

"I have a lot to live up to," Vex adds.

Chapter 24

Vex

"Don't make plans for tomorrow. We have things to do," I tell Taja as I'm driving us to Dreams for our shift. Yes, I lost the argument about her working, but it's a temporary loss. I'll get my way; I just have to think up a new angle to hit her with.

"What things?" she asks.

I prepare for the explosion but forge ahead.

"We're looking at some homes to buy. Nothing wrong with your home, but we need something bigger with the baby coming. And I want land with our house, so our little one has room for a large yard, pool, and pets. We'll have your house updated and maybe rent it out until Tessie's ready to move back there."

I wait a full minute before glancing her direction and find her just staring out the windshield. I gently squeeze her hand but still no reaction.

"Taja? You okay?"

"Yes, I'm fine. I've decided to pretend you don't exist. That's my new defense when you start talking nonsense about cars, homes, and pools," she finally answers.

I bark out a laugh at her trying to take a stand against me. It's so cute. Adorable really, but it's going to be ineffective. I'm giving in on her working for now because it's early in our pregnancy, but she's not going to be on her feet slinging drinks later on. I pull her hand to my mouth and drop a light kiss on the back of it. Taja continues to stare straight ahead.

I park my truck, and we walk silently into the already busy club. Taja walks directly behind the bar without a word to me. I grin at her retreating back before walking to Freddy's office to check in on what's going on tonight.

Freddy and I have a quick chat before I make a complete round of the club and speak with various employees and regular customers. I eventually make my way to the bar and step behind to grab a beer. Both Suki and Taja are busy, and I don't want to interrupt them. I grab a chilled glass, fill it from the beer on tap, and turn to walk away when I stop quickly. Suki's directly in front of me, the glare from hell gracing her face.

"Ohhhhh hell, woman! Let me the fuck go! Owwww!" I bellow as Suki latches onto my junk, fingernails digging into my ball sack. I don't jerk away because I have a pretty good idea what kind of pain that would cause. I feel an instant sweat break out across my body with goosebumps following close behind. The woman has one hell of a claw on her. Fuck me, I should've worn tight jeans instead of these baggy ones. She might not have been able to get such a tight grip on all my favorite fucking parts.

"Suki! Jesus, fuck! Let go!" I try to say without screaming like a nine-year-old, but I'm not sure I succeed. At this point, I don't care.

"You got her pregnant?" she screeches up at me.

"Please, God, Suki! Ease off the nails, or you're going to decapitate me!" I tell her while trying not to breathe or do anything else that might jiggle her hand.

"I will decapitate you if you ever think you're bailing on Taja or that child! I'll decapitate this one first!" Suki screams as she jerks and squeezes her hand at the same time.

I'm positive I see a bright white light off in the distance, and I'm thinking that I should go toward it. End my suffering. If Suki didn't have a such death grip on my favorite muscle and his roly-poly friends, I would. My mind blanks, and I, stupidly, reach for Suki's hand only to experience a pain so intense it's indescribable. I have to lock my knees to keep from dropping to the floor. I throw both my hands in the air, splashing beer everywhere, and keep them the fuck there. I watch as Taja walks calmly past us without a word.

"Taja, baby. Now would be a good time to make this woman get her hands off my junk," I shout at her. "Show her my body's off-limits to all but you!"

Taja walks back to us, leans her arm on Suki's shoulder, and grins. I know this isn't going to have a happy ending like most encounters that involve my cock.

Keeping my hands in the air, I try reasoning with these two demonic women.

"I would never bail on Taja. I want this baby with her. I've even offered to buy us a new, larger home. Can you just let go, and we can discuss the terms of the agreement we're about to come to?" I plead.

Suki releases her hand, and for a moment, relief hits me. Then the blood starts rushing back into my abused appendages, and another round of agony commences. As soon as my vision clears and my stomach contents stay down, I hobble to the other side of the bar and gingerly take a seat. Very gingerly. I hear the snickers and comments coming from around my stool, but I ignore them. After a few deep breaths, I manage to lift an arm and point a finger at Suki's face.

"We're no longer friends. You're my enemy to my fucking dying day," I inform the evil witch.

"Better change your mind about that, Vex," Suki grins.

"Why the hell would I do that?"

"Because Suki's going to be our child's godmother," Taja informs me with her own grin in place.

"Take that back! Take that back right the fuck now!" I holler, now pointing my finger at Taja's face.

The two women fist bump and walk off to fill drink orders. They've just given me another reason why Taja needs to quit this job. Suki.

"Come on, Vex. Don't be like this. Suki was just looking out for her girl," Taja says as we're lying in bed that night.

I have my back to Taja, but she's spooned herself up against me and is softly stroking my abs. It's given me a raging boner, but I'm not sharing it with Taja. Taking my cues from Gunner, Taja's now on LOCP. Loss of Cock Privileges.

"She's like a fucking pitbull on crack," I argue.

"She's protective, yes. Maybe overly so."

"She is NOT going to be my child's godmother."

"Well, yeah, here's the thing. We've always promised each other that we'd be the other one's children's godmother. So, you can be pissy and deny me all the orgasms you want, but Suki *is* going to be the godmother. And I can outlast you on going without sex," she responds in a smug tone.

"How do you figure you can go longer than me?" I ask because I'm now curious.

"I'm female. Being stubborn's in my DNA. You're male, and everyone knows men can't go without it. If you want to test this, fine by me. Your loss. I'm going to take a quick shower before bed," Taja states as she climbs out of bed. She swings a long leg over me and slides her body across mine as she gets out on my side. Of course, she makes it a point to have her breasts within inches of my face while doing this.

I take a quick peek in her direction when I hear the bathroom door open. I get a quick glimpse of her naked ass before it disappears. I flop onto my back and grab my dick. Why? Because I'm male, and that's what we do. We fix things and fondle ourselves. I make sure to not touch my balls, though, because they're sore as hell. I looked earlier and found half-moon-shaped marks on both sides of them where Suki's nails did damage. I'm still trying to decide if I should wear a cup for my next shift just in case she decides to go for round two.

I hear scratching at the door, and I don't even bother trying to ignore it. Duffy's a persistent little fucker, and he'll either scratch the door down or start howling until I open it. As I do just that, he gives me an angry meow before strutting to the bed and jumping onto it. Now I have an angry female and an angry cat on my hands, and I'm not sure which is worse.

"Who let you roam free at this time of night?" I ask him.

Duffy ignores me and starts cleaning himself. I stretch out on the bed beside him and wait for Taja. It's not long before Taja strolls out of the bathroom wearing one of my t-shirts and using a towel to dry her hair.

"Who's a pretty kitty?" she coos.

"Meow."

"Prettiest kitty ever with the grumpiest of faces."

"Meow."

"He's been known to be a little possessive of me, so you may have to do some serious sucking up if you want to get back in bed," I tell her with a smirk in place.

"He loves me," she replies while hanging the towel over the back of a chair and laying down on the other side of Duffy.

I prepare to save her ass if Duffy decides to hand out his form of punishment, but he starts purring instead. Within seconds, he's stretched out on his back, enjoying his tummy rubs from Taja. I'm more than a little floored at this turn of events. I had expected at least one round of switchblade warfare like he's done so many other times when he's found a female in my room. Fuck me. Even this bad-tempered cat likes Taja.

I reach over Duffy to tuck Taja's bangs behind her ear when it becomes game on. I jerk my injured arm back and bolt upright. What the fuck?

"You bit me!" I accuse.

Taja giggles, Duffy purrs, and I'm not a happy biker.

"I can't believe that fat rat bastard just bit me. He's chased more whor…" I stop my sentence suddenly.

"Guess it's me he's protecting from the whores now," Taja states smugly.

"Reformed whore!" I shout back.

"Better be true, or I'll give Duffy and Suki free rein on you," Taja threatens with a laugh.

"Make him leave so we can get some sleep."

"You make him leave, and good luck with that," Taja says.

I try. I lose. Duffy spends the rest of the night cuddled up to Taja between our bodies.

After my shower in the morning, Taja graciously applies antibiotic cream and bandages to my many wounds, though the wench laughs the entire time.

"He was going to claw my door down, so I had no choice," Gunner tells me with a grin.

"Not my problem, Prez. The chubby prick took a unit of my blood last night," I continue complaining to no avail.

"Did Vex finally find someone, or something, that doesn't think he hung the moon?" Trigger adds his two cents worth to this useless conversation.

"Cat's interfering with the honeymoon sex. That's why he's in a pissy mood today," Pooh says with a laugh at my expense.

Petey takes a seat next to me and without a word, grabs my wrist and lifts my arm to look at it from all angles. Still not talking, he raises one eyebrow and stares at me. I jerk my arm away and give him a glare.

"They were the only band-aids Taja had in her purse, okay? No, I'm not turning into Axel. I just needed them to stop the bleeding!" I shout at the look Petey continues to give me.

"Hello Kitty? How appropriate," Pooh murmurs.

"Why are you wearing pink bandages?" Craig asks from beside me.

When I look his direction, I'm again amazed at how dirty one child can get. He's got one hand down the back of his pants, scratching at his ass, Bart the skunk, and Gee the pig standing next to him.

"Duffy scratched the hell out of me," I tell him.

"Axel says only real men wear pink. Guess that means you do have a dick," Craig responds before walking off, still scratching, with his entourage in tow. All that ass itching makes me wonder if the kid has fleas.

"Need advice. What kind of car should I get Tessie?" I ask the men.

"To keep her or the world safe?" Gunner asks with a grin.

"Both, I guess."

"Some old boat of a car from the 70s," Pooh declares. "Like a Lincoln Continental. Huge, slow. Lots of metal on them to keep her safe during the numerous accidents she's going to cause."

"That girl needs something newer. Something with a lot of airbags. Lots of airbags," Petey says.

"Get her whatever you want, Vex. I'll tinker with it so it has no speed. None whatsoever," Trigger grins.

"I'm thinking a Jeep Wrangler. They have blind-spot monitoring and collision warning. She needs both. They're good for off-roading, and she'll do that whether it's intended or not. And I can get one in bright orange so others can see her coming and get the fuck out of the way," I explain.

I get several nods in agreement, and my mind's made up.

"911! 911! Call 911!" Mac screeches as he waddles across the floor, wings flapping out to the sides of his body. He starts running around in circles in a complete bird tizzy, continuing to scream 911.

"What's wrong, Mac?" Gunner barks at him.

"We've been robbed! 911!" Mac answers in a high-pitched scream.

During Mac's drama, Loki walks into the room and flops down on his belly, not concerned in the least. I reach down and give Loki a head rub while knowing Mac will eventually get around to telling us what's got his feathers in a twist.

"What was stolen, Mac?" Petey patiently asks the noisy bird.

"Cashews! My cashews!" Mac answers. "All my cashews! Fucker stole them!"

"Who stole them?" Pooh asks.

"Axel! Fucking Assman! Cashew thief!" Mac informs us.

"Did not. Quit accusing me of shit I didn't do," Axel states as he enters the room. Bright pink baby sling in place, hands cradling his cargo.

"Did too!"

"Did not! If I want cashews, I'll buy my own. You're just trying to get me into trouble again. You know what, Mac? You're going to come up missing one of these days, and I'll enjoy every second of it!" Axel threatens loudly.

"Mom would hurt you," Mac says confidently.

"He's got you there," Petey laughs. "Ava was looking for you yesterday. Did she ever find you?"

"Fuck no, she didn't. I've had to employ my best ninja biker moves to avoid that two-legged bloodhound. Thanks to Gunner and the two formerly known as my nieces, I've been forced into stealth mode. I can't even walk down the street without feeling her eyes on me. Gives me the skeevies. I've been reduced to slinking through the woods if I want to get out of the house," Axel says with a whine to his voice.

"Quit whining and give me my grandchild," Petey orders.

Surprisingly, Axel transfers little Alex to her grandpa without arguing. We find out why right away.

"See how that's done, Gunner?"

"How what's done?" Gunner, clearly confused, asks.

"Sharing of one's child with those that love her. Easy-peasy for someone who's not a selfish ass," Axel responds smugly.

"Jesus Christ, Axel. Quit whining and pouting, and I'll lift the LOTT ban, okay?" Gunner concedes. "But teach the twins another cuss word, and I'll hold you down for Ava's punishment myself."

"Deal! Where's my girls?" Axel shouts.

"Right behind you. With their mother, the two-legged bloodhound," Ava answers.

Axel freezes in place for a quick second before bolting out of the room. No looking back, no slowing down. He nearly knocks Toes on his ass as they collide, but Axel keeps pushing forward until he's out of sight. After hearing the back door slam shut, laughter erupts throughout the room.

"You never told him I wasn't upset, did you?" Ava asks while cocking an eyebrow at Gunner.

"Fu… uhhh, no, I didn't. Guess it slipped my mind," Gunner answers while scooping up one twin while Trigger does the same with the other.

"You enjoy his fear. That's just mean. Funny, but mean," Ava says with a laugh.

Weeks have passed, and things are better than ever in my life. Tessie's the little sister I never had, and Taja's the woman I never thought I'd want or need. She gets testy when I buy things for her or Tessie still, but the Jeep has finally been accepted after Tessie and I explained how she's going to pay me back. It's not a gift but a loan we insisted to Taja. Every dollar that Tessie pushes into my hand as payment goes into a bank account for her future. No need to tell either of them that because it saves me grief. Two stubborn-ass women to contend with, and I've found ways to save my hide.

Taja isn't showing yet, and I'm getting impatient to see the baby bump. Her morning sickness hasn't went away, and she's sleeping more. It worries me that she's lost weight instead of gaining, but Bailey assures me that's normal in the beginning. Suki hovers over her at work, as does Freddy, so I've kept my mouth shut about her quitting. Word's leaked out that I'm off the market, but that hasn't stopped some of the strippers from pushing up on me. Taja deals with that fairly well by not blaming me, but trouble is brewing with a few of them.

Rooster's gone into hiding, but he'll reappear at some point. Axel says it's like playing the game Whack-A-Mole. We're waiting for his head to appear before it gets whacked. Gunner's not playing around or taking chances. On his orders, Taja and I are still at the clubhouse with Tessie at Petey's. The sisters see each other daily, but I know Taja wants to get back to a normal life. With Tessie and Bella being like conjoined twins, I think Taja's feeling a little left out. What's helped with that is the other women. Taja's formed great relationships with all of them, especially Pippa. We spend a lot of time at Pooh's house, and the women are tight.

Little Craig still has a crush on Taja and takes every opportunity to do nice things for her. He even brought her flowers once when she was having a particularly bad bout of morning sickness. He'd asked Axel how much flowers cost and Axel took him to the flower shop to pick some out. Both scored points with Taja for that.

While Taja, Pippa, and Tammy, along with Pooh for security, are off shopping today, I'm meeting with a realtor. I'm wanting to plant roots, and since Taja bailed on looking at homes with me, I brought

Trigger instead. He's knowledgeable and not afraid to be honest. The man's a wealth of information, and I need that.

"There's property available that butts up to the club's property. You could build there. Be close to the compound but still have some distance for privacy. What kind of budget are we looking at?" Trigger asks.

"No budget. If we find something I like, and I think Taja and Tessie will too, I'll buy it. I like the idea of being close to the compound, but I don't want to wait the time it takes to build. I want Taja settled before the baby comes," I answer.

"Makes sense. No budget, though? Don't tell the realtor that," Trigger says with a laugh.

After looking at several homes, none of which I think are good enough for my girls, we return to the realtor's office. I had given her an idea of what I was looking for, but the properties she showed us are nowhere close. They had the right number of bedrooms but were basically dumps. When I told her the homes weren't nice enough, I got a once-over look and a raised eyebrow. My biker boots, jeans, and hoodie apparently scream low-class neighborhood to her.

Trigger mentions the property near the compound, and the realtor pulls it up on her computer. Behind Gunner's house is a section of land that borders several acres with the compound. It would put us as Gunner and Ava's backdoor neighbor but with a lot of woods in between. I like it instantly. Private, secluded, but close to my family. Building a trail or a road to connect the two pieces of land would be easy. Also smart because Rex could wire the club's perimeter security to include my land and home also.

"I don't know if the owner's interested in breaking up the land into smaller parcels, though. He's a bit of a recluse and bought a full section of 640 acres so his home would be well hidden from the road and all other people," Theresa, the realtor, says.

"What's his home like? Is it close to what I'm looking for?"

"It's a huge stone and timber home. Three levels, six bedrooms, five bathrooms, four-car garage. It's beautiful, and it's been on the market for quite a while because of the cost of the home, all of its amenities, and the amount of land that it sits on," Theresa says while naming the asking price with a condescending smirk.

I shoot a grin at Trigger when he coughs loudly at the price.

"When can I get a walk-through?" I ask, still grinning at Trigger's response.

"Here's the problem. The owner's very fussy about showing the home unless the person can validate that they can afford it first. He doesn't want to open his home for showings to people that are simply curious about it with no means to acquire it. Or people that might simply be wanting to case the home for possible future criminal activities. And I don't like to waste my time either. I can contact him and see if he's willing to sell you a few acres, though. Maybe you could afford five or ten acres and put something cheap on it for the time being," Theresa informs me in a slightly arrogant tone.

Realtor chick doesn't think biker boy can afford a nice place. Interesting. I listen to Trigger snort, and I know she's on his bad side now. I speak quickly before Trigger's temper flares.

"What's his name? I'll contact him and see if we can get a walk-through."

"That's not how things are done," Theresa says while giving Trigger the side-eye.

"Alright then. We're done here. Have a great day, Theresa, and thank you for your time," I tell her with my best smile in place.

Trigger and I exit her business and park our asses in my truck.

"Rex can get you the info you need. He can also pull up the property so you can get a view of the house," Trigger says.

"Let's go put Rex to work."

"I want it. How do I go about buying it without the realtor twit getting a commission?" I ask Rex.

Rex had quickly pulled up all the specs on the house and property. He even showed me the pictures the realtor had neglected to mention. The home's stunning, inside and out, and perfect for what I think Taja, Tessie, me, and our baby need. Definitely what Taja and Tessie deserve.

"Let me do some digging around and find out what I can. He can't sell it outright if he's still under contract to the realtor, but I'll find out when that ends," Rex says.

"Owe you a steak dinner, my brother," I tell him with a slap on the back before I walk away.

"That's the brake. That's the gas pedal. Neither need to be stomped on, Tessie. Let's try this again but no…"

The Jeep bolts forward, and I'm trying to wrap my head around the fact that I'm going to die a fiery death. I don't get why this is so hard for Tessie. The girl has no coordination and no sense of speed whatsoever. As we fly past the clubhouse, I see most of the guys outside laughing their dumb asses off at my predicament. Again. This is our third attempt, and I'm ready to toss in the towel. I get a tiny glimpse of Pooh, phone out, probably getting ready to call 911 when Tessie takes a corner way faster than I would've thought possible.

"Stop!" I scream while bracing for what I know is coming.

Tessie immediately stands on the brake pedal and brings us to a quick stop, dust cloud billowing everywhere. We're feet away from broadsiding Reeves' truck.

"Too fast?" she asks.

I don't answer, but I do climb out of the Jeep, squat down, and place my palms on the ground. I need to feel grounded for a moment. I look upward when I see Tessie's Chucks in front of me. She's got her hands on her hips, one hip cocked outward, and a frown marring her face.

"Am I just too stupid to learn something as simple as driving a vehicle?" Tessie asks in a small voice.

Fuck, now I feel bad for making her feel that way. I've got to fix this in a way that she's safe on the road but also so there's no hit to her confidence in herself.

I stand and wrap my arm around her shoulders, giving her a gentle hug. No way do I ever want her to feel bad about herself.

"Don't ever say you're stupid. That'll piss me off. Nobody's good at everything, and you're good at a lot of other stuff. Trigger and Petey say you're the best apprentice they've ever had, and that's saying a lot. You're the best sister I know. You're going to be the best aunt ever. You work and are a straight-A student. Bella adores you because you're a great friend. We'll figure this out, honey, I promise. No matter how many vehicles we crash together, I'm not giving up on you. Ever. For anything. Got that?"

"Yeah, Vex. Got it. Thank you," she replies.

"I've got an idea. Come on."

I make a few calls, and it's not long before Craig and Bella have joined us outside the clubhouse. When I explain what I want to try, most of the men agree it can't hurt, and everyone loads up into vehicles. We drive to the nearest go-cart track. I speak privately with the manager. A short wait and everyone's getting into their go-carts, helmets on. The track is ringed in stacks of tires. It's as safe as it's going to get for Tessie to practice her skills. Even Craig gets a cart of his own, and his smile couldn't be bigger. Off we go.

I keep my go-cart close to Tessie, shouting instructions. She bounces off the tires more times than I can count, and everyone quickly learns to keep their distance. Eventually, I can see improvement in her driving. She's staying between the tires more and using her brake better. I give her a thumbs-up, and her smile says it all.

It's a great afternoon, and Tessie's learning while having fun. She's safe from harm, and her confidence has been restored. She's grinning and then laughing out loud when Craig goes sailing past us shouting, "Go, Tessie! Go, Tessie!"

Chubs is following Craig with a hotdog in one hand and a big smile on his face. I chuckle when Axel bumps Tessie from behind with his go-cart, and she flips him off. Axel speeds past, shooting her a pout, and then bounces off the tires because he wasn't looking where he was going. That, in itself, made the outing worth it to me.

"You made Tessie's day. Thank you," Taja says while sitting astride my thighs on a couch in the main room.

"Glad to do it. We all had fun. I promised her and the other kids we'd go back next week, and half the men have insisted on going too. I'm anxiously looking forward to seeing Gunner and Cash try to fit their asses into a go-cart. Gunner's knees are going to be against his ears. And I don't think a go-cart has been made that's wide enough for Cash. Should be good fun."

"Vex!"

I hear my name shouted and look to see Gunner and Cash hauling ass across the clubhouse toward the main door. I lift Taja to her feet, set her on the floor, and stand.

"Go to Pooh or Petey's house. Stay there until you hear from me. Don't leave the compound," I order before running out the door behind the others.

"What's going on?" I shout to Gunner as Pooh's truck slides to a stop next to me.

"Explosion and fire at Dreams," Gunner says before he and Cash jump into his truck and tear out.

I hurry to get into Pooh's truck, and we're off right behind them.

The fire department's finishing their job while Gunner and Freddy are speaking with the cops. I'm standing in the lot with several of the Devil's looking over the damage. The fire department was quick in their response and did a great job in minimizing the damage, but there's still enough that Dreams is going to be closed down for a while. No injuries, and that's all that really matters to any of us.

Freddy and Pigeon were both there and got everyone, employees and customers, outside safely. We've sent everyone home after making sure they were okay to drive. Suki was here working but wasn't near the kitchen when the explosion occurred. It was a small one but only because it failed. If it hadn't, countless injuries and probably a few deaths would've occurred. I sent Suki to the compound to be with Taja and let her know what happened.

Gunner and Freddy approach our group, and Gunner lays it out.

"We have no choice but to let the cops do their thing. We'll let them chase their tails. It'll keep them out of our way. Rex has the video feed, and I'm heading back to view it. Story to the cops is that the security cameras weren't working. Stick to that if asked. Meet at the clubhouse for Church."

"Do you know this guy's name?" Gunner asks Taja as he points to a still image from the video feed.

"Road name is Tats. One of Rooster's guys," she answers quietly. "That's all I know about him. He's the one who hit me right after Mom died, and Rooster showed to get payment for Tessie."

"He's going to be a dead man when we find him," I tell her with no hesitation.

Taja looks me in the eye for a moment before giving a quick nod of her head. She gets the life.

She understands how things work in an MC, even though she was young when Rooster left. Smart girl.

"I'm so sorry that…"

"This isn't on you or Tessie. This is all on Rooster," Cash interrupts.

Gunner asks a few more questions, and Taja answers as many as she can before I walk her back to my room. Standing just inside it, I pull her close to me and hold tight. I know she's feeling guilty and to blame, but Cash was right. Rooster's made a fatal mistake by taking on the Devil's. He made that choice, and he'll pay for it.

"Get some sleep. I'll be back as soon as I can," I whisper to her.

I give her a brief hard kiss and close the door behind me. I know she's not going to sleep much, but I can't help that right now. The club has business to take care of.

Chapter 25

Taja

When I hear the scratching noise I've been expecting, I get out of bed and pad over to the door. When I open it, in walks Duffy, tail swishing. He rubs against my legs on his way past and lands with a thump on the bed. I curl up with him, stroking his fur, and listen to his purring. I think I can sleep now.

Sometime later, I feel Vex sliding in behind me and wrapping his arm around me to place his hand on my stomach. He does that often, and I've come to need it from him. I push back slightly, so we're touching back to front the full length of our bodies. He's solid, warm, and all man.

"Everything okay?" I ask sleepily.

"Will be. Get some sleep and grow our baby," Vex murmurs in my ear.

I fall back to sleep knowing that things are a mess right now, but Vex won't bail and leave me to deal with it alone. The club won't bail on Vex, Tessie, or me. For the first time in my life, I can clearly see what a good MC club can be. It doesn't matter if you ride a bike or drive a truck. All that matters is the caliber of the people you surround yourself with.

"You *are* going to take the credit card, and you *are* going to buy everything our little one will need," Vex tells me while pushing his card into my hand.

"Vex! You're being ridiculous. I'm not racking up a huge credit card balance buying all the stuff you keep saying we need. We can pick things up a little at a time. Until Dreams is back up and running again, we're both out of work. Dude, seriously, you might want to listen to me on this. I know how to budget like nobody's business," I continue to insist to the stubborn-ass man.

"Dude? Did you really just call me Dude?" Vex asks with a shit-eating grin.

"Oh my God! You're driving me nuts. Sit and listen for a minute, please?" I implore.

Vex takes a seat, but he's still grinning like I'm the crazy one here. I step between his thighs and rest my hands on his shoulders. I can't help but let my fingers weave in and out of his hair while looking down at him.

"Money's been tight my whole existence. Mom could stretch a dollar until it was paper-thin, and I learned from the best. There were times that we barely had enough food in the house to eat, but she made it seem like we owned the world. Neither Tessie or I ever felt we went without because Mom couldn't always hold down a steady job with her illness. We felt blessed to have her in our lives. She found out she had breast cancer when I was eight. Tessie was barely a year old. Rooster bailed and took every penny we had, but Mom kept us clothed, fed, and happy. She beat her cancer and was free of it for almost five years when another tumor showed up in the scar tissue from her mastectomy. Us girls were terrified we were going to lose her that time, but she beat the odds again.

Or so we thought for a few more years," I explain in a quiet voice.

"Taja, I don…"

"Time to listen, Vex," I whisper before continuing. "It was harder on Mom the last time around, and she had more bad days than good. We weren't raised to let others handle our problems. Mom had a lot of pride, and she'd instilled that in Tessie and me. I got a job, different ones, over the next few years to help with the bills. I graduated, got better jobs with more hours, and started taking classes on the scholarships I'd won. Mom was let go from her job for missing so much work, and that alone about killed her. Suki helped get the paperwork done, so Mom's disability checks came through and those saved us. Those checks and the money I made. But Mom was devastated when that first check came in because, in her mind, she'd failed. In my mind, she was a fucking rock star for all she'd overcome and battled through. In the end, we lost her, but we'll never lose the example she set for us. What I'm trying to say is going without all the newest gadgets and fancy clothes aren't important to Tessie and me. We know what's really important in this world, and we learned that from our mom. This baby doesn't need the name-brand diapers and fancy stroller to be happy. This baby just needs the basics along with a lot of love and a good family."

Vex is quiet for a moment, but I know he's heard every word. It's showing in his eyes that he understands everything I said. It's also showing that he wishes like hell he'd been around to help us through those tough times.

Vex drops his head and places a kiss on my abdomen, right where our baby is residing. It's a sweet and very telling gesture, and it warms me throughout.

"Those days are over for you and Tessie. You two will never have to make ends meet again. I have mad respect for your mom, and I wish like hell I'd had the pleasure of meeting her. She sounds like one hell of a woman. I'm glad you two had that in your life. She sounds like pure beauty. But, baby, you don't need to be concerned with money anymore. You don't have to budget every cent and worry about bills coming up months from now. I've got you, and I've got this. You just need to trust that your man can and will always provide for you. Can you give me that?" Vex asks in a deep, serious tone.

Looking down into that gorgeous face, I realize how important this is to him. I never intended to imply that he couldn't provide for his own child. I need to give in on this and buy the things he wants for the baby. I will, but I'll do it Taja style. Bargain shopping, coupons, and pinching pennies where I can without it being too noticeable.

"I can give you that," I answer as he grins and drops another light kiss on the baby.

"I don't have time today because the guys are waiting on me, but when I do, we'll have a thorough conversation about finances. There are things you need to know, and one of them is why money isn't a concern. Until then, go shopping. Buy the stuff we discussed, but stay close to Chubs. Him and Lucy will be with you anytime you need them, and I don't want you out of his sight if you leave the compound," Vex says.

"Okay. Be careful, Vex. There are people needing you to come back safe," I say because I need him to know that he's important too.

He stands and wraps me up in a tight, hard hug. After a lingering kiss and a shout from Axel at the door, Vex lets go and walks off. I miss him already.

Spending time with Chubs and Lucy has kept my mind busy from worrying about Vex being gone. Him, along with Pooh and a few other members, are on the hunt for Rooster, Tats, and other members of the Spirit Skulls. The Skulls made this battle personal for all of the members when they set fire to Dreams. Now, there's hell to pay, and the bill is due.

Chubs, being who he is, has been sticking close. I've enjoyed his company immensely. My morning sickness strikes at all hours of the day, and Chubs is a calm presence when it does. I seriously wouldn't mind being left alone during the throes of it, but nobody, including Duffy, agrees. With Lucy and Chubs staying in his room across the hall since the guys left, they're close if needed and close enough to know when all is not well with my stomach.

I couldn't have picked a better woman for Chubs, even if given years to find one. Lucy's his perfect match. Watching them together, I'm allowed the privilege of seeing how a real relationship works. I didn't have that growing up, but I do now. I'm grateful that Tessie's experiencing it too. Mutual respect, compromise, and a huge dose of humor seem to be the glue that keeps this club and their women together. They bicker and disagree, argue and tease one another, but in the end, there are couples here that will always be a unit.

Only odd thing I've noticed is that weird shit happens when Lucy's around. I don't know why, but it does. She sits at the bar, and a shelf will break when no one's near it. Or she'll walk across the room, and a picture will fall off the wall. Oddly enough, as cool and nice as Lucy is, I've noticed Toes keeps his distance from her when he can. He actually looks like he's scared of being near her. I want to ask Vex about all this stuff, but I'm afraid I'll sound like a crazy person.

When I'm not sleeping or feeling sick, I've been starting to get stir-crazy. I've never been off work this long before, and I envy Tessie for having a job. I scrubbed Vex's room from top to bottom today and then tore into the kitchen. It's spotless, and I feel better now that I've got something to do. I have four loaves of zucchini bread baking in the oven, and it smells amazing.

I've re-stocked the bar and am dusting the shelves when Chubs appears on the other side of it. He's got Craig, Bella, and the pets tagging along today and his ever-present grin.

"Hello, customers. What can I set you up for?" I ask.

"Root Beer," Craig says.

"Coke," Bella answers.

"When's that zucchini bread going to be done?" Chubs asks.

"How do you know what kind of bread it is?" I ask.

"It's a gift," Chubs responds.

"It's his super-power," Craig informs me in a serious tone. "We were doing our learning things in the woods today, and Chubs smelled the bread. So here we are."

"In about… oh God. Sorry!" I say as I bolt for the nearest bathroom.

After the latest round of pregnancy hell has passed, I stretch out on the nearest couch, not caring what deviant behavior has occurred on it. Duffy curls up next to me and promptly starts snoring. Soon after that, Bart gets set on my thighs, and he's off to snooze land too. Craig sits on the floor in front of me, one hand patting my arm.

"Bailey used to be sick a lot too. When she got better, she spitted a kid out," Craig states. "Little Alex is cute now but wasn't when she first came to live here. Her face was all red, and she looked mad all the time. Axel let me hold her once. He made me get cleaned up first. Wasn't really worth it. When you get tired of being sick and spit your kid out, do I have to be clean to hold it?"

"Sorry, Craig, but yeah, you do. Babies can get sick really easy, so we have to be careful not to let germs get around them. Clean hands are important."

"I think pets are better. No need to be clean to be around them. Loki's girlfriend is having puppies soon. Maybe you should get one of them instead," Craig says in a serious as hell voice. He's obviously put some thought into this.

"You really don't like baths, do you?" I ask with a small laugh.

"I just get dirty again, so why bother?" he answers while holding out a black licorice stick to me.

We munch on our candy silently for a few moments before Bella walks over to stand near the couch.

"You okay now, Taja?"

"Yeah, Bella, I am. Thank you."

"I took the bread out of the oven for you. I tested it with a toothpick like Ava showed me to do, and it was ready. I hope it wasn't for something special because Chubs was waiting and took it off my hands. He said it was hot, and he was doing me a favor," Bella says while rolling her eyes and laughing.

"That's fine. I was just baking for something to do."

"You're studying to be a nurse, right?" Bella questions while stroking Bart's little skunk head.

"Yeah, I'm close to having my degree. I've already gotten to do quite a few clinical hours in the hospital, so I don't have much left to complete."

"One of these days, would you mind teaching me some first aid? I think it's something we should all know, and I thought you might be the best to ask," Bella questions softly.

"Bella, that's a great idea. I'd love to. Rex mentioned they keep a well-stocked first aid kit here. We'll go through it together, and I'll show you what each thing is good for. Basic first aid's very important, even for small cuts or burns. How about tomorrow we get together and do that?"

"Sounds perfect. Thank you."

I pull myself up and off the couch after relocating the cat and skunk and walk to the bar to take a seat next to Chubs. Mac's strolling back and forth on the bar top singing a song I don't know. Something about a fat donkey with a bad attitude and a bird saving the day. I think he makes up half the songs he sings around here. Glancing at the plate in front of Chubs, I feel my stomach roll again.

"Oh God, Chubs. Please don't eat that," I beg in a tortured voice.

He instantly shoots me a guilty look but has already taken a bite. Swallowing slowly, he shoots me a contrite look. I know I'm about to lose this battle again.

The plate contains slices of the zucchini bread, smeared in what I think is butter and BBQ sauce, fresh jalapeno peppers sliced in half (stem still in place) laying on top of the sauce with guacamole on top of them. Next to the sickening sight of the sandwich is nacho cheese Doritos and a tall glass of orange juice. The smell of this concoction hits my nose, and it's off to the bathroom again.

When I return to the bar, Chubs is gone, but the kids and pets are hanging out. I pour some ginger ale and sip at it slowly until my stomach feels normal again.

"Where's Chubs?" I ask Bella, but it's Craig who answers.

"At the gate. Toes called him and said he was wanted down there. Two men wanted to talk to Mr. Cooper. I don't know who that is, but Chubs left."

"How do you know all that, Craig? Chubs didn't say who called or why he had to leave. Just that we were to stay here with Taja until he got back," Bella asks.

"I heard Toes telling him that on the phone," Craig replies with a grin.

"You weren't sitting anywhere near him!" Bella insists.

"Still heard it. Axel says I have bat ears," Craig says proudly.

"Guess you do," mumbles Bella while giving him the side-eye.

Mr. Cooper's a popular guy around here, it seems.

I spent the late afternoon hanging out with Tessie and hearing all about the latest projects she and Trigger have been working on. I've missed having sister time, and having Bella hang with us just made it nicer. I must have fallen asleep at some point because when I wake up, I'm alone in the clubhouse except for Duffy and Loki. It's still daylight outside but darker inside. I must have slept for quite a while. I let Loki outside to go potty, but he insists on coming back in when he's finished. I don't mind this at all. He's a beautiful dog, and regardless of the things I've heard he's capable of doing, he's friendly with me.

Sitting on the couch petting Loki, I see a small figure slip through the kitchen door and go behind the bar. A moment later, I see Craig creeping back toward the kitchen with two cans in his hands.

"Craig? What'cha got there, buddy?" I ask and smile when he jumps slightly.

"Nothing. Go back to sleep, Taja," he answers.

"Craig, show me what you have."

He holds up two cans of ginger ale, and I'm relieved because I was worried for a second that he might have been sneaking beer out of here.

"Why do you have ginger ale?" I continue questioning him.

I watch as his little shoulders slump, and he walks over to stand in front of me. Making eye contact for the first time, he shrugs his shoulders.

"We're friends, right, Taja?"

"Yes, you're definitely my friend. Why do you ask?"

"I like being your friend. But I can't answer your question, okay?"

"You're going to have to explain that to me, Craig."

"Pooh told me that a good man should always tell the truth to his friends. He should also always protect his family, no matter what. I don't know how to do both. Pooh's not here for me to ask. Neither is Chubs. So, I figure if you don't ask me that question, I don't have to lie to a friend."

Huh. This is interesting but confusing.

"It's just ginger ale, Craig. Why would you have to lie to me about why you have some? Aren't you allowed to have it?"

"I'm barely five years old, Taja. I don't know how to answer these questions without getting someone in trouble or doing one of those things Pooh told me I shouldn't ever do!" Craig says in an exasperated voice.

"Let me ask you this. Is anyone hurt? Anyone in trouble?"

"Nobody's hurt. Nobody will be in trouble if you'd just quit asking me questions," he mumbles. "I'm just trying to be nice and to take care of my family."

"Okay, Craig. No more questions. If you need help taking care of your family, come get me. I won't say anything," I tell him as I watch his face relax with relief.

"Thanks, Taja," he says before placing a knee on the couch, climbing up close enough to place a kiss on my cheek. After that, he climbs down and races out the door. How sweet.

Curiosity's killing me, but I don't want to break his trust by following him either. To take my mind off whatever he's up to, I pull my phone out and text Vex.

Me: Hi. Everything okay?

Vex: Hey babe. All's well so far

Me: Any idea when you'll be back?

Vex: No. Not until we find Rooster though. How you feeling?

Me: Pretty sure I died twice today but otherwise okay. Bored though

Vex: When Bailey was preg. Axel thought he had morning sickness too. We had a lot of fun with that.

Me: Omg! I can imagine him thinking that. Pretty sure he's convinced he half carried Alex to term lol

Vex: He does think that. He even thought he had swollen ankles

Me: He's a nut

Vex: Am not! I'm adorable and sexy as fuck with big manly muscles!

Me: WTH?

Vex: Axel just grabbed my phone. That was him, not me

Me: He's special – but you have to say "special" in a high pitched voice for it to apply to him lol

Vex: *Yeah, he's special alright. Pooh's got him pinned to the floor now so my phone's safe.*

Me: *I miss you. I want you back here*

Vex: *Same for me. But I want this taken care of first. You've never said what you want – boy or girl*

Me: *Doesn't matter. Just healthy*

Vex: *Boy, for the reasons I already told you*

Me: *Yes I remember. Girls bring about murder and mayhem*

Vex: *Ain't that the truth*

Me: *Hey!*

Vex: *Been thinking on names?*

Me: *No. It's so far away yet*

Vex: *Boy – Isaac*

Me: *Really? Isaac? Never thought about that name before*

Vex: *Boy – Joshua, Noah, Jaydin, Ethan, Mason*

Me: *You've put some thought into this. What about a girls name?*

Vex: Don't want to jinx it. Not thinking any up

Me: You know there's a 50/50 chance you're going to have to think up a girls name

Vex: I like Hattie, Olivia, Isabella, Sophia. Your mom's name would be the middle name. Now we're jinxed. Thanks doll

Me: You have so totally put thought into a girls name too. You know you'd love one

Vex: I'll absolutely love any child we create. If it's a girl though I want her to be Axel's special kind of ugly so I can remain a free man and help raise her. I said that part out loud and now Cash is helping Pooh keep Axel pinned

Me: I better let you go before Axel gets hurt

Vex: Get some sleep. I'll call later so we can FaceTime. Need to see you

Me: Need to see you too. TTYL

The following day finds me ready to pull my hair out from boredom. Luckily, Bailey calls and invites me to come to her and Axel's home. Upon arriving, she hands me a cup of decaf coffee, and I watch her fuss over little Alex. It's probably this exact moment when I realize how excited I am about becoming a mom. With everything that's been happening, my mind has been occupied elsewhere. Now seeing the complete adoration Bailey has for Alex has brought home to me all that I have to look forward to.

I spend a few hours with Bailey and Alex before walking back to the clubhouse. Once there, I pull out my laptop and sign online. Vex will be happy to know that I finally agree with him. I have shopping to do. After a few hours of looking at the cutest baby things, I take a break and hit the kitchen for a snack.

"Hey, Taja."

I turn and see Tessie and Bella standing in the doorway, both looking nervous. This can't be good.

"Hey, ladies. What's going on?"

"Can we talk for a minute?" Tessie asks while picking at her nails.

That's her tell. When she's nervous, upset, or guilty, she picks at her nails. Now I'm positive I'm not going to like what I'm about to hear. Keeping a calm face, I wave my hand toward the main room, where we all take seats at a table.

"We screwed up. Made a mistake, and we're sorry," Tessie says softly.

"It won't ever happen again, Taja. Promise it won't," Bella adds.

"We decided we needed to tell you what we did because we don't want Craig to get into trouble for trying to help us. We know you saw him yesterday, and he promised he didn't tell you what he was doing. He was just trying to help, and he was looking out for us. So please don't be mad at him or get him into trouble. It was us that messed up," Tessie explains.

"Okay. I promise I won't get Craig into trouble. What do you mean you messed up, though?" I ask.

"Bella and I were talking about things. About how both of us have been kidnapped and what happened when we were. Before you get upset, neither of us were sexually assaulted. I promise that. But it was good that we talked, even if we both ended up in tears. Both of us got beatings, Bella more than me, though. We talked about how scared we were and how relieved I was when I saw Vex. I knew I was going to be okay then. I knew it because I knew to my soul that Vex would make it that way. Bella felt the same way when she saw

Pooh and the other guys. She somehow knew they weren't there to hurt her. Anyway, that's not an excuse, though, for what we did," Tessie says.

"I'm glad you two talked about those things and have each other to do that with. Either of you can always come to me too if there's things you need to talk about. I hope you know this," I answer firmly.

"I do. We do," Bella responds, glancing at Tessie.

"We grabbed a couple of beers from here and sat in the woods drinking them and spilling our guts to each other," Tessie blurts out.

"They were disgusting, so neither of us drank the whole beer. I swear! Even the small amount I had made me feel sick, though," Bella says.

"And Craig came across you, came here for ginger ale to settle your stomach, and ran into me," I say, having worked out what Craig's part was in all of this.

"Yeah," Tessie agrees.

"Craig took us to his fort in the woods to hide us from everyone. He thought that since the ginger ale helped settle your stomach, it would for us too. He also poured out our beer, then lectured our butts off," Bella adds with a small smile.

"He was just trying to help," Tessie states.

"Yeah, he was. I know that. He made a comment about taking care of family. He didn't want you two to get into trouble and was worried when you didn't feel well," I tell them.

"We're really sorry, Taja. I swear it won't ever happen again," Tessie vows.

"I don't like it, but I get it. But drinking isn't the answer—ever. I'm not mad, and I trust you two to do the right thing next time. Maybe you should both apologize to Craig, though. You put the little guy in an awkward position yesterday," I say.

"We will. We owe him that. Are you going to tell Mom?" Bella questions quietly.

"No, I'm not. Unless it happens again, this will stay between us. And I'm positive Craig would have to be tortured before he spilled the beans, so I think you're safe on that count."

"Thank you, Taja," Bella and Tessie both say at the same time. Both sound relieved, and I think they've learned their lesson. Time to move on.

"Want to see the things I've picked out for the baby so far?" I ask the girls.

"Yes!"

Chapter 26

Vex

I'm getting impatient with being away from Taja. I want to end this with Rooster once and for all, but I need to get home to her too. I know Axel's feeling the same since he talks about Bailey and Alex non-stop. We know Rooster's in Los Alamos, New Mexico, and that's where we're at waiting for intel from Rex.

One of our support clubs has contacted Gunner. They're extremely interested in Rooster's whereabouts also. Guess we're not the only club he's crossed. He definitely has more enemies than friends, and that's playing in our favor. Some of his club members have bailed and let the word out that they've stripped themselves of their own patch. We've heard that there's been dissension amid his club for a while and talk about voting in a new president. A few of those who've spoken out against Rooster are now MIA. We know that several have gone to ground. Whether by his hand or their own choice, we're not sure. That doesn't matter to us. We eliminated four at their clubhouse, so we know their numbers are dwindling. We definitely have the advantage, but we have to find him first.

While waiting for Rex's call, I step outside the hotel door and pull out my phone. I hit dial and wait for her to answer. When she does, I can hear the surprise in her voice. I haven't called nearly enough, and the guilt of that rides heavy on me.

"Hello? Vex?" Mom says in her soft voice.

"Yeah, it's me. How you doing, Mom?"

"I'm good, Vex. I'm so glad you called. How've you been?"

"All's good with me. How's everyone?" I ask, knowing she knows I mean my brother and not my dad.

"He's good too. Working for your father still."

There's a pause, and I wait through it, knowing what's next.

"When will you be home for a visit? I miss you, Vex."

"Every time I'm near him, it's nothing but a fight, Mom. You know this. I'm never going to be the person Dad wants me to be, and he's never going to quit being the person he is. Nothing's ever changed. Nothing ever will," I remind her.

"I know, honey. I hate that it's like that with you two. I pray every night that he'll learn to accept you as you are. You're not like him, and that's okay. But I fear he'll never come around," Mom admits.

"He won't, and neither will I. I'm not going to be bent into something I'm not. Discussing Dad isn't why I called, though," I say.

"I did what your attorney requested. I didn't tell your father, though, because I didn't want another argument with him over you. Who's this woman? Taja Davis? She must be important to you."

"She is. Her and her sister Tessie have never had it easy. They watched their mom slowly die of cancer and have struggled their whole lives. Dad wasn't in the picture. We met and have been seeing each other. She's important to me, Mom. We're pregnant, and I'm happy as hell about it. I wanted to get my affairs in order in case something ever happened to me. I need to know that Taja, Tessie, and our baby will always be taken care of if that happens," I say firmly.

"Oh God, Vex. A baby? That's so exciting! I'm going to have a grandchild!" Mom shouts excitedly.

"Yes, you are. I want you to meet Taja and Tessie. But I won't subject them to the comments Dad would make. They've had enough shit dumped on them from their own dad. Maybe you could come here for a visit. Meet my woman and get to know her a little. I'm looking at buying a home. You could stay a while and help Taja furnish it."

"I'd love to, Vex. I really would. But I don't know how your dad would react to that. He's bitter that you won't come back or even take his calls anymore. Let me see what I can do because I'd love to come see you and meet Taja. Give me some time to work on your father, okay?" she ends in a hopeful voice.

"Sure, Mom. Anytime you could come would be great. Let me know if you can make that happen," I say.

We chat for a few more minutes before we hang up. I have my doubts that Mom will make it to Denver. Dad's only let her come once before, and that's because he was coming for business. We had dinner together one night, and that's the last time I've seen them. Maybe knowing I have a woman and a baby on the way will help her strengthen her backbone when it comes to Dad.

Pooh, Cash, and I are sitting in Pooh's truck. We had to use his since mine's in the shop getting the door repainted. Trigger was shaking his head and muttering that he's getting tired of repainting the same damn door when I left it with him. Thanks to Tessie, this is the third damn time. It's also the last since she's starting to get the hang of driving now. Fucking finally.

Cash's phone rings, and he answers. When he disconnects, he tells us we have a possible location for Rooster. Pooh starts the truck, and we're on our way to meet up with the others there.

As Axel kicks in the door, I move past and scan the right side of the room. When I see movement, I aim but don't pull the trigger. Rooster's here but holding a half-naked woman in front of him as a shield. He's backed them into a corner of the room and now has no way out. Why doesn't it surprise me that he'd hide behind a female?

"Let her go, Rooster. Only way out of here is through us. No need for her to die tonight too," Gunner barks.

"Fuck you!" Rooster shouts back.

I take my eyes off Rooster long enough to see Cash and Reeves march two other men into the room and seat them on chairs by the kitchen table. Both have the barrels of guns pressed to their temples. They're no longer a threat, and they're not going anywhere soon.

Looking back at Rooster, I see a moment of surprise on his face. I think the dumb bastard actually thought we were too stupid to know there were others here with him. He thought they'd get the drop on us instead. So sad, too bad. His life has just taken a suck-ass turn, but at least it won't suck for long. Rooster's life can now be measured in minutes rather than years.

I look the two men over carefully and note that neither of them is Popeye. That means we're missing one that we need to find. We're not missing Tats, though. He's sitting in the chair that Cash is standing behind, and he looks like he may be pissing himself. If not yet, he will be soon.

"Missing Popeye," I say and watch Rooster shoot an evil grin my direction.

"No, we're not. Security system at the clubhouse went off. Rex and Chubs were expecting him. Horse Nuts clotheslined the simple fuck, and now Popeye's hanging out in the basement. Literally. He'll be there when we get back," Reno says with a chuckle.

"Time's up, Rooster. Let her go and settle your debt like a man," Gunner says.

"You the Mexican fucking Taja?" Rooster says aiming his eyes my direction while the woman whimpers.

"Half Hawaiian, douchebag. But yes, Taja's mine. Baby on board, in fact," I grin at him.

"You could've made a mint off her if you'd left her intact. And the younger one too. Had a goldmine in your hands, but you couldn't keep your dick to yourself. That's what's wrong with your club. It used to be a club to fear. 1% all the way. Now you're all soft, young wanna-bes. Not an outlaw among you. Pansy-assed cunts, each and every one. Patty raised those girls soft too. Neither could handle a real biker's life. How do you think it's going to go down with them if you kill their father? Pretty sure you'll never dip your dick into Taja again if that happens," Rooster spews.

"You don't even know your own daughters. Spines like steel. Patty raised them right, despite giving them shit for a dad. You have no idea what those girls are really like. But let me clear one thing up for you right quick. Taja and Tessie know exactly where we're at and why we're here. Both are praying we end you. Both begged us not to come home until you're dead and out of their lives forever. I promised them that's how this would go down. And I never break my promises to either of them," I say, laying it out for him.

Rooster's sneer holds in place for a moment while all that sinks in. Then, in a quick movement, he pulls his gun up and fires it into the side of the woman's head. He swings his gun toward me, but it's already too late for him. As the woman dropped, we all opened fire. I watch with satisfaction as Rooster's body jerks from all the lead entering and exiting it. I don't know which of us fired the kill shot, and it doesn't matter. He's deader than dead. Good riddance.

"What do you want done with these two?" Cash asks.

"I want Tats. He's mine. Don't care about the other one," I say.

No hesitation, Reeves ends his guy's life. Now it's Tats and me time.

"Cuff him and get him into the van. He can come back to the clubhouse with us and join Popeye. They can share their misery before we end it," Gunner orders.

I like this idea better because it'll give me more time to play with Tats. I watch as Axel cuffs him and marches him out the door. He'll be chained to the floor of the van that Freddy and Reno will drive back home.

Pooh pulls the cuts off the two dead guys, and we'll burn them later along with Tats' and Popeye's cuts. Probably their bodies too. That'll be decided later.

"Torch the place and head for home. You know the drill. What's left of their club has scattered. They wanted no part of Rooster's master plan anyway. This is done for us," Gunner says as he walks out the door.

I slide into bed behind Taja and pull her warm, soft body tight to mine. I don't want to wake her, but I need her close. I push my face into her neck and breathe her in. She has a unique scent that never fails to make me hard. Tonight's no different.

I feel her shift, and then her hand reaches back and strokes my cock. I push myself deeper into her hand and lightly nip at her throat. She releases me and turns her body around so we're facing each other. I raise up enough to rest my head on my hand and look down at her. She's beautiful even when she's half-awake and not wearing a drop of makeup.

"Is it done?" she whispers.

"It's done. Nothing to worry about for you and Tessie," I tell her.

"Thank you," Taja says with feeling.

"Give me your mouth, woman."

She does and then gives me so much more. We spend hours exploring each other's bodies. We take things slow and sensual. No need to hurry. I want to know every inch of her. Taja must have felt the same because she took her time tracing every tat I have with her tongue and fingers. We have sex, yes, many times. But we also have more than that. We have what I never thought I would. We make love, and we do it looking into each other's eyes. We're connected in ways we weren't before, and I'm loving every minute of it. Her hands in my hair, she nips my bottom lip until I give her what she wants. Taja's inexperienced, but she's not shy about learning. She's not afraid to ask for what she wants, and I love that about her. That and many other things. Life is good.

Lola Wright

Chapter 27

Taja

With Rooster out of the picture, we've moved back to the house. Vex and Pooh are always fixing something or updating things around it. Trigger's often here to assist or bark orders at them. Tessie and I especially enjoy those days because Trigger's such a teddy bear with us. It drives the guys nuts.

Vex is still pushing me about buying a home and some land before the baby comes. I get why he wants to do that, but I hate to spend the money when we already have a roof over our heads. He wants to fix this home up and rent it out. I want to stay here, even though it'll be crowded with a baby too. We need to save money, not spend it.

After the Rooster problem was ended, Vex told me that Tats was in the basement. He asked if I wanted to say anything to him before that business was ended too. I did. I followed Vex, along with Pooh, Cash, Gunner, and Petey, downstairs to a small cement room. In it, I found Popeye and Tats both naked and hanging by their hands from the ceiling, feet barely touching the floor. Neither were in pristine shape, and I knew their time here had been unpleasant. I took a quick look at Popeye but felt nothing when I saw the bruises and blood caked on him. I turned my eyes to Tats and watched in amusement as he swallowed harshly. I know it's not me he's scared of. He knows that me being here signifies the end is near for him, and he's scared shitless about that. He knows Vex is giving me time to say what I want or need to say, and then when I leave, Tats will die.

"Remember me? What's my name, Tats?" I ask him softly.

"Taja, honey, please. Please tell your man that I had no choice but to do what Rooster ordered! I didn't decide anything! I just took orders! You…"

His words end in a harsh gasp when my foot collides with his dangly bits. I kicked as hard as I could, and I'm now watching his face change colors. I hear a few groans from behind me and know the guys can almost feel Tats' pain. As soon as Tats' eyes focus back on me, I swing. I'm not trained in any self-defense or fighting techniques. I'm not like Ava, but now I wish I were. My fist connects with his cheekbone, and his head snaps back. Pain radiates up my arm, but I ignore it and swing a second time. Plastering a poker face on mine, I stare Tats down.

"I hope you rot in hell. Both of you. But before that happens, I hope you feel pain like you've never felt before. Taking orders? You enjoyed hitting me. And both of you enjoyed terrorizing Tessie and me. You would've sat back while Rooster sold his daughters to the first piece of shit with enough money. You're scum," I tell them in a steady voice.

Before walking out of the room, I spit in Tats' face.

As soon as the door closes behind us, I see grins on the men's faces. As soon as we make it up the stairs and are standing in the main room, Vex turns to me and grabs my arm gently.

"You broke your hand, didn't you?" he asks.

"Ouch. Oh fuck, yes, I think so. Ow, ow, ow, ow," I whimper as he guides me to a chair and helps me take a seat.

Petey pulls another chair up in front of mine and takes a seat. He takes my arm from Vex and starts examining it. I force myself not to flinch or pull away. Glancing up, I see Gunner, Pooh, and Cash all grinning at me.

"What?" I ask.

"Fuck, woman. Thought you were going down there just to say your piece. Didn't realize you were going to go all MMA on his ass," Cash says with a big, beautiful grin. There's also some pride showing in his eyes, I think. He gives my shoulder a squeeze before speaking again.

"When that heals, come to the gym with Vex. I'm going to teach you the proper way to throw a punch so only the asshat gets injured. But, with that said, you did good, girl."

"I will. Thank you, Cash. Thanks to all of you, actually. For everything. Taking care of Tessie and I. Giving us jobs. Getting Rooster out of our lives. Thank you."

"No thanks needed. You're family," Gunner says in a soft, sincere voice.

"What the fuck happened?" Axel asks as he stops next to Petey's side.

"Taja broke her hand. Trip to the ER for you, girl," Petey says while Pooh sets a bag of frozen peas on the table.

I carefully set the peas on my hand and rest it on the table.

"How'd you do that?" Axel questions.

"By punching Tats," Pooh says with a laugh.

"You punched Tats? You took her downstairs and let her punch him? Why the fuck wasn't I called? I would've loved to see that! You're always leaving me out of the fun times! What the fuck, people!" Axel shouts in an annoyed voice.

"Calm yourself, Axel. I videoed it. I knew there was no way she would only bitch him out. Girl had vengeance in her eyes all the way down the stairs," Petey states while winking at me.

"Oh, thank fuck! Let me see it!" Axel says, reaching for his dad's phone.

"While you're reliving the fun, we'll be at the hospital. Let Tessie know so she doesn't worry," Vex cuts in while helping me stand.

Things have settled down, and Vex and I are on solid footing. It's been several weeks since the Rooster drama, and life is great. He's easy to live with, never demanding, and picks up after himself. I shouldn't say he's never demanding because he can be, but I've learned to ignore most of it. He's bossy, but it's cute, so I just grin at him when he does it. He usually just throws his hands up in the air and stomps off. Five minutes later, and he's back trying another angle. The man is persistent, but that plays well for me in the bedroom.

Suki doesn't help matters when she's here. She likes to tease Vex on how we're still living in this house and not some new one yet. She knows that's a sore spot. And she's here a lot. She almost always comes through the door with coffee and one of those head-sized cookies. Vex always grabs the coffee she brings for me away from her because she never remembers to get decaf. That starts round one. Suki also likes to tell Vex to only look at homes big enough that she can move in too. She told him yesterday that with her, me, and Tessie living in the same house with him, we could be called Vex's Harem. Her other favorite name is Vex's Angels. He likes neither. They bicker and battle like brother and sister, but it's all in good fun. I think.

Dreams has been repaired and will be opening up again next week. Vex is dead set against me working there. He wants me to finish college and grow our baby instead. I may give in and do just that. That way, I could have my degree before the baby's born. I'm just a little concerned about money and worry about taking advantage of Vex. He says we need to have a talk about finances, but we've just not found the time yet.

The cast is off finally and just in time. Vex's mom's coming to visit us. I'm nervous about it and terrified I won't be what she wants for her son. Vex just laughs and says not to worry. But I do. I know nothing about her except that she doesn't have a good marriage. Vex grew up in a home with a tyrant for a father and a mother who bows to his every wish. I'm concerned she won't like me because we're so different. I don't back down when Vex and I disagree if I feel I'm right. I stand toe to toe with him and will always be that type of person. Not that we disagree much. Just over big things like buying a new house or buying me a new car. That's his latest kick. He wants me in an SUV so it's safer for me and the baby. Vex is big on safety, I've found.

Catherine Dagen will be arriving in one week. Vex is looking forward to seeing her, and he's not afraid to show that. I've decided the house needs a thorough cleaning before she gets here. Vex and Tessie disagree.

"Baby, she's staying at the Ritz-Carlton, not here. You don't need to kill yourself spit-shining everything. We'll meet her there for dinner," Vex says.

"At the Ritz-Carlton? Holy shit, Vex. Do you know how expensive that place is? I don't even own clothes nice enough to walk inside it," I say in an exasperated voice.

"Then go buy some that are. Order online or go to town and get what you need. Quit worrying about money, doll. I've got us covered, okay? And take Tessie. She'll probably need some too."

I stare at Vex like he's grown an extra head. Men are so clueless as to what clothes like that cost. One outfit can be more than my grocery budget for a month or more.

Vex stands, walks to me, and pulls me to his chest.

"Call Tessie down here. I'll take you two to town, and we'll get the clothes you want and need. Okay?"

"Can't we just meet her at KFC instead?" I ask with a tiny whine in my voice.

Vex barks out a laugh and hugs me tighter. I can feel his body moving with his amusement. It's a nice feeling, so I move closer and rest against him.

"Honey, listen. My mom came from old money. My dad didn't, but he married into it and took it over. He's good at what he does, and he's made her money double itself many times over. My mom wouldn't even know what KFC was, let alone be caught dead eating in one. I don't care what you and Tessie wear. You can wear jeans if you want. I like you in anything or nothing. But if you feel you need to dress up, then let's go shopping and get you and Tessie set up. Okay?"

"How dressed up will your mom be?" I ask in a weak voice.

"I doubt that she owns an outfit or dress that's worth less than $1,500. I know her shoes are always $800 and up. That's how she was raised, and that's all she knows. I want you to just be yourself. She's going to love you and Tessie no matter what you're wearing. I promise. What do you want to do?"

"What are you wearing?"

"Fucking jeans with a button-down. The shirt is my only concession to dressing up," Vex states with a laugh.

"Then I'll wear something I already own. You're right. I need to just be who I am, and Tessie does too."

"I happen to like who you are. A fuck of a lot. Don't want you to try to be someone else. Ever. It's the Taja Davis I met at Dreams that I care about. That's the Taja I want my mom to meet. That's the Taja that's growing my kid and will someday be growing more with me. Yeah?"

"Yeah. Thanks, baby," I answer.

"Thank fuck that's done with. Now pull your shirt up so I can see my baby."

I have a small baby bump now, and Vex can't get enough of it. If we're close to one another, his hand's usually on it. Resting, rubbing, or caressing. He kisses it often, and I know he's anxious for the baby to start moving. I have a feeling he's going to be as bad as Axel when the baby arrives. And that makes me smile every damn time I think it.

Vex's mom is meeting us at a local steakhouse. It's upscale but not to the point of being snooty. Tessie and I are both dressed in nice slacks and blouses, while Vex has on nice jeans and an untucked, fitted dark grey button-down. He looks delicious. Vex has a hold of my hand as we enter, and Tessie's only a step behind us. Vex gives his name, and we're led to a large table in a darkened corner, and I feel Vex's body stiffen. Looking past him, I see why. His mom's not alone. There's a handsome older guy sitting to her right. I know instantly it's Vex's father. The resemblance is remarkable. His father stands, without a smile, as we approach. I watch his eyes do a once over of me, then Tessie, and finally Vex before they go blank. No emotion at all. First time he's seen his son in years, and he doesn't seem to care. Wow.

"What's he doing here?" Vex says quietly to his mother. His voice has a bite to it, though, and I move closer to his side.

"Vex, please. Your dad insisted on coming so he could see you too. Please, honey, take a seat and introduce me to these lovely ladies you've brought," Vex's mom says in a soft, pleading voice.

Vex hesitates for a moment, then turns to help seat me and Tessie. He sits between us and does the introductions. His body and voice are stiff. I slide my hand onto his thigh and give it a gentle squeeze. His eyes meet mine, and for a brief moment, I see rage. His eyes warm, and his hand lands on the top of my mine, lacing our fingers together.

The waiter takes our drink orders and disappears, leaving an awkward silence behind.

"What do you do for living now, Vex? Do you work or just live off your trust fund?" Michaeli Dagen asks with a slight sneer.

"I work security for a strip club," Vex answers with a grin.

"You what?" his father barks.

"You heard me," Vex replies with yet another grin.

"I'm guessing that's where you met her at?" Mr. Dagen says in a condescending tone.

"Yes, as a matter of fact, that's where we met," I answer.

"I figured as much. Classic story. Rich guy meets stripper. Stripper gets pregnant. Rich guy pays through the nose for a baby that may or may not be his. Make sure you have the kid DNA'd, Vex," his father says while giving me the side-eye.

"Michaeli!" Catherine says on a gasp.

Vex is on his feet before she gets the whole name out of her mouth. This is bad. This is very bad. I hang tight to Vex's hand and try pulling him back down but to no avail. He's seething mad, and I'm surprised his dad's not on the floor knocked out yet.

"Is that what you've done, Father? Got them all DNA'd?" Vex spits out.

"Sit down, Vex. You're causing a scene. God, you're so predictable. I'm giving you sound advice, and you know it," Michaeli says in a perfectly calm voice.

"Not sure I like what you're implying about my sister. She's never been a stripper or anything close to that. She's studying to become a nurse, so she can care for people. She was a bartender there when she met Vex. And she was only bartending to help pay our bills after our mother died of cancer, and my dad demanded payment for me. If she didn't pay him, he was going to forcibly become my pimp. Yes, my own father. And yet, I still think we scored higher in that department than Vex did. And one more thing before I walk out of here and leave you to your pathetic life, you stuck-up snobby bitch. I'm a sixteen-year-old girl who dreams of becoming a mechanic. Ha! Bet you're glad I'm not your daughter. Blue-collar all the way, baby. No shame in getting your hands dirty," Tessie says on a rant before standing up, tossing her napkin on the table, and turning to Vex's mother.

"I like you. You seem like a nice lady, but you can't be very damn bright. What kind of woman allows a man to keep her from her own child, her son? A son that's good through and through. A son who fought for two women who had no one else to fight for them. Only death could make our mom leave us. Never some man. I'm sorry it's went down like this, Mrs. Dagen. But you should be ashamed of yourself," Tessie finishes with a soft voice before giving Vex a quick hug, me a shoulder squeeze, and walking away.

I stand, set my napkin on the table, and turn to Catherine.

"It was nice meeting you. You're always welcome in my—in our—home. If you want to meet your grandchild, we'd love to have you. But your husband is not welcome. Completely your choice, but I have to agree with Tessie. You allowing your husband to keep you from Vex shows weakness. And Vex deserves better than that. He deserves everything good and nothing bad in his life. I aim to see that's exactly what he gets."

"Of course, you do. On his dime. How long before you got your name on his bank account?" Vex's father says with a sneer.

"She doesn't know anything about my money. We've never discussed it before. Taja isn't with me because of my bank account, Dad. That's how things go in your life, not mine. Don't come back. Mom, love you but don't come back either if you're bringing him. You won't be welcome if you do," Vex declares. "Warning, Dad. The next time you insult Taja, in any way, you're going to get the beat down you've deserved for many years. I kind of hope you make that mistake again. I want to cause you pain. You've been warned."

Holding hands, heads held high, we walk out and leave his parents behind. Tessie's waiting on the sidewalk, and she's fuming. Before she gets her mouth open, Vex tosses his other arm over her shoulders and pulls her tight to his side.

"Love you, little sis. You did good in there. The prick had it coming," Vex tells the top of her head before dropping a light kiss on it.

Turning to me, I get a light kiss from Vex also.

"I'm sorry you two had to go through that. She never said one word about bringing him, or I wouldn't have brought you guys with me. Hell, I wouldn't have come myself," Vex mutters as we reach his truck.

"You've met our father, Vex. We can't really say much about yours," Tessie says with a grin as we all climb in the truck.

"It's fine, Vex. I'm sorry about your mom, though. I know you were looking forward to seeing her," I say softly.

"Yeah, I was. But you two were right. She's to blame as much as Dad is. She doesn't fight for what she wants, and spending time with her son isn't worth a battle, I guess."

"She'll have to figure it out on her own, baby," I tell him.

"Now that the drama is over, where we eating tonight? Because I'm starving back here," Tessie interjects from the back seat.

"Call Suki, and you three pick a place. Have her meet us there. Dinner's on me. Might as well have the whole damn harem together," Vex mutters with a grin as he starts the truck.

"You have lost your effing mind, Vex! What the hell? Nobody can actually afford this place!" I shout at his grinning face.

"We can. Just walk through it with me before you pass out, okay?"

I give in and decide to humor him. Rex hands over the keys, and we walk inside. I hear Tessie gasp and then see her start running through the big-ass living room, stopping long enough to look out each window. And there are a lot of them. They circle the entire room except where the fireplace is. The fireplace is large enough for me to walk inside and not be touching my head. It's humongous and beautiful with its flat stones and glossy wood mantle. Tall cathedral ceiling over the living room portion. Balcony on the second floor overlooking it. The rooms organically blend from one to the next. Open floor plan and every inch of it's gorgeous. The kitchen is all white cabinets with black granite counters, and everything shines. I'm in love already but don't want to admit it. No way anyone I know can afford this place.

The exterior of the house is made of flat stone and huge wood timbers. It has a deck that circles it all the way around to the pool. The pool's a work of art with natural stone surrounding it and making up a small waterfall on one side. Hot tub in one corner with a huge BBQ pit made of brick. The entire lawn is beautifully landscaped and well-maintained.

"The basement is finished. Game room with pool table and a pinball machine. Small bar with fridge and sink. Huge-ass TV that would be perfect for watching the game. A few small rooms that could be made into anything you'd want. Craft room, maybe. A large bedroom and bath for guests. On the main floor is the master bedroom and bath. It has huge closets and a connecting bedroom that would be perfect as a nursery. Come see," Vex says excitedly as he pulls me by the hand.

Standing in the door of the master bedroom, I feel my mouth drop open. It's as large as the downstairs of my house. French doors that open to the deck. I slowly walk to the bathroom and forcibly close my mouth. Again, it's huge. Double sinks, a large claw-footed tub sitting in front of a window overlooking the backyard. The shower is like walking into a stone cave. It has a large arched doorway with no door. Eight people could easily stand in it. Showerheads are placed in several locations around it. What looks like a state-of-the-art security system is mounted on one wall. It's the control panel for the showerheads, temperature, on/off, steam, and God knows what else. Walking out of there, I open the door to the connecting bedroom, and my heart sinks. I love it, and I want this for our baby, but I know it's way the hell out of our range. The room is empty and looks like it was never used. It would need painting, but I can easily picture Vex and I in here with our little one.

"Taja! Taja! Come see this!" Tessie hollers down the staircase.

I hear Rex and Vex chuckle as I brush past and go looking for my sister. I find her twirling in circles with her arms out to the side, huge grin on her face, and eyes twinkling.

"Tessie?" I ask to get her attention.

"Check this out! This would be my room! French doors that go to a balcony overlooking the Front Range and the pool. My own friggin' bathroom. No more sharing with you! It has a tub, a separate shower that's big enough to throw a party in, and the toilet is closed off in its own little room. It has a makeup table that's lighted and about a dozen plugins. And I'm guessing they don't blow the breakers when I have my blow dryer and the coffee maker going at the same time! This is the bomb!" Tessie ends on a shout.

"Tessie. Honey. You know we can't afford…"

"Yes, we can afford it," Vex cuts in.

"Vex, no, we…"

"Let the man talk, Taja. It's rude to interrupt," Tessie interrupts me to say while walking to Vex and wrapping her hands around his bicep. "Talk to me, pretty boy. Are you serious that we could actually live here? And still have food to eat?"

"Yes. If you ladies like this place, we're buying it."

"I call for a vote. Majority rules. I vote yes," Tessie says while waving one hand in the air.

"It doesn't work that way!" I shout at her.

"Should. Be a lot easier if it did," Rex mumbles. "Not sure I've ever seen a woman so hell-bent on *not* spending money, Vex. You need to have that talk with her. Now. Tessie, why don't you and I go explore the pool and property and let Vex convince Taja that you all need this place."

"Great idea! Use whatever means necessary, Vex. We'll stay gone until you call us back inside. Just please, use another room to convince her in," Tessie says while tossing a wink at Vex and walking out with Rex.

I watch as Vex chuckles over Tessie's sassy remark, and then I brace as he walks up tight to my chest. Grabbing my hand, he bends and places a sweet kiss on my mouth. Then pulls me behind him until we've walked through all the rooms upstairs. We move down to the main level, and he leads me to a table and chairs. We sit, and Vex rocks my world.

"Before we get into anything else, I want you to know a few things first. I'm not asking you this because we're pregnant. Please know that. I'm asking because it's what I really want for my life, even if it seems quick. Will you marry me?"

I hear and see the words leave Vex's mouth, but I'm not comprehending them. I see his mouth jerk up on one side in a small smile before he gives my hand a shake.

"Taja? Will you?"

Holy shitballs, I did hear what I thought I heard.

"Making me nervous, Taj."

"Yes. Absolutely, yes," I answer in a hushed voice. I think I'm a little shell-shocked.

"You can't take that back. I heard you say yes. It's official. We're getting married. And it's going to be soon, so prepare your mind for that. Taja? You with me, doll?" Vex asks with a smile in his voice.

I focus and see his gorgeous face close to mine. I lean forward enough to kiss him. He's not into a quick kiss, and I know that when he throws his arms around me and lifts me from the chair. Feet off the floor, Vex spins us in a circle. Arms around his shoulders and neck, I deepen our kiss until my feet are back on the floor.

"I can't believe you just asked me to marry you."

"I don't like to fuck around once my mind's made up. I spent a few months wanting you but not going after you. That was a mistake. I'm not making another one like that. We're getting married, and it can be as big or small as you like, but it needs to be soon. I want our baby born with my name. That's important to me, but it's not why I asked. I asked because I fucking love you and want you with me no matter where life takes us."

"I want that too. I want you as mine legally, spiritually, every way possible, Vex."

"Then you better get this on your finger so every swinging dick knows you're taken," Vex says while holding out a small jeweler's box. "We're going to have our wedding bands tattooed on our ring fingers, but you deserve an engagement ring too. Open it up and try it on."

I open it to find a beautiful chocolate diamond solitaire glittering back at me. It's set in a silver-white palladium band, and it's stunning. Vex removes the ring from the box and slides it onto my finger. He then places a soft kiss on it. I'm at a loss for words. The stone reminds me of his eyes, and I love it even more.

"Baby, I'm not joking when I tell you we can afford this place and a few more just like it. My mom's family were wealthy, and my grandmother left me an inheritance. I've never really touched it, to spend, I mean, so it's been sitting there for years drawing interest. I've managed it and learned how to invest wisely, so it's done nothing but grow. This place will not make a dent in it. I want this place for you and Tessie. For us and our baby. For the family we'll continue to grow in the future. But if you really don't like it, we'll find something you do. We'll look until we do, or we'll build exactly what you want."

"I love this place! It's beautiful, but I thought it was just too much for us! I didn't want you feeling like you had to give us the world when all I need is you," I say with tears streaming down my face.

"I love you, Taj. I don't feel like I need to give you the world, but I want to do just that."

"Love you too, Vex. So much."

Those words bring a beautiful, perfect smile to Vex's face as his eyes warm. I know hearing them meant something to him. His did to me too. God, I love this man.

"You can come in now, Tessie. We're buying the house!" Vex shouts over my shoulder.

"Yes! Yes! I knew you could do it, Vex! Score!" Tessie screeches from the doorway as it swings open.

Vex turns my body so that my back is pressed to his front. His hand naturally slips down to rest on my bump. He grasps my left hand and holds it out in front of me. It takes Tessie a few seconds to notice because she's doing some weird kind of happy dance. But her face is priceless when she does.

"You didn't ask my permission," Tessie states oddly.

"Sorry. Didn't know I was supposed to," Vex replies.

"Well, yeah! I'm her only living relative. You have to get past me first. Then you ask her. That's the order of things," Tessie states like she's talking to a child.

"Can I marry your sister?" Vex plays along while Rex's fighting laughter behind Tessie's back.

"Do you remember the house rules we discussed before?" Tessie questions.

"Yes. No boxer briefs, but boxers are fine. Jeans are better. Toilet seat down at all times. Blah, blah, blah. I remember them," Vex answers with a laugh.

"Those rules still apply when we're living in your house and not ours?" Tessie asks.

"It's not mine or yours. It's always going to be *our* home. All three of us. So yes, Miss Tessie, the rules still apply."

"Will I get an allowance now?"

"Tessie! Oh my God, girl!" I shout at her smiling face.

"Just joking. Yes, you have my permission, biker boy. Marry my sister and give me lots of nieces and nephews."

"I look forward to granting your wish, Tessie."

Chapter 28

Vex

My offer on the house and property was accepted. I close on it tomorrow. We have a lot of work to do, but the women have already started packing things and preparing to move. Horse Nuts came to Taja and I and asked about renting their home for now. We agreed, and the rent he'll be paying will go directly into Tessie's savings account.

Taja finally agreed to not go back to work, at least until after the baby's born. She's taking a few classes, and that's fine by me. I spoke with the club, and they agreed I could cut back on hours at Dreams. Freddy hired a friend of Rod's. He's been working out well so far. I still work there, just not as much. I have enough to do right now, and I want to be with Taja as much as possible. She's still having some issues with morning sickness, even though the doctor said it should have ended by now. That keeps me worried.

Taja has developed cravings for black licorice, and I often see her with a stick of it in her hand. Craig takes full credit for that and makes sure to always have some for her when we're at the clubhouse. He's still carrying a torch for Taja, and they're so cute together. He willingly takes a bath and always wears his "romantic" shirts when he knows Taja will be on the compound. He often pushes himself between us to stand closer to her. It's cute, but I often find myself jealous of a five-year-old boy. Sad, but true.

Taja's also missing Duffy since we don't see him as much. She visits the compound often just to get her Duffy fix. He's back to being mellow with me, but only if Taja's lavishing her attention on him. If I'm receiving it, I often have my blood drawn by the ill-tempered cat. I'm learning what the club sluts must have dealt with when Duffy would ruin their day instead of mine. At least the fat bastard doesn't live with us.

I decided to speak with Ava and Reno about one of Loki's puppies. They're due any day now, and I want one for Taja and Tessie. Our house is isolated. Even with Rex setting up a security perimeter, I want the women to have a large dog with them there when I'm not. I know both women will love the idea. They both fuss over Ava and Craig's pets constantly, so getting them a puppy will not cause an argument. After speaking with Ava, I'm on the list in the number four spot to choose. That will be a fun day for the sisters.

My mother has reached out to me numerous times since the restaurant incident. I know she's torn, but she's an adult and needs to stand up for what she wants. I can't make it easier for her. She also texts with Taja often, and I'm hopeful the pull of a grandchild will get her to make the right choices. Time will tell.

Even knowing that I can afford anything she might desire, Taja's still hesitant to spend money on things she deems unnecessary. Tessie's become my best ally in helping me get around Taja's refusal to spend money. We've spent hours together online picking out baby things. Taja will walk past, look at what we're buying, and gasp at the cost. Tessie has no qualms about picking out the best, and neither do I.

Luckily, the guy we're buying the home from has moved out and is allowing us to move things in already. The first order of business was Rex getting the security system up and working. Second, Chubs and Pooh helped me paint the nursery. I now wished I hadn't teased Gunner so much when he kept repainting the twin's nursery because I'm just as bad. I couldn't decide on a color and then changed my mind twice after it was completed. Chubs just smiled and continued painting with one hand while eating with the other. Eventually, the nursery ended up being a very pale gray with white trim. It turned out awesome.

Bailey agreed to sketch some pictures for the walls. She did animal sketches, and they're adorable. The "Pooh" bear is sniffing a flower, the cat is curled up in a blanket, and the puppy has a ball next to it. All will work whether we have a boy or a girl. She also sketched my favorite bike, and it's perfect. It has every tiny detail, and I'm debating whether I want it in the nursery or the living room. With the mountains in the background, I'm leaning toward the living room.

While buying furnishings for the house, I hear, "You've lost your damn mind!" often from Taja. I just grin and click add to cart. If I don't do it, she'll never spend the money, and my girls are not going to live with second best anymore.

I had to enlist Tessie's help when it came to maternity clothes. Taja needs them, and she's broke down and bought some but not nearly enough. She usually wears my shirts, which I love seeing, but she needs more than that. Tessie didn't hesitate to take my credit card and hit the stores. Taja now has a beautiful maternity wardrobe. And she loves it.

We had a doctor's appointment yesterday with an ultrasound. We both chose not to know the sex of the baby. Taja wants to go the old-fashioned way, as she called it, and find out at the birth. I'm scared to hear it's a girl, so I'm putting that off for as long as possible. Yes, I can be a scared little child sometimes, and I'm not afraid to admit it. To myself at least.

The doctor's concerned, though, and told us the baby isn't as large as it should be by now, but everything else seemed okay. Taja asked a lot of questions. We left the appointment with her being quiet and worried. She's doing everything the doctor told her to do, so I think all will be well. She's tired all the time and sleeps a lot, but the doctor said that's normal and not to worry about that. She wants us back in two weeks.

I closed on the house, and we've been moving things into it. Taja isn't allowed to lift anything, so she does a lot of directing. It takes us a week, but we're finally moved in and loving it. Tessie and Bella got free rein on decorating Tessie's room. They did a great job, and the room is perfect for Tessie.

While some of the guys helped us move in, others got to work making a road from our backyard to the compound. It's just a dirt trail, but it's wide enough to drive a truck through. It ends up connecting to the road that Gunner, Pooh, Axel, and the rest live on. Someday I may have it paved, but for now, it's perfect. We own 640 acres with the house nearly in the center of it, so we have a lot of privacy. Chubs and I have already discussed him buying a corner of it so he can build a home for him and Lucy. He loves the idea, and I love that he'd be close to us. He doesn't know it, but no way will I take money for the land he'd like. Chubs could ask for the moon, and I'd try to get it for him. No better person in the world. And Lucy? Best ever.

Lucy and Taja get along great and hang together often. Lucy has approached Taja about helping out at New Horizons. Taja's excited about it and has agreed as soon as the baby's born. Once she has her nursing degree and license, Pippa, Lucy, and Tammy have asked her to become New Horizons nurse on-call. They get women who need treatment for wounds that refuse to go to the hospital. That's where Taja would come in. She's thrilled at the idea of being able to help there. Gunner and Axel have also asked her to do the same for the MC. Of course, she agreed before she hugged the hell out of both guys. She's still smiling over being asked. I've mentioned a few times now that if she wants to go forward with her education and become a doctor, I'm all for it. I'm proud as hell of her as she is, but if she chose to do that, I'd back her every step of the way.

"What's got you thinking so hard?" Taja says softly as she wraps her arms around my waist from behind.

"You. Tessie. The baby. Us. Just thinking about how perfect my life is now. Meeting you changed my whole world. I'm getting married, having a baby, and bought a home. I'm going to have a sister-in-law that I get to watch grow into a beautiful adult. Everything's coming together. I'm just amazed that in such a short time, everything's changed, but it's all for the better."

Taja moves to my front without letting go of me. I look down into her beautiful face and again think how lucky I am. I wrap my arms around her and pull her snug to my chest.

"I wish so much that Mom were here to meet you and our little one. She'd be so happy that I met someone like you. She'd love being a grandma," Taja says in a quiet, sad voice. "She'd love you."

"I wish I could give you that, Taj. I would have loved meeting the woman who raised such beautiful daughters. But, baby, she's here. She'll always be with you and Tessie. She's a big part of both of you. I like to think she's smiling, knowing her girls are happy and safe. I also like to think she'd approve of me being with her daughter," I confess.

"She would've. Now, quit staring out the window and come to bed. It's our first night in our new home, and we have a bed to break in," Taja says with a laugh as she pulls away.

Taja walks slowly backward toward the bed as she starts removing pieces of clothing. She doesn't understand it, but her pregnant body's a cock-hardening sight for me every damn time I see it. She was self-conscious in the beginning when she first started showing, but she's gotten over it. When her bra hits the floor, my mouth waters. Her breasts have always been perfect, but now they're slightly larger, fuller, and I can't get enough of them.

While I stand watching the strip show, Taja drops her yoga pants and panties. Naked, she climbs on the bed, lays on her back, and plants her feet, knees raised. Looking at me from between her spread thighs, I watch as her hand drops to slide across her clit. That move puts me into action. My clothes are off without me remembering that I removed them. I walk until I'm standing at the foot of the bed, eyes still glued to Taja's hand. I stroke my cock a few times before lifting my eyes to see hers locked on my hand.

"I'm getting a taste of you before you get my cock, baby," I rasp out.

"That's what I'm counting on," she replies softly.

I pounce and grin at Taja's surprised laugh. I get my taste, taking my time until Taja's writhing on the bed and begging for my cock. Climbing up her body on my hands and knees, I pause long enough to place kisses on her swollen belly. It's the most beautiful sight to view, and I can't get enough.

Eventually, my mouth finds her breasts, and Taja sighs. Working one nipple with lips and teeth, my hand does the same on the other. I feel Taja's hands gliding up and down my sides and then into my hair. Balancing on my forearms, I keep my weight off of her.

"Vex, baby. I need you in me. Now. Please," Taja quietly begs.

Hearing those desperate words makes my cock weep. Moving to the side of her, I urge her to turn over and raise up on hands and knees. I slide under her top half far enough to latch onto a nipple and suck hard. She moans, and I know she's close already. That's my girl. Always ready for my cock.

Letting go of her nipple, I rise and move behind her body. Pressing tight to her ass, I rub my cock along her pussy. I use a hand to hold onto my cock and slide it back and forth along her wetness.

"Honey, please! I'm going to come, and I want your cock in me when I do," Taja orders.

I grin. I know I'm torturing her, but it's in the best way possible. Letting go of my cock, I slide a finger deep inside her. She's sopping wet, and no woman will ever understand what that does to a man.

"Baby, now! Oh God, I'm coming! More Vex! I need more," Taja moans as I feel her inner walls twitch.

I remove my finger, grab my cock, and slide it into her. Taja instantly slams her body back against mine with a hiss. I lick my thumb and slide it around her other opening that's right in my view. I press it slightly in while pumping my hips. Taja's body jerks, and I know she's coming hard. I can feel her tighten like a vice on my cock, and I push my thumb inside her a little more. Twirling my thumb, I use my other hand to hold her hip. Using the leverage I have on her, I pump hard. She stiffens for a moment, slamming back against me, then she shudders.

"Not even close to being done yet, baby. I want another," I tell her.

I continue pumping into her, stopping to swirl my hips every few seconds, and I know I'm going to get another orgasm from her.

Moving my hand from her ass, I move it back down to her clit. I rub gently and then pinch it harshly. Taja responds by widening her legs a little for better access.

"So close, Vex. Don't stop, please!"

It only takes another moment before I feel her getting wetter. She's taking all of me and wanting more. I move my legs a bit to change the angle, and I hear Taja let out a gasp. Yeah, that's the spot. I keep my cock sliding across that spot until Taja starts panting. When I feel her come, I let loose of my control and join her. There's nothing better in this world than sharing an orgasm. Taja pants, and I hold my breath through it. When it's over, I stay planted because I love the quivers that continue deep inside her body. When I notice Taja's arms shaking, I reluctantly withdraw from her. She collapses on her side, breathing hard. I lean down and drop a kiss on her cheek before exiting the bed.

After cleaning myself up, I take a warm washcloth back to the bedroom to find Taja in the same position, though her breathing has slowed to normal. I drop another kiss on her shoulder before gently cleaning her up. This is something I found I love doing. Something I never thought of doing before with any other female. But with Taja, I like bringing her that small comfort after we've been intimate.

After returning the washcloth to the bathroom, I slide into bed behind Taja and pull her close. Placing my hand on her belly, I'm where I want to be for the rest of my life. As I'm drifting off, I feel

Taja move, and it brings me fully awake. Lying still for a moment, I realize it's not Taja moving but our baby. I press my hand fully against her belly and smile a huge grin when I feel fluttering against it.

"Taj! The baby's moving," I say in her ear.

She jerks awake, and I grab her hand to move it where mine has been. After a moment, the baby moves again.

"Oh my God! She's moving! I can feel her!" Taja whisper-shouts at me.

"He! He's moving! Quit saying she, or you'll jinx me!" I shout back.

Taja bursts out laughing while we both wait for more movement. It doesn't happen, but we drift off to sleep, hoping.

Taja's morning sickness has finally disappeared for the most part. She still has some bad days but not nearly as often as before. Certain smells will set it off, and bacon is one of them. There's no bacon in our home, and Ava has quit cooking it at the clubhouse to help Taja. Chubs pouted for a few days, but Ava told him she'd still make his candied bacon treats at the bakery. He goes there to get his fix now. Along with cupcakes, cookies, and pies.

We're at the twenty-eight-week mark, and the time's not passing quickly enough for me. Taja's following everything the doctor says and is eating healthy and exercising regularly. She's cut back on the licorice to only a few sticks of it a day, but she craves it constantly. She never forgets to take the prenatal vitamins, and she looks and feels healthy.

I'm at Dreams working when I glance up to see Taja sitting at the end of the bar, chatting with Suki and Freddy. She misses working and comes here occasionally to see her friends. I walk over to her and lean in for a kiss.

Placing my arm across her lower back so that my hand rests on the side of her belly, I smile down at my woman. I get a breathtaking smile back before I feel someone pat my ass. Thinking it's Taja, I laugh. When she looks at me oddly, I swing my head around to find Kristy leaning against the bar next to where I'm standing. It was her hand.

"Don't do that shit, Kristy. Keep your fucking hands off me," I bark at her.

"You don't seem to mind when she's not here," Kristy blatantly lies while smirking at Taja.

"That's bullshit, and you know it, Kristy. I, my own damn self, have heard him tell you that several times now," Freddy states loudly.

Freddy doesn't ever raise his voice to any employee here. He's a laid-back guy who always has a smile in place. He's got to be really annoyed for his voice to raise and the smile to be gone. And both are happening right now.

"Not making me jealous, Kristy. Just making me pity you even more than I already do," Taja calmly says while taking a sip of her water.

"Fuck you, Taja! You come in here all innocent like and disrupt what was a good thing we had going. Getting yourself pregnant to hang onto a man's the most pathetic move ever!" Kristy spits in anger.

"You're just pissed because Vex decided to trade in his old, tattered, used toys and go for an upgrade. Back off, bitch. We're having a conversation here," Suki snarls from behind the bar.

"Stay out of this, Suki! Doesn't concern your lesbian ass!" Kristy snarls back.

"Bi, baby. It's bi, not lesbian. I like all sexual parts regardless of shape. But I don't sell mine for cheap-ass shoes and perfume. Get gone, whore," Suki bellows back.

Kristy whirls on her stripper shoes and gives Taja a hard shove, completely catching me off-guard. Having my arm around her back keeps her seated, but I see fire shooting from Taja's eyes. Instinct kicks in, and she tries to stand, but I wrap my arm tighter around her and don't allow it. It takes a second but reason seeps into her, and she relaxes. There will be no momma-to-be brawl tonight. Placing my body between the two women, I aim my eyes at Kristy.

Before I can tell her she's fired, Suki sails over the bar and pounces on Kristy. They go down in a heap of legs, arms, and squeals. Suki fights her way to the top and starts swinging.

"I can't see, Vex! Move yourself," Taja hollers at me while pulling on my shoulder.

I slide to the side so she can enjoy the fight with me and Freddy.

"How long should we let this go on?" Freddy asks in a calm voice.

"Don't you dare stop this!" shouts Taja.

We've drawn the attention of the entire club, and several patrons are tossing money at the fighting women. A few of the other strippers have rushed up to see what's happening. Kristy's not well-liked, and it shows when the strippers start cheering Suki on.

Freddy eventually gets a grip on Suki's arms and pulls her off Kristy's battered body. Suki and Taja fist bump with big smiles. Other than wild-ass hair, Suki looks fine. Kristy, not so much. Bleeding nose and lip, wig laying on the floor, and bruises already starting to form, she's a mess. Not one stripper or security personnel offer to help her up. Freddy releases Suki with an order to go take a break and then assists Kristy to her feet. Fake boobs hanging out, skirt raised above her ass, one shoe missing, she limps away toward the dressing room. Taja slides off her stool and starts picking up the loose bills laying all around where the women were battling. She straightens them into a neat stack and drops them into Suki's tip jar with a grin. I just shake my head at her, grinning.

"I'm off to go fire Kristy. Something I should have done a year or so ago. Sorry about that, Taja. You okay, girl?" Freddy asks with concern.

"I'm fine. No harm done. Thank you, Freddy," Taja replies while still grinning.

Freddy walks off, and I turn to Taja.

"You sure you're okay?"

"Yeah, it was nothing. But watching Suki kick-ass on her was friggin' awesome. The bitch has had it coming for a long time now. Just wish I could have gotten in a few shots too."

"And earn yourself another cast? No, honey. Just no. After the baby's born, you get some lessons on how to do damage, and then we'll see about letting you kick some ass. But not until then," I tell her with a laugh.

"Yeah, you're probably right."

"You going to explain what's going on?" I ask Chubs.

"No," Chubs replies.

"Let me rephrase. You *are* going to explain what's going on," I spit back.

I've been on Chubs' ass for a while now. I know that whoever keeps showing up here looking for him is not giving up. Chubs has been quieter lately, and I know he's dealing with something serious. I'm concerned and frustrated. Chubs is always helping the rest of us and yet not letting us return the favor. I don't like that he's keeping secrets from the club. Not that I don't trust him, but because we can't help while being kept in the dark. I won't quit until I know what the fuck is happening with him. And I have no problem fighting dirty to get that info.

"Let it go, Vex. I'll deal, and all will be well," Chubs says in a tired voice.

"Not letting it go, Chubs. You can tell me, or I'll be forced to bring it up at Church," I threaten while meaning every word.

"Rather not, brother. I don't want to bring trouble to the club," Chubs answers.

"What kind of trouble? There isn't a person connected to this club that wouldn't back you against anything out there, Chubs. What the fuck? You know you can trust us!" I insist.

"I'll only tell you this, but the less you know, the better off you'll be. You know my name's Brock

Cooper. Nobody's called me that in years, though. Here in The Devil's Angels MC, I'm Chubs. Period. That's who I am, inside and out, and who I want to be. Just Chubs. The club brother who's dependable and always there to help anyone. The Chubs that loves Lucy. And Ava and the rest of the women and kids here. The Chubs with an unexplainable eating disorder. But Cooper isn't my real name. It's the name the Feds laid on me when they placed me in WitSec. I left the program when I was a teenager because I didn't feel safe with them. I had good reasons to get gone, so I did. Gunner's dad found me starving on the streets and brought me in. That's how I came to be a Devil's Angel. The Feds have finally tracked me down and want to pull me back in for reasons I'm not going to explain. I've told them no, and they've threatened to expose who I am if I don't do what they want. I'll disappear before I'll let them bring that kind of trouble to the club," Chubs says passionately.

I don't doubt him for a second. Chubs would give up everything and everyone he loves if he thought it would keep them safe. He has a heart of gold, but we need him here.

"Does Lucy know about this?" I ask.

"She knows my history, but she doesn't know the Feds are snooping around here," Chubs says with a miserable tone to his voice.

"We need to have Church. Explain everything to the guys and let the club decide what's the best course of action. We make big decisions together, as a club, and you know that. This isn't just your problem. It's ours too because you matter to us. You're one of us. Bring this to the club, Chubs," I implore him.

"I'll think about it. I've got to go. I have wrecker calls to make," Chubs says with a slap to my shoulder before walking out of the clubhouse. Fuck!

I drive my truck to work because it's snowing and icy outside. In Denver, it can snow one day and be sunny and warm the next. Today, it's decided to be nasty.

When I leave for work, Taja and Tessie are playing video games and arguing up a storm about who's the better player. I give each a kiss on the forehead and leave. Opening the door, I find a wet, cold Duffy sitting on the deck, pissed-off look on his face. He's also breathing heavy, so I'm assuming the walk from Ava's to our place was long for his little kitty legs. I wave him in the door and hear Taja squeal in delight as I shut it behind me. I don't think just a puppy will be enough for the sisters. I see a trip to the animal rescue for a kitten in our future. As long as it's not the size of Duffy, I'm good with that.

Work's boring but easier now that Suki's put the message out, in her own unique way, that I'm off-limits. I grin, remembering the battle between bartender and stripper. Go Suki!

Pooh calls to give me shit about something, but the storm is wreaking havoc with our connection, and I can't hear half of what he says. I do hear the phrases "pussy-whipped" and "pregnant sex" so I know the call's not an important one. Hanging it back up, I stick my phone in my back pocket and get to making rounds.

A few hours later, music booming, I see Freddy run into the room coming from his office. His body movements are frantic, and I feel my blood run cold. Bolting across the room, pushing patrons out of my way, I feel real fear when I see the look Freddy gives me when our eyes meet.

"What?!" I shout before I even get to him.

"Let's go! You're riding with me," Freddy shouts back as he rushes toward the door, barking orders to Rod on the way.

I don't waste a moment of repeating myself. I just run. Making it to Freddy's truck, we get inside, and he starts it up. Once on the road, I then repeat myself.

"What's wrong, Freddy? What's happened?"

Freddy visibly takes a deep breath and calms himself. He's driving like a bat out of hell, especially considering the road conditions, but he speaks in a steady voice.

"Tessie drove Taja to the compound. Taja's bleeding. Bad. More like hemorrhaging, and their phones wouldn't work. Tessie got Taja into the Jeep and hauled ass. Axel saw Tessie's Jeep sliding onto the road by his house and jerk to a stop. Tessie saw him and started screaming for help out the window. He ran to see what was wrong and found Taja slumped in the backseat. He tried calling for an ambulance but didn't have cell service either. He sent Tessie inside to use the landline. Ambulance arrived, and he's following it to the hospital now."

My heart in my throat, I can't even reply. God, no. I can't lose Taja or the baby. I need them. My thoughts are scattered, and I'm fighting not to lose it completely.

Freddy's driving attracts a cop's attention, and lights are flashing behind us. Freddy doesn't slow in the least. I'm still incapable of speaking, so I try to slow my mind and wish the distance away. I hear the siren kick on, but we're only a few blocks from the hospital. I know Freddy's going to get me there regardless of a flashing blue light.

As we slide to a stop outside of the ER, I bail out of the truck at a run. I leave Freddy to deal with the cop and rush frantically up to the nurse's desk. I'm told the ambulance's ETA is two minutes. We beat it here. I rush back outside and can hear its siren in the distance. Freddy's still explaining things to the cop when Cash suddenly appears beside me. Hand on my shoulder, he's always the calm one.

"She'll be fine, brother. Just keep positive thoughts," he murmurs.

"I can't lose them," I barely whisper my fear.

"She's a fighter. You know that. Right here for you, any way you need me."

When the ambulance comes to a stop, I see nothing except the stretcher they remove with Taja on it. I run beside it, holding her limp hand as they rush into the hospital and down a short hall before coming to a stop. Instantly, doctors and nurses are in motion around us, but my eyes stay locked on Taja's face. When her eyes open, they hit mine immediately. Hers are filled with fear, and I know mine probably are as well. She grips my hand, and I bend to kiss the back of hers.

"It's going to be okay, Taj. I'm right here. We'll do this together," I say, trying to ease both our fears.

The doctor places Taja's feet into the stirrups and covers her the best he can with a blanket. The nurses are calling out Taja's stats as the doctor barks orders. It seems like chaos to me, but I'm sure it's controlled chaos from their perspective.

After a few terrifying moments, the doctor moves to Taja's side and raises her shirt to expose her belly. Using an ultrasound, he watches the screen intently. While doing this, Taja's OB-GYN, Dr. Spitz, walks into the ER bay and starts speaking quietly with the on-call doctor.

I lean down and place my lips on Taja's forehead and hold them there. I know she's in a lot of pain, and I wish to hell I could take it for her. I feel helpless. I'm not good with that.

"Taja. Vex. Please listen. We have to deliver this baby immediately. Things are not good, and we have no choice," the doctor informs us.

"It's too soon. It's too early!" Taja moans while gripping my hand and her belly.

"I'm sorry, Taja. I'm so, so sorry. We have no choice, and we need to do it now."

"Is she alive?" Taja whispers the words I'm too terrified to ask.

"We're not sure yet, Taja. We've got your bleeding stopped, but you lost quite a bit of blood, and we've not been able to locate a heartbeat. We're taking you into surgery now."

I hear the words, but they're not sinking in. I know what the doctor said, but my brain is refusing to allow them to make sense. I drop my forehead to the pillow next to Taja's and press our heads together. Still gripping her hand, I stay close to my girl. The doctors and nurses get busy, and in a few minutes, we're on the move again.

I'm surprised when I'm allowed to scrub in and sit near Taja's head during the C-section. As much as I hate why I'm here, I wouldn't be anywhere else but close to Taja.

Stroking her hair off her face, I see her staring sightlessly at the ceiling. No emotion on her face, nothing showing in her eyes. She looks like a beautiful corpse, and even that thought makes me feel panic.

Moving slightly to the side of her head, I squeeze her hand.

"Taja? Look at me, baby," I order softly.

No reaction whatsoever.

"Taj? Please, honey, look at me. I need you to focus on me," I try again.

Slowly her eyes meet mine, but they're blank. It's like her soul has been ripped from her body, and I'm left with a shell. No tears, no sobbing, nothing.

I place my forehead on hers. I hold tight to her hand while my other one cups the side of her face. I stay that way during the entire ordeal. I tune out the doctor and nurses' voices and focus all my energy on Taja.

When it's almost over, I look up and see them placing a perfectly formed, tiny little boy into an incubator, and I feel hope for the first time. I can't see him now with the medical staff in the way, but I hold my breath waiting for that first cry. While that's happening, the doctor finishes up on Taja.

I finally have to breathe, and yet I don't want to. There still hasn't been a sound from the baby, and I see the truth on the staff's faces. It was not meant to be. I feel my body shut down against what I know the doctor's going to say.

"I'm so sorry. Your little boy didn't make it. He wasn't developed enough yet to survive outside the womb. The nurses will bring him to you in a few moments if you'd like to hold him."

I nod my head once and ease back so the nurses can finish up with Taja. Once that's done, we're moved to a nearby room. Taja's bed is propped up, so she's in a comfortable position. She still hasn't spoken a word, and her face is still blank. I don't know how to comfort her or myself at this gut-wrenching time. I just stay close, and she clings to my hand like it's the only thing keeping her on earth.

A short time later, a nurse walks in, cradling our dead child in her arms. Taja reaches out immediately and accepts our baby. Pulling the blanket back a little, we both lay eyes on the most perfect miniature face ever created. He's so tiny and so beautiful. Without making a sound, I watch tears fall from Taja's eyes onto our child. It's something I never want to see again. A mother grieving over a child lost to them forever. Reaching down, I brush my finger over little baby Dagen's head. Even knowing he's gone, his cold body is a shock. He looks like he's sleeping, and I wish to God that were the truth.

After our time with our baby, the nurse returns and takes him away forever. Taja collapses against me, and sobs erupt from deep inside her. They're painful to hear. I lay beside her on the bed and hold her tight. I fight my own tears, wanting to be strong for her, but it's killing me. After a long time of trying to expel her grief, exhaustion sets in, and Taja falls to sleep.

I hear the door open quietly and look to see Tessie standing there. One look at us and her face crumbles. I ease off the bed and walk to her. Wrapping my arms around her, I let her cry it out while I explain what happened. When she gains control of herself, I ask her to stay with Taja so I can speak with the family that I know will be waiting to hear what's happened.

I walk into the waiting room to find it overflowing with family. Pooh reaches my side first, and I know by his face he knows I have bad news. Gripping my arm, he waits.

"Taja's fine. Health-wise, she'll be okay. The baby didn't survive. Um, uh, the doctors said something about IUGR and problems with the placenta. Sorry, I'm not even sure what that all means. They had to do an emergency C-section, but the baby wasn't developed enough to survive it," I explain in a quiet rasp. "He was so fucking beautiful, though."

Lucy's tiny body collides with mine, and she holds on tight, sobbing. Pooh wraps an arm around my shoulders and holds me steady. I'm not sure I wouldn't have hit the floor if it wasn't for those two. In time, I get hugs and sorrys from everyone gathered here to support Taja and me. This has been the worst night of my life, but at least I'm surrounded by those who care.

Tessie and I stay by Taja's side right up until she's discharged. Both women have been quiet and withdrawn but leaning on each other. I'm not faring any better. We're a unit, a family, and this has been hell for each of us.

Leaving the hospital, Freddy's waiting out front in Bailey's SUV to give us a ride home. Upon arriving there, we find the fridge stocked and numerous bouquets of flowers placed around the main floor. We also find Duffy waiting on the deck. Tessie picks him up, before Taja could, and carries him inside. Setting him down, he stalks over to the couch, jumps up on it, and turns to face Taja. She carefully sits down next to him, and he settles his considerable body weight against the side of her thighs. I watch Taja's hand land softly on Duffy and start stroking. Maybe he'll be a comfort to her.

At the end of the week, we held a small service for our baby, Joshua Dagen. Only family and close friends were invited. It was a beautiful and quiet service. My mom showed in time for it, and she came alone. Taja invited her to stay with us for a few days, and she readily agreed, much to my surprise. I'm happy she's here, though.

We laid baby Joshua to rest next to Taja's mom. We know without a doubt she'll look over our little angel for us. Taja stood strong throughout the day with Tessie on one side, me on the other. She even gave a small smile when she held her arms out, and

Axel placed little Alex in them. I was worried it would be too much for her, holding another baby so soon, but she's stronger than that. Spine of steel.

Taja and I haven't talked much about all that's happened, but she hasn't pulled away from me in her grief either. Instead, we've quietly grown closer. While she doesn't say much, her actions speak volumes. She stays close to me and doesn't shy away from clinging to me when the tears come. I'm not ashamed of them either, and don't hide mine from her. We hold tight and ride the waves of grief together. We'll get through this and be stronger because of it. Time won't heal this wound, but it'll dull the rough edges of it eventually.

Chapter 29

Taja

Physically, I've healed. Mentally, I'm not sure I ever will. I know the pain will lessen eventually, but there will always be this horrible feeling of loss. The pain of watching Vex cradle his baby so tenderly about stopped my beating heart. The grief etched on his beautiful face was almost too much to bear. Being cheated from experiencing all of our baby's life's moments. Learning to walk, going to school for his first day, learning to ride a bike. I try hard not to dwell on those things because it guts me when I do. Of course, I'll never forget his tiny, perfect features and what could have been, but I have to move forward and stay strong. Not just for me but for Vex and Tessie too. They're grieving just as hard, but we're doing it as a family.

Subconsciously, I blame myself. I know I shouldn't, and I know what happened wasn't my fault, but it's hard not to. I lived and he didn't. Survivor's guilt, maybe? I'm not sure of anything except that I need my mom more than ever before. But she's gone, and I'm supposed to be the mother now, but I'm not. Guilt is a heavy weight to carry.

Each day, I climb out of bed and face the day. I want to stay curled up in a ball and hide from the world, but I don't. I push forward, and when a bad moment hits me, I cling to Vex and his strength. Instead of tearing our new relationship apart, it's brought us incredibly closer. We're connected through love and tragedy, and I firmly believe nothing can tear us apart. He's been there with me through every tear, every bit of rage at the world, and even my doubt in God. He's been strong for me, but we're stronger together. And that's the way we'll stay.

"I want that one! No, wait! This one!" Tessie says, changing her mind again.

Loki's girlfriend has had her puppies, and we're arguing over which one we want. Tessie, Vex, and I are all sitting on the floor at Gunner's house while several puppies climb on us. Each one is adorable, and it's hard to pick just one. Most of them bear a strong resemblance to Loki. He definitely put his stamp on his brood.

"I think I like this one best," Vex says.

"Why that one?" Tessie questions.

"Because I've moved her away from Taja several times now, but she returns to lay by Taj's leg. Every single time. She wants to stay close, and I think she's picked Taja to be her human," Vex explains.

I know exactly which puppy he's talking about because the second we walked in the door, she claimed me. She's not as hyper as some of the others but demands my attention by pushing gently at my hand with her nose. Yes, I want this one, but I didn't want to break Tessie's heart by not letting her get to choose.

"She is really cute and fluffy," Tessie says while moving to sit closer to the puppy.

The puppy must sense that Tessie's considering her because she leans over enough to lick her hand.

Tessie's face softens, and I know who'll be living with us soon.

"I agree. That's our girl," Tessie says while petting the beautiful grayish-brown head.

"You sure? You liked some of the others too," I ask Tessie.

"Positive. Vex is right. She's chosen you to be her human, and she should have some say in who she spends her life with. She'll be protective of you, of us, and I like that. Besides, most of the puppies are going to other club members, so it's not like I won't get to see them all the time."

Ava hands Vex a cute purple collar, and he puts it on the puppy. She's ours when she's old enough to be away from her mom. I'm in love already.

A few months have passed since losing our baby, and things are a little better each day. Not saying I don't still have moments where I feel depression setting in and pulling me under. I do, and it's hard. But I remind myself that my mom is taking care of Joshua now, and that eases some of my pain. Vex and Tessie are also having more good days now. It's fundamentally changed us all, but we're coping and slowly healing.

"We need to set a date and start making arrangements, Taj. You keep putting me off about the wedding. Are you having doubts about getting married?" Vex asks quietly.

We're lying in bed doing nothing more than being together. He's flat on his back, and I'm cuddled tight to his side, head on his chest. Vex has one hand in my hair with his other linked with mine resting on his chest. He's been bringing up the wedding more often lately. I've been trying to avoid this discussion because I don't want the fight it's going to cause.

"There's no rush anymore, Vex," I carefully say.

"Told you before that getting married wasn't about you being pregnant. Just that if you would marry me, I wanted to do it before the baby was born so he'd have my name," Vex answers in a terse voice. I feel his body tense, and I know I've angered him.

I sit up, bracing myself on a hand in the bed, and look him in the eye.

"You no longer have to marry me," I say, and even I can hear the sadness in my voice.

"Never had to before, Taja. Wanted to and still do. That hasn't changed. I want you as my wife, and I want that as soon as I can get you in front of a minister."

I can hear the truth in his words. Words I needed to hear.

I smile down at my man and know life will always be good with him in it.

Epilogue

Vex

"Taja! You're going to be late!" I shout toward the master bedroom.

"Coming!" she shouts back.

Tessie, sitting at the kitchen island, rolls her eyes. This is a daily occurrence on the days Taja's training at the hospital. As she rushes into the room, I hold out the travel mug of coffee and a bagel in a napkin. She snatches them from me, turns her face upward for her goodbye kiss, and bolts out the door after she receives it. We hear a faint "Bye, Tessie" as the door shuts.

"Does she have any idea about the party?" Tessie asks as she finishes off her toast.

"I don't think so. You women have been pretty sneaky about getting it planned."

"She's going to cry, you know," Tessie informs me.

"Nah, she won't. But she'll be happy."

"For being a man whore, you sure don't understand women," Tessie states with a sad shake of her head.

"Reformed man whore! Reformed!" I shout.

I watch as Tessie breaks into laughter. The little wench likes to get under my skin and knows all the quickest ways of doing just that.

"I might not totally understand women. But I do understand enough to know that if Taja finds out you've been texting Horse, she's going to skin him alive. And that's if he gets off lucky," I tell her with a smug smile.

I watch as her face freezes, mid-laugh, and then gets a slight pink tinge to it.

"How'd you find out I texted him?" Tessie questions loudly.

"I was sitting next to him when his phone went off. Now that he's a patched member, he attends Church too. Advice, Tessie. Nothing's secret for long in an MC. Too many eyes watching everything. Please don't make it so I have to kill and bury a good friend of mine. Or watch your sister lose her shit and watch this place turn into a war zone."

"I don't get why Taja's so against him. He's a nice guy. And he's hotter than hell. And I'm not a nun!" Tessie exclaims.

"Because you're underage, and he's not. Simple as that, Tessie."

"I'm almost seventeen now," she mumbles.

"And that's still underage. Give it a few years. Maybe at that point, Taja won't feel the need to stack bodies next to the barn."

"She's cramping my style," Tessie shoots back. With a grin and a toss of her hair, she disappears upstairs to what she calls her lair.

The day Taja has completed everything necessary and is officially a registered nurse, I take "my harem" out for dinner to celebrate. My mom, who's been visiting often, meets us there. I'm astonished to see her dressed in more casual clothes, and she appears comfortable wearing them. She's made changes in her life, and they seem to have made her a happier person. Her and dad are still married, but she does what she wants now and isn't afraid to argue with him to get her way. She speaks up for herself, and she's never done that before. I'm proud as fuck of her. She's always welcome in our home.

After dinner, I tell Taja I need to stop at the clubhouse on the way home. Upon entering, I quickly step aside and watch with a smile as Taja registers all the "congratulations" and "surprise" shouts she encounters. The entire club turned out to celebrate her accomplishment, and she's moved to tears.

"Told you, biker boy," Tessie says as she bumps me with her shoulder as she walks by.

"Gloating is an unattractive trait, Tessie," I inform her, only to get a smug grin in return.

The party rages into the night, and every single person takes a moment to congratulate, hug, or pick up and twirl (Chubs) Taja during the party. She's smiling more tonight than I've seen in months. I'm relieved to say that while we grieved and grieved hard, we've made it through and are making our new life together work. Taja struggled for quite a while, but she kept getting up each day and fighting her way forward. Nobody can ask for more than that.

Surprisingly, it was Axel who ended up being Taja's sounding board one day while I was at work. He'd went over to our house to bring Duffy back to Ava's and found Taja sobbing. He sat with her, listened, and handled her with care. I'm not sure what all he said to her, but that day seemed to be a turning point. The old Taja started to re-emerge and slowly became the norm again. Axel, even though he can be a nut, can also be the exact right person to talk to when needed. He was just that for Taja, and I'm grateful to him.

I've been pushing Taja for a wedding date for a while now. I want to marry that woman, and I wanted to do that yesterday. She said she would and that she wants to, but she's still been dragging her feet about it, so I demanded to know why.

"I was never that little girl who grew up dreaming about my wedding day," Taja softly says. "I've always wanted to get married and have a family, but the whole big-ass wedding thing has never been something I wanted. I hate all the fuss and details needed for a wedding like that. I don't begrudge them to anyone else, but for me, I just want something intimate. A ceremony that's meaningful to us and not so much a celebration for other people. I'm not comfortable with the whole queen for a day thing. I don't like being the center of attention and hate having all eyes on me. Does that make sense?"

"Perfect sense. How about this? We fly to Hawaii and have a quiet, intimate ceremony on the beach. I miss my home state and want to show it to you. Mom, Tessie, and Suki can come. Afterward, we honeymoon there. When we come home, we have a large wedding reception with the club. If we don't include them in some part of our wedding, we'll never hear the end of it," I suggest.

"That's exactly what I'd like!"

That's exactly how it went down. Simple, elegant wedding under a falling sun. Tessie, Suki, and my mom there, all with tears in their eyes. Taja loved Hawaii, and our honeymoon was off the charts. While there, we saw an old friend of mine for our ring tattoos. I showed him the design I had Bailey sketch for me, and he said it would be no problem. The design is tribal in form, but if you look closely, you can see letters intertwined. Our initials connected by a tiny heart. They came out perfectly. Taja didn't want her engagement ring to cover hers, so she's now wearing the ring on her right hand. It doesn't matter to me which hand her ring's on because the wedding band tattoo is permanent.

Life is great for me. I don't miss the different women and different dramas in the least. Never even think about my old lifestyle because my new one is so much more. Nothing I like better than cuddling on the couch watching a game with Taja. Or working on the lawn with her. Lazing around the pool with her. Anything that's with her is one of my happy times. We've spent long hours riding the bike, not able to talk over the noise of it, but our connection is always present. We don't always need words to communicate. A look, a touch, and we know what the other's thinking. Some of my favorite times together involved little speaking and more just being us.

I haven't broached the subject of another baby yet. I'm ready, but I'm not sure Taja is. There's no hurry, but I'm definitely on board when she's ready. She shut the nursery door when we came home from the hospital, and it's not been opened since. Nothing's been moved, and I don't know whether to strip it out or leave it there. For now, I've decided to leave it as it is. I'll follow her lead and be there to support whatever decision she makes.

Chubs hasn't said anything else about the Feds, even though I've asked him numerous times. He's still with us, and it's my sincere hope it stays that way. If the world crashes down on him, the club will be there to back his every move. Lucy and Chubs announced their engagement, and the club celebrated like never before. It was the party to end all parties. Ava and the women outdid themselves with the cooking and decorating. The club kids were a huge hit when they flew a drone over the compound, pulling a "Congratulations Chubs and Lucy" banner behind it. It was a good day for everyone. I still smile when I remember the look of pure love that Lucy's dad's face showed when he watched the two together. Fatherly love and pride. Lucy's a lucky girl to have been raised with that and to now have Chubs too.

"What're you doing standing out here alone and in the dark?" Taja asks as she leans against me at the deck railing.

I turn so my ass is against the railing and pull her flush against me. Wrapping my arms around her, I hold her tight.

"Just thinking about how fucking lucky I am that Suki had to stand up in her sister's wedding. You filling in for her. Us meeting. Luckiest fucking day of my life, Taj."

Taja's arms wrap around my waist, and she settles her body against mine. Tilting her head back, she rests her chin on my chest. I look down into the face I want to see every day of my life.

"Luckiest fucking day of my life, too, Vex. I love you so much it hurts," she responds.

"Love you, Taja. For fucking ever."

The End

Lola Wright

About the Author

Lola Wright currently lives in the great state of Michigan with her husband. She has enjoyed living in several different areas of her home state and the USA, but Michigan is home. Her kids are grown now, and between them, her grandchildren, and numerous furry family members, Lola keeps busy.

When Lola has free time, she will most likely be found outside riding her horses or being entertained by her rescued minis, her dogs, and cats. Lola has a passion for feeding the wildlife and enjoys watching them come and go on her property. If indoors, Lola is usually cooking up new recipes, reading, or is in front of her computer dreaming up who she hopes is the perfect couple.

Amazon
In the Kindle Store on the Amazon site, search for "Lola Wright"

Facebook
On Facebook search for "Lola Wright, Author" to find *Lola's Profile*, *The Devil's Angels Page*, *Lola's Angels Group Page,* and the *Angels Spoilers Group Page*.

Twitter
@LolaWri47124635

Join Lola Wright's Mailing List for the latest news on her books! Go to the **Lola's Home page**—https://www.lolawright.store—and scroll to the bottom of the page.

Also by Lola Wright

The Devil's Angels MC Series

The Devil's Angels MC: Book 1 - Gunner

Ava

Left to die as an infant, Ava Beaumont has not had an easy life. Being raised by the system has taught her to be independent, hardworking, and cautious. When Ava becomes a victim, she uses her inner strength to put it behind her and move forward. Now she lives a good life with the family she's created through adopting pets that were also throwaways, including a smart-mouthed parrot and a skateboarding pig. When Ava meets Gunner, she realizes what her life is lacking but does she have the courage to trust a big, rough biker enough to let him into her safe little life?

Gunner

Being the President of The Devil's Angels MC was not something Gunner asked to become, but through the loss of his dad, the job was thrust upon him. While he loves his club and club brothers wholeheartedly, Gunner wants his club to move in a better direction. And when Gunner spots bakery owner, Ava, he realizes that's not the only change he wants to make in his life.

Nothing worth having is easy to acquire.

This is an MC story with a heart. Come meet the crazy pets and even crazier club members of The Devil's Angels MC.

The Devil's Angels MC: Book 2 - Axel

Bailey

I'm the sensible, independent, quiet, and hardworking accountant girl next door. My life is safe, sane, predictable, and boring. My biggest concern is dealing with my free-spirited, wild-child parent.

Until it's not.

The day I see something I shouldn't have and crash into the crazy lives of The Devil's Angels MC is the day my life changes forever. That's the day I looked into the bluest eyes I have ever seen and knew nothing would ever be the same.

Axel

My life is perfect. I'm the Vice President of my club, The Devil's Angels MC, and we've moved the club in the right direction. I manage the club's gym, own my own home, and have women around that are always up for a night of fun. I have my club brothers, the world's best dad and a new sister. Family is everything in my world, and I have a great one. What more could a guy want or need?

That question is answered when a tiny, little woman slams her way into my life. I never saw her coming, but I'm not letting her leave.

The Devil's Angels MC: Book 3 - Pooh

Pippa

Owning and operating a home for victims of domestic violence doesn't leave a woman wanting a man in her life. Not a permanent one anyway. Having been a victim myself, I chose to open this refuge to help others that are in a similar situation that I had been. I was one of the lucky ones because my foster mom was always my rock, my safe haven. It was never me alone against the world. We decided, together, that we wanted to be just that for others. New Horizons is born, and we are on a mission to save all that we can.

Pooh

I'm restless, bored, and I want more. I want what some of my club brothers have found. I want that one woman that is meant to be mine.

The problem is I don't know any women that qualify. Being in a motorcycle club brings women around in flocks, but they're not meant to be mine when they're clearly everyone's girls.

Then I meet her. The One.

Now the problem is that she is not interested in me or a relationship and not a big fan of men in general. She's a strong, independent woman, and a little spitfire when it comes to protecting those she's sworn to keep safe.

She will be mine, and I'll prove to her that men like me and my club brothers from The Devil's Angels MC are nothing like the men she's known before.

The Devil's Angels MC: Book 4 - Vex

Vex

I've lived my life free and easy. No attachments, no entanglements. I easily move on after an evening with a woman. For a night, they get all I have to give. After that, it's time to go. They're warned ahead of time, so tears and ploys have no effect on me. I love my MC family, The Devil's Angels, and my bikes. Not much else. Certainly, none of the various women I've known.

Then I meet someone who changes all my rules, thoughts, and beliefs. But as luck would have it, she's the unattainable one. She seems immune to my charm, and that tweaks my ego. After being warned away from her, I try to push her to the back of my mind. She doesn't stay there for long, though. Now I'm determined to have my night with her, consequences be damned.

Taja

Trying to raise my sister, working any job I can while fighting to keep a roof over our heads, I don't live the life of a normal woman my age. I don't have time for dating, sex, or men. Especially a member of an MC. My father's an MC President, and I want nothing to do with that lifestyle. Not even for the gorgeous biker whose nearly golden eyes follow my every move. Common sense tells me he's in it for a night, and that's not my style. Best to keep my head on straight and ignore what my body's craving.

Actions have consequences, and fate has a way of messing up the best-laid plans.

The Devil's Angels MC: Book 5 - Cash

Livi

Being a female in a male-dominated career can be daunting, but I refuse to allow others' attitudes to deter me. I always try to be professional, compassionate, and non-judgmental. Through hard work, I have earned respect within my department. Wearing a badge and uniform, I've seen the best and worst of humanity. Heartbreaking, dangerous, hectic, or hilarious, I approach each shift and person with an open mind.

As all cops know, the partner you're teamed up with makes all the difference in the world, and I struck gold. Work partners and best friends, James and I have a tight, unshakable bond. We're each other's support system when things get rough and defend each other's right to wear the uniform against anyone who believes otherwise.

Cash

Muscled, tall, tatted, and The Devil's Angels MC Sergeant at Arms, some see me as an intimidating man. Others see me as quiet, thoughtful, and dedicated to my blood and MC families. I'm the first call everyone makes when things are going sideways. Whether it's bullets or fists flying, I'm the man you want at your back. Highly respected within my club, I live by a strict biker code.

When a life-altering event occurs in my life, I will not waver in doing what's right. With the love and support of my two families, I'll face my new circumstances with determination.

The Devil's Angels MC

More books to follow in this series!